To [illegible]

Enjoy!!

[illegible]

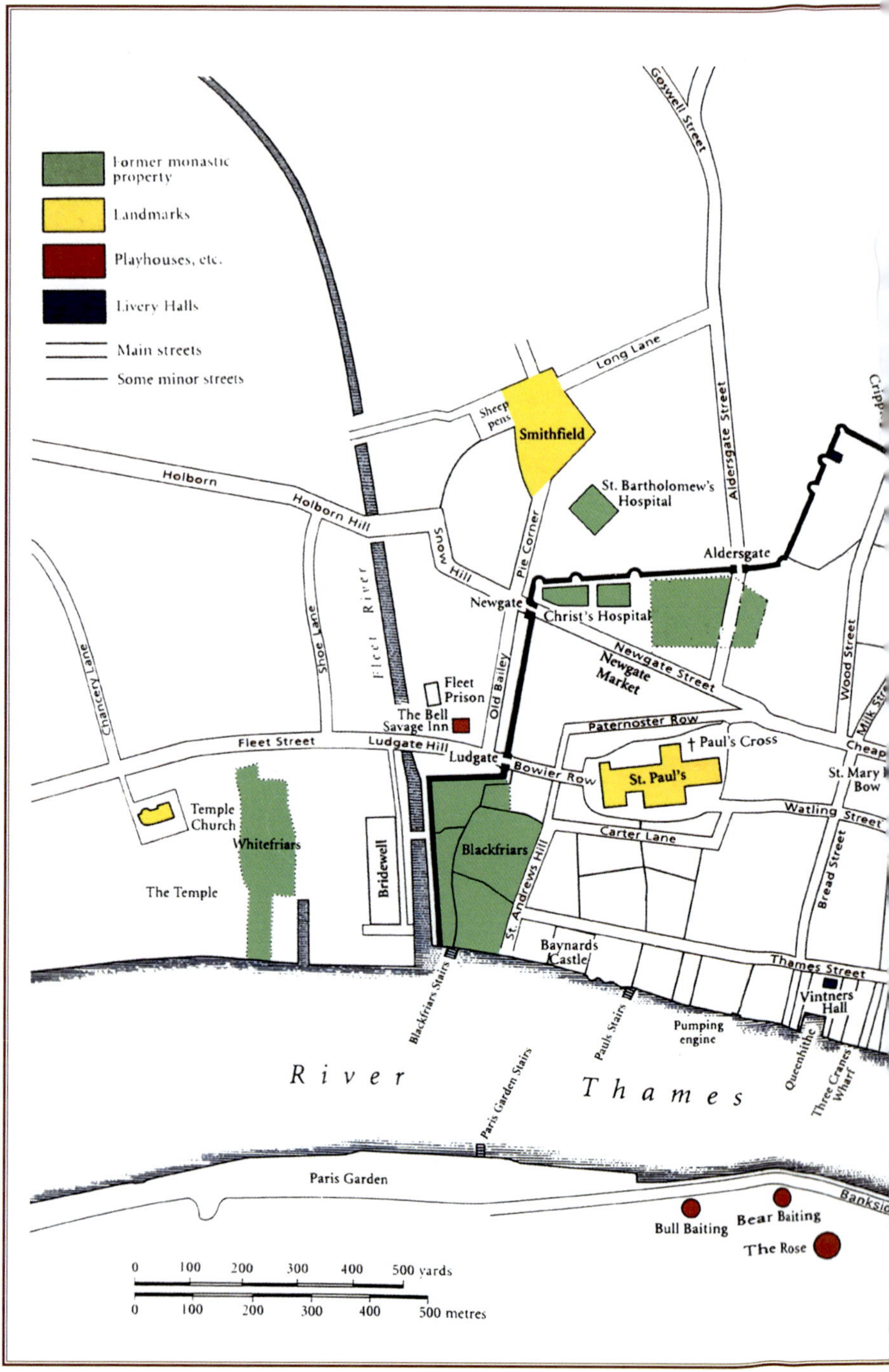
Former monastic property
Landmarks
Playhouses, etc.
Livery Halls
Main streets
Some minor streets
Goswell Street
Long Lane
Sheep pens
Smithfield
Aldersgate Street
Holborn
Holborn Hill
Snow Hill
Pie Corner
St. Bartholomew's Hospital
Aldersgate
Newgate
Christ's Hospital
Newgate Street
Newgate Market
Wood Street
Chancery Lane
Shoe Lane
Fleet River
Fleet Prison
The Bell Savage Inn
Old Bailey
Paternoster Row
† Paul's Cross
Fleet Street
Ludgate Hill
Ludgate
Bowier Row
St. Paul's
St. Mary Bow
Temple Church
Whitefriars
Bridewell
Blackfriars
Carter Lane
Watling Street
The Temple
St. Andrews Hill
Bread Street
Baynards Castle
Thames Street
Vintners Hall
Blackfriars Stairs
Pauls Stairs
Pumping engine
Queenhithe
Three Cranes Wharf
River Thames
Paris Garden Stairs
Paris Garden
Bull Baiting
Bear Baiting
The Rose
0 100 200 300 400 500 yards
0 100 200 300 400 500 metres

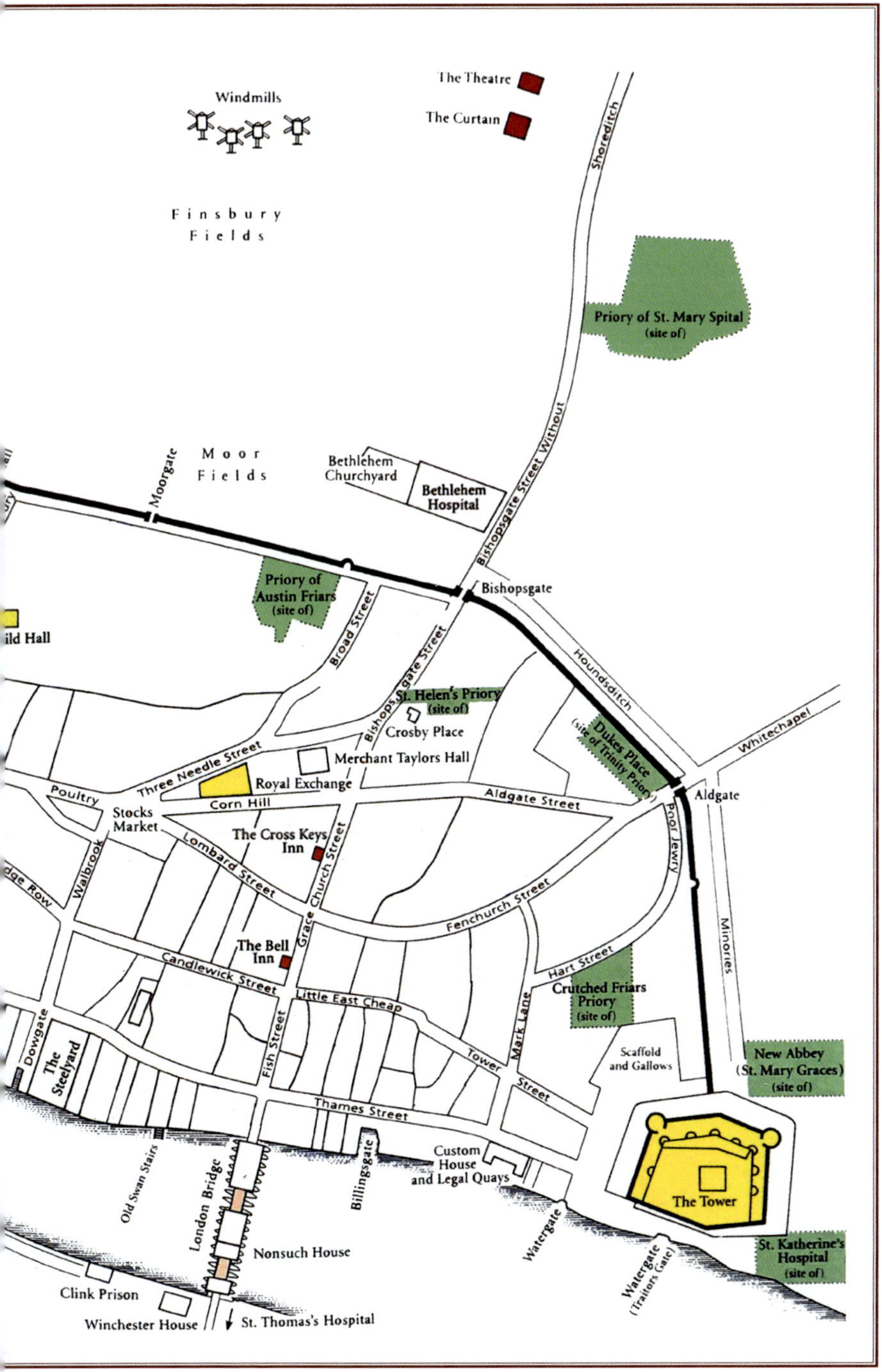

The Theatre
The Curtain
Windmills
Finsbury Fields
Shoreditch
Priory of St. Mary Spital (site of)
Moor Fields
Moorgate
Bethlehem Churchyard
Bethlehem Hospital
Bishopsgate Street Without
Bishopsgate
Priory of Austin Friars (site of)
Broad Street
Bishopsgate Street
Houndsditch
St. Helen's Priory (site of)
Crosby Place
Merchant Taylors Hall
Dukes Place (site of Trinity Priory)
Whitechapel
Three Needle Street
Royal Exchange
Aldgate
Poultry
Stocks Market
Corn Hill
Aldgate Street
The Cross Keys Inn
Lombard Street
Grace Church Street
Poor Jewry
Walbrook
Fenchurch Street
Minories
The Bell Inn
Candlewick Street
Hart Street
Crutched Friars Priory (site of)
Little East Cheap
Mark Lane
Dowgate
The Steelyard
Fish Street
Tower Street
Scaffold and Gallows
New Abbey (St. Mary Graces) (site of)
Thames Street
Custom House and Legal Quays
The Tower
Old Swan Stairs
London Bridge
Billingsgate
Watergate
Watergate (Traitors Gate)
St. Katherine's Hospital (site of)
Nonsuch House
Clink Prison
Winchester House
St. Thomas's Hospital

A MURDEROUS AFFAIR

A John Lovat Mystery

JONATHAN DIGBY

First published 2013 as an eBook by Endeavour Press
This edition published 2022 by Jonathan Digby/One Ear Up Books

ISBN: 978-180352-360-6

Prologue

December 16th, 1567 – Mouth of the Mitomba river, Guinea

The deceitful English have engaged us in war.

After an uneasy standoff lasting three days, during which time our fleets eyed each other warily across the wide bay, the tension finally snapped. I awoke to the sound of cannon-fire and was on deck just in time to see a large man-of-war bearing down on the Santo Francisco out of the dawn haze. The Chagras and the Mossem Gaspard were both struck in the early skirmishes, and the piercing cries of wounded men were soon intermingling with the sound of the guns.

The catalyst for the English attack – a fleet of barracoons from upriver, laden with slaves, which arrived yesterday afternoon. It was too much to hope that the English pirates could resist such bounty.

I take to my diary now to denounce this enemy with all my heart. I have come to observe that there is no man so villainous as an Englishman, no creature so treacherous. Only days after assurances, not to mention gifts, given to us by these perfidious devils, they blatantly go against their own word. The heathen behaves like a spoilt and flattered child, which, nevertheless, thinks only of its own imaginary neglects and wants.

The attack was swift and calculated, and unleashed terror across the bay. We were ready for them, of course. Our sailors are as great in number and even more battle-hardened than our contemptible foe, but there is something desperate, jealous even, in the English character, which makes them a formidable enemy. Their aim is to take what we Portuguese have worked hard to forge, and they are determined to grab it by any means, however base. The battle has raged all day but we have held firm.

As I write this, my parchment is lit by the bright glow of the fire from one of their ship's, which blazes not a quarter of a league away. I feel certain that we shall repel them emphatically tomorrow and secure the trade that is so rightfully ours. May all their ships burn so, and their sailors, in an inferno of hell.

JONATHAN DIGBY

December 17th, 1567

Curse the fates that have forsaken us!

A damned act of foolishness has undone us at the last. We had all but defeated the enemy when one of our ships broke rank to pursue them in retreat – and here I lay the charge of gross negligence against that ship's captain, Blasius d'Aragon, whose vainglorious behaviour has handed the English a crucial advantage. Even now they are engaging the remainder of the Portuguese fleet with d'Aragon's ship, the Christavaldes, lost when the imbecile disobeyed orders and was captured. The Christavaldes outguns anything that we, or indeed the English, have in their fleet. But all is not yet lost and I must return to the deck.

I will now entrust this diary to my son. If anything should happen to me, I hope he will carry my poor record of events back to Lisbon, where the truth can be brought to light. Merciful God hear my prayers, and spare us defeat to this most hated enemy.

Part 1

Old London Bridge
November 1588

Chapter 1

'In men of base degree may raign the very same vertues that are in Gentlemen.'
(Castiglioni; The Book of the Courtier)

Thud, thud …

London. City of fortune. Where cajouxs and cants are kicked aside to starve in foul ditches, while those more fortunate in birth glide forth on their quest for riches and influence …

Thud, thud, thud …

London. City of barrators and broggers – the dark underbelly that each day breaks out of its iniquitous haunts – the gaming inn, the trugging-house, the conyman's lair – and brazenly roams the streets, facing down the constables, who would rather pitch a guiltless man into the Clink than deal with these fiends …

Thud, thud, thud, thud, thud …

London. City of the dispossessed. Burgeoning each day with foreign refugees, landless countrymen and disbanded soldiers. Where a cuttle-bung can cut a throat as quick as a purse, innocence be blackened for the price of a few angels, and a fortune conjured from the Indes or sunk to the bottom of the jewelled sea ...

Thud, thud, thud, thud, thud, thud, THUD!

London! Where, on a frosty and foreboding day, I found the interweaving threads of my troubled dreams harshly interrupted. Which one of the city's dark hearts had wended its way to my door?

Already assaulted by the twin hammerings of excessive liquor, and the churn of the waterwheels some thirty feet below my bed, it took a while for my addled brain to register the knocking as something quite distinct.

My first conscious thought told me it was wrong side of lunchtime. Through the criss-cross pattern of the mottled glass, I could discern with, admittedly blurry vision, a low sun poised to start its cheerless descent towards evening. The only movements against the muted, marble sky were the effortless swoops of raptors, circling high above the rich pickings of the rancid city.

Gradually, my fractured senses became aware of an unholy blend of smells hanging in a fug around my bed. Hungary Water, Dutch brandy, tobacco – the remnants of a night of excess – all conjuring vivid, but broken recollections of the previous evening. I tried to push these unwelcome memories aside. With each new thud, I felt fresh sweat pricking on my nauseous brow and a rising tension growing in my empty gut. Suddenly alert to the threat, I threw off the crumpled sheet and reached instinctively for my dagger. Just as my fingers grasped the hilt, the banging on the door ceased.

Stock still, head swimming, I noticed the cloudy interaction between my breath and the cold draft that was seeping through the gaps in the window's lead casing. With any luck, whoever it was had decided I'd got lucky and stayed out the previous night. I listened intently for the sound of footsteps carefully negotiating the narrow flight of rickety stairs, of the brief bustle of the street outside and the door banging shut – but there was only a stillness to match my own. It must be someone who knew of my reputation, or lack of it, with the ladies.

'Master Lovat? Rouse yourself, Master Lovat?' A nasal voice squeaked through the keyhole. 'It is I, Nesbitt.'

Nesbitt – chief steward to my aristocratic brother, the perennial ghost at the feast. My shock at the abrupt awakening morphed quickly into a gnawing sense of unease. There was no likelihood that the persistent and dogged Nesbitt would desist, but his visit could only mean some onerous chore for my brother. I tried thinking of an alternative, but my head hurt too much. There was nothing else for it – I opened negotiations.

'I'm here Nesbitt, what the hell do you want you great clucking Margery-prater? Keep the noise down, can't you, for pizzle's sake.' This time the silence spoke of reproach at my insult. I sighed, dragged my disconnected body to its feet and began inching my way across cold, creaking floorboards.

After fumbling with bolts and lock, I opened the door to reveal a skeletal, serious man, with a closely cropped head of thinning, grey hair. He was a good foot taller than me and had a natural stoop, doubly accentuated by the low-slung ceiling of the attic corridor. This and the black cloak he was wrapped up in reminded me of the popular image of *La*

Mort. All he lacked was a scythe.

'What do you want?' I said, glaring at him with as much hostility as a half-naked, unwashed inebriate could manage. The doleful figure in black appeared unmoved.

I took a couple of unsteady paces and flung open the window, acutely aware of the lack of fresh air in the cramped space. Another wave of dizziness washed over me, as I looked down at the wooden roof tiles of the house jake, which jutted out over the river. Below that, the swirling waters of the Thames were fighting their way through the narrow arches that supported the bridge. I momentarily contemplated pitching myself in – the dangerous waters looking far more inviting that anything Nesbitt might have in store for me.

'Get dressed, Master Lovat.' Nesbitt's tone was terse, insistent.

I glanced wearily over my shoulder, the resistance draining out of me. Nesbitt was standing in the doorway as if loath to set foot in the room.

'You realise with all that noise you've been making, you'll have woken Father Thames himself.'

'Father Thames is unlikely to be asleep, nor are most Christian souls at this hour.'

'What hour would that be?' I said, just about mustering a scornful laugh, knowing that it was hardly likely to be an hour to make me proud.

'The time, *de facto*, is half past the hour of one.' There was no disguising the contempt in Nesbitt's voice. A chime from the nearby bell of St Magnus-the-Martyr neatly emphasised his point. 'Sir Robert sent me. He requests that you accompany me. Immediately.'

'Requests? Ha!' I staggered back onto the bed and sat with my sore head propped in my hands, the room swirling around me. 'But where, Sir Apple-Squire? Can't you see I'm …'

'There's a body in the river.'

A momentary pause, while I searched his inscrutable face for more clues.

'There are always bodies in the river, what does this particular one have to do with me?'

'His Lordship is concerned he might know the man.'

'I see.' I said, though I didn't. 'And fishing him out is deemed a suitable task for the bastard brother?'

Nesbitt ignored this remark, letting my words hang in the frigid air. Instead, he fetched a bowl of water from the corner of the room and dumped it roughly in front of me, water splashing onto my naked feet. 'You'd better hurry. We've the best part of a league's journey ahead of us. *Tempus neminem manet.*'

Defeated, I glared bitterly at a black knot in the floorboards, before reluctantly splashing water onto my face.

The next ten minutes were farcical. Whilst I stumbled around my lodgings collecting various items of strewn clothing, Nesbitt stooped in the frame of the doorway, studying me contemptuously. Occasionally, he would cast his eyes disdainfully around the room. The man's puritan views were well known in my brother's household and, judging by the curdled expression on his cadaverous face, the state of my lodgings suggested that it was dissolute young men like myself who were putting his immortal soul in peril.

I found myself blearily following his gaze, as though Nesbitt's disapproving eye was helping me to see the cramped, angular space for the first time. Clothes strewn about the place, half empty glasses and half cleaned plates scattered with no discernible pattern. I had to admit that it was hardly an advertisement for clean living. The lodging, four floors up on London Bridge did, though, merit a couple of strong points. One was the tremendous panoramic view of the wide river and the teeming city along its banks, which always caused maids to gasp with appreciation, but was wasted on Nesbitt. The second was that, due to its claustrophobic nature, I belonged to that tiny minority of Londoners lucky in the privilege of not having to share their bed. Unless I wanted to, of course.

This latter advantage also meant that, with no one to borrow them, it was a complete mystery as to why I should be missing any of my possessions – chiefly amongst them a pair of new boots. After searching in vain, they failed to materialise. Nesbitt's impatience reached its limit and he said we should go, regardless. Reluctantly, I pulled on an old pair found wedged under the truckle-bed, which had grown stiff with age and sported a number of gaping holes. As an afterthought, I began buckling on my short sword and dagger.

'You won't need those where we're going.'

'I'll take them all the same,' I said, meeting Nesbitt's gaze evenly, 'if it's all the same to you'

As soon as we alighted on the narrow street that ran along the bridge, my face was slapped with a width of cold air. Nesbitt didn't waste time, striding purposefully towards the southern entrance, I following in his wake, fighting with my cloak which was wrapped too tightly and catching the hilts of my weaponry. We hustled and bustled along the narrow, covered street and under the finery of the newly erected Nonesuch House. Here, a boisterous crowd, following the entertainment afforded by a constable whipping an obstinate beggar across the bridge, and, presumably, back to the charity of his Kentish origins, halted us momentarily. We shuffled with the crowd out into the daylight across the Old Drawbridge, as they cheered and jeered the spectacle, their cries mingling with the shouts of 'Eastward-Ho' and 'Westward-Ho' floating up from the watermen on the river below.

At Traitor's Gate, with its silhouettes of beheaded skulls against the bruised sky, my eyes were briefly drawn to a colourful flag hanging directly above the portcullis. It had been taken from one of the Spanish galleons captured during the Armada and placed there so that revellers crossing to the Southwark Fair could either marvel, or simply hurl things, at it. The flag was torn and stained with gunpowder but partly showed the shield and emblem of some proud Spanish captain, who was now most probably residing at the bottom of the English Channel.

Finally free of the revellers, Nesbitt's mark became clear as a set of treacherous wooden steps, which dropped to the river. A rowing boat was moored alongside the bank, in which sat two oarsmen, whom I instantly recognised from their blue-and-black livery as belonging to my brother's household. Also in the boat was a scruffy young boy, who Nesbitt introduced dismissively as Pinchkin, explaining cursorily that the boy's father had discovered the body.

Pinchkin was no older than ten, but already had a worldly-weariness about him. A shock of his fair hair stood up, in what I assumed was a permanent state of perplexity at the injustices and iniquities his pimply young face had already witnessed. He was dressed in what amounted to little more than rags, making me wince at the sight of him, and was awkwardly perched at the front of the boat shaking involuntarily with cold. As we stepped aboard, he looked relieved that we had finally returned.

I offered him my cloak, which, after a moment's hesitation, he gratefully accepted, and berated the oarsmen for not doing likewise. Once the men had grudgingly pushed off, Pinchkin turned away from us and stared earnestly into the distance as if willing our destination to arrive as quickly as possible.

Now that I was committed it seemed a good time to ascertain more details of our journey.

'Where is this body, Nesbitt?'

'Washed up by Rotherhithe marsh.'

'When?'

'Some time in the early hours.'

'And this boy's father found it? What business did he have on the river?'

'The boy claims his father is both a fisherman and a member of the Watch. Which particular activity he was engaged in this morning has not been made explicit.'

Nesbitt's tone made it clear that whatever the father was doing, it was unlikely to help the nation achieve a state of Godliness.

'No doubt he was fishing for Papist eels?' I said flippantly. Nesbitt merely grunted but offered nothing further, so I gave up trying to provoke him into conversation and slumped into a morose silence. The cold seeped through the exposed shoulders of my doublet, and into the holes of my boots. I was already regretting my generosity with the cloak.

Once we had cleared a long line of merchantmen, chained in the middle of the river, we drifted towards the left bank, passing the silhouetted Tower, and the sprawling tenements of St Katherine's hospital. The afternoon light was starting to give way to a brooding dusk, which loomed ahead over the distant hills. As the city began to recede from view, we were left with only the company of other boats, plying their trades up and down the banks. Soon we were clear of most of those too and the only sound was the rhythmic clinking and splashing of the oars. The tide was rushing out and we were making good progress – I said as much to Nesbitt

'You can be grateful for that,' he replied matter-of-factly. 'Otherwise I'd have awoken you a good deal earlier.'

We had been hugging the Middlesex bank as it curved gently northwards, but now the oarsmen began to strike out into the middle of the flux towards the opposite, low-lying shore. The boy suddenly stiffened and, pointing, cried 'Over there, sirs'.

I squinted into the distance. There was the shape of what looked like a huddle of men, but what was more arresting was a tall, thin object situated on a spit of land where the river turned southwards. As we pulled nearer, it gradually became clear as a multi-coloured wooden pole, roughly twelve feet high, with a sizeable pair of deer's antlers fixed at its apex. Other animal bones and skulls were attached up and down its length with ribbons, whose brightly-coloured tails fluttering in the wind were the only things moving in that desolate spot. I glanced at Nesbitt, who had pushed his hood back and was eyeing the spectacle distastefully. The backdrop of the low marshes certainly provided an incongruous setting for this strange feature in the landscape, which had an eerie air of paganism about it.

Our reverie was broken by one of the men walking to meet us.

'Joseph Pinchkin, Captain of the Rotherhithe Watch, at your service sirs.' He doffed his flea-bitten cap in our direction and then pulled his son roughly from the boat, giving him a clip round the ear for his trouble. A less inspiring 'Captain', one could hardly hope to encounter. 'If you were pleased to follow me, the parcel is along 'ere.'

I prepared to disembark, mindful that my old boots had holes in them and thus determined to place my first footstep on dry land. I stood at the front of the boat, waiting for an opportune moment, but just as I thrust forth, a larger than average wave caught the boat, causing it to pitch sharply, and I fell face first into the freezing surf. Momentarily confused and disorientated, I scrabbled about in the mud, the water soaking to my skin, before I felt the wrench on my shoulders as Pinchkin Senior extracted me roughly from the water and heaved me onto the shore. I stood on the bank displaying a comedic mixture of stupefaction and anger, as the men of the Watch gaped at me and barely smothered their sniggering.

Nesbitt, having successfully negotiated his way to dry land, hadn't time for such niceties. 'Come now, Lovat. Enough fooling,' He strode off towards the 'parcel' letting me drip on the shore. So much for sympathy.

'What in a Jesuit's name is this about, Nesbitt?' I asked tetchily, as I caught up with him, any lingering feeling of tiredness and drunkenness now thoroughly dispelled. 'You drag me out here against my will, and don't even have the decency to tell me why. I've had enough of your damn reticence.' Despite his position in the household, Nesbitt wasn't a blood relation, which still gave me some sense of superiority. Sensing the newly found edge in my voice, he looked at me coldly but thought better of a rebuke.

'As I told you, a body in the river, Master.' I decided to ignore his sarcastic stressing of the word 'Master', as he continued meaningfully: 'There is suspicion of foul play, which is why we are here.'

'How did this rabble connect the body with Robert?'

'*A posteriori* …' Nesbitt had practised as a lawyer before going into my brother's service, and had an irritating habit of sprinkling his speech with legal phrases, '… they found this seal around the man's neck.' Nesbitt produced from somewhere under his cloak a seal attached to a thick, silver chain, which I recognised as sporting my brother's insignia. 'One of the men from the village identified it as your brother's coat of arms and so, reasonably enough, sent word there. Sir Robert requested that you investigate the matter and report back to him forthwith.'

The body was lying at the foot of the colourful column – twisted and inert. The face was badly disfigured and the clothes, although once rich in appearance, were badly torn. A closer inspection of the face showed one eye blankly acknowledging the sky – the other missing, revealing an open socket. All around the swollen, bloated hole, the flesh was cut and bruised and the man's features were barely recognisable. From the gaping mouth a veiny, swollen tongue protruded, like some ancient creature that had died in its hole.

I knelt down beside the man, drawn closer by a vague feeling of recognition, despite the disfigurement. I yanked the cloak, still grimly clinging to its owner, to one side, and, feeling the heavy, sodden material in my hand, it began to dawn on me. Despite the rough treatment it had suffered, I recognised the cloak with its fine red velvet and rich embroidery. A fresh glance at the shape of the cheekbones, the curve of the hooked nose and the colour of the skin, and I was certain.

The dead man was, in a loose sense, known to me.

Chapter 2

'Under the glorious spreading wings of Fame,
I saw a virgin queen, attired in white,
Leading with her a sort of goodly knights.'
(George Peele; The Arraignment of Paris)

Sunday the 24th November 1588, the day before the Rotherhithe Watch had pulled the mangled body out of the Thames, had been the day of the Queen's procession to St Paul's Cathedral to celebrate victory over the Spanish. As God had been firmly on our side, it was only right that the *Virgin Queen* and an entourage of worthies should thank him in person, and I, and my fellow Citizens of London, line the streets to bear witness. It was also a holiday and the beginning of the Southwark Fair on Bankside, and thus a day that many of those same Londoners had long looked forward to with feverish expectation.

I had left my lodgings early that morning and joined the larger-than-usual throng forcing its way along the narrow passage of the ancient bridge. My route took me past the little church of St Magnus the Martyr, at the foot of the bridge, through the bustling and noisy Billingsgate Harbour, before I darted away from the river up a thin, curving passageway, called Love Lane, which took its name in honour of the women who plied their trade there. It was a short cut which offered ample opportunities for escaping the city crowds, providing one could put up with the stench of refuse and the proximity to the rats that fed on it. I covered my face with my cloak and moved quickly, keeping to the wall to avoid the open sewer running down the centre of the lane. Fortunately, as the lane's notorious itinerants avoided daylight like the plague, for once I wasn't invited to engage in a bit of *stair-work* in some indignant inhabitant's doorway. The most serious danger that early in the morning was being showered by a piss-pot emptied from one of the higher storeys on either side of the narrow alley – an illegal but all-too-common occurrence.

My first port of call that previous morning had been a draper's shop on Tower Street, the home of one of my few close friends Harry Bucklesbury, or Buck as he liked to be known. The shop, belonging to Buck's stepfather, catered to the clothing needs of gentlemen living in the affluent lanes north of East Cheap, but unlike many 'sons' in his position, Buck had so far avoided getting roped into the family trade. Instead, from an attic room not dissimilar to my own lodgings, Buck indulged his ambition of becoming a poet and writing plays for the burgeoning London theatres.

On my arrival in the shadowy workshop, I politely greeted Buck's stepfather, who I knew disapproved of me, and received a curt nod in response. The shop was quieter than usual and I surmised that the apprentices had been freed for the holiday. Buck's father was an austere, hawkish man of about fifty, who was less than enamoured of Buck's chosen career and never tired of reminding his stepson of his 'duty'. Buck's own father had died when the family lived abroad, and his mother had brought the children to London and re-married before being swiftly reunited with her first husband in the afterlife, following the requisite bout of fever. A young Buck, and his even younger sister Emmalina, had been left in the hands of a man who neither had time for, nor cared very much about their existence until, that was, they had become old enough to be useful. I had heard many uncomfortable tales of their cruel and neglectful upbringing, not all of which had been fashioned by a poet's mind. There was certainly no love lost between Buck and his stepfather, and my friend was largely craving artistic success so he could escape the latter's clutches.

At the rear of the shop, I could see Emmalina sewing by the light of a window. Emmalina was the paste which just about held the family together. Numerous were the times that I had witnessed her diffuse a potential row between stepfather and stepson with a clever use of wit, or a disarming change of topic. She smiled at me, as I caught her eye, and before I could escape her gaze, called out to me:

'Wherefore are you out so early, Master John? Are you going to the procession?'

'Ay marry! If your brother's awake and hasn't been struck by the muse?'

'He is awake and has already entertained a fine visitor this morning. Father was most upset that it wasn't a customer. Weren't you papa?'

'Probably some good-for-nothing from one of the theatres,' the old man mumbled grudgingly, fixing his eyes on me suspiciously. Buck supplemented his income from writing – or lack of it – by taking small parts in the plays of others, a profession considered to be on a level with whoring or thieving by many of the better-heeled members of society.

Emmalina had put down her work and joined her father on the opposite side of the counter. She reached over and quietly began doing up the highest buttons of my doublet with slender, delicate fingers. 'There was a frost this morning, Master John. You need to wrap up warm, even if you are going to bathe in the warmth of *Gloriana* herself!'

I meekly let her adjust the frilly ruff of my shirt, enjoying the attention. Until recently, I had regarded Emmalina as a slightly vexatious younger sibling, but lately had become aware of a quite different set of sensations whenever I encountered her, ones that her protective brother might not altogether approve of. I glanced at her furtively now, acutely aware of her breath on my neck. She brushed aside a thick tress of auburn hair and took a pin from between her teeth, with which she proceeded to sure up my doublet against the cold. Catching my enthralled gaze, she stretched her soft, coral-coloured lips into a broad, delectable smile.

'Won't you let me accompany you? You could do with a chaste maid on your arm to give you some respectability.' Before I could think of a suitably witty reply, her stepfather relieved me by pouring cold water on the suggestion.

'Don't be ridiculous child. It may be an undeserved holiday for some', that 'some' was Buck and I, 'but there's still plenty of work to do. If your idle brother won't help us, we'll have to do everything ourselves.'

Just as he finished speaking, a shadow darkened the shop and the little bell above the door rang as someone entered. On seeing the newcomer, Emmalina released my collar, her expression changing abruptly from playfulness to apprehension.

I turned to see who could have produced such a reaction. The man who had entered was not old but not exactly young either. His face was made up of large slabs of flesh, seemingly put together at random, out of which the only signs of life were tiny, moist eyes and a darting tongue. Nevertheless, he sported the rich clothes of a merchant, in particular showing off the black cloak which marked him out as a member of a guild. Emmalina's stepfather's reaction was in marked contrast to hers. He bowed obsequiously and held out his hand to the stranger.

'Good day Master Shuttleworth, good day. I hope this fine morning finds you well.'

'Quite well, thank you, draper. Business is advancing profitably now that we have seen off that Spanish mob. And how is your charming daughter?' he leant across to Emmalina as he spoke, tongue darting across his lips. 'Keeping her little lady's fingers busy, I see.'

She curtsied awkwardly, mumbled something under her breath and hurried back to her sewing, putting as much distance between herself and the stranger as possible. I stood there awkwardly for a second and then decided to make myself scarce.

Buck was usually a late riser because of equally late nights spent pulling his hair out while staring at half written lines, the floor filling up inexorably with crumpled parchment. I was therefore surprised to find him sitting at his writing desk, quill in one hand and head in the other, eyes staring glazedly at a blank scroll.

'Ah, Lovat,' he greeted me, with an air of muted enthusiasm. 'You witness the noble scene of a writer with a commission.'

I looked at him quizzically. 'The last I knew you were still working on your Roman tragedy. Don't tell me old quatch-buttock Burbage is finally going to pay you for it?'

Buck had been working on the same play for a number of months but, to his frustration, the theatre manager had consistently rejected it. Combined with his increasing fatigue at having to play bit parts in other writer's plays, this rejection had recently been wearing Buck down to the point where I had started to become quite worried by his sudden plunges into depression or anger – usually manifested when locking horns with his stepfather.

'Alas not, dear friend, although the incredulity in your voice betrays a worrying lack of faith in my talent. Not to mention the fact that 'old quatch-buttock' Burbage, as you so poetically describe him, could one day conceivably be the docket to my success.' He looked at me sideways, his handsome face prematurely marked by fatigue, and I felt it prudent not to scoff.

'No, this commission comes from an altogether loftier source. A young gentleman, shortly to be presented at court, has commissioned me to write an *impresa*. And what is more, and of much greater import, he is paying three shillings for the bounty of my genius.'

'An *impresa*!' I chuckled unkindly. 'Next you'll be writing odes for love-sick lawyers.' An *impresa* was a gift presented to the Queen at the Palace of Whitehall by the knights invited to participate in the Accession Day Tilts celebrating the Royal Birthday. The Queen herself had instigated the practice and on the only occasion I had visited the palace, on a messenger-boy errand for my brother, I had witnessed a gallery leading off the Thames crammed with row upon row of pasteboard shields, each with their own obsequious, personal messages in Latin, designed to flatter or cajole the Queen. I remembered shuddering at the sight of them.

'The only problem is that I can't think of anything original to write and his high-and-mighty Lordship wants it by tomorrow morning.'

'There's little point asking for my advice, unless you want to test Her Majesty's tolerance, and the strength of your own neck.'

'You know Lovat, for one so closely related to aristocracy, you display an alarming lack of respect for the finer points of society. I think the strength of your own neck will be tested long before mine.' With this comforting thought, Buck brightened considerably. 'No, I intend my young knight to curry great favour with Her Majesty before entering battle.'

'Who is he?'

'The Honourable Richard Hardwick, eldest son of Sir Christopher, merchant adventurer, entrepreneur and erstwhile favourite of good queen Beth.'

'Dick Hard-wick? You jest. With a name like that it will be difficult *not* to offend.'

'He certainly is a poperine pear of a young gent.'

'Stuck up you mean? Well, let's just hope the little pillicock gets his cardinal's cap knocked off during the jousts!'

'Providing he coughs up first, eh?' He gave me a sideways glance. 'Money, that is.'

'Naturally.'

Buck went back to staring at the blank sheet of parchment. After a few moments of glassy-eyed consideration, he let out a big sigh and turned back to me. 'How's the Pointer?' he asked wearily.

The Pointer, owing to the shape of his nose, was the nickname we gave to our master, John Wolfe, at the publishers where we had met and occasionally worked, translating foreign texts into English. We both had strong Latin but my specialities were Greek and French, Buck's Spanish, Portuguese and German. Buck supplemented his meagre acting wages by putting these translation skills to work, but he hated doing that almost as much as playing 'third lady-in-waiting'. He had failed to turn up to work the whole of the previous week, feigning illness.

'As sharp as ever,' I replied. 'Your absence was duly noted.'

'It's of no consequence. When *Vespacia* is finished I won't have to work for the old gown anymore.' *Vespacia* was the mooted title of Buck's supposed hit play. Feeling overwhelmed with the hopelessness of my friend's prospects, a wave of sympathy came over me

'Come on,' I said. 'We'd better get this other matter out of the way first. Where's your *Lily's*? I reached for the Latin grammar book on a shelf above the desk. 'Remind me, what's the Latin for cocksure, upstart, prick?'

* * *

Buck and I had left his lodgings at midday, having drafted an *impresa* that we hoped would satisfy young Hardwick, and walked westwards to join the huge crowds flocking to the Queen's procession. The truth was that neither of us had much enthusiasm for the event itself, and I had more or less been ordered to attend by my brother – 'to demonstrate the love of the common man for his sovereign' was how he had put it, conveniently forgetting that we were of the same noble blood – but it was an excuse to venture abroad across the city on a day of feverish excitement. Buck had convinced himself that it would be good research for his play, and I had convinced myself it would be fun to cavort around the city for the day, like a Flemish tourist.

On the way we collected Greville Mortimer, a friend of Buck's, from the Old Swan Inn on the corner of Thames Street and Old Swan Lane. Greville and Buck were old school pals but Greville had only recently returned to London after spending time abroad and I barely knew him.

The Old Swan was the lowest class of ordinary, but an attractive option because it had been given special dispensation for pipe drinking. Tobacco was still a relatively new phenomenon, and was regarded with suspicion or awe by many, although fashionable young men considered it a social necessity. The strange apparition of smoke being breathed into and expelled from another man's mouth was still a novelty for most citizens, and when we reached the tavern we had to shove our way through a crowd of ragged children who had gathered at the bowed window to marvel at the strange goings on inside.

To our dismay, Greville had already made a head start on the day's revelry and was loudly pursuing an argument with a dangerous-looking gentleman over a game of dice. Greville had lost but was refusing to pay his debt on suspicion that the other man's dice were loaded. This was a common enough accusation but it was better to be absolutely sure of one's ground before launching into the kind of verbal assault that Greville had embarked on. Knives had been drawn on both sides and the situation was threatening to escalate. Buck and I quickly extricated Greville by settling the debt of two shillings, and hustling him into the open.

The procession started on the Strand, entered the city at the newly restored Ludgate and proceeded up Ludgate Hill before arriving at St Paul's for the service of celebration. A display of fair blue cloth in the distance announced that we were getting close to the procession route. Glimpses of St Paul's showed it swathed in colour from the captured flags of Spanish galleons. The streets in the vicinity had been expurgated for the event, with the usual array of beggars, disbanded soldiers and street hawkers nowhere to be seen.

'Probably been rounded up and invited to spend an afternoon in the Clink,' quipped Greville, when I commented on it.

'As you will be, if you don't keep that dagger out of sight,' warned Buck good-naturedly in return. Weapons were banned in the city, especially today of all days.

Lacking their usual inhabitants, the streets were a strange mixture of proud merchants and their families, wide-eyed foreign visitor clinging to their purses, blue-clad apprentices looking for mischief on a rare holiday and an array of other citizens and commoners, all caught up in the febrile air. Amid the chaotic hubbub, street stalls cashing in on the event sent tempting aromas into the air. Musicians, dancers and street performers were drawing crowds of young and old alike. Even the three of us began to drop our natural cynicism as we started to get transported by the mood – not to mention the proximity to many pretty maids, who had ventured out in force for the day and could often be caught pointing at the three of us and giggling.

It is difficult to explain the euphoria that had gripped the country since the Armada had been defeated. Months of worry and insecurity had been followed by preparation for war and a grim determination against what amounted to overwhelming odds. Buck, Greville and I had all been mustered to fight, Buck and Greville at Tilbury with the Earl of Leicester, where they had already witnessed a visit from the Queen. When the threat had finally materialised, we had all gone through the same emotions of fear, bravado, and real courage, followed by rejoicing, patriotic fervency and a downright feeling of superiority as the Spanish ships had been washed away, like the excrement of Love Lane on a rainy day.

Along the route of the procession, people were leaning out of windows, standing on balconies and ranged along the city walls, even climbing flag poles and drainpipes in order to get a better view. Wifflers in coats of velvet and chains stood along the edge, halberds raised, to prevent the crowd from spilling forward. Ludgate itself, whose recent renovation followed years of falling into disrepair, was filled with people at every vantage point including the turreted roof, where some even gripped onto the statues of King Lud and his sons.

The three of us pushed our way through the crowd, which was as much as a dozen people deep, trying to find a good vantage point. It was not made easier by the obstacle of a set of railed stairs, set up along the route to give preference to merchants and artisans – the true *citizens* of London – who wore long black gowns lined with red, and held ensigns and flags denoting their particular trades. Although these flags made a very fine spectacle, they made it difficult for those with a less privileged position to actually see what was going on. Eventually, after being shoved on a couple of times by over-zealous wifflers, the three of us managed to clamber onto the Ludgate Hill stocks, fortunately emptied of their occupants for the occasion, where we stood a head above the crowd in a rather precarious position from which one or other of us periodically toppled off, usually when trying to have a surreptitious swig out of one of the flagons of ale Greville had had the foresight to bring.

There was still some time to wait before the procession and so we passed the time sharing provisions and good-natured banter with our neighbours. Suddenly though, a new mood of anticipation transmitted itself from the crowd outside the gate to those inside, and we knew that the procession was on its way.

The Queen was preceded by a fine pageant of a thousand men on horseback, including nobles, admirals and even foreign allies of importance. Many of the latter were dressed in clothes of overtly continental fashion and some of the more fervid members of the crowd took great delight in heckling these gentlemen as they rode past.

There was one gentleman, in particular, who stood out. He was wearing a bright red-and-gold doublet and hose, cut in the Italian style. Enveloping his neck was a fat, cream-coloured ruff, made up of intricately-woven lace, which impressively set off his handsome, if somewhat haughty, features. The outfit was embellished by a rich velvet cloak, which was slung stylishly off one shoulder to flow down the flanks of his horse, and a wide-brimmed hat sprouting feathers representing all of the colours of the rainbow, and some others besides. The overall effect was to make him look like one of those exotic talking birds that sailors were fond of bringing back from the New World.

This poor gentleman's humiliation was increased by the fact that he had a Mediterranean complexion and looked every bit the Spaniard, increasing tenfold the jeering and laughter flung in his direction. I had to grudgingly admit, though, that he did a good job of holding his large, crooked nose in the air, adopting a manner of complete disdain for the seething masses, as he passed along the narrow channel.

The exotic stranger was soon forgotten as more and more riders came through the arches of the gate, many of them carrying keys, crosses and other symbols of their standing in society. By now fully committed to the path that would see me at such a disadvantage when Nesbitt arrived at my lodgings, Buck, Greville and I continued to drink voraciously and cheer or jeer, according to what the occasion called for. Suddenly the crowd subdued into a muted hush as the Queen's train passed through Ludgate – part admiration, part awe, part fear caused by the proximity to her bodyguard, the Gentlemen Pensioners, who ran along beside her wielding halberds. The Queen, resplendent in a silver dress, sat on a raised chariot, pushed along by footmen in crimson velvet running suits and black skullcaps, with a golden canopy raised above her head. Her pale face was expressionless, cold even, as though she was somehow from a different sphere altogether. Accompanying her walked the great heads of state – Burghley, Hatton, Somerset, Walsingham – their faces a mixture of determination and pride. My brother was amongst the gentlemen following the Queen's chariot and I found myself staring at him – he all to oblivious to my presence amongst the crowd. As the remnants of the procession passed, I was left with an impression of him – aloof, dignified, belonging – his future secure.

* * *

That chilly, overcast afternoon on the Rotherhithe bank, I threw off thoughts of how the rest of the previous evening had developed – celebrations and jousts in the streets, the dash south across the river for the beginning of the Southwark Fair, games and drinking in diverse inns and taverns, eventual oblivion in my lodgings – and concentrated instead on the pitiful, battered remains of the dead man.

There was no sign of the huge cream ruff, nor of the feathered hat, but much of his rich clothing was still intact – there was no doubt that the proud foreign gentleman from the Armada procession was raising his nose indifferently to the sky one last, and final, time.

Chapter 3

'We are continually dying: I while I am writing these words, you while you are reading them.'
(Francesco Petrarca; Letters)

The discovery of a foreign corpse on the banks of the Thames was quite a coup for the Rotherhithe Watch. There were six of them in total, including the boy, and judging by their eager, curious faces, discovering washed up bodies on the beach wasn't a everyday occurrence.

For months the whole country had been rife with paranoia about the threat of invasion from Spain, or the infiltration of undesirables such as spies and Catholic priests, and the '*Watch*' had become a regular feature of life around the English coast. Their instructions were to look for anything suspicious along the miles of empty stretches of coastline and report it to the *Parish Constable* or *Officer of the Watch*, who, in turn, was supposed to inform some higher authority.

Just like the ragtag group standing before me, the '*Watch*' usually consisted of small bands of men and youths deemed worthy to protect their country, whilst foregoing the burden of payment. The country was still on high alert and the Thames estuary was considered a particularly likely place for an illegal landing. Looking for spies, however, was nothing like as much fun as it sounded and being a member of one of these numerous groups was largely a thankless task – conducted during the night, invariably in intemperate weather, and tending to yield little by way of success, let alone excitement. They were also poorly trained and not particularly adept at spotting their target. Consequently, most of them were ready to lynch the first innocent stranger, just to liven their routine up a bit.

Besides, landing a boat on a deserted coastline was a risky method of entering a hostile country. Most undesirables preferred to simply arrive in disguise at one of the main ports and walk straight into the country with little by the way of bother. I remembered my father laughing as he told me about the Jesuit priest, Robert Persons, still unaccounted for, who had swaggered his way into the country disguised as a captain of the army returning from the Low Countries: 'dressed in a coat with a gold lace trim and a feathered hat'. My father, usually a mild-mannered man, could barely conceal his scorn as he recounted how the port authorities were so impressed by this brave adventurer returning from battle that they went out of their way to find him a horse and send him on his way to London with their sincerest blessings. With that kind of professional security in place, it was hard to imagine the amateur patrols achieving much success.

There was one odd one out, an older man with a forced air of respectability and a marginally better quality of clothing, which is to say that it wasn't muddy, torn, and reeking of fish. There was something pious about him, which indicated the church. He kept himself slightly apart from the others as though wishing to avoid any misinterpretation of his status, although I sensed that he wanted to be just as involved as they were.

I turned back to the body, feeling the cloying dampness of the men closing in around me. I ordered them to stand back so I could have some light, although it was mainly to alleviate their unholy stench.

Although a stranger, it still felt eerie to be examining the lifeless body of a man seen alive in all his glory and finery only a day earlier. I looked closely at his disfigured face and tried to concentrate on what more it could tell me, rather than getting distracted by the shocking injuries. He was closer to forty than thirty, although still with a thick head of dark black hair and a short, fashionable beard. Also, there was no doubting his foreign appearance, despite the ravages of the river, his skin being far darker than the pasty faced natives surrounding me.

Other than that, the features were hardly recognisable and I doubted whether anyone who knew the man well would have been able to convincingly identify him by his face alone. The nose was broken and cut, there were large patches of red and purple bruises covering the surface of the skin, and, most tellingly, the gruesome eye socket, which was now of use only to one of those modern doctors interested in how the human body was put together. There was also severe bloating of the skin, caused by being in the water, which gave the head an eerie appearance of unreality, not to mention the unnatural position of the tongue. It best resembled some of the more mistreated craniums that Nesbitt and I had seen earlier on Traitor's Gate.

I turned the skull from side to side, looking closely at the ears. On one side there was a neat hole where I imagined I'd espied a large, studded earring during the procession. On the other side there was a nasty tear through the skin. Had the force that had caused the injuries to the face been sufficient to rip out an earring as well, or was that the work of the men standing around me? Hard to tell.

I concentrated on the rest of the man's body, trying to ignore the eager gaze of my audience. Immediately, I could see that the trauma continued down the whole torso. The fine red-and-gold striped clothing, that had looked resplendent in the late Autumn sunlight, was torn and shredded, and one of the sleeves had been partly torn from the shoulder. Down the arm and through the gaps in the remainder of the clothing there was evidence of the same bruising and colour disfiguration of the skin.

Thinking of the man's wealth, I searched for a purse around the waist but there was no sign of one. Reaching for each hand in turn, I also saw that there were no rings on his fingers, although an impression on one finger suggested that he had clearly worn at least one. The nails on both hands were well manicured, but the unnatural position of some of the fingers implied they were broken.

With my own digits trembling in the cold, I started to undo the clasps of the rich velvet doublet, which fastened right up to the chin. It took me an inordinate length of time to undo the first hooks and start to pull the doublet and woollen undershirt apart. Underneath, the flesh was just as bruised as the face but there was something even more sinister, a deep unnatural line pressed into the dark skin of the man's neck that contrasted markedly with the rest of the injuries. I chose not to undo the doublet further, preferring to hide what I had seen from the men of the Watch, although a quick glance up at Nesbitt, who had taken up a position to one side of me, indicated that he had seen the tell-tale signs of strangulation.

'Help me turn him over,' I said.

Nesbitt knelt beside me and we heaved the stiff body onto its front. There were more tears in the cloth and under clothing, and more cuts and bruises on the man's back. Glancing further down, I noticed, rather incongruously, the man's boots were still on his feet and that rich, blue stockings were visible around his knees. I eyed the boots enviously.

They were in fine condition and looked to be exactly my size.

Slightly ashamed that this thought had so readily crossed my mind, I turned my face upwards towards the men who were standing round staring intently at what I was doing.

'Where did you find him?' I asked Pinchkin Senior.

'Right 'ere on the bank, Master, as the tide went out. We pulled 'im from the water's edge and put 'im on this piece of driftwood.'

'What time was this?'

He thought for a moment, a calloused hand scratching his stubbly chin. 'Reckon t'was an hour before dawn.' He looked at the others for confirmation, receiving one or two nods. 'We passed this spot a few hours earlier and it weren't 'ere then.'

An hour before down was roughly six o'clock. I did some loose calculations in my head. It couldn't have taken more than two hours for Pinchkin Junior to reach my brother's house and Nesbitt had come calling after one. Assuming that Pinchkin senior wasn't lying, that allowed for a few missing hours when I supposed the men had stood around discussing what to do with the body, whilst probably helping themselves to any trinkets that were still intact. For the moment, I decided to let that pass.

'Why didn't you go to the local constable?'

'Well 'e was … unavailable, sir.' The hesitation suggested that the constable was either asleep, drunk or both. Those particular methods of evasion hadn't done me much good.

A thought occurred to me: 'How did you know the seal was Lord Rokesby's?'

At this question, the better-dressed man pushed himself forward from the position he had taken up, slightly apart from the men of the watch. He had an obsequious manner and clearly loved the sound of his own voice.

'That was my contribution, your Honour.' His address caused me to smile grimly to myself – if only he knew who I really was.

'Go on,' I said, baring my teeth in what I hoped was an encouraging manner.

'Thomas Radclyffe, sire, the verger of the local parish. Sir Robert Rokesby is the Over-Marshall of our glorious county of Kent. I naturally recognised the seal at once.'

'I took the seal to Master Radclyffe as soon as we found it,' piped in Pinchkin Senior, eager not to be left out of the glory. 'I knew if any round 'ere would know it's true meaning, it'd be 'im.'

'Where was the seal and chain?'

'Around the man's neck but caught on the clothing so it hadn't come loose.'

'You've had a good look at the body, have you? Was there any jewellery on the man when you found him? Or a purse?' I addressed this directly to Pinchkin Senior, looking him squarely in the eye.

'None sir.' A slight hesitation, nothing conclusive.

'You realise of course that stealing from a corpse is a serious felony?'

The men shuffled uneasily but no one said anything. I looked at the verger, Radclyffe, in particular, but he had suddenly discovered a speck of dirt on his tunic. It seemed his aloofness didn't stretch to missing out on a share of the booty. However, I decided not to pursue it. The men had demonstrated a modicum of honesty by identifying the seal and sending word to my brother. They could have pocketed that as well and tipped the body back into the water. Besides, I was pretty certain they hadn't murdered him, which, under the circumstances, seemed a more pressing matter.

'Who else knows about this man apart from the six of you?'

'No one, sir. I went to fetch Mr Radclyffe, and we returned forthwith.'

'And none of you have any idea who he is? There were no clues when you found him other than the seal?' They shook their heads in unison.

'When I saw his skin colour, we thought 'e must be a Spaniard from one of 'em 'mada ships.' This opinion was offered by a belligerent-looking fellow who had hitherto gone unnoticed. His jaw jutted out in an aggressive manner and appeared to support only a solitary tooth. I considered his suggestion as I stood up, knees aching from crouching over the body. It wasn't completely stupid, the country was awash with stories about Spanish sailors clogging up English beaches, but I dismissed it.

'Unlikely. No Armada ships have been close enough to London to deposit a body in this area.'

'Perhaps he's a spy?'

'Or a Jesuit priest?' another of the men chipped in. 'I 'eard that they caught a Papist trying to land on the North bank only a month ago.'

'So no one else knows about this?' I snapped, eager to put an end to the speculation they had clearly been rehearsing before my arrival. 'No wives or children wondering where you've got to? No passers-by?'

'Like I said, just the six of us standin' here. We ain't let a soul see the body, nor discussed it with anyone.'

'Well let us keep it that way shall we?' I knew that this request would most likely be in vain. I imagined that, even if Pinchkin's protestations were true, the temptation to discuss it would soon overwhelm them, especially when tongues were loosened in the local tavern.

Wondering what to do next, I turned away from the group of men and gazed across the expanse of river towards the North bank. Since our arrival, the tide had already receded a few feet further, leaving in its wake a thin expanse of glistening mud. By now the sun was in its dying throws, causing a yellowy-brown sheen to shimmer across the clay infused water. Small fishing boats could be seen skirting the northern shore and a large merchant ship had moored itself half a mile away towards the sea, waiting for the tide to turn and help it run into the waiting ports of London, where it would disgorge its exotic goods.

My main concern was what to do with the corpse. We couldn't very well leave it where it was, but I wasn't at all sure where responsibility for it lay. In the end I decided that, unpleasant as it was, we should row it to my brother's house. I didn't see why he should avoid the pleasure of viewing the mangled body, and at least he could confirm the man's identity. It would also give me a chance to further examine the stricture on the man's neck without an enthralled audience.

Whilst deep in thought, I had leant back against the colourful pole towering over the dead body. Now I became aware of the men stifling laughs and exchanging glances with each other.

'What's so funny?' I demanded; my impatience obvious.

Pinchkin Senior tried and failed to wipe the grin off his face before saying: 'I take it you're not married, sire.'

'What's that got to do with anything?' I said, taken aback for a moment by his impertinence.

'You wouldn't want to touch that, if you were married, sire – that there's the Cuckold's Pole.'

At this, all the men burst out laughing, apart from Nesbitt, whose face was sour with disapproval. I had heard of Cuckold's Point – a monument erected to the age-old custom of wives jumping into bed with men other than their, supposedly, impotent husbands. Evidently the foreign gentleman had washed up at that exact spot.

I broke the merriment by telling the men to cover the body with the cloak and carry it to the boat. The body was completely stiff as they lifted it, but bent in unnatural ways. What on earth had happened to it?

'I saw you noticed the mark on his neck,' I said quietly to Nesbitt, when the men had cleared away. 'I want to take a closer look at it away from the prying eyes of these oafs. If they see that he's been strangled, we'll never be able to shut them up.' Nesbitt merely nodded in agreement. 'Do you think he lost his jewellery before or after he went into the river?'

'I've no doubt these cozeners wouldn't hesitate to steal.' Nesbitt replied, displaying little sign of that famed Puritan Charity.

'Perhaps, though not easy getting a ring off that bloated finger, and why didn't they take his boots as well? They're a perfectly good pair of leather and they've had all morning to think about it.' Looking down at the useless pair I was wearing, I hoped my true thoughts on the subject weren't too transparent.

'Perhaps they don't value leather as highly as pretty trinkets,' mused Nesbitt, looking at me sideways.

Before we pushed off, I addressed the *Watch* as a group, asking them again to keep the discovery of the body a secret, and telling them they could expect a reward for their vigilance and discretion. I tried to convince them that it was most likely an accident up in the city and that there was nothing untoward afoot. However, their faces told me they weren't convinced. The state of the body, and the fact that two gentlemen from upriver had come down to cart it away, was enough to convince them that some greater mystery than a hapless stranger falling in the river had occurred. Their expressions contained a mixture of incomprehension and suspicion, not to mention disappointment that the morning's entertainment seemed about to end. Only the verger was different, looking at me meaningfully as I finished speaking. I decided to ignore him and turned to get in the boat but as I did so he caught my arm and spoke to me in a tone low enough to conceal his speech from the other men.

'Your Honour, if Lord Rokesby wishes, I will happily call on him to give a description of the events that have occurred here. I believe that an eloquent account of what I have observed may be of use to him, and I am somewhat of an expert in the local area.' An expert footlicker more likely, I thought unkindly. 'Perhaps I could accompany you and the body?'

'That won't be necessary,' I said, taking him into my confidence. 'But if you could ensure that the men here keep their discretion, I am sure you will earn Lord Robert's favour.'

He smiled conspiratorially but still held tightly onto my sleeve. I began to discern what he wanted. 'Send word to Master Lovat, sign of the watch-maker on the bridge, and I will ensure your reward is forthcoming.'

This seemed to do the trick. He released my arm and I left him on the shore wearing a conspiratorial expression. I slung myself into the back of the boat and we set off with a firm shove from two of the Rotherhithe Watch. As we rowed away, the men stood for a moment staring at us sullenly, the strange pole with its antlers silhouetted against the gloaming sky above them, before turning and slowing starting their journey back to the village across the marsh. I watched the disparate bunch for a while as they reluctantly trudged off.

I now had ample time to study the body, wedged awkwardly in the curved bottom of the boat. Nesbitt had taken a position in the stern allowing me the dubious pleasure of having the corpse to myself. I opened the neck and breast of his garments again and looked closely at the mark around his neck. Although at first it was hard to distinguish from the extensive bruising, there was one deep maroon line seared into the skin about half an inch thick. I had an idea about that and a quick comparison proved that the size of the mark corresponded exactly with the width of the chain to which my brother's seal was connected. Not only that, as I turned the neck slightly, I could even identify where the seal itself had left an impression.

I opened the clothing further to reveal the man's chest and stomach. Again, there were marks similar to those on the face, neck and arms suggesting that the entire body had been badly battered.

'Anything further of interest?' Nesbitt asked me. He had been standing up and leaning over the backs of the rowers, much to their annoyance, trying to see what I was doing.

'The tongue sticking out, the mark on the neck – it all points to strangulation. Apart from that nothing new.'

'A nasty deed. Rokesby won't like it one bit.' Nesbitt sat back down and folded his arms with what seemed like grim satisfaction. He appeared to be relishing the task of delivering the bad news to my brother. I felt only apprehension. It was the first time I had encountered a dead body in such a manner and I was a loss to know what it might have to do with Robert.

By now the weather had closed in and freezing rain was starting to spit down on our heads, but the tide had changed in a moment, making rowing far easier for the two oarsmen. Both of them had relaxed slightly and were talking as they rowed, turning to look at each other.

Suddenly we heard the urgent clattering of a loud bell behind us. I turned sharply to see the bow of the huge merchant ship we had seen moored further downstream, coming out of the gloom only a few feet behind us and gaining quickly. We were directly in the ship's path and I could clearly see the figurehead of a mythical sea creature as the vessel loomed up behind us. The two oarsmen chatting away had barely noticed the huge ship, sped on by the changing tide and increasing winds. They quickly scrambled with their oars to take us to one side, as Nesbitt and I looked back in horror at the great shadow towering above us.

It was a close-run thing as the bow of the merchant ship cut past us but the men just managed to manoeuvre the exposed boat out of the ship's path, though not beyond its wake. As the first wave hit us, we rocked violently and Nesbitt and I, lacking the luxury of oars, both grabbed onto whatever we could to avoid falling over the side and suffering the same fate as our passenger. In my haste to secure myself, I took hold of the dead man's shirt but couldn't avoid falling straight on top of him, my head disappearing into the space between his head and shoulders. The dampness and stench of the dead body caught me and for a moment I felt as though I was held in the grip of the dead. I broke into a cold sweat and the hairs on my back shot up in an animalistic terror. As I tried desperately to push myself away, another wave hit the boat causing me to fall helplessly again, awkwardly landing in a twisted mass and with my arm still clinging to the man's shirt under my body. The irony of holding onto a dead man for dear life was not lost on me.

Gradually, the waves from the ship subsided as it pulled ahead of us. I unravelled myself and pushed myself upright, the colour drained from my face. Cold, wet, tired, hung-over – all in all it was too much excitement for one day. I cursed the men for allowing the ship to almost ram us and told them to concentrate on their jobs.

I realised that I was still kneeling on the dead man's body with my white knuckles clinging to his under-shirt. I was about to loosen my grip, when it occurred to me that the material I was holding contained an unnatural bulge at about the height of the man's chest, under his left armpit. Feeling my way around the area, which was about two inches thick, I turned the shirt outwards. On the inside was a pocket sewn into the shirt. I ripped the stitching to reveal two items: a brooch and a golden ring. It seemed I had discovered some valuables that had not been fleeced from the body by the river or the Rotherhithe Watch.

I glanced back at Nesbitt to see if he had spotted my discovery, but he was busy watching the stern of the boat that had only moments earlier tried to carve us in two. I studied the items as discreetly as possible. The brooch was a delicate piece, about an inch in diameter, and of the most exquisite craftsmanship. I cupped it gently in the palm of my hand, admiring the concentric ring of opaque pearls, inlaid in gold, surrounding a bulbous red carnelian stone.

By its narrow diameter, I judged the ring to be that of a lady. There was slight staining on the gold but the water had done it no harm. I gently rubbed my fingers around the band, tracing the inscriptions imprinted on both sides and strained my eyes to read them. On the outside were the words: RATHER DEATH THAN FALS FAYTH and the initials C.H. On the inside, the simple statement: MEMENTO MORI. These heavy-handed inscriptions somewhat cheapened the ring which must have once been beautiful in its simplicity.

Memento Mori – remember you must die. I slipped the ring and brooch furtively into the sleeve pocket of my doublet and sat back heavily in the bow. The Latin inscription was common on wedding bands: remember you must die and therefore live virtuously. The outside inscription only appeared to enforce this message of chastity. The wedding gift of a suspicious husband, perhaps, but what was it doing sewn into the dead man's shirt? And who was C.H. – the wearer or the giver?

It was only then that I realised my whole body was shaking, from the cold and the wet, from the shock of nearly capsizing, and from my brief encounter with the clammy grip of the dead.

Chapter 4

'The name of brother is indeed a beautiful and affectionate one.'
(Michel de Montaigne; Essays)

The Chancel House, my brother's London home, was situated along the Strand, the principal route linking the city with the state buildings at Whitehall. It was one of a number of large estates laid out between the road and the curving stretch of river, which for years had been home to rich and influential families. This reflected their growing appreciation over the centuries that their fortunes (not to mention the opportunity of having some fun in life) were as closely linked to the sprawling city as their country estates.

Formerly the residence of a Catholic bishop, the house had been appropriated for the crown during the dissolution of the monasteries fifty years earlier and bought by my father at a knockdown price, with the blessing of the boy King, Edward, as a reward for his loyalty. For thirty years my father had bucked the trend by more or less ignoring his London residence, preferring to spend his time in the countryside. Since his death, however, its ownership had passed to my brother, who spent a great deal of his time there. Compared with the flashier estates on either side, the Chancel House still had a certain antiquated charm, although I knew my brother was planning to redress this as soon as funds allowed.

Cold, damp and tired on that November morning I was hardly in the mood for my brother's company, let alone the little jaunt down the river that he had sent me on. For much of our upbringing, our relationship had been one of mutual antipathy. Robert and I were only half-brothers. We had the same father but different mothers and there were eight years between us. When my father sired my brother he was careful to do it with the agreement of his then wife, her Ladyship, and my brother burst forth into the world squalling and screaming as the legitimate heir to a title, a fortune and a life of uncomplicated ease, at least so it seemed to me. I never knew my brother's mother. She had died by the time that my ageing father went for one final fling with a servant on his Cotswold estate. The result of this frowned-upon conjugation – my good self – came timidly into a life characterised by lack of prospects, uncertainty, and the constant reminder of being a bastard, both for the amusement of friends and the advantage of enemies.

I never knew my own mother, either. The act of my birth was the final part she played in life. I am told she was a pretty girl with a winning smile but that's all I ever gleaned. Not surprisingly perhaps, no one in the household wanted to talk about her. It wasn't all bad news though. My father, kindly and generous in his dotage, was happy to accept me into the family and my childhood was spent in his house, where I had the run of his large country estate, and was able to learn all of the trappings of being a gentleman, a title that the circumstances of my birth barred me from ever obtaining.

My father's indulgence of this unexpected late arrival had been the main source of antagonism between myself and Robert, who felt, somewhat condescendingly in my opinion, that I should be brought up in the cowshed attached to my late mother's family cottage in the local village. It was only when I was about five years old that my teenage brother started to see how I might become useful to him as a dogsbody and our relationship changed to one of unerring superiority on his part and a life of drudgery on mine. At least I no longer had to worry about my back becoming the target for his daily archery practise.

To begin with, my brother began to employ me as a glorified servant, carrying his coat of arms at pageants, fetching his horse, polishing his armour. It amused him to have his bastard brother act as a slave in a way that my father could hardly object to. The one time I complained to my father about it he laughed heartily and said in his enigmatic manner:

'A man's character, John, can be determined by how he deals with servitude both as servant, and master.' I looked at him for explanation but he merely clapped me on the back. 'Come on, get the cards out. There's a new dodge I've been dying to teach you.'

Perhaps mindful of the struggles I would face later in life, my father was always keen to instruct me in the 'black arts'. His particular enthusiasm was for sharp-practise with cards but he also took great delight in teaching me how to cheat at dice and even pick locks.

In the meantime, my brother continued to refer to me loudly as his 'pageboy' whenever we were in company and make use of me at all opportune moments. My early childhood was littered with instances where I remember standing alone at some joust or fair feeling isolated and aggrieved, while my brother amused his friends by sending me on some laborious and demeaning errands. There was to be no sudden reverse in fortunes, as in the King Arthur stories I consoled myself with at night; no sword to draw from the stone to prove myself a worthy gentleman after all – or simply to run my brother through with!

Fortunately, this period was relatively short-lived. Well-to-do families have unusual ideas about how to raise their children and Robert was invited to spend long periods in the homes of other aristocratic friends and relations. As illegitimates like myself were hardly considered good role models for other children, these aristocrats conveniently forgot to invite me, much to my relief. I stayed at home learning dubious skills from my rogue of a father, and making strategies for avoiding my brother when he returned.

It wasn't long before Robert left home permanently to continue his education at Oxford. From Oxford he had gone up to London and, after not too long, a seat on the Privy Council. He was a rising star of Queen Elizabeth's court and for a few years it seemed as though he had quite forgotten about my existence.

Then two things happened in quick succession to bring me back into his sphere. My father, whose health had long been threatened by his excessive way of life, died suddenly. His death left me with a mixture of profound grief, and fear of what was to become of me. Despite his indulgences, his acceptance did not extend to anything by way of an inheritance, apart from a small bequest of money and the few items from the house that I now treasured as my prized possessions, most of which I had simply taken without asking. I knew I could expect little else. As a bastard, according to the laws of the land, I could legally neither own nor inherit property, nor marry into it. My prospects seemed bleak.

Then, unexpectedly at my father's funeral, my brother offered me the chance to come to London with the promise that some work could be found for me. The arrangement included him funding lodgings for me on London Bridge and finding me part time work in a publishing house, where I could put the language skills I had learnt during my childhood to good use.

It soon transpired, however, that he was most interested in rekindling our former relationship; the one where he said 'jump' and I asked 'how high?' Mostly the tasks he employed me for involved benign matters such as delivering letters of state, bringing him information, or accompanying him as a kind of bodyguard.

Occasionally the tasks were more exciting. At one time he had even sent me to witness an execution – that of Mary, Queen of Scots. That death was legitimate, however. The trip down the Thames was the first time I had been asked to investigate a freshly murdered body and the escalation of my duties did not appeal to me in the slightest.

* * *

Stone steps from the Thames ran up to the house's manicured garden and it was here that our boat finally docked, after a further half-an-hour's journey up river. The remainder of our passage had been uneventful, despite a discrepancy in the tide at London Bridge, which had been skilfully negotiated by the oarsmen, eager to prove that their earlier carelessness had been an aberration. As the arches of the great bridge receded behind us, I looked back wistfully at the room of my lodgings high up on the west side of the bridge, longing to be still there curled up comfortably in my bed.

I told the men to carry the body into the cellar, and Nesbitt and I went on through the garden to the house. We skirted round a tight pattern of box hedges forming a complicated knot, designed to amuse guests who could contemplate it from the upper rooms of the house. There were also a number of exotic plants from foreign lands placed at conspicuous vantage points, that my brother was often to be heard boasting about.

A servant informed us that my brother was expecting us in the hall overlooking the garden. Ascending the carved oak staircase, we were accosted by a grossly overweight man coming down, with a red face and a mop of brown hair on his head – Marmaduke Drummond, my brother's protégée and resident poet. Typical of the breed, he spent his days idling about the house composing flowery odes, all unctuously dedicated to my brother. Blocking my path, he addressed me in the usual contemptuous tones he reserved for me.

'My dear J-Jackie boy, always the centre of fashion,' he said, with his usual stutter, which always seemed to me to be an affectation. 'I must remember to take you to B-Bankside with me one night – what a sensation you will p-prove to be.' His fat cheeks wobbled as he spoke, allowing the rouge, which only heightened his grotesqueness, to glitter under the candlelight.

'I'm perfectly well aware of the establishments you frequent, Drummond, and frankly I would rather visit a leper colony. Would you mind stepping aside? I need to see my brother urgently.'

Drummond stiffened slightly and refused to budge. 'Urgently, you say? What little errand could the d-dogsbody be sent on that required any urgency?' His eyes narrowed in his head and he stared at me unnervingly for a second before looking back towards the garden, through the door we had entered. 'Some little task on the river, perhaps?' He looked at me shrewdly expecting a reply, eyes sunken behind balloons of fat. I declined to answer.

'If you wouldn't mind, Master Drummond, we are in rather a hurry.' Nesbitt, always the diplomat, began to edge forward. Drummond reluctantly moved sideways to let us pass but I felt the noxious heat of his gaze on my neck the whole way up the stairs.

* * *

The hall was a long, oblong room running the length of the house on the riverside. It had three sides of warm timber wainscoting, set-off by two wide bay windows, which jutted out over the garden and gave a breath-taking view of the bend in the river, now all sparkles of light in the darkness. Covering the oak panelling were a number of broad *arrases* depicting scenes from Greek myths, as well as one or two paintings, which were said to be good likenesses of the Italian School.

Robert stood with his back to the stone fireplace that stood at one end of the room, with two large mastiffs lying by his feet. Behind him a vibrant fire crackled in the grate. As ever he was immaculately dressed in a black doublet and hose, set off by an elegant ruff, silk tights and velvet shoes with lace bows. His hair was neatly cropped but his beard was long and straight, in the manner of other courtiers. In all outward appearances he portrayed the confident peer of the realm. However, his manner was impatient, and an uncharacteristic nervousness punctured his usual haughty confidence. This soon turned to anger as he sized up my rather contrasting appearance.

'My God, Lovat, what the hell do you look like?' His handsome face was a picture of long-suffering exasperation. 'Even if I didn't receive constant reports of your excessive behaviour, I could see the evidence for myself right here.'

At the sound of his master's raised voice, one of the mastiffs raised its head to eye me in a bored manner, before its jowls slumped back onto its paws. I could only imagine how I must look with my crumpled boots, damp clothes, and unshaven chin, but feeling that the day's task had already been enough of a penance for the enjoyment of the previous day, and embarrassed by his outburst, I allowed my own anger to rise despite my better judgement.

'Naturally I would be delighted to attend on you dressed as the rest of the perfumed fops that hang about this place, like refugees from Bohemia, but sadly the meagre pittance you pay me doesn't allow the wardrobe. Rather than berating me,' I added for good measure, 'perhaps you would be kind enough to offer me a bath.'

My brother chose to ignore this outburst, and instead turned pointedly to Nesbitt who was standing by my side with his head bowed submissively.

'Well? Did you find the body?'

'Yes, your Lordship, it was where the boy indicated. We've examined the body and brought it back here. We have placed it in the cellar, awaiting your further instructions.'

'It can stay there for now. Where exactly was it?'

As Nesbitt began to explain with his customary Latin flourishes exactly where the body had been located, I edged as close as possible to the fire to relieve some of the cold that had saturated through to my bones. My attempts were thwarted, though, by the two hostile dogs, who eyed me coldly as if they were quite aware of my place in the pecking order, and were fully prepared to assert their rights to warmth above mine. One of the slavering mutts even sparked up a low growl, warning me I had got too close. Averting my gaze from their unfriendly interest, I chose instead to study the gilded plaster patterns on the ceiling, something I knew my brother was extremely proud of, as he had only had the work done in the previous year by Flemish craftsmen.

Having described our journey down river in needless detail, Nesbitt started to describe the rabble we had met on the Thames shore that morning. However, before he got very far my brother, evidently losing patience, cut him short and turned instead to me.

'Anything to add?'

'Nesbitt failed to mention that we found the body under an ancient monument dedicated to the age-old pastime of cuckolding.'

'What has that to do with anything?'

'Oh nothing. As a student of the city I thought you might be interested that's all.'

'Don't be frivolous. This is a serious matter. What about these men who found the body?'

'The Rotherhithe Watch?' I replied as nonchalantly as possible, 'What can I say? Fishermen, rough types, pretty ignorant though far from stupid – I tried to impress upon them the need for secrecy in these dangerous times, so I suspect that the story will be all over Kent by now. I did make them promise of a reward,' I beamed broadly at my brother, 'which may stay their tongues for a short while at least. However, if they do talk I think they'll only be spreading rumours of a tragic accident befalling a rich foreigner. It's hardly an unknown occurrence after all. I don't think any of them saw the tell-tale marks around the man's neck.'

'What marks?' My brother asked, the words sticking in his throat.

'The man was clearly strangled. Although I am assuming you suspected something like that or you wouldn't have sent me.' As I spoke I took the seal attached to the chain out of the pocket in my sleeve and held it out to my brother. 'This item would seem to point to you as the prime suspect,' I added breezily, still annoyed at the way he had spoken to me earlier. I expected an angry reaction but instead Robert looked at the weighty chain with an expression of shock. I tried to hand it to him but he recoiled as if it might burn him. The colour drained from his cheeks and he sat down heavily in one of the chairs close to the fireplace, bidding me to take a second chair with a limp flick of his hand.

Sensing his mood, I decided to change tack and simply give him the facts just as they were. As I did so, my brother listened intently, breaking the flow only once to invite Nesbitt, who had been hovering awkwardly above us, to take a stool. I described the man's Mediterranean appearance, his rich clothing and the mangled state of the body, trying to picture it all clearly.

Finally I said: 'There is no doubt in my mind that the death was caused by strangulation and that the other injuries were caused later, possibly in the water itself.' I paused, before asking the question that had been on my mind ever since I had seen the seal. 'Can you tell me the man's name?'

Robert ignored the question. Instead he asked 'Why do you think the injuries were sustained after death?'

'I can't imagine why anyone would want to strangle a body that had already been beaten to death. The injuries on the body are so severe that no one could have survived them.'

'Is it possible that the beating of the body was an attempt to hide the strangulation?'

I thought for a moment: 'it is possible, although the neck is relatively free of damage. The worst injuries are to the head and the torso. I suspect the man was strangled and then pushed into the river. As he floated he might have been struck by a boat.'

'Unlikely. Surely the river is too wide for something like that to happen.'

'You'd be surprised. Nesbitt and I were almost run down by a merchant ship sailing into the city this evening. Your men fell asleep on the job and failed to see it coming.'

Ignoring this rebuke of his staff my brother continued.

'And the men who found him, they were *all* fishermen? I find it hard to believe that the men you describe would have the wherewithal to connect the dead man with me.'

'No that's right.' I realised that I had forgotten about the obsequious Radclyffe. 'There was someone else – the verger from the village church. He was the man who recognised your seal. A natural busybody who seemed overjoyed to be part of the macabre proceedings. He fancies himself as a bit of a local historian and guardian of the niceties of society, such as recognising the Over-Marshall of the county's coat of arms. Incidentally, brother, he seemed keen to make your acquaintance. It was all I could do to keep him from squeezing into the boat.'

'I hope you didn't insult him.' My brother returned evenly. 'We don't want him making trouble unnecessarily because you put his nose out of joint. One day you might learn to be diplomatic.'

'Perhaps you would like to give him his reward in person then. I promised him the same as the other men, although I fancy the opportunity to kiss your ring would suffice in his case.'

'What exactly did you promise them?'

'Only a few shillings – I gave them the address of my lodgings to spare you the inconvenience. However, if you could advance me the sum?'

'Yes, yes'. My brother waved a hand dismissively and sat thoughtfully, worry still etched on his face. I glanced at Nesbitt, who had been quiet for some time, seemingly happy to let the two brothers slug it out. Having been relegated to a bit part in the proceedings, he had reverted to an impassive, attentive manner.

'So,' my brother said after an interminable pause, 'all you can tell us is that the man was most likely a stranger of Mediterranean extraction, he was probably strangled and then put in the river and that the only people who know about it are the three of us in this room, and the five gentlemen and one youth of Rotherhithe.' He let out a huge sigh of pent up breath. 'Is there anything else you've left out?'

'There is one thing.' I replied. 'I've seen him before not two days ago, and most assuredly alive and kicking.'

'What? Where?'

I started to explain to him how I had recognised the man from the Queen's procession, but my brother cut me off sharply.

'Judging from what I've heard about you at the procession you were too drunk to even notice your own shadow.' He stared at me directly as if challenging me to disagree and I felt the colour rising in my cheeks. But something in his manner caused me to check and I said nothing further.

'Go back to your lodgings for now.' He said, dismissing me. 'I want you to return here at eight and I will send a boat for you. There is someone I want you to meet and in God's name clean yourself up a bit. This is an important gentleman and I don't want you looking like the farm hand you aspire to be. That is all for now. Nesbitt stay a moment. I have an errand for you. Till eight then.'

I walked out of the room, still at a loss as to what the morning's events were about. It seemed my brother was troubled about the death of the stranger but he seemed to prefer to discuss his concerns with Nesbitt. There was little point feeling slighted.

Rather than return to the river gate, I went to the Strand entrance, preparing to walk home in the knowledge that I was unlikely to get a free ride in a boat now that my usefulness was temporarily concluded. Walking through the rabbit warren of the house, I passed an open door. Looking in I could see Robert's wife, Anne, sitting at a sewing table in a bay window surrounded by maids and three young children. Two were playing on the hearthrug and laughing loudly, whilst an older child, sitting next to her mother, read confidently from a large book. I watched as the girl, whose name was Mildred, held the book up for her mother to decipher a word for her.

Sitting opposite Anne was a young woman I didn't recognise. She was elegantly dressed, with dazzling jewellery adorning her hair and neck, and a face to match, although her beauty was somewhat spoiled by an expression of barely concealed scorn as she regarded the domestic scene before her.

I paused in the doorway, momentarily caught by this contrast between family bliss on the one hand and ill-concealed contempt on the other. Sensing my presence Anne looked up. For a moment our eyes met and a smile of recognition formed on her lips. The other woman turned her head, following Anne's gaze, and regarded me with direct, honey-coloured eyes. Her look seemed to be challenging me to provide an interesting diversion. I was about to greet both ladies when suddenly an alert maid noticed her mistress's gaze. Letting out a slight cry of indignation, she walked swiftly to the door and shut it firmly in my face.

So much for family bliss, I thought, as I walked stiffly out of the house, trying not to let the gate porter discern my embarrassment. The church bells of St Martin's-in-the-Fields struck six o'clock as I stole into the chaos of the restless city, a place where I felt more at home.

Chapter 5

'Above our life we love a steadfast friend.'
(Christopher Marlowe; Hero and Leander)

Only a few hours had passed when, for the second time that day, I found myself in a boat on the Thames bound for The Chancel House. I had made some effort to smarten myself up and had exchanged my cloth breeches for a velvet doublet and hose – a green and gold combination – set off by a smart pair of leather boots, borrowed from my landlord, and a thick velvet cape. The boots were a size too small for me and pinched my toes painfully, but other than that I felt in comparative comfort and had been relieved to get out of my damp clothes.

As I left my lodgings, I could hear a Bellman on patrol calling the hour of seven. The city gates would be closed by now but it made little difference to the traffic on the river. At night it became even busier, with a lot of trade passing between the North and South banks.

Only one oarsman had been sent to fetch me, an old servant by the name of Matthew Jordan. We were well acquainted with one another, as he had been in service to the family for many years, and we chatted amiably as he negotiated our way upstream through the cross traffic.

Matthew was about fifty years old and physically strong. He had bird-like features with a large, pointed nose and keen, black eyes. His single, bushy eyebrow was permanently set in a slope of inquisitiveness and, when not reciting poems or singing ballads, he was always very quick to pick me up on anything I said and to engage in good humoured debate.

As he rowed, Matthew cheerfully described his recent encounter with a man he had met whilst walking in Holborn fields. Apparently the man had been picking a variety of plants from fields around the law courts. He had explained he was collecting specimens for the College of Physicians physic garden in Chelsea, where he was the chief gardener. During their conversation, the herb collector remarked that he had seen Matthew limping and Matthew explained that this was the result of an old injury to his knee. After some further conversation, he invited Matthew back to his house between Chancery Lane and Fetter Lane, where he promptly made up a poultice of herbs and strapped it to Matthew's leg.

Matthew proudly lifted his leg to show me.

'Highly, Master John, I tell thee this Master Gerard has studied the secret art of physic most surely, 'e can cure wonderfully with all kinds of materials – vegetives, metals, stones, all the wonders of the orb.' I took this to mean that the plant collector was some kind of quack.

'Are you sure he didn't stone you on the head, you old fool?' I teased.

'Highly, Master John, it isn't meet that a man as young as you should be so cynical. Mark my words it'll twist your gut. No doubt Master John Gerard can cure your cynicism as well as 'e has cured this 'ere knee.' He waved his leg in the air again, making the boat rock disconcertingly. 'It an't felt this good for many a year.'

'I shouldn't let my brother hear about it if the leg improves too much. He'll have you replacing me as his errand boy.' With that we both laughed and Matthew launched into a rousing rendition of *Bonny Sweet Robin*.

***

Ever since leaving the Chancel House earlier that day, my mind had been occupied with thoughts of Anne, my brother's wife. Her affectionate face, glimpsed briefly, had haunted me as I passed over the Fleet and into the crowded city streets. It was hard to believe that she was now the mother of three children; I could still remember clearly the first time I'd met her.

It was the summer of 1575 and I was eleven years old. My brother was away and I was living in relative happiness. Anne, along with her older brother and sister, had come to live with us after her father, a Catholic rabble-rouser, had been tried and executed for treason. She had been a shy and confused girl, and for the first few weeks of her stay no one in the household could get so much as a sound out of her. My father, never one to avoid fun and games if the opportunity presented itself, went to elaborate lengths to cheer and amuse her but to no avail. I was the only person she responded to in the household.

It was hard to explain the affinity between us. Maybe the connection between a newly orphaned daughter, her mother had died some years earlier, and a bastard son. Maybe it was natural as we were the same age. Whatever it was, Anne chose me as her sole companion. We spent the whole of that first summer together, running out to the fields in the morning to avoid her brother and sister. At first it was like a game, but we soon became inseparable friends, sharing adventures and secrets as easily as we shared our hastily prepared lunches in the fields.

Anne had been my inseparable companion for the next four years, until one day a messenger arrived to summon her to Court. Her father's crimes had been temporarily forgiven, if not forgotten, and she was to become a lady-in-waiting to Queen Elizabeth. It was an honour that no subject in her right senses would refuse, and especially not one with a cloud hanging over her past. Up until that time, we had done everything together, from learning French and Latin, to horse riding and dancing. I'd never had to question my feelings towards her, but I felt a great loss following her departure; although, it wasn't the first, and wouldn't be the last time that reality broke into the fantasy world I had carefully fashioned for myself.

My sense of loss turned to one of seething injustice a year later, when Anne returned to the house as my brother's wife. They had met at Court, an institution that was as far from my reach as the Heavens. To rub salt into the wounds, the marriage had angered the Queen, who often took exception to her ladies-in-waiting getting wed, and Robert had temporarily been exiled from court. The newlyweds therefore came to live in the country and the only way to avoid them was to stay away as much as possible.

Within a few months, Robert and Anne were forgiven by the Queen and returned to London. I reflected as I walked that six years had passed since that day, and during that time the gulf between Anne and I had widened ever further, to the point where even her maids mistook me for an insolent servant, rather than the childhood friend I had once been.

* * *

On leaving my lodgings to meet Matthew and get my ride to the Chancel House, I had noticed, as I passed through the Bridge Gate on the city side, that one of the great waterwheels below had been forcibly stopped and a group of men were working on it. I briefly joined a small crowd that had gathered on the side of the bridge to watch the work. Standing slightly apart from them was a man who was shouting instructions down, and whom I assumed must be their foreman. When he broke from bawling down to them for a moment, I took the opportunity to ask him what had happened. He eyed me suspiciously and didn't seem inclined to answer but then his annoyance at having to work seemed to get the better of him.

'Drunken youths throwing rocks down on the panels.' He looked at me as though he rather suspected that I might have been one of them. 'Happens every year during the Southwark Fair. At least four of the damn things are smashed and I've got to have them fixed by sundown. And on a holiday too! It's unbelievable what the city burghers expect from us, and all so they can pump water up to their expensive houses.' He scowled at me and then turned his back leaving me in no doubt that he wanted to end the discussion. I had left him, and the enthralled crowd, to it.

A while later, as Matthew hauled us expertly up to the stairs of the Chancel House's river gate, we drew alongside a distinguished boat with a crest on its side. It was empty and I assumed that the oarsmen must have gone inside to keep out of the cold, whilst my brother entertained its illustrious passenger. The large house seemed strangely empty as I entered. There was none of the usual bustle of servants about the corridors, nor did I hear any laughter of children. It was as if my brother had cleared the house in anticipation of his guest. Without thinking, I knocked on the large door of the hall and entered.

Two men, my brother and a stranger, were seated in front of the fireplace. Otherwise the room was empty and I was pleased to see that there was no sign of Nesbitt, or my nemeses, the dogs. Both men turned sharply as I entered. The immediate impression I got was that they had been sitting in an uncomfortable silence and were relieved by my interruption. Despite this, my brother couldn't resist immediately putting me in my place.

'You see, Sir Francis, my brother's manners are very much the product of the farmyard. Nevertheless, I have no doubt he will be up to the task we have for him.'

The man, who was aged around sixty, watched my entrance with an interested, slightly bemused expression – the way one might calmly observe a stranger's child that is over-reaching itself. He had a deeply lined, gaunt face and an air of sickliness about him, but his bright black eyes displayed great intelligence. Despite having never met him before, I knew immediately who he was. The mention of his name merely confirmed what I had already guessed from the crest on the boat. Before me sat none other than the Principle Secretary to the Privy Council, Sir Francis Walsingham.

A number of thoughts immediately collided in my mind. For one thing, I was very surprised to see Walsingham in my brother's house. On a number of occasions my brother had been overheard disparaging Walsingham as being a member of an old cabal that had too much influence at court and stood in the way of the 'coming men' – one of which my brother considered himself to be. A more worrying consideration was that Walsingham's presence indicated there might be a political connection to the dead man. More than anything, the word 'task' reverberated ominously. Walsingham's reputation as chief of the country's murky intelligence networks was well known – a world I had no desire to be mixed up in.

For a moment, Walsingham's dark eyes regarded me unblinkingly. Lit by the flickering flames of the fire, they seemed to be the only sign of life in his dark face, which remained completely passive. Eventually his lips moved slowly and the ghost of a smile formed.

'Come Robert. Your brother has done us great service this morning and we must thank him for it. I never trust a man who puts manners before hard work and simple country ways are far preferable to the over-elaboration we see at court these days. At least to my mind.'

If this was a reference to my brother, or the type of courtier he represented, it was hard to tell. Walsingham's gaze remained fixed on me as he spoke. The speech was delivered in a deliberate manner, and as he spoke his fingers, which were joined together like a vaulted ceiling in front of his chest, tapped along as though they were counting out the rhythm of the sentence. His manner was reminiscent of the insipid lawyers who had attended my father's estate after his death, but unlike them, his words commanded absolute attention. I found myself frozen to the spot not knowing whether to bow, reply, or simply bolt for the door.

My brother evidently decided to play the diplomat. 'Of course you are right, Sir Francis,' he said, breaking the spell that Walsingham had conjured over me. 'John, come and warm yourself by the fire.'

I broke out of my reverie, bowed low, stammering 'your Lordship', and moved clumsily to a third, high-backed wooden chair that had already been set for me. My brother directed me to help myself to a glass of hot wine from a metal decanter on a nearby table and also to replenish their glasses. But Walsingham refused and instead reached for a bottle containing a green liquid, and poured it into a glass. Even over the sweet scent of the wine, I could smell its musty, acrid scent and assumed it must be some sort of physic for his condition. Walsingham kept his level gaze on me, as he took a sip of the strange brew, as though he were weighing up some unfathomable equation. Rather than return his gaze, I took comfort in eyeing the deep red colour of the glass cradled between my hands before taking another draft of the warming wine, which, like all of my brother's cellar, was of the highest quality.

Seating himself between us, my brother began to speak in a quiet voice. 'John, please repeat to Sir Francis what you discovered this morning. Just as you did earlier – leaving nothing out.'

I finally found the courage to look at Walsingham directly, and began recounting my tale of the dead foreigner discovered by the Rotherhithe Watch. It occurred to me that there was still a great deal that my brother hadn't told me, but it seemed as though I would have to wait. When I had finished Walsingham waited a moment before speaking.

'Excellent. Your brother is as observant and diligent as you avouched, Lord Robert. I think he could be very suitable for the little assignment we have in mind.' He paused to take a sip of the strong-smelling medicine, before adding: 'First, if you don't mind, Master Lovat, I would like to tell you a story and perhaps you will do me the goodness to hear me out before you ask any questions, though no doubt you will have many. Shall I begin?'

I sank back into my chair, nodding uncertainly. Apart from Walsingham's mellifluous tone, the only other sound was the crackling of flames coming from the fireplace. Even my brother sat in complete silence, listening attentively to every word.

As he started to speak, a strange stillness settled on the room and a feeling of uneasiness swept over me, as though my soul was being carried away on an invisible tide.

Chapter 6

'I speak the truth not so much as I would, but as much as I dare.'
(Michel de Montaigne; Essays)

'The man washed up in Rotherhithe, who you so observantly described, Master Lovat, was a Portuguese nobleman. Not strictly Mediterranean, but your reasoning was sound. I would have recognised him by your excellent description alone, but I believe your brother has since confirmed his identity. His name was Don Alphonse de Sousa.'

My brother nodded solemnly in confirmation, his eyes cast down at the base of the fire. He still held that same worried demeanour I had witnessed earlier.

'Don Alphonse has been an ally of this country for many years, and a personal friend to a number of its leading statesmen, including your brother and myself. He first came to these shores through his trading connections and by virtue of the fact that, like many of his countrymen since the Spanish occupation, he could no longer live safely in Portugal. You were a young man at the time, Master Lovat, and I hardly expect you to remember the circumstances surrounding the Portuguese wars. However, as I am sure you will be only too keenly aware, Portugal is a Spanish colony, ruled from the Escorial Palace, and the estates of men like Don Alphonse have long since been confiscated.'

Although I felt his confidence in my political knowledge was somewhat misplaced, I thought it prudent not to mention it at this juncture.

'I don't need to go into great detail. Suffice to say that Her Majesty, in her graciousness and wisdom, offered Don Antonio, the Portuguese King in exile, a home in this country. Sadly Don Antonio is an impetuous man, and his frustration with our, admittedly, laboured attempts to support his claim to the Portuguese throne, has led to him being somewhat abased in the eyes of the Sovereign. He still remains a guest in this country but continues to seek help from other, less agreeable sources. We need say no more about him, except to mention that his presence in this country has induced many of his fellow countrymen to make their homes here.'

Walsingham suddenly broke off to cough violently, a bout which was followed by a large helping of physic from the green bottle. My brother glanced at him anxiously. Walsingham's condition was serving only to increase his anxiety. His composure recovered, Walsingham continued. Although he did his best to hide it, the pain caused by his ailment was evident in his eyes, which had slight traces of water around them. I wondered what it was that he was suffering from. Knowing the expertise of most doctors, it was probably prolonged by the medicine he was taking. The pungent liquid in the green bottle hardly smelt like a healthy tonic. Momentarily these thoughts distracted me, until I was brought back to the story by Walsingham's resonant, bass tone.

'Our story here concerns the dead man, Don Alphonse. Whilst living in London, Don Alphonse was an extremely useful source of information to the Crown by virtue of the fact that his trading links spread far and wide. The circumstances surrounding the growth of these networks are somewhat murky, but, notwithstanding, he was extremely successful. Naturally, his mercantile interests afforded him the opportunity of a great number of contacts, and from time to time he was most helpful in passing on any information that he felt would be of interest to our security as a nation. I believe that his intentions towards us were always friendly but at heart he was driven by the desire to see his own country once again able to determine its own affairs. To this end, I am only sorry that his unfortunate demise has come before he could witness such an event, although I fear that he would have had a long wait.'

All the time Walsingham spoke, his fingers remained joined together in front of his chest, occasionally tapping out a rhythm to accompany his words. His narrative was only interrupted by Robert standing to throw a log on the fire, which was lighting Walsingham's impassive face as he spoke. The rest of the room – tapestries, furniture, portraits – had sunk into the gloom, only occasionally alluded to by a flickering shadow. The whole world seemed to consist of the three of us in that small arc of intense concentration, defined by the dancing flames of the fire.

'Don Alphonse's trading networks enabled him to have contact with a number of countries and individuals that we would consider undesirable, although in the interest of our nation's wealth, and intelligence, we turned a blind eye. He, naturally, had strong connections with Mediterranean and Spanish markets, many of which are Roman Catholic and do not accept the legality of a Protestant Queen on the throne of England.

Nevertheless, as I have always believed, trade is the bedrock of a nation and these links will inevitably make us stronger in the future.' Another pause for a productive cough, the result of which was washed down with more medicine. I wondered nervously when he was going to get to the point.

'Six months ago, Don Alphonse sent a letter to my country home at Barn Elms requesting a meeting. It was an inopportune moment. Preparations to repel the impending Spanish invasion were at their height and my secretaries and I were awash with all manner of intelligence. I was spending most of my time at Court and, furthermore, I was undergoing an indifferent period of health.'

If that was an *indifferent* period, I wondered how he would describe his current condition.

'Howbeit, Don Alphonse was resolute. He sent another letter, one week later, imploring me to see him.' Walsingham momentarily regarded me with an incisive glance. 'The letters, you see, Master Lovat, were just a forerunner to further contact – the information he had to impart was, in his words – *too sensitive to be written down, even in code* – and he wished to deliver the said information in person. I admit my interest was piqued. I sent word that he should come and visit me at my country house the next evening. He duly arrived, apologetic for disturbing me at such a time but still insistent.'

I sensed that we were getting to the heart of the story and found myself again holding my breath, with the same feeling of weightlessness I had experienced earlier. Even my brother's mood of despondence had momentarily subsided. We were both absorbed in the tale.

'What Don Alphonse had to tell me was simply this. Knowledge had reached him of a sea captain who was conducting illicit trade with Spain. In return for being allowed to trade certain goods, the English captain, a Papist sympathiser, was passing on information about English preparations for war. Not only was the trade illegal but many of the goods being traded were not recorded - that is, they were smuggled. More importantly, the English ships under this captain's command were the property of a high-ranking member of the Queen's Court who, at that precise moment, was an important advisor on the Armada defence preparations.'

Throughout this passage, Walsingham had been staring gravely at the fire, but now he looked up slowly to make sure we were both listening.

'You must understand that Don Alphonse felt unable to put names to these allegations. Even the source was described only as a 'trusted friend', who had boarded one of his ships in the Canary Islands. The ship had been part of a fleet sailing from the coast of Guinea in January with a cargo of textiles, palm oil, millet and the prized commodity of Ivory. The fleet had then journeyed to the Canary Islands, where it picked up Don Alphonse's source, before sailing along the North African coast, where it stopped to exchange goods for saltpetre, an essential ingredient of gunpowder, as you must be well aware, Master Lovat, at a Moroccan port. The ships then sailed past the hostile waters of Spain and thence to Plymouth via the Bay of Biscay and the English Channel. Rough weather had delayed the trip and the flotilla had been forced to put in for shelter in a French port. All in all, the prolonged voyage and other unforeseen hold-ups had meant that potentially serious intelligence had taken four months to reach these shores. Nevertheless, the message was clear. There was treason at the heart of the English establishment, which could have very grave consequences for our nation and sovereignty.'

'My initial reaction was one of disbelief. Treason at the heart of the government was disturbing to contemplate. I insisted that Don Alphonse name the men involved but he told me that he was not yet in a position to do so. I am ashamed to say that I was somewhat angered by his stance. My fear was that it was an enemy plot to destabilise the government and that without proof, it would likely cause more harm than good. On reflection, I was under great pressure preparing the country for war, but I must admit I sent Don Alphonse away quite coldly, insisting that to back up such accusations he must give both names and proof.'

'The next day I received long-awaited intelligence that the Spanish Armada would set sail in the middle of May – one month away – and this news was the catalyst for the final efforts of preparation, which were to consume all of my energies. I pushed Don Alphonse's story from my mind, convinced even more that the intelligence must be false, and consoling myself with the thought that by now, in any case, it was too late for the conspiracy, if it existed, to do much more damage. Robert, I think I would like a little wine now, my throat has become exceedingly dry.'

This sudden jolt in the narrative caused me to break from the grip

Walsingham's words had exerted over me. My neck and back had become quite stiff as a result of sitting still for so long on the hard wooden chair, and the ornate carving on the back was starting to make deep, uncomfortable impressions into my skin. Robert indicated to me and I poured a glass of wine for both him and Walsingham, before replenishing my own glass, only to catch my brother eyeing me with displeasure. I ignored his look and sat back heavily in the uncomfortable wooden chair, taking a defiant swig from my glass. Walsingham's expression showed a hint of amusement, as he took a slow draft of the wine, nodded his approval and then continued his narrative.

'As I am sure you can imagine, the Armada occupied all of my thoughts and energies throughout the summer. When final confirmation of the defeat came in September, there was still much to do. Even now preparations are being made to engage the enemy further. I had long forgotten all about Don Alphonse's visit. I was surprised therefore to receive a letter from him, only days ago, saying that he had acquired the proof I had asked for and hoped I would now listen to him. Although I still felt it unlikely that his accusations were well founded, I was eager to repair our relationship and so I wrote in reply that I would see him on the morning after the procession to St Paul's. This morning to be precise.' Walsingham turned his gaze on my brother. 'The morning after, I believe, he spent the evening in this house.'

As the conversation had turned to more recent events, my brother had begun shifting uncomfortably in his chair. Walsingham's clear challenge now forced him to speak.

'Don Alphonse was an occasional visitor to this house for some months. We have some mutual, um, business arrangements.'

Walsingham let these words settle as though he were sifting the weight of each one. An uncomfortable silenced ensued, which my brother again felt compelled to break.

'Last night he attended a dinner at which we celebrated the Armada victory.' So, Don Alphonse had been my brother's guest on the night he was murdered. Is that why he had been pondering the fire morosely all evening – a sniff of a scandal was threatening to halt his meteoric rise to the top?

'Yes, he had informed me he would be your guest last night, and, naturally, when he didn't turn up this morning I sent word here, only to discover that tragic events had overtaken him. Had he been in England prior to that?'

'Yes. As far as I'm aware.'

'In London?'

'Naturally.'

'Interesting, but, of course, I must have failed to mention that his most recent letter, the one that spoke of proof, was dispatched from the coastal town of Rye, only three days ago.' Almost imperceptibly Walsingham had moved from narrator to interrogator. The atmosphere in the room had become thick with tension. 'I wondered if he had returned from some voyage?

'He never mentioned Rye to me. I thought he was in London.' My brother spoke tersely, as if wishing to end this exchange.

'Quite so, Robert,' Walsingham paused long enough to show he had recognised the change of tone, and then went on in a more temperate manner. 'It appears that his movements, whatever they may have been, are to remain a mystery for the time being. As a proud man, I fear my initial failure to take his story more seriously may have hurt him deeply and, perhaps, driven him on recklessly to get the information I required. Any sea voyages at this time would have been quite dangerous; the sea is littered with desperate Spanish galleons fleeing homewards. Wherever he had been, in his letter he wrote of conclusive proof. Unfortunately, as I was not able to speak to him on his return, we are currently in the dark as to what that proof might be and, more importantly, who it implicates.'

The tension in the room had subsided slightly, but Walsingham seemed reluctant to let it die completely.

'So, we have come to Don Alphonse's last hours. On returning to London from Rye, ostensibly to take part in the procession, but also to give me the information he has gathered to convince me of a plot, Don Alphonse attends the Armada celebration and then comes to dine in this house. As you related to me earlier, Robert, after spending an enjoyable evening in the company of yourself and others, he takes his leave of your household. Did he give you any indication as to where he was going?'

My brother paused for a moment, as though reluctant to contribute anything to the narrative. 'It was late. However, he did mention that he had something to attend to – business or pleasure, I couldn't say. All I can say is that he was in perfect health when he left this house.'

Walsingham ignored the last sentence. 'And that is the last we hear of him until this morning, when his body is discovered washed up at … what did you say the name of the place was, Master Lovat?'

'Cuckold's Point.'

'How very curious.'

'And, at some point in between, someone took that rather fine seal and necklace you gave him, presumably as a gift, brother, and strangled the poor fellow?' Robert glanced at me sharply, his look showing the unmistakable sign of fear under his anger, but Walsingham only nodded in agreement.

'I am very much afraid it would appear so. The question is who and why? It seems to me that there is every likelihood that Don Alphonse was killed before he could speak to me because he did indeed have intelligence that was of a compromising nature to a person or persons unknown. However, there is also the possibility that he was killed for some other pertinent reason, unknown to any of us in this room.'

'He could simply been the victim of an unpremeditated assault in the street. Such things are far from uncommon.' My brother's tone suggested he would find that a satisfactory solution to the mystery.

'Marry, Robert, granted you could be right, but, personally speaking, I think his death is too much of a coincidence. However, let me hear your brother's thoughts on the matter. After all, he will be the one whose task it is to discover the truth.'

And with that he turned his level gaze on me.

Chapter 7

'Nothing is so firmly believed as that which is least known.'
(Michel de Montaigne; Essays)

By now we were deep into the far reaches of the night and, despite the fire, the cold had taken a firm grip on the room. Walsingham and my brother were both afforded the luxury of deep upholstered armchairs, whilst my hard, fussily carved wooden chair offered no protection at all and even lacked a cushion. I shifted uncomfortably, trying to find some solace for my numb limbs, but also buying a bit of time before answering the direct question that Walsingham had put to me.

'Well, Master Lovat?' he prompted.

I ran my mind across the various permutations and tried to spell them out in as measured terms as possible, aware that my brother was watching me closely. 'As far as time of death is concerned, it seems to me that if he was, as seems most likely, strangled with the necklace you gave him brother, then it happened soon after leaving this house. Although I am sure he deemed it a great honour, I doubt he would have continued to wear for long due to its weight.' I took a sip of wine and ploughed on. 'As far as the matter of who did it and why, we can reach no firm conclusions at present. Certainly the story of treason is a compelling one. Let me be certain that I have understood that correctly – a sea captain with Catholic sympathies has been giving secrets to the Spaniards in exchange for being allowed to trade illegal goods? A common enough temptation, I don't doubt. And this captain's fleet is under the command of someone who has access to government?' I paused for a moment. 'My first thought would be that the sea captain's actions in no way imply the senior man's guilt. He may be operating in complete isolation, the ship's owner quite ignorant. To suggest treason at the heart of the government seems somewhat of a stretch.'

'Spoken with admirable caution, Master Lovat,' Walsingham said approvingly. 'Although, Don Alphonse was adamant that there was a link. Besides, what secrets could the captain leak that were worth a candle, without, that is, information from above?'

'Without any names to investigate, or the proof that he spoke of in his letter, it will be difficult to determine one way or the other.'

'Just so,' my brother interjected.

'With no evidence to go on concerning the plot, perhaps we should concentrate on the other end – Don Alphonse's murder,' I continued quietly, almost to myself. 'The possibility that Don Alphonse may have also had a pre-arranged meeting after the dinner is an intriguing one. There is certainly some ambiguity in his remark about an appointment, and if he was meeting someone last night that could point us directly to the killer. As far as your theory of a random attack is concerned brother, the city is certainly a violent and dangerous place. However, I'm afraid I have to point out that a thief would hardly have needed your necklace as a weapon, nor would have expected it to be round Don Alphonse's neck. They have plenty of their own tools of the trade, in my experience.'

'An excellent assumption Master Lovat,' said Walsingham, glancing towards Robert, who grunted in grudging acknowledgment.

By now I was warming to the task in hand. 'Perhaps we should start with the dinner itself, seeing as that was the last time anyone saw him alive. How many guests were there in total Robert?'

'I hardly see how that is relevant. My guests had nothing to do with this sordid affair.' My brother's statement was a little too assertive, as though he had been ready to deflect any questions in that direction. For the time being, I thought it prudent to pursue a different theme.

'What is the history of the seal and chain?'

'I presented him with the seal out of gratitude for his service. Don Alphonse gave some financial support to the regiment I mustered at the time of the Armada crisis. The regiment you should have been part of, incidentally.' This was a reference to an on-going argument we had been having. With the impending threat of the Armada, Robert, required like all noblemen to provide men for the oncoming battle, had wanted me to muster with his troops on the South coast of England in Kent. I had chosen instead to join up with the trained band of the Bridge Within Ward, as required by the city laws. Robert thought I should have put family duty first. I was always considered part of the family when it suited him.

'When did Don Alphonse leave, brother?' I said trying to hide any exasperation I felt at my brother's inability to let sleeping dogs lie.

'At around nine o'clock.'

'And was he alone?'

'I've no idea. Perhaps a servant will remember. I've asked Nesbitt to make enquiries amongst the staff.'

'Where does … did Don Alphonse live?'

My brother hesitated for a moment 'I don't know. He has a port office in Billingsgate.'

I looked at Walsingham to see if he could enlighten me further as to Don Alphonse's home address but he too shook his head. 'I'm sure it won't be hard to find his lodgings in the city but he certainly never confided its whereabouts to me.' It struck me as unusual that neither Walsingham nor my brother knew where Don Alphonse lived, but I put it down to the fact that he hadn't been one for throwing parties. 'Has anyone informed his port address that the body has been found? They could inform his family perhaps?'

'As far as I am aware, there is no one to tell. He was not married and has no children.' This was typical of my brother. The fact that there might be servants who were now wondering where their master had got to would not have occurred to him. Those who sat below the salt barely existed in his eyes – attendants might as well be invisible.

'Was there anyone at the dinner who might be considered an enemy of Don Alphonse? Anyone who might have had a grudge against him, Robert?' Without thinking, I had again trespassed on sensitive ground.

'You are surely not suggesting that any of my guests would have been involved?'

'I merely ask, brother. It seems expedient to check, that's all.'

'There is absolutely no need to disturb anyone who was a guest in this house. As Sir Francis has explained to you already, we have good reasons to suspect the killer was in some underhand business to do with spying.' So, Robert had decided that might be likely after all! 'There are darker forces at work.'

As though aware of Walsingham silently directing me, I ploughed on recklessly. 'But, brother, the man was killed shortly after a visit to your house. At the very least you and your guests were the last people to see him alive. Perhaps he said something to one of them about where he was going? Perhaps he had an argument with one of them?'

'Don't be damned impertinent, Lovat.' Lovat was my mother's name.

I hadn't been allowed the family name, and Robert always called me Lovat when he wanted to put me in my place. The colour was rising in his cheeks above his distinctive beard and despite himself his voice rose in volume. 'I won't have a common spy interrogating people who are above suspicion. You need not concern yourself with anything outside of your assignment. Do you understand?'

'On the contrary, Lord Robert.' It was the first time Walsingham had spoken for a while and his low, measured tone made a sharp contrast with my brother's high-pitched anger. 'I think we should allow Master Lovat to have free rein in this matter. After all, we have no idea who represents those 'darker forces', as you so aptly put it. I'm afraid no one can be above suspicion, at least until proved otherwise. Perhaps you could ask one of your servants to prepare a list of your guests of that evening for your brother.'

'Sir Francis, I must insist that my guests are not harassed.' My brother said, struggling to hide his exasperation. 'You must take it on my word of honour that none of them could have been involved in this squalid affair.'

'Perhaps we can make do for now with only those who knew Don Alphonse,' I said, coming to my brother's rescue.

'There were certain gentlemen present known to him but I can't believe that any of them were involved in his death.' It was obvious that my brother was obstinately refusing to mention their names.

'Was Don Alphonse attended on by anyone? Friends, a servant perhaps?'

'Don Alphonse was a singular individual. I can't recall him ever mentioning friends. As for servants...' My brother trailed a hand through the air as if the mere thought of minions was beneath him.

'Don Alphonse did have a manservant,' Walsingham interjected. 'A rather unusual one as it happened: an African from Guinea. I believe he had been in service to Don Alphonse for many years. I'm surprised you don't remember him, Robert. Whenever I've seen him in Don Alphonse's company he has been remarked upon. His name is Cassangoe.'

'A savage?' I knew my brother well enough to see immediately how his mind was working. 'Then he must be accounted for immediately. I will call Nesbitt at once.' He stood and pulled on a long chord hanging by the fireplace, which I knew from experience set a bell ringing deep in the bowels of the house. Nesbitt had obviously been on standby because a few moments later his hunched frame was filling the doorway. My brother went straight to the point.

'Nesbitt you spoke to the servants earlier? Do you have any light to shed on the mystery.'

'I have, your Lordship, but there is little of use I am afraid. Don Alphonse is remembered both arriving and leaving by the river gate last night but as to where he came from or went to, no one is the wiser.'

'Did he have a servant with him? An African man?'

'No one recalls him being accompanied by anyone on his arrival.' Nesbitt calmly raised his eyes to survey the faces in front of him. 'I'm sure they would have remembered an African servant. I am reliably informed, however, that he left with some other gentlemen. They took a boat together, though it is not known where.'

I sensed immediately from my brother's reaction that Nesbitt, in his efficient, eager to please manner, had said too much. Walsingham immediately pounced on the information.

'How interesting. Do you know their names, Master Nesbitt?'

Too late Nesbitt realised that this information was confidential as far as my brother was concerned. Fortunately for him, he wasn't able to give any names but this only led Walsingham to turn his level gaze on Robert. The question didn't need asking again but even so my brother was reluctant to answer. After a moment he said:

'I believe one of them was a gentleman called Simon Turney. He is also a merchant adventurer. There had been some discussions between them during the evening but more than that I honestly can't say. Yes, casting my mind back, I think they left together.' I could tell that Walsingham wanted to pursue this information but there was an invisible barrier that prevented him from questioning my brother lest his persistence should appear impertinent. He decided to turn to me instead.

'Well, Master Lovat, it would appear you have two lines of enquiry to pursue – Don Alphonse's servant, Cassangoe, and this man Turney, who I am sure it will not have escaped your notice is, by trade, a 'sea captain'. No doubt one or the other can shed some light on the matter.' He rose to his feet indicating that he wished to leave. 'Your laying out of the case and the questions you have already asked suggest that you are very much the man for the task of getting to the bottom of this mystery. I would like to see the murderer brought to justice, whether it has anything to do with treason or not. Your brother has willingly offered your services, and, therefore, I suggest you visit me in three days' time at my house in Barn Elms and report what you have discovered. Now Robert, if you don't mind, I think I must be on my way. Ursula will be worried and a late journey down the river in this cold will hardly be good for my ague. Could Master Lovat call my oarsman perhaps and then see me to my boat?'

I left the hall and went quickly to lodgings above the stable yard at the side of the house, where I found Matthew Jordan in jovial conversation with a giant of a man. Having ascertained he was the man I was looking for, I told him Sir Francis was ready to leave and walked with him to the river stairs. Walsingham, with the aid of a stick, had already reached the garden and was resting against one of the carved stone pillars by the side of the steps. Just as we reached the foot of the stairs, he turned and handed me some papers he had been carrying.

'This letter gives you official authority to interrogate people in my name. Please use it. You should also know, Master Lovat, that as well as anything your brother feels obliged to recompense you for this service, I will happily add a generous reward of my own, should you resolve this matter satisfactorily.' I doubted my brother was planning on paying me anything but thought better of mentioning it, in case Walsingham withdrew his offer. 'I have faith in you, Master Lovat. I know you have grown up on your wits alone and do not live with the complacent illusion of a secure life. I know also that you are not a man to whom trust comes easily. Such men, I have found, are invaluable.' I felt the hairs rise on the back of my neck, startled that this man who I had never met before could pinpoint my state of mind with such accuracy.

'One other thing. Although I understand your brother's reluctance to suspect his guests, it is always better we suspect those that are innocent than blindly hold the guilty to our bosoms.' It was hard to tell if Walsingham was referring specifically to my brother's friends or merely stating an eternal truth. 'Please leave no stone unturned.'

He fixed me with a razor sharp gaze, full of intent, and then turned and climbed into the boat with the help of the huge oarsman. Once seated comfortably in the stern he looked up at me with a serious expression on his face.

'Until three days' time, Master Lovat. Visit me around midday and I will have lunch for you. We will talk more then. I wish you luck in the meantime.' With that he signalled to the oarsman and the big man began to row effortlessly Westward.

Feeling shaken by Walsingham's words, I stood watching until the swirling fog on the river swallowed the boat's lamp. Had I imagined it, or had Walsingham implied that I had a clear choice between pursuing the truth and finding Don Alphonse's killer, or alternatively helping my brother construct a cover-up?

I didn't like the implication of that one bit.

Gradually the splashing of the oars faded. On the far bank I caught occasional glimpses of lights burning brightly in the theatre district but there was only the odd cry of a crazed voice or the sound of a dog barking. On this side of the river, all was silence and darkness – the gentry were clearly asleep, or not yet home. Turning slowly to the house and looking up at the window I could see a dim flickering light but most of it was in darkness – impossible to tell if my brother had watched my exchange with Walsingham from the shadows of the room.

A sudden, biting gust of wind, sweeping in off the river, brought home to me how cold it was and I moved quickly to the shelter of the house. Back in the great hall I found Nesbitt and my brother in earnest conversation, which broke off as I entered the room.

'Has the dark moor left us?' my brother said, and then continued as he saw my raised eyebrows. 'I believe that is the affectionate name Her Majesty reserves for him – when his back is turned, of course.' He smiled grimly to himself. 'He may have done great service to this country but he is an old man and he won't be around much longer. There is a new generation of meet men and it's time they were allowed to undertake their responsibilities without the interference of these relics of the past.' It was rare for my brother to express sentiments like that and I took it as an indication of the pressure he was under.

'As to this mystery, I wouldn't get too carried away by Walsingham's assertion of a plot. You said yourself that the link was tenuous. Men like Don Alphonse are always coming to the council with stories of plots and intrigue. It is a shrewd method of gaining favour and influence, not to mention ready money. No, I think we should look much closer to home. I wouldn't be surprised if this African servant proves to be responsible. God knows what men like that are capable of.' By 'men like that' I assumed that he meant black savages. 'Find him and bring him here. We'll soon get the truth out of him.'

Robert was clearly fixed on the idea that the black servant, Cassangoe, would make a convenient scapegoat and deflect his own responsibility in the matter. I knew how these things worked and that if we weren't careful it would soon become a stone-cold fact that Cassangoe was guilty. It seemed a little early to be so certain.

'Nevertheless brother, Sir Francis was insistent that I should also include your dinner guests in my investigation. I don't think we should jump to conclusions just yet. What about Simon Turney and the other three men who left with Don Alphonse?'

'Well there unfortunately Sir Francis is out of luck. Turney is due to sail on the morrow. He'll already be aboard ship preparing to depart. I'm afraid you won't have time to speak to him.' So my brother had cleverly offered up to Walsingham the one person who was practically already out of the picture. 'Anyway, it is a ridiculous suggestion that he could be involved. The man is above suspicion.'

'But he is captaining a fleet?'

'As are hundreds of other men.'

'What about those he left with? Are they are above suspicion?'

'I wouldn't concern yourself with them. The servant – he is the man to concentrate on.'

'But brother, Sir Francis insisted …'

'Enough! There's a reason why I suggested you to Walsingham for this task and it wasn't so that you can become one of his damned snoopers. Walsingham may be unavoidably involved in this matter but you will remember at all times that this house comes first. I'm quite convinced that no one present last night was involved. Why should they be? Don Alphonse left this house a good while before he was murdered. Your job is to prove this to be the case. Not amuse yourself by playing at being a spy.'

'So you want me to effect a cover up? Brush things neatly under the Turkish carpet? Is that it?' I raised my chin towards him, challenging him to pick up the bait, but sensing my anger he continued in a more reasonable tone.

'You have to understand John, Sir Francis Walsingham, despite his great abilities, does not have our family's welfare uppermost in his mind.' In particular, your own welfare, I thought unkindly. 'It is not a 'cover-up'; I have no idea who murdered Don Alphonse any more than you do. There is simply no need to stir up any unnecessary aggravation. We have to make sure that the family comes out of this matter without the slightest stain on its character. Besides you work for me, not Walsingham. Remember that.'

'Well, that's quite clear then,' I said, failing to hide a note of sarcasm. It was anything but clear. Robert and Walsingham seemed to have quite different ideas about how I was to proceed and what my aims were. However, I saw little point in arguing. Robert already seemed severely rattled by the business and I would only aggravate him further. I was acutely aware that I depended on him for everything and falling out with him could only hurt me. I couldn't help thinking, though, that his protestations of ignorance had a hollow ring to them. What was so important to him about his dinner guests that he was determined to protect them at all costs?

'What's Nesbitt's role to be? Will he be dogging my every move? Making sure I preserve the family honour?'

'Not if you do what I tell you to. Nesbitt has been a good servant to this family. You would do well to learn from him. I want you to report to him in my absence.' I scowled but his mind was clearly made up. 'You can stay here tonight. There should be plenty of rooms in the servant's quarters. In the morning I want you to find this man Cassangoe and bring him here. You can take Matthew Jordan with you. He'll row you where you need to go and help bring the man back if he resists. I should imagine he will be easy to identify.' With this dismissive remark, my brother departed to his bedchamber and Nesbitt to wherever it was he slept.

I stood obstinately for a moment and then pulled a chair up close to the grate. I stoked some life back into the fire and then helped myself to what was left in the wine decanter, all the time pondering the mess I was in.

Chapter 8

'If a man will begin with certainties, he shall end in doubts: but if he will be content to begin with doubts, he shall end in certainties.'
(Sir Francis Bacon)

The dissonant bells of St Clement Danes awoke me suddenly from a troubled sleep, notwithstanding the fact that my sleeping arrangements had been more comfortable than Robert intended. Rather than taking up his offer of a dreary servant's bed, I had carried on drinking by the warm fire until the decanter was empty and the house was quiet. Then I had crept quietly into one of the staterooms on the other side of the courtyard, which I knew was always empty. It was called the King's Chamber and rumour had it that Henry VII had slept in the huge bed, as a guest of the old bishop who had been in residence. Alas, I hadn't slept like a king, my mind swirling with conspiracies.

Venturing downstairs through the layers of the grand house, my mood rapidly darkened on espying Nesbitt hunched over the table in the large kitchen parlour. In front of him lay a large helping of eggs fried with breadcrumbs. He was tearing strips off a small round Manchet loaf before dipping each one fastidiously into the scrambled mixture. I stood watching him distastefully for a moment, reflecting that this finicky way of eating endeared me to him even less. Noticing me, he leant forward across the table and offered me the basket with the bread rolls in. I obstinately refused to accept one.

'Where's my brother?' On the way down through the house, I had looked in at my brother's dining room but it had been empty.

'Good morrow to you too, Master Lovat,' Nesbitt paused whilst bringing a dripping strip of bread slowly to his mouth. 'His Lordship has already left for Court.'

'What already? The Queen must be an early riser.'

'Her Majesty is certainly not one to idle time away, that's for certain.' The tone of his voice suggested that I could take a leaf out of her book. I didn't bother mentioning that it was still dark outside.

'You're acquainted with Her Majesty's daily habits are you Nesbitt?' It was hard to keep the annoyance I felt out of my voice that my brother had left before speaking to me. What made it worse was being chided by this complacent crook-back, who clearly felt more at home in this house than I did. Nesbitt must have heard the irritation in my voice but simply looked sanctimonious. He continued eating in his pernickety manner, and didn't deign to answer.

I sat down and took a roll from the basket. The soft white bread was still warm and smelt delicious. It also tasted distinctly different from the coarse rye bread, common amongst most households. Bread, like everything else in my brother's house, was a symbol of his social status but it only served to remind me of the childhood I had enjoyed and the privileges I had lost since my father died.

Chewing idly, I studied Nesbitt across the table. He had been in my brother's service for only a few years, employed at the same time that I had come to London, and I often felt resentment towards him and the position he held at my brother's side. It wasn't beyond a flight of fantasy that his position should be mine. That morning, though, it dawned on me that I knew next to nothing about this deliberate, dour man, with his impassive face, who was adept at giving nothing away.

After swilling the bread down with some small beer, I felt impelled to speak.

'Where is everyone Nesbitt? The emptiness of this place is starting to give me the creeps.'

'Her Ladyship has gone to the country estate and taken a good part of the household with her. I believe it was decided quite suddenly yesterday afternoon. Knowing the delicate nature of her Ladyship, I presume that his Lordship wanted her to be as cosseted as possible from any likely scandal resulting from this unfortunate business with the Portuguese gentleman.' I didn't recognise the Anne of a 'delicate nature'. The Anne I had known had been hardy and adventurous and wouldn't have needed packing off to the country as soon as danger reared its head. It galled me to hear him speaking of her like that.

'You were here the night of the dinner weren't you? '

'Naturally. I was in attendance on your brother as always.'

'Good party was it? Stuffed duck followed by frog blancmange, blanched almonds and custard?'

'I believe his Lordship lays on one of the finest banquets in London.'

'I'll wager he does.' I brooded over my bread and beer. 'You know, Nesbitt, there's something that's been puzzling me. If Don Alphonse was a regular visitor to this house, you must have seen him and, if so, you surely recognised him on the riverbank and yet you never mentioned it. I can understand you not wanting the Rotherhithe Watch to get wind of it. What I don't understand is why my brother needed me to be there at all. I never met the man and had nothing to do with the business. Surely you could have identified him without me.'

'You had better ask his Lordship about that, Master John. All I know is that he wanted you there and I fetched you. Although I recognised the man, I felt it was better to let your brother inform you who he was. But, as it happened, you already recognised the man, did you not? Something that you failed to let on yourself. So perhaps it is best if neither of us reproaches the other in the matter. *Quid pro quo?*'

I regarded Nesbitt warily. I had to admit I didn't fancy sparring with his solid and measured intelligence. He was right that I had tried to score points off him by not revealing I'd seen Don Alphonse at the procession, but it was also obvious that my brother had used me as a substitute for Nesbitt when it came to dealing with Walsingham. So far I could only come up with negative reasons for his doing that, none of which sat easily in my mind.

'Is Matthew Jordan waiting for me?'

'You'll find him by the river gate preparing a boat.'

'Good,' I said, finishing my breakfast and pushing my wooden stool back. 'First I want to take another look at the body.' For a moment, I thought Nesbitt was going to tag along but he seemed to think better of it.

'It's in the cellar. His Lordship expects you here this evening with the black servant. He said to remind you of his wishes.' I felt my irritation rising again but bit my tongue.

'In that case, let's hope I can find him.' Despite my brother's wishful thinking, I thought it unlikely the African, Cassangoe, would be easy to find. True, there were a smattering of black servants kept in some of the better houses in London, exotic additions brought back from overseas adventures, but if he had murdered Don Alphonse, it seemed unreasonable to expect him to wait around politely for me to take him into custody. The best I could hope for was to find Don Alphonse's port office and see what turned up.

Narrow stones stairs wound down to the cellar from a passageway adjacent to the kitchen. I am not someone that takes great delight in mooning over dead bodies, especially not battered ones that have been pickled in the Thames, but I had an ulterior motive that morning, which was to relieve the Portuguese gentleman of his fine leather boots. I had already decided they would make a good substitute for the pair that had mysteriously gone missing the previous day.

Down in the dank bowels of the house, lit only by a dim light coming from a small window at the height of the ceiling, I was dismayed to find that my scheme would be thwarted. Don Alphonse had been stripped of all his clothes and now lay on the cellar floor with just a thin muslin sheet preserving what was left of his dignity. There was no sign of his clothes. It occurred to me to exit forthwith but some strange fascination drew me to the corpse. I gently lifted the sheet and pulled it away from the body.

If anything, Don Alphonse looked even worse now than he had done a day earlier. The sallow skin of the face had turned a pallid grey colour and had sunk in against the cheekbones. The empty eye socket had become puckered and there was evidence of more bruising around the forehead and scalp. The handsome, proud features were now just a memory. Further down, the livid cuts and bruises of the day before had dulled into muted greys and blues that had no place on a human body. There was barely an inch that had escaped the battering.

I bent forward to examine the neck closely. The mark there was distinctive by its uniformity compared with the rest of the injuries but what was interesting was how clearly it sat underneath the later, more random injuries. There was no doubt that Don Alphonse had been strangled first and then battered.

The sight suddenly became too much. I felt nausea rising as I hastily replaced the sheet, but not before a further glance down the prostrate body had drawn my attention to an interesting detail.

Back in the parlour, I asked Nesbitt what had happened to the clothes in a forlorn hope that I might still get my hands on the boots.

'Burnt on his Lordship's orders. He didn't want the risk of disease spreading.'

So much for that idea.

* * *

At the bottom of the river stairs, I found Matthew bobbing up and down in a small rowing boat. He was rubbing his hands together for warmth and watching the traffic going up and down the river. On seeing me, he gave me a big, gap-toothed grin and offered me a hand into the boat.

'Highly Master, I hear I'm to have the pleasure of ferryin' you about town.' He rubbed his nose and winked at me conspiratorially. 'The utmost privy work, so I've been told.'

'Ah, my brother has had words has he?'

'That's the rub of it. Called in first thing, I was, and told most surely that if I was to give away so much as a whistle, I would find myself at the wrong end of the lash.' We both laughed at this, but, knowing the occasional severity of my brother's justice, it was rather a hollow gesture.

'Well, you can start by giving me some information.'

'Oh, how's that?'

'The dinner in the house two nights ago. Were you on river duty?'

'Always on duty is Matthew, Master John. What of it?'

'There was a Portuguese gentleman here that night. Do you remember him?'

'The stranger with the hooknose do you mean? Portingale was he?' Matthew sniffed disapprovingly. 'Yes I remember him. And heard he recently tried swimmin' his way home an' all.'

I nodded grimly: 'That's the one. Apparently, that night he left from here with three or four others. Do you know where they went to?'

'Highly Master, I can't say I do, seeing as I didn't row them myself. They was a-taken off in a hired boat.'

'Was there anything out of the ordinary that you noticed?' I didn't have much faith in Matthew remembering anything but, after furrowing his brow for a moment, he surprised me.

'Well, now you comes to mention it, young Master, there was some disagreement, if memory serves.'

'Disagreement? What about?'

'I can't rightly say – only that it was between the foreign gentleman, him as had the hooknose, and some other party. A heated exchange it was, in the garden, before gettin' aboard. The other three gentlemen were waiting on the steps. That's how I remember. There was an embarrassing moment, while the fine gentlemen all stood around pretendin' not to notice.'

'You didn't hear what the argument was about? Any snippets at all?'

'None Master. Them were out of earshot up in the garden and the likes of me an't paid to listen to private parlances, howsoever amusin' it might prove.' He cocked his head to one side and stroked his grey stubble for a moment. 'If you asked me to lay a bet, and I only say *if* mind, I'd wager it was about a woman.'

'A woman?'

'You've got it – pretty thing that'll break your heart and empty your purse – not necessarily in that order. Ever encountered such a wonder?'

'I met one once who ripped out hearts and kept them in a purse she'd already emptied. What makes you say such a creature was the cause of the argument?' My tone suggested that the last thing I trusted was his old-man's intuition, but Matthew surprised me further.

'Only someat one of the other gentlemen said before they all laughed.'

'And what did he say?'

'Someat about the foreign gentleman being free with other men's wives. That's all I heard. The foreigner come down the steps soon after and the others pretended like they hadn't heard nothin'.'

'Do you know who any of them were?'

'Only one of them, it were the poet.'

'Who Drummond? I can't imagine that molly knowing much about women, let alone about other men's wives,' I said, with a knowing grin at Matthew, which he returned in kind. 'What did the man the Portingale was arguing with look like?'

'Highly Master, I never saw him – it were pitch black here that night. Word came that they were leavin' and a-wanting a boat so I came down here and called for one. The argument took place near the house.'

'What happened to the man?'

'I don't know. I assumed he returned to the house. Like I said, the foreigner came down and they all departed.'

'So Don Alphonse and Drummond were two in the boat, and a third must have been this Simon Turney. I wonder who the fourth man was.'

'Why don't you ask Drummond who it were?'

'That line of enquiry has been expressly forbidden by my brother.

If I ask Drummond, it'll get straight back to Robert that I've disobeyed his order. We'll have to find out some other way. Do you know where they went?'

'Downriver for certain but more than that … ' Matthew shrugged forlornly.

'Would you recognise their pilot again?'

'Doubtful Master, every face looks the same on the river, especially at this time of year.'

'We need to find him if we can. Another thing, the Portuguese had a black servant. Do you recall ever seeing him at all? Our official job now is to go and find him and bring him back here.'

'A savage?' Matthew exclaimed using the same term of endearment as my brother. 'I can't say as I have Master. I think I'd have remembered someone like that.'

'They might be savages to you Matthew but I've read sailor's accounts that say when the first boats arrived in Guinea they found neatly laid out towns and villages, a healthy population, and even political systems in place. Just remember that the next time you're picking your way through the plague, shit and beggar ridden streets of our fine city.'

Matthew merely looked surprised at my comment: 'You shouldn't believe everythin' you read, Master? I heard some of them have two heads and four legs, and that they eat one another for breakfast.'

'*You* shouldn't believe everything you hear on the river.'

'Why, young master, I believe I overheard that said in this house.'

I shook my head with mock despair at that last remark and bade Matthew start rowing.

Out on the river I felt my spirits lifting. As we coursed into the traffic, I could see, through the occasional gaps between the great houses along the bank, new buildings being erected on the opposite side of the strand, where only a few weeks ago green fields had stretched into the distance. Amongst the new great houses being erected by the rich, there would also be new tenement accommodation built to soak up some of the ever-burgeoning population of the city that had been increasingly spilling over the city walls. The outskirts of the city were fast becoming home for all kinds of immigrants – some fleeing poverty in the countryside, others persecution abroad.

It was happening within the walls too. Comfortable, well-worn wooden framed town houses, and their gardens, were being raised and replaced with cramped, steep-roofed houses – all with a cellar, a shop, two more floors and a garret – the whole thing thrown up in a trice to release the newcomers of their coinage as quickly as possible. I chuckled inwardly at the thought of my brother's view being obscured by these brash new buildings, which would soon be the nesting place for a whole host of undesirables. This thought, combined with the crisp, clear weather that greeted us on the Thames, served to raise my spirits even further, as we jostled with the wherries and barges on the wide, viscous river.

As the daybreak crept slowly over the horizon, I mulled over my task. It had become clear the previous evening that Walsingham and my brother were far from in agreement on how to tackle the questions of who killed Don Alphonse and why. I was, effectively, working for two masters with two different objectives – and two competing outcomes.

The biggest conundrum I had been struggling with overnight was how involved, if at all, my brother was in the murder? At the very least, Robert's reluctance to reveal the names of his dinner guests, combined with an indecorous haste to pin the crime on Cassangoe, served only to make him look guilty of hiding something – a fact that hadn't gone unnoticed by Walsingham.

But the thought of my brother's involvement in murder jarred in the mind like a bone in the throat. Both his staunch Protestantism and sense of aristocratic honour were at odds with that view. However much I disliked him at times, I couldn't see him as a murderer. More likely he was simply protecting one of his guests who he suspected might be, and Matthew's evidence of a quarrel after the dinner added fuel to that particular fire. Yes, I thought, my brother's position could credibly be put down to a combination of loyalty to a friend and obstinacy in his dealings with Walsingham, whose involvement he clearly resented.

Whatever the truth, I knew that I had to be careful about uncovering any evidence that contradicted Cassangoe's guilt and would thus embarrass my brother. At the same time, if all I came up with was the same weak reasoning as my brother – ergo savage equates to murderer – Walsingham was hardly likely to be satisfied. I had a very tricky path to negotiate.

I paused momentarily in my thoughts to shoo away a belligerent swan, with two nicks marked in a V-shape on its beak, which was taking exception to Matthew's course. The mark denoted one of the Vintner swans, which appeared to think, like all of its brethren, that it owned the river. The momentary distraction dealt with, I got back to thinking.

Loyalty to Walsingham or loyalty to my brother? I confess I felt little of it to either of them – it was more a question of who was the more dangerous to disappoint. My brother provided a roof over my head, and an existence of sorts, but he had hardly gone out of his way to instil feelings of loyalty and kinship. He simply took these attributes for granted. A life with my brother's patronage offered no possibility of advancement and a permanent role somewhere below the dogs in the general pecking order. Walsingham, on the other hand, represented a myriad of opportunities. It was well known that he was at the centre of a spider's web that spread over the whole of Europe and able men of all backgrounds had risen to height in his organisation. Impressing him was one thing though, failing him another entirely. It could mean creating a powerful enemy, especially if he felt I was obstructing his suspicions of my brother.

I didn't like the situation one bit.

* * *

Soon I was walking through the bristling streets of Billingsgate, looking for Don Alphonse de Sousa's port office. The cold weather hadn't dampened activity in the port, which was full of pinnaces, galleons and every sized ship in between, all gorging their wares onto the London markets.

Matthew had stayed with the boat under instructions to find the waterman that had rowed Don Alphonse and his companions down river two nights previously. We had agreed he would berth at Three Cranes Wharf because it was a popular alighting points for boats going to and from Southwark, as well as those going East and West along the river, and was therefore deemed as good a place as any to start looking for someone who plied their trade as a wherryman. Still, the chances of finding the man were extremely remote – there were thousands of watermen working on the short stretch of the Thames from the Strand to the Tower, it would be as likely as finding a virgin in a Shoreditch playhouse. Not to mention the fact that, despite his assurances, I wasn't totally convinced Matthew would recognise him.

After some serious thought on the matter, I had also asked Matthew to glean any information he could about Simon Turney, and from where he was sailing. Although my brother had expressly forbidden me to approach his friend and guest, not to mention making it as difficult as possible, Walsingham had wanted me to pursue this line of enquiry. It was the first of a number of such contradictions that I realised I was going to have to deal with, if I was to satisfy two masters. I consoled myself with the thought that Turney had probably set sail with the morning tide and my brother would never know I had considered talking to him.

Finding Don Alphonse's port headquarters didn't prove as easy as I'd hoped. London Pool, as Billingsgate was affectionately known, was a huge port and hundreds of merchants had their offices and warehouses on the scores of wharfs and quays that surrounded it. After an hour's worth of fruitless enquiring, someone told me that I wanted Lion's Quay. I was pointed to a hitherto undiscovered stretch of quay, where the frenzied activity of the main docks had subsided.

A sign of a lion, badly drawn and with flecking paint, told me I had found my destination.

Chapter 9

'There is no sin but ignorance.'
(Christopher Marlowe)

Lion's Quay consisted of a terrace of low-slung warehouses on one side of a rickety dock, a stretch of fetid water on the other. There were one or two ragged barks, but they hardly filled the harbour, which was wide enough, and must have once been a docking point, for large mercantile vessels.

Beyond the stretch of foul-smelling water, the back walls of the central Billingsgate docks rose claustrophobically, throwing shadows across the harbour. A few doors were open and one or two people were working on the jetty but there was no sense of urgency in the day's work. Even the snow had refused to settle here as though the rotting timbers of the jetty were somehow deemed unworthy. At the far end, ships could be seen passing on the main stretch of the river, whose surface glittered in the low winter sunlight. None stopped at Lion's Quay; it felt unloved and ignored.

I walked carefully along the greasy, gnarled timbers of the jetty, peering closely at the writing on each of the buildings in turn. None of them appeared to be what I was looking for until I came to the last one. It was a solidly constructed timber shack, which looked in better condition than most of the run-down warehouses I had passed till now. Large black letters painted above the door announced:

A.DE.S. – MERCHANTS SHYPPING TRADE

My instincts told me immediately that I was to be out of luck – the building had an eerie stillness about it. I tried the door but it wouldn't budge. There seemed little point in knocking but I did so anyway, careful not to attract too much attention from the few stragglers along the quay. Even so, the hollow emptiness of the warehouse echoed loudly along the pier. There were grubby linen windows, set with thick iron bars, to either side of the door but peering through the grime only revealed the backs of shutters that were firmly locked on the inside. Stepping to the edge of the pier, I surveyed the low, sloping roof. There was a tubular metal chimney, where I would have expected to see smoke emerging on such a cold day, had the building been inhabited.

At the river's edge the pier ended abruptly and it occurred to me that the place would be an ideal location to commit a murder – secluded and quiet, with the only inhabitants seeming intent on minding their own business. Was this the murder scene – there was nothing to suggest it, apart from the desolate nature of the spot. It was a relatively short distance from here to Cuckold's Point – a body could make it in under an hour given the right tidal conditions. Certainly a good working hypothesis, although it didn't account for the battering the body had received.

I looked dejectedly into the sandy-brown water and thought of all the things I didn't know concerning Don Alphonse. The waters of the Thames lapped hard against the legs of the wooden pier, as though trying desperately to undermine them. I had reached a dead end – both literally and metaphorically.

I stood there gloomily pondering my next move, when I noticed a thin trail of smoke coming from the adjacent warehouse in the line. It was a much shabbier version of the same design, with the same uniform door and windows and the same thin metal pipe sticking out of its roof. There was also writing above the door but this time it announced, somewhat more prosaically and in much older paint:

'H. SMYTH & SONNES – HYDDES and SKINNES. FINE WINNES.'

It seemed an improbable combination.

The warehouse door was slightly ajar and I knocked briskly before pulling it open and stepping through. The interior was smoky, and smelt of a mixture of coke and what I took to be animal skins. It took a while for my eyes to adjust to the room – through the gloom, I could just about make out all manner of crates and boxes but otherwise it appeared to be empty. The smoke started to make my eyes water and I was about to step out again, when a voice spoke to me from one corner.

'And what can I do for you young man?' Startled, I peered into the darkness. 'If it's hides you're wanting then I'm afraid the next shipment isn't due until next week. Or the week after. There's never any telling these days. If, on the other hand it's fine wines you seek, then you are about twenty years too late.' During the course of this abstruse statement, I had gradually made out the figure of a man huddled over a desk in one corner, working to the light of a low-burning candle. He had a black hood over his head out of which sprouted a bushy grey beard. I could just about see that he held a quill in one hand and was making notes in a thick leather-bound ledger that lay on the table in front of him. Behind him the fireplace smoked, rather than blazed, making it look as though his cloak was smouldering. I moved closer towards him, taking care not to trip over the debris that lay about the floor.

'Excuse me interrupting your labour, sir, I came to the warehouse of Master De Sousa.' I said, wafting smoke from my eyes before adding helpfully, 'Your neighbour.'

He put his quill down slowly and raised his eyes towards me, then fixed me with a playful, mischievous look. 'Would that be Don Alphonse de Sousa? Scourge of Spanish shipping and English husbands? The libertine of Lion's Quay? He may well be known to me, young master, he may well indeed.' His voice was slightly nasal, as though he had a cold, though it was more likely his nose was bunged up with smoke. 'And what business might you have with the Don, Master…?'

'Lovat, sir.'

'Come closer, Master Lovat. Let old Hercules have a look at you.' He beckoned me forward with bony fingers and then stretched out his hand to be shaken 'Hercules Smyth at your service.' I gingerly held his fragile, mottled hand, whilst the diminutive Hercules surveyed me up and down. He wasn't slow to tell me what impression I gave.

'Now you don't look the jilted husband type – altogether too young and innocent-looking, if you'll forgive my saying so. So it can't be revenge you're after. Expensive hand me down clothing, coupled with an air of superiority – a gentleman fallen on hard times, perhaps? Old Hercules has seen plenty of those in his lifetimes. No, I've got it – a disinherited son? You have that touch of mordancy about you. Only a touch mind. Are you hoping the benevolent Don Alphonse will whisk you off to foreign parts where you can recoup your fortune?' I smiled at the old man's summing up.

'Alas, no fortune lost to recoup, and no desire to be a mariner either.'

I studied the old man's twinkling grey eyes on either side of his thin, red nose and wondered just how well he knew Don Alphonse.

'Then what business with Don Alphonse, pray, brings you to the lepers' end of Lion's Quay?'

'Actually it's his servant who I seek. A moor named Cassangoe.'

At this the old man snorted dismissively. 'Ah, the luckless Cassangoe? What has he done now? Been in the general vicinity of some ill-deeds? Scared a rich old lady by looking in her direction?' He sat back in his chair, his early playful expression morphing into one of contempt. 'Or are you paying him that rare courtesy of a social call?'

'He has done nothing as far as I am aware sir,' I replied carefully, at pains to ignore the sarcasm in his words. 'I merely wish to speak with him.'

'Well I expect you'll find him by his friend's side. The faithful Cassangoe rarely ventures onto the London streets by himself. Far too dangerous – for him, that is!'

'I am afraid not. Unfortunately Don Alphonse has met with an accident.' Ever since the beginning of our conversation I'd been wondering whether or not to mention Don Alphonse's death, but the change in the old man's manner towards me seemed to trigger the information involuntarily.

'An accident? Is he dead?' Hercules Smyth shot these words out almost as if he had been expecting the news.

'His body was found yesterday morning, given up by the river at Rotherhithe.' I explained briefly how Don Alphonse had been found, without mentioning anything about strangulation. Nevertheless, the news was clearly a shock to the old man. He slumped forward on the table and all of the earlier playfulness and pride dissipated from his frail body.

'Don Alphonse dead? I can't believe it.' He shook his head slowly and I noticed a lone tear running down his face into his beard. He suddenly regarded me coldly as if, as the bearer of bad tidings, I must somehow be involved.

'And why are you here Master Lovat? What does Don Alphonse's death have to do with you?'

'I work for a friend of Don Alphonse's who wants to know what happened to him.'

'What happened to him? So he didn't just fall in the river? Don't try pulling the wool over my eyes Master Lovat.'

'I can't say.'

'Can't or won't?' The old man's sudden fierceness towards me was disconcerting. I hadn't expected to be on the receiving end of an interrogation. 'A friend you say? Don Alphonse had no *friends* as far as I am aware. Not amongst the English gentry, who you so clearly represent. He held them in the greatest contempt.' His manner had now become bitter and hostile. I realised I'd lost any element of empathy and decided to cut to the chase.

'Can you at least tell me where I might find Cassangoe?'

'No. I haven't seen him.'

'Perhaps he's at Don Alphonse's home?' I asked, hoping the old man would tell me where that was, but he either he refused to take the bait or genuinely didn't know – the shake of the head he gave me was difficult to interpret.

'Cassangoe might be in danger. Are you sure you don't know where he would go if he was alone?' Hercules Smyth hesitated for a moment, his eyes flitting about the room. I thought for a moment he was going to tell me something, but he evidently thought better of it.

'Danger? From whom? I really can't help you Master Lovat. I'm sorry I must continue with my work.' There was nothing for it but to go. I paused in the doorway and turned back to the hermit-like figure in the corner.

'You called this the 'lepers' end of Lion's Quay'. What did you mean by that?'

'It was an expression coined by Don Alphonse. You Englishmen want the trade us foreigners bring but you don't want to be reminded of our success, and you certainly don't want to associate with us. So you stick us at the end of these backwaters and pretend that we don't exist. Now would you kindly leave.'

There was nothing for it but to leave with as much dignity as I could muster, the passionate force of his words echoing in my ears. My overriding feeling was one of having bungled the interview, despite not knowing what, if anything, I could have done differently.

* * *

The light and air outside the warehouse came as a relief, even though sleet had started to fall. I huddled inside my cloak in front of Don Alphonse's port-house door, a feeling of frustration building up inside me. Cassangoe was nowhere to be found and I could see no means of unearthing him. I could stake out Lion's Quay but would he return there, particularly if he were guilty? Without Cassangoe there was very little else to go on and failing to find him would hardly impress either my brother, or Walsingham.

As I again stood despondently by the river's edge, the semblance of a vague plan forming in my head, Hercules Smyth suddenly appeared in front of his warehouse. Without looking at me, he quickly locked the door before hurrying away along the greasy boards of the quay. After a moment's hesitation, I followed him, making sure to keep some distance between us. As I reached the passageway beyond Lion's Quay, I momentarily lost his slight figure as he disappeared into the crowd, but after a few seconds panic, I caught a glimpse of his hood disappearing down a side alley. I ran quickly after him squeezing round carts and buffeting into disgruntled strangers.

After that brief moment of concern, shadowing Hercules Smyth was child's play. He kept himself out of the crowds by using a variety of short cuts and alleys, and it was simply a question of keeping him in sight as he wound his way up the tight passageways that led away from the river. He kept moving at a brisk pace, never once looking back.

I stalked him as he beat a path past St Dunstan's Church and out onto Tower Street, where he turned right towards the Tower, whose turrets loomed ominously against the skyline at the end of the street. Now that we were out on a broad thoroughfare, I held back and allowed him to pull further ahead, aware that at any time he could turn round and spot me, but he continued on, seemingly oblivious to my presence. When he reached the end of the street, he turned right along Petty Wales in the direction of Crutched Friars and I lost sight of him for a few seconds. I turned the corner a few seconds later but there was no sign of him.

It was an unusual street with the houses along one side overshadowed by the foreboding wall of the castle on the other. In between ran the wide moat filled with black, reflection-less water. At the north corner of the Tower the cobbled road opened out into an empty grassless patch of scrub, known as Tower Hill, where executions regularly took place but which today was completely deserted. Hercules Smyth must have gone into one of the houses.

I walked along trying to peer discreetly into windows, until I reached the porch of a church at the end of the row. There was no sign of Hercules Smyth. Rusty signs occasionally swung jerkily as gusts of wind blew unhindered across the hill. The odd passer-by scuttled across the desolate spot. There seemed nothing for it but to wait.

This plan was soon thwarted, however. A parson walked out of the church door, and began eyeing me suspiciously – before telling me that there was nothing of value in the church and advising me to clear off. Choosing not to explain that I was actually an upright citizen rather than a thief intent on robbing His house, I sloped back past the tenements. It was depressing to contemplate the impression I gave of myself. I was thinking of loitering at the other end of the street but as I reached the corner two gentlemen of the watch, who had noticed my exchange with the parson, began walking towards me. Suddenly I found my nerve giving way. The last thing I needed was to end up in the Clink for a night for no good reason at all. Without glancing back, I turned into Tower Street and decided to cut my losses.

* * *

As it was close by, I decided to pay a quick call on Buck. I hadn't seen him since the night of the procession and I was still intrigued to find out what had happened to my boots, suspecting that he and Greville had stolen them as a prank. More than that, I was looking forward to sharing my new adventure with him, and discussing what to do next.

On entering the shop, I could immediately sense there was something wrong. The only person behind the counter was one of the two apprentices, a gangly youth called Clochiard, who Buck had nicknamed 'cloth-ears' on account of both his name and the two crumpled-up features on either side of his head. Before I reached the stairs, he stopped me in my tracks.

'If it's Master Harry you're after, you won't find him. He's gone.'

'What do you mean gone?' I assumed that he only meant to the theatre.

'Cleared out. The boss and him had an almighty row last night and this morning he was gone. Must have done a moonlight flit.' I stared at him amazed for a second. Despite having removed his blue cap as he spoke, in supposed deference to my rank, he voice contained a certain relish. 'I'm surprised you don't know anything about it? The master says the pair of you are as thick as thieves.'

My heart sinking, I turned and ran up the four flights of stairs to Buck's garret. Instead of Buck, I found Emmalina sitting on the bed. When she saw me she stood up and threw her arms around me, before sobbing wordlessly on my shoulder. I was at a loss what to do but after a moment began to gently stroke her fine hair, which was falling down around her neck and shoulders. Gradually she stopped shaking and seemed to get a better hold of her emotions. She pulled away slightly and looked at me directly. Her pretty face was distraught.

'What happened?' I asked her gently.

'Last night Father and Harry had a terrible row. It's been brewing for a while – they have hardly said a civil word to each other in months – but this time it was somehow different.' Her words came out in short, breathless bursts.

I knew that Buck's moods had been darker than usual recently but I never expected that something like this would happen. Of more immediate importance, where could he have gone? I found myself grasping for rational explanations

'Perhaps he's gone on tour with the theatre – players are always touring around the country?' I knew it sounded unlikely but felt I needed to offer her something. 'He's probably gone to Warwickshire or some other God forsaken part of the country. As soon as he gets bored he'll be back. There's no need to worry.' Emmalina simply turned her solemn eyes to me and shook her head.

'He's left everything. If it was anything to do with the theatre, he at least would have taken his writing.' I looked on the desk – Buck's papers were in their usual mess. The room seemed just as we had left it two days earlier.

'Where's your step-father?'

'He went to report Harry to the Constable. Harry threatened him during the argument. He'll be back soon,' she shuddered at the thought. 'I've been staying up here to avoid that odious merchant Shuttleworth, who is coming into the shop more than ever.'

'Do you mean that man who was here the other morning? What has he got to do with anything?'

She looked at me as though I was brainless. 'He wants to marry me of course. And now that Harry has disappeared there's nothing to prevent it happening. God help me.' The thought was too much for her and she burst into another bout of sobbing. I felt a sudden urge to be protective welling up inside me.

'Come on,' I said. 'Gather your things. You can stay with me until we work out what to do about Buck.'

Within minutes she had collected her belongings. Downstairs there was still no sign of Emmalina's stepfather or the unwelcome merchant. Clochiard and the other apprentice watched us threateningly but they made no attempt to intervene.

Neither Emmalina nor I thought twice about the consequences of our actions as we burst out of the oppressive house and into the rain.

Chapter 10

'The eagle suffers little birds to sing.'
(William Shakespeare; Titus Andronicus)

Three Cranes Wharf was its usual busy, bustling self. The cold weather hadn't impacted on the river trade and the narrow wharf was awash with human river traffic, embarking or disembarking from the stairs that ran down to the river.

Emmalina and I found Matthew chatting to the bookseller, whose stall was situated outside the Tavern at the end of Three Cranes Lane, where he had a good view of the watermen dropping off and picking up their fares but was out of the main bustle of the street. In characteristically ironic style, the tavern sign showed three waterfowl cranes with plump bodies and long beaks, rather than representing the three mechanical cranes that stood on the dock for loading wine barrels, after whom the wharf was named. Today, only one of the cranes was in operation, lifting barrels from a barge and swinging them high across to the vintry warehouse. A glance at one of the barrels, as it rose over our heads, showed that the wine was imported claret from a certain T. Lurton of Bordeaux.

Matthew and the bookseller both had their hands wrapped around a cup of warm sack, and were debating how much colder it needed to get before the river froze over. The consensus seemed to be not much. I briskly introduced Emmalina and asked Matthew if he'd had any luck finding the waterman.

'Alas no, Master John. I've spoken to one or two who were in the vicinity that evenin', but none so far as have rowed the Portuguese gentleman and his companions.'

'And this man Turney? Any news of his ship, or where it might be sailing from?' The thought of tracking down Simon Turney had occurred to me as soon as my brother had mentioned him the night before, more through bloody-mindedness than anything else. I resented being asked to perform a task and then having my hands tied. The subsequent failure to find Cassangoe at Don Alphonse's warehouse had made quizzing Turney an imperative, as he was, along with Marmaduke Drummond, someone that I knew for certain had been with Don Alphonse in the hours before his murder. Besides, my brother had been so obstructive that it seemed clear he was hiding something – maybe I just had a natural propensity for sticking my nose in where it wasn't wanted?

'On that score,' Matthew said brightly, 'I have more satisfactory news. A lighterman I spoke to tells of a ship a-harboured at Deptford captained by a Master Turney, and due to sail this very day. He says he delivered goods to that very same ship. The Lady Merrydance it was called. None others, as he knew, were so ready to slip anchor along the whole stretch of the Thames.'

'Only one ship, I thought Turney was captain of a fleet?'

'That's what he told me.'

'Deptford? That's at least a league by river isn't it Matthew?'

'Nearer two I'd reckon, master.' It was too far to expect Matthew to row and I didn't much fancy joining him in the effort. I was on the point of suggesting we hire a boat with professional oarsmen, when the bookseller made a suggestion.

'The best thing, young sire, would be to take a tilt-boat from Billingsgate. That's how all these damned foreigners come and go. Their ships dock in Kent and the tilt-boats pilot them to the city. If you get there anon, you shouldn't miss the fleet afore she sails.'

'Well, let's catch it then.' I said decisively, before commanding Matthew to row us to Billingsgate with all haste. Coming to the great bridge, I only had time to glance up briefly at my lodgings as Matthew excellently propelled us through one of the arches and down the chute created by the higher water on the city side.

At Billingsgate, we left Matthew once again with instructions to continue his search for the waterman and went off in search of the tilt-boat to Deptford. I had wanted to leave Emmalina in Matthew's charge but, ever since we had left Tower Street, she had been clinging onto my arm (even more so as we shot the bridge), as though I might abandon her at any moment.

The tilt-boat was easy to identify. It was a larger than average riverboat with eight oarsmen and an arched canvas *tilt* at the back to shelter the heads of wealthier travellers. As well as passengers, the boat also carried goods, livestock and even horses – a veritable Noah's Ark, as I remarked to Emmalina on our approach.

Boarding was almost complete and we found ourselves caught up with the servants and belongings of a young, overweight German merchant, who was standing to one side and commanding the people around him in an arrogant tone. The man seemed to have every accoutrement bedecked about his person as befitted a gentleman, including an assortment of furs and a broad brimmed hat with feathers sticking out of it. I pointed him out to Emmalina, who laughed spontaneously at the spectacle. It was the first time I had seen the semblance of a smile since I had found her in Buck's garret and her whole face lit up. She noticed me observing her and gave me an anxious look, as though her happiness somehow displayed a disloyalty to Buck.

We forced our way through the German's impedimenta and onto the boat, finding space on a bench towards the stern, close to the oarsmen and just in front of the area covered by the canvas. Intermittent sleet was still falling, and I glanced enviously at those who had managed to secure seats beneath the tilt. A kindly gentlewoman, sitting behind us, leant forward and asked if my 'sister' would like a covered seat. Emmalina looked at me uncertainly but I bade her take refuge, which she did, leaving me wishing that my smart outfit had come with a hat.

The over-dressed German had finally secured his belongings and was casting his small, piggy-like eyes around for somewhere to sit. He hadn't managed to find a place for everything and was holding in his hands a metal birdcage. Inside was a large, colourful bird, which was also looking about with an indignant expression. Only too late I realised that I'd invitingly left open the space that Emmalina had vacated, and before I could rectify matters the German was squeezing his well-fed arse into the gap, the bird giving an offended squawk as he slumped down heavily on the bench. I shifted awkwardly as feathers and furs invaded my already cramped position. Before I'd had a chance to compose myself, he turned to me and started speaking.

'I shall miss your beautiful city.' This remark came out as a sigh, and was accompanied with a wink. His accent was thick, and his breath smelled like sour damsons.

'Really?' I grunted, trying to suppress a sneeze brought on by having a pheasant feather stuck up my nose. I don't think I could have been less communicative but it made no difference.

'Yes Herr Englishman. I shall miss the taverns and especially the girls, yah?' He accompanied this remark with a leer in the direction of Emmalina, who was sitting directly behind us, followed by a fleshy elbow into my ribs. The latter action very nearly pitched me into the water, which was already moving quickly by us as the oarsmen exerted themselves. 'Du verstehst mich? Aha – I bet you a gold sovereign you do!'

'I'm sure zeee ladies will miss you too.' I replied, once I had recovered my breath, being careful to lay the sarcasm on as thick as a tanner's facemask. I might as well have poured a piss pot over his head for all he noticed.

'Allow me to present myself. I am Karl Würtembatter of Lübeck. And this is my bird Lucius.' He indicated his gaudy-feathered friend, who was looking distinctly unimpressed with river travel, and then pulled off a leather glove in order to present a chubby hand. I produced my right arm from its crushed position against the side of the boat and reluctantly took his, introducing myself in the name that I might have been able to use, had I been fathered under different circumstances.

'Sir John Lovat of London. At your service sire.'

'Naturlich, an English nobleman – I felt certain you must be. Sehr angenehm, sehr angenehm.' Würtembatter stood up comically to bow, causing consternation in the birdcage, as well as amongst the passengers packed in around him. Eventually he got himself seated again and I decided to have a little fun.

'You go back to zee home country, Herr Warted-butter?' I asked, gently mocking his thick accent.

'*Würtem-batter*,' he corrected me in a schoolmasterly fashion, 'and, ach yah, Herr nobleman. I embark on a journey that leads me home this very day. Just two days ago I received a letter from my father demanding that I return there without delay.'

'Why? Is your father ill or does some other reason cause him to beg your return?'

'Between you and me, Herr Lovat, my suspicion is that someone has been telling him of the fun I have been having in London. Too much fun – du verstehst mich, Herr noble Englishman?' As he said this, he again jerked his thumb in the direction of Emmalina and made an obscene gesture with his tongue. I decided I couldn't let him get away with that.

'Allow me to present my cousin, Herr Würtembatter, the Honourable Emmalina Bucklesbury.' I leant back indicating Emmalina and drawing her into the conversation. Emmalina, who had been rolling her eyes at the German's remarks, quickly caught on and offered her hand demurely. The look on Würtembatter's face was priceless.

'Your cousin?' He spluttered. 'Mein Gott, Herr Lovat, you really should have warned me.' He stood up again and went through the whole rigmarole of bowing and scraping, this time nearly falling over the benches in front. Eventually, he sat down heavily in an explosion of feathers.

'I believe you were saying to my brother how your father has forced you to return home, Herr Würtembatter,' said Emmalina, in what must have been a perfect imitation of the aristocratic ladies that frequented her stepfather's shop.

'Ah yah? Miss… er…?'

'Bucklesbury.'

'Miss Bucklesbury. He has sent a cousin to replace me. Meanwhile, I have one more adventure before returning home – aboard an English ship.'

'And what ship might that be?'

'The Lady Merrydance, I am on my way to her now. She sails directly from Deptford.'

'The Lady Merrydance?' I exclaimed, exchanging a meaningful glance with Emmalina. The desire to mock him instantly drained out of me, replaced instead with a bristling excitement, tempered by my relief that the ship had yet to sail. 'And what is the nature of your – adventure?'

'The nature – how is it you mean?' I explained what I meant. 'Ah yah, ich verstehe. After some dealings in France,' he tapped his nose conspiratorially, 'we go on a trading expedition to the German States and the Baltic – Bremen, Danzig, Visby, Novgorod. A winter in the freezing Baltic, fending off frostbite and Swedish pirates – not everyone's idea of fun but it is better than being stuck in Lübeck! Sadly, I then have no choice but to return home, where I shall go back to counting the beans in my father's warehouse … until I can think of a good reason to persuade him to let me return to our *kontor* in London.' He seemed genuinely depressed at the prospect, his fat frame slumping into the seat and spilling even further onto mine.

'Cheer up Herr Würtembatter,' said Emmalina, warming to the task and feigning companionship. 'Your voyage sounds like quite an adventure. Why don't you tell us about it?'

'Indeed,' I chimed in. 'I wonder who can afford to fund such an expedition?' The German averted his gaze from Emmalina and squinted at me sideways.

'That is not my area of concern. I am merely employed as *factor* but it's – how do you English call it – a joint-stock company. A number of financiers are involved. They all contribute a share of the cost and divide up the loot at the end – if there is any, of course.'

'I thought the Baltic was off limits for English vessels?'

'Don't you believe it. It used to be of course, when the Hanseatic League was stronger, but now we are weak and the area has become a complete handgemenge. Poles, Swedes, Russians – you name it – we are overrun with vermin.'

'So adventurers like you are filling the void?' Emmalina fluttered her eyelids coquettishly, 'How brave.'

'Und warum nicht, Milady? You see the last two years have been terrible for trade in the north. Those Hapsburg schweine shut us out of the port at Antwerp and we've had nowhere to buy or sell anything. But since the Armada, who knows? We are Protestants in the north and you are Protestants here – well some of you anyway.' He had by now completely recovered his composure and seemed to think this last remark a great joke. He suddenly thought of something, turned back to Emmalina, and lifted the birdcage towards her.

'Excuse me Lady Miss Bucklesbury. Would you please to hold Lucius for me?' Before Emmalina could protest, the cage had been dumped unceremoniously in her lap and she was obscured temporarily behind a bright display of ruffled feathers. Würtembatter reached into one of his large leather sacks to extract a bag full of cured venison, which he offered to us cheerfully.

'The defeat of the Armada will make you English very rich,' he began again between chews. 'Until now the Spanish and Portuguese have divided up the routes between them – the English have been living off piracy – but now the enemy is weak.' He eyed me thoughtfully. 'A nobleman like yourself ought to be chartering a ship and making his fortune, like Turney and his partners. Yes, you English are about to get rich and my father has ordered me back to Lübeck. Unglaublich?'

He chewed morosely for a moment and I glanced back at Emmalina, who was befriending Lucius. The bird seemed much happier now that he had some female company. Perhaps he took after his owner.

'Turney? Would that be Simon Turney by any chance?'

'Freilich. He is Master of the Merrydance. You know him?'

'Not personally, no.' I said, trying to maintain an air of vague interest. I was about to ask more about the expedition and Simon Turney in particular, when Herr Würtembatter alarmingly dived off on another topic.

'These London youths – vot is their problem please, Milady and Herr noble Englishman? Gotten himmel! All I am is a humble merchant trying to pursue some business but two weeks ago …' He went into a detailed story about being chased and pelted with mud from the street by a bunch of young ruffians who had seemingly taken great offence to the undeniable fact that he was foreign.

It was the custom on festivals, which became their Saturnalia, for rampaging mobs of blue-clad apprentices, ably supported by street-boys and ruffians, to go alien baiting about the streets of London. The cry of 'Clubs' would be their rallying call and woe betides the unsuspecting travellers whom they happened across. It had been bad enough for Don Alphonse at an official procession and so one could imagine what it was like for a lone foreigner hemmed in by the narrow streets and lacking any protection.

Emmalina and I offered him some platitudes and some advice for his next visit, which was predominantly along the lines of suggesting he be a bit more discreet in his appearance. The sour look he gave us suggested he wasn't about to change that in a hurry but, as he appeared suitably mollified, I took the opportunity to continue our gentle interrogation.

'Are you familiar with a merchant called Don Alphonse de Sousa?'

'Don Alphonse? I've come across him once or twice. A Portuguese. I don't know him well. He is one of the few that prospered in the last few years. No doubt because he is Portuguese. People like him have been able to operate fairly freely.' He remembered something which made him smirk, and then looked at Emmalina quizzically as if deciding whether he dare impart the information. His verbosity got the better of him. 'He is a bit of a character that Don Alphonse. I tell you that for free.'

'In what way?'

'Well let's say he didn't always play the game at home. Not at his own home for sure. You understand me?' followed by another irritating elbow in the ribs. 'And not just in anybody else's home either. Excuse me, Milady, but he never had to worry about the painted whores that your brother and I meet on the Southbank.' Emmalina looked at me sardonically over the top of the birdcage as I felt my face flush. Either Würtembatter had already forgotten that I was supposedly a peer of the realm or maybe he just subscribed to the universal worldview that all English gentlemen were perverts. The truth was that the 'painted whores', as he so delicately referred to them, tended to laugh in my young, beardless face.

'Don Alphonse is not part of the joint-stock enterprise?' I said, my manner somewhat terser.

'I doubt it. Why would he join? He doesn't need the money – why take the risk?'

'So the voyage is a risk?'

'Naturlich! For one thing there are always pirates and other dangers but more likely the boat will sink! Have you seen the leaky tubs you English go to sea in? How Drake ever – how do you call it – circumnavigated the globe I will never fathom?'

'And is the Lady Merrydance seaworthy?'

'Good question, I've never seen her.'

'Never seen her?'

'No. The strange thing is I was only offered the position one week ago. It seems the expedition has been arranged in somewhat of a hurry. I was looking for some way of delaying my trip home and this job comes along. Perfekt!' He went back to chewing musingly on a dried stick of venison.

'Don Alphonse.' The German let out a chuckle. 'Always a thorn in some poor husband's side. Always making them play the cuckold. Always so full of life.'

I couldn't respond to that so I just looked away across the increasingly stretched waters of the Thames.

* * *

The trip to Deptford took about an hour and a half from Billingsgate, which was a good deal longer than anyone would want to be stuck with the delightful Karl Würtembatter. I actually pitied the poor fools who were going to sea with him. His principal topics of conversation were drinking in Shoreditch, gambling in Dowgate, whoring in Southwark, or any combination of the three.

Once he had got up steam, he showed no delicacy in respect to Emmalina. His particular speciality was brothels. When he wasn't thumping me tiresomely in the ribs, following the punch line of some tedious joke – which usually involved the decidedly unattractive image of him with his breeches around his knees – he was regaling us with some intimate story about a stew he'd visited in some godforsaken part of Europe, and what the girls therein had got up to. The man seemed to have an encyclopaedic knowledge of brothels encountered on his travels and his favourite pastime was comparing the virtues, or more accurately the vices, of the poor unfortunates who operated in them. Fortunately, finding me to be mute on the subject, and Emmalina taking an ever-greater interest in Lucius, he eventually gave up with a shrug, instead consoling himself with more sticks of venison.

Relieved, I concentrated on the external views across either side of the river and the internal mystery going round in circles in my head. We were speeding rapidly across the silky waters of the Thames, the oarsmen straining in their exertions. Not long after passing Rotherhithe Marsh, the boat began to turn a sharp right hand bend in the river and I saw clearly the pole with the antlers on it defining the area known as Cuckold's Point.

First one of my brother's guests, then Hercules Smyth and now Karl Würtembatter had all volunteered the information that Don Alphonse had a reputation for seducing other men's wives. Murder had been committed for far less than that.

***

After Würtembatter had run aground, as far as stories of his leisure activities were concerned, I decided to have another go at interrogating him. We still had some distance to travel, and there were myriad questions I wanted to ask about the voyage of the Lady Merrydance. Principally, I wanted to establish the extent of my brother's involvement.

'Robert Rokesby. Is he a member of this joint-stock company?' I asked with the same air of disengaged interest but, for the first time, the German eyed me suspiciously.

'Lord Rokesby. I believe he is the chief investor in the company. Why, may I ask, are you so interested in Turney and Don Alphonse and Lord Rokesby?' He shifted his ample arse uneasily in his seat, waving a stick of venison under my nose in a mildly threatening manner. 'Are you one of those withered puritans trying to sabotage our trip, yah?'

'A puritan? How amusing!' I bluffed, realising that I hadn't prepared myself in the least for a direct question of this kind. 'I am merely a distant kinsman of Lord Rokesby.' Practically an invisible one, if my brother had anything to do with it; at least Würtembatter seemed momentarily put off guard.

'Ah I see. Perhaps you come to see seek an adventure on one of his ships and your cousin comes to wave you farewell?' His voice held a note of regret, as though he rather liked the idea of taking her with him. 'I thought for a minute you might be a spy, or one of those puritans who object to tobacco and all other pleasures in life. Like that fanatic Walsingham.'

This remark opened up a tantalising line of enquiry. 'Walsingham? Is he opposed to your adventure?'

'You would have to ask him, Herr Englishman.' He sniffed and wiped some spray from the oars from his face – his demeanour suddenly brightening. 'Mind you, everyone knows that Walsingham is jealous of successful merchants.'

'What do you mean?'

'Herr Walsingham hasn't had much luck with trade himself.'

'No?'

'Hah no! Ask him about Fool's Gold next time you see him!' He broke out into a fit of laughter. Although I had no idea what the flatulent German was on about, it seemed to amuse him greatly, so I let him enjoy it. Until, that was, he started to choke on the venison and needed a good thump on the back. He hunched forward, red faced and breathless. When he had started to recover his composure, I leant forward, my arm still on his back, and spoke quietly but directly into his ear.

'Actually, I work for Sir Francis Walsingham.'

'Don't jest with me, Herr Lovat.' Würtembatter turned his rotund face towards me with a mocking smile playing on his lips, but he very quickly realised from the look in my eye that jesting was the furthest thing from my mind. I produced the papers that gave me Walsingham's authority to act on his behalf. 'I'd be very careful what you say about him in future if I was you.'

'Then you are a spy after all?' A look of sheer terror passed across Würtembatter's face. Behind us Emmalina had become quite still and was watching me intently. I still held Würtembatter tightly, the staleness of his breath all too present.

'His Lordship happens to be very interested in The Lady Merrydance and her crew.' As far as I knew, Walsingham had never even heard of the ship, but he had given me the authority and I might as well use it. 'I would be grateful for anything you could tell me about them.'

'Really, Herr Lovat. I know nothing about anything.' Würtembatter tried to pull away from me but I held him tight, in as intimidating a manner as I could muster.

'You said Lord Rokesby was funding the voyage? Who else is involved in the joint-stock company?'

'Ich weiss es nicht!'

'I think you do. Turney?'

'Yes of course Turney.'

'Who else?'

'I know of no one else. Bitte, du hast verstehst mich falsch. I mean no disrespect to Herr Walsingham. Let's say no more about it.' He had started raising his voice and thrashing around in the seat so I was forced to let him go in order not to attract the attention of the other travellers.

Würtembatter couldn't get further away but he spent the remaining ten minutes of the voyage looking out across the river, refusing to acknowledge me. I could tell from his agitated manner that there was something causing him deep concern.

When we reached Deptford he practically leapt out of the boat, issuing rapid instructions regarding his belongings, before setting off at great pace across the dock. I watched him disappear into the crowd, reflecting that he could move quite nimbly for a man of his size, and wondering what on earth could have disturbed him so greatly.

Chapter 11

'A prudent question is one half of wisdom.'
(Sir Francis Bacon)

Deptford was a small town on the south bank of the Thames, given elevated status by virtue of the fact that the Royal Docks had been built there in the time of King Henry, Elizabeth's father. The town nestled right up against the riverbank but, rising beyond it, could be seen the rigging and masts of great ships in the harbour. The tilt-boat dropped us at the Upper Watergate, a few hundred yards north of the dock, which meant that we had to scramble through the narrow streets around the port to reach it. This, and getting caught up in the unloading process, meant that Karl Würtembatter had made a good start on us by the time we eventually reached the ships.

There was no mistaking the Lady Merrydance. Even if her size hadn't been a clear indicator, the fact that I recognised our family crest on a flag flying high on her central mast was a strong clue. She was a three-masted vessel of approximately a hundred tons, and with her high poop deck, seemed, to my untrained eye, more suitable for warfare than merchant shipping. She was strangely calm for a ship that was about to embark on a lengthy tour of the high seas. Only a small group of sailors were employed at the end of a rope, hauling crates onto the deck, but there was very little sense of urgency.

Emmalina and I negotiated our way around a maze of wooden jetties and bridges, trying to reach the ship. As we approached, I spotted Karl Würtembatter standing in the centre of the main deck, talking excitedly with a tall man, a youthful shock of sandy-coloured hair on his head. We were still a good fifty yards away from the boat but could clearly see the action taking place, as if we were watching a theatrical dumb show. Würtembatter's arms were waving about frantically and every inch of his corpulent frame was employed in conveying a seemingly urgent message. The fair-haired man seemed at first disinclined to take interest, then paused to listen more attentively and finally became rigid as Würtembatter re-emphasised a particular point. They turned towards the dock and began to cast their eyes around until Würtembatter's gaze found what they were looking for and he pointed – directly at us.

I had stopped stock-still on the jetty to watch this pantomime and Emmalina was eyeing me quizzically.

'That's the man you were talking to on the ferry, isn't it? Why's he pointing at us?'

'I don't know,' I said, 'but I seem to have caused quite a stir.' This remark was prompted by the fact that the fair-haired man had run over to the group of sailors on the end of the rope, and issued new orders. Suddenly the ship became a whirlwind of activity – sailors appearing from below deck and advancing up the rigging, sails beginning to be dropped. It took me a moment to realise what was happening. Emmalina said it for me: 'She's about to sail.'

'Quick,' I said, seeing my final opportunity of getting any information disappearing on a gust of wind. I broke into a run, reaching the ship in a matter of seconds, and, without thinking, grabbed a rope and hauled myself up onto the central deck. Almost immediately, I spotted the sandy-haired man standing on the upper deck, where he was conducting the organised chaos going on around him. Up close I could see that he was a good deal older than the boyish shock of hair had made him seem from a distance. His face was wide and weathered, and he was certainly a hardy seaman, though I got the impression that his most forceful days were behind him. He immediately spotted me and advanced threateningly.

'I warn you sire, this ship is about to sail. Stand ashore unless you want to be party to a lengthy voyage.'

'Are you Master Turney?'

'What of it sire?'

'I need to speak to you.'

'Can't you see I'm busy? Stand ashore I say. The men are making the sails ready. You are a landloper sire, I won't warn you again.' He began to motion to a couple of sailors to come and remove me physically. My options were narrowing dramatically.

'I work for Sir Francis Walsingham,' I said, trying to dredge up some authority. I hoped dropping Walsingham's name would have the same effect as it had with Würtembatter, but it served only to make Turney more belligerent.

'Who you work for is irrelevant to me, my lad. If Walsingham wishes to speak with me he can produce an official summons and then await our return – a good six months hence, perhaps longer.' He waved the two sailors urgently to come and deal with me.

'Sir Francis doesn't wish to speak to you. I do, on his authority and also on the authority of my brother, Lord Robert Rokesby. I'm investigating the death of a man called Don Alphonse de Sousa.' This volley of information, rushing out without a breath as I saw the sailors approaching with intent, finally seemed to do the trick. Turney's manner changed abruptly.

'What did you say? De Sousa dead?' An expression of incredulity fixed on his face. 'Würtembatter said nothing about that.'

'I hadn't told him.'

But I was only with Don Alphonse two nights ago.'

'That's why I wanted to speak with you. You must have been one of the last people to see him alive.'

'I don't understand. Why does his death need investigating?'

'Because he was murdered.'

'Murdered?' The look he gave me was less one of surprise at the news, but more one of shock. As though the news, though dreadful, was somehow expected. 'How?' It came out as a croak.

'Strangled, with a necklace my brother gave him as gift. Then thrown into the river. His body was badly beaten.'

'Strangled, you say?' The sailors had reached my side and were awaiting orders to pitch me overboard.

'Yes. Can you tell me anything about it?'

'No!' The word exploded forcibly from his lips, as though, if he suspected anything about the murder, he certainly didn't wish it to be true.

'We're ready to cast off, Master.' One of the sailors had picked up on Turney's hesitancy and was helpfully offering him an escape route. Turney, himself, stood as though in a state of confusion, a thousand thoughts cramming into his stunned head. Thoughts that I dearly wanted to get at. I tried again.

'My brother told me that you left his house with Don Alphonse. Don Alphonse was murdered later that evening. Where did he go after you left him? Anything you can tell me might help to find his killer.' One of the men stepped forward but Turney raised his hand to prevent him accosting me.

'You or Walsingham think I might have had something to do with his murder?' It was more of a musing than a threat.

'I make no accusations, nor imply any such thing. I simply want to establish his movements, and the whereabouts of his black serving man Cassangoe.'

'Cassangoe isn't a servant.'

'Well, whatever he is, I wish to find him.'

His pale blue eyes appraised me warily. 'I can't help you with that. Nor can I shed any light on what happened to Don Alphonse.'

'You left my brother's house with other men. Can they help me? One was the poet Marmaduke Drummond? Who was the other?'

'You're fishing Lovat? I can assure you that none of the men with Don Alphonse that evening had anything to do with his death. He was quite alive when we left him. Now you will have to leave my ship.' For a moment I thought that he would give me some useful information but it seemed his mood had changed. 'See this gentleman off the ship, men. Do it gently mind, he claims to be the brother of our patron. I'm sorry I can't help you further. Give my regards to your brother – if indeed he is your brother. He certainly never mentioned you.'

As I was being escorted to the edge of the deck I tried one last throw of the dice. Looking back over my shoulder to Turney who was beginning to climb the stairs to the poop deck: 'Are you married sire?'

He stopped and turned. 'What do you mean by that?'

'Don Alphonse was a womaniser. Could a jealous husband be the cause of his death?' The look he gave me showed that, in some imperceptible, way I had scored a bulls-eye. 'There was an argument in the garden that night between Don Alphonse and another man. Who was that Master Turney?'

'I don't know, though I assumed it was hard …' He stopped abruptly.

'Hard? What do you mean by that?'

'I can assure you Master Lovat I am not married and Don Alphonse has never given me any concerns in that direction. Leave the ship, now. Quickly men.'

There was no reprieve this time. I was forcibly handled over the side of the boat and dropped unceremoniously onto the deck where I landed in a heap. There was a great lurch and the huge ship started to move beside me, although I felt disorientated as though it was I, and the jetty moving, such was the size of the ship. I suddenly became aware that, above the noise of the sailors and ship, Simon Turney was shouting down at me from above. I scrambled upright on the wooden planks, almost stumbling into the sea, and then ran alongside the ship, forcing my way through the crowds of onlookers who were thronging the jetty.

'What was that?' I cried up.

'I said, if you want to know who Don Alphonse was fooling around with I would look much closer to home if I was you. There is a very attractive proposition in your own household.' And then the boat passed the end of the jetty and I had to stop running to avoid continuing headlong into the water, clattering as I did so into a load of paraphernalia standing at the end of the dock. Simon Turney raised his hand in mock salute and turned away. Was he a murderer slipping out of my grasp? A huge sense of frustration overwhelmed me. That coupled with the anger I felt at the distinct slight he had laid on Anne's character. I looked back at the ship and to my amazement saw Karl Würtembatter's fat features peering anxiously over the back of the high deck. He was waving his arms frantically at me and shouting – I think I caught the words: 'Keep them for me, Sir John' before the galleon carried him inexorably out of earshot.

I looked around at the objects I had clattered into – animal hides, furs, trunks, furniture, and a colourful bird that looked decidedly relieved at being left behind – Würtembatter 's belongings; the ship had sailed without them.

* * *

'I can't help you if you won't speak to me.'

It was beginning to get dark, the distant firelights of the city guiding our return journey. The tilt-boat was relatively empty and we had found space under the canvas – something to be grateful for at least. For the past twenty minutes, I had been sitting with my chin wedged between clenched fists, eyes fixed despondently on the fading Middlesex shore. Emmalina had decided that she'd had enough of my morose humour.

'You allowed me to come with you, you might as well tell me what it's all about.' I looked into her eyes, which had softened to a deep green in the twilight. She twitched her brow questioningly. 'Come on, Master John. What did that man say to you on the boat? What's it all about?'

Being stuck with my own thoughts was hardly an attractive option, so I relented. I quietly explained everything to Emmalina – the discovery of Don Alphonse's body at Cuckold's Point - the meeting between myself, my brother and Walsingham and the conflicting tasks they had set me – my fruitless search for Cassangoe at Don Alphonse's warehouse.

Once I started talking, I found that a lot of pent up thoughts came tumbling out. I went into detail about my brother's intransigence, and how it was obvious he was hiding something from Walsingham. I described my strange encounter with Hercules Smyth, who I also felt sure knew more than he was prepared to tell. And lastly I explained that, in the absence of Cassangoe, Turney, who had sailed off into the sunset, was probably my last hope of discovering the truth about Don Alphonse's final hours. It was a relief to speak it all aloud but I was also making it quite clear from my tone that the whole thing was a complete mess and I was at my wits ends.

'If I can't find Cassangoe and my brother won't tell me who else Don Alphonse departed with on the river that night, then that's as far as the trail goes.' I said it with an air of finality, but my attempt to garner sympathy fell on deaf ears. Emmalina immediately began setting out the facts in a pertinent and sensible manner:

'I don't agree with that. Anything could have happened in between the time that Don Alphonse left the boat and when he was murdered.'

'Not that much really. It was quite late when they left and for the body to have reached Rotherhithe by the hour it did, it must have been in the water for some time.'

'Some time? You see – that's the problem. We need to be precise about these things.' She glanced up at me to check she wasn't being too assertive and I gave her an encouraging grunt. 'What time exactly did the men leave the Chancel House?'

I paused for a moment, getting used to this new approach. Emmalina had surprised me on the boat with her cleverness towards Würtembatter and she was surprising me again with her pragmatic attitude. 'My brother puts the time at nine of the clock, corroborated by Matthew.'

'What time did the men find the body in Rotherhithe?'

'They said an hour before daybreak – so let's put that at six.'

'Six. So that leaves nine hours from the time he left the Chancel House with Turney and the others until his body was found. Now, wherever he went on the river that night, it can't have taken more than an hour, two at the most. How long would it take for a body to wash down the river to Rotherhithe?'

'The question is: from where? We don't know where the body went in.'

'True. But it was most likely somewhere in the city and the distances from one end to other aren't that great, especially when the tide is rushing out. Perhaps a difference of half an hour overall for a body floating downstream. The poor man, it disturbs me to think of it.'

'I don't think it would have taken more than four hours for the body to reach Rotherhithe from, say, the bridge,' I said, encouraged by her reasoning. 'So, roughly speaking, there is a possibility that he went into the river as late as three in the morning. It is very roughly speaking though.'

'At least it's a start. It means there is a possibility of around four hours when we can't account for his whereabouts. That's what we have to discover. As for knowing more about Don Alphonse, there must be lots of other people who knew him. We'll simply have to look for them. We need to ask around the ports, go to the harbour offices, talk to other merchants. Someone will have records of his associates and his ships.'

'We?' I said.

'Well if I'm going to be lodging with you, I may as well help out.'

'What about finding Buck?'

'We can do that together too. It seems to me that until we discover who killed Don Alphonse, you're not going to have much time to look for Buck.' She paused for a moment. 'The thing I don't understand is why you're so opposed to the idea that the moor, Cassangoe, killed Don Alphonse? Surely you can't dismiss him out of hand?'

'I went to look for him didn't I?' I said, rather harshly, before giving the question more consideration and softening my tone. 'It just seems a bit too convenient, that's all; bit too neat, from my brother's point of view. If Cassangoe is guilty, the mystery is solved. I suppose that I'm worried that if I do find him, events will overtake him and he will be held accountable, whether he's guilty or not.'

'And that wouldn't satisfy Walsingham.'

'Exactly.'

'Well so much for what we don't know, let's think about what we do. Tell me about your discussions with Hercules Smyth and Turney again.' I recounted the conversations, trying to remember as much detail as possible. With Hercules Smyth, I still felt at a total loss, but there were a couple of things that had been nagging about my meeting with Turney.

'The strange thing was that the news didn't so much surprise him as shock him, it was almost as if somebody had unexpectedly carried out a threat.'

'You think he knew who killed Don Alphonse?'

'Or at least suspected. He also said one thing that I didn't understand. When I asked him who had argued with Don Alphonse in Robert's garden, he said: "I don't know, though I assumed it was hard …" and then he stopped in mid-sentence.'

'Assumed it was hard? What did he mean by that?'

'I haven't the faintest idea.'

'Perhaps he meant it was hard to tell who was arguing?'

'Perhaps. But I don't think so. The man arguing with Don Alphonse didn't join the others on the boat, so presumably he went back into the house.'

'Another guest, perhaps.'

'Perhaps.' I didn't mention that Turney's parting words had thrown suspicion on Robert, by suggesting that Don Alphonse had been interested in Anne.

'We do have one clue,' I said, suddenly remembering something. 'Or rather a pair of clues, to be exact.' I fumbled in the pocket of my sleeve and produced the brooch and ring that I had found stitched into Don Alphonse's shirt. I handed them to Emmalina who took them gently and eyed them in wonderment. There was just enough light still left in the day to bounce off the pearls and stone of the brooch, and shimmer along the gold of the band.

'They're beautiful,' exclaimed Emmalina. 'Where did you find them?'

I explained about the rowing boat nearly capsizing and how it had led to the discovery of the secret pocket stitched into Don Alphonse's shirt. 'I don't know what I intended to do with them. Keep them I suppose,'

I admitted rather sheepishly. 'I had no idea who he was at the time and was feeling a lot of resentment towards my brother for sending me to collect the body. Afterwards, events simply overtook me and I completely forgot about them.'

'I can understand you wanting to keep them. This brooch is the most beautiful thing I've ever held. But whose are they and why were they hidden?'

'My guess is that they belonged to a woman whose husband was being made a cuckold by Don Alphonse. Her initials are L.H. Both Hercules Smyth and Karl Würtembatter said that Don Alphonse had a reputation as a libertine.

'*Rather death than fals fayth*,' Emmalina said, reading the inscription on the ring. 'What do you think it means?'

'I think it tells us that it's a wedding ring. On the other side it says *memento mori*.'

'If it was mine, I would hate to lose such a beautiful thing.'

'Perhaps you'll be able to keep it.'

Emmalina suddenly shifted to look me directly in the eyes: 'What did you say to Würtembatter on the tilt-boat that sent him scuttling off like that?' She said, a note of reproach in her voice.

'Don't tell me you feel any sympathy for that fool?' Würtembatter had continued to try my patience severely, even after the Lady Merrydance had sailed. We had spent an hour at Deptford dock trying to secure a repository for the bulk of his belongings, eventually finding a seedy host of an even seedier tavern, who had agreed to hold the German's possessions indefinitely for an extortionate fee. Even then, we hadn't felt entirely comfortable leaving everything behind and were now surrounded by some of the more precious items – a casket of valuables, some silver items and, of course, the parrot Lucius, who had perked up considerably, having narrowly avoided a life on the high seas, and had started to chirp away quite happily. Emmalina had developed a fondness for the bird and had insisted on bringing him, although I wasn't entirely convinced as yet.

'I merely told him that I worked for Walsingham and that he ought to be careful what he said. The man was a garrulous fool.'

'Well you certainly put the fear of God into him. You can be quite intimidating when you put your mind to it.' The way she said it suggested that she didn't wholly approve.

'He couldn't open his mouth without putting his foot in it,' I said, in a conciliatory tone. 'Maybe I taught him a valuable lesson? I don't understand why he was quite so disturbed though.'

'He certainly moved a lot quicker than I thought he could.' Emmalina gave a small chuckle at the thought. 'Well that is just another mystery that we are going to have to solve together.' Saying this, she slipped her arm through mine and laid her head on my shoulder. 'Something to take my mind off the fact that I am homeless, have lost a brother and am now truly an orphan.' She looked me meaningfully in the eye for a moment, before laying her head back on my shoulder.

I took her hand and squeezed it, wrapping my cloak around her shoulders as I did so. A distinct chill had arrived with the onset of nightfall. Our floating world carried on in silence for a while.

'At least you're not an illegitimate orphan,' I said, after a while, trying to make her feel better. She didn't respond. I didn't dare move fearing she was already asleep. We drifted on together locked in stillness. The only sounds accompanying us were the splashing of oars and the hushed conversation of strangers.

The city was looming close, the shadow of the great bridge blocking views further upstream. Hundreds of thousands of strangers packed tightly into an area no larger than my brother's estates. For a while, when discussing the case with Emmalina, I had felt a renewed surge of optimism but now, left alone with my thoughts, doubts began to creep perniciously in again. The huge scale of the city seemed to merge with the enormity of my task, blowing it up like a vast, impenetrable black cloud.

Chapter 12

'Think as you like but behave like others.'
(Robert Greene; The 48 Laws of Power)

The next morning I set out from my lodgings for the Royal Exchange on Cornhill, eager to learn what I could about joint-stock companies.

Emmalina hugged me before I left and then bolted the door securely behind me. Neither of us was under any illusion as to the dangerous path we had embarked on by her coming to live with me. Although unloved by her stepfather, she was a valuable asset to him and one that he would not want to lose lightly, particularly if he had plans for her to marry the rich merchant Shuttleworth, thus further advancing his own interests. He would know from his apprentices that she had left with me and it was doubtful it would take him long to search me out and demand the return of his property. We needed to create a plan to thwart him but in the meantime she needed to stay secure and out of sight.

All of this we had discussed the previous evening, in the relative comfort of my lodgings. On our arrival, I had at first watched Emmalina's bemused expression with interest as she cast her eyes around my cramped, mess of a room and the eclectic mix of possessions I owned. Naturally, I had quickly introduced her to the view of the city, which she cooed at approvingly, whilst I quickly tidied as much as I could behind her.

Whilst doing this, I cast my eyes around the room as though seeing it through Emmalina's eyes for the first time. It hardly took a moment to take it all in:

A rickety, open cupboard holding a few meagre treasures – a Venetian-style drinking glass, made in Antwerp, and a salt-glazed stoneware jug, both smuggled out of my father's estate when my brother ordered me up to London, along with a lead-glazed mug with a silver mount carrying his initials – H. R. for Henry Rokesby. There were also some rather garish, rib-patterned green glass and a pair of earthenware candles, all borrowed from my landlord and long overdue for return, and a few *simples*, collected from the apothecary on Thames Street for various ailments.

There was also a grandiose, astronomical clock, which I had also taken from my father's estate, and was the companion piece to an even more splendid telescopic eyeglass on a tripod – currently being utilised as a clothes stand – which I occasionally used to gaze at the stars above the city.

On the wall to the left of the cupboard was a small portrait of a young man, which must have been forgotten by a previous tenant and was the only *objet d'art* that I owned. The young man spent his days regarding me with a sardoni expression of amusement, which appeared to deepen when I was at my most foolish or vulnerable. He also stood guard over a pretty, inlaid elm box, in which I kept the miserly number of trinkets, jewels and letters in my possession, next to which I now piled up Würtembatter 's belongings.

Squeezed into the space below the window was a cramped oak table overflowing with a collection of books, plays and pamphlets, some of which I owned outright but others borrowed from the translating house. The collection consisted of a few pamphlets on astronomy, copies of sonnets and other poetic works, and, taking pride of place on top of the pile and wrapped in an opaque vellum cover, my most recent 'acquisition' – the philosophical *Essaies* of a French nobleman called Michel de Montaigne.

Finally, there was the low-slung truckle bed, with its scratchy straw mattress, under which I was shoving things out of the way. More than anything else in the room, the bed had seen better days, to the point where, if the truckle was pulled out, the mattress sagged onto the floor. I wondered nervously what Emmalina thought of the sleeping arrangements.

The young man in the portrait had watched me sardonically, as Emmalina had brewed us some delicious vegetable soup – firstly complaining about the state of the only pot I possessed, which admittedly hadn't been used for a while – and we had sat down to supper. His mocking expression had appeared to deepen when I hesitated before offering Emmalina the use of my bed, myself taking the extended truckle.

He was still watching in the morning when we both arose from a restless night – Emmalina complaining that she couldn't sleep because of the noise of the waterwheel continuously thumping away beneath us – something I was well used to. My own excuse was that the mystery going round in circles in my head had kept me awake – that and the proximity to my friend's beautiful sister. Only Lucius, whose cage Emmalina had thoughtfully thrown a cover over so that he was spared the gaze of the young man, had appeared to get a decent night's sleep.

No one had seen Emmalina and I enter together and I hadn't had to answer any awkward questions about 'lodgers' but I suspected it was only a matter of time. The Bridge Within Ward beadles were always poking their noses into living arrangements and were required to give constant details of inmates and aliens. Keeping Emmalina a secret from my landlord Charles, and his family and servants, would be the first challenge.

We hadn't found Matthew when we returned to the city, and I suspected that he had sloped off early to shelter from the biting cold. But, not long after we returned, a message had arrived to say that he had followed a lead to the village of Chelsea, further upriver, and he would attend on us the next day. In return, before leaving the next morning, I left a message for him to continue his search and to await me at my lodgings later that evening.

The Royal Exchange, or Gresham's Exchange, as it was still known in some quarters, had been built during my lifetime and its shining stucco-clad walls stood out in marked contrast to the old wooden dwellings that surrounded it. That had been the point of course. The Exchange, built on the design of a Flemish Bourse, was designed to show the world that, far from being the inhabitants of some backwards island, the English were now masters of trade and wealth and could rival any of their continental cousins. It was also a testament to the city's gradual pre-eminence over more traditional forces – the kind of symbol that held a deal of inspiration for young men without names or prospects.

But it wasn't all perfection, rumours had it that the building had been constructed somewhat hastily and cracks were already starting to show – as I entered via the South arches, stopping briefly to buy some fruit from a foul-mouthed women camped at the gate, I noticed that the gratings by the door had given way and were swinging loose. Nevertheless, the building was still impressively grand and even Gresham's iconic grasshopper, perched on the top of the bell tower that loomed high above the edifice, managed the semblance of a glint in the overcast day.

Inside, the open courtyard was relatively quiet at this time in the morning, allowing the clip of my heels on the paving stones to echo off the marble colonnades surrounding the square. All around me, the statues of English kings and queens gazed down solemnly. Apart from a few early shoppers, the inhabitants at that time were mainly vagabonds and other masterless men, either hoping for an offer of work, a handout, or simply a roof under which they could idle the best part of the day away. Any public space in London was plagued by this phenomenon. I was approached by one who had a burn hole through his ear lobe, a sign that he had already been convicted once of vagrancy. A second conviction would likely result in him being hanged. He seemed to size me up more in hope than expectation, but backed off, after I gripped the hilt of my sword meaningfully, and I was able to climb the stairs to the balcony unmolested.

The man that I had come to see occupied one of the hundred or so small shops housed on the floor surrounding the courtyard below. The shops were home to an eclectic mix of traders: booksellers, glass-sellers, armourers, milliners, and goldsmiths all jostling together for space and custom – hardly the fine array of merchants Gresham had envisaged leasing the building to, when its design was first conceived.

Davy Bennett was a good case in point. His apothecary shop, squeezed into one side of the arcade overlooking the courtyard, offered a range of goods, which seemed much broader than the relatively narrow title of 'apothecary' allowed. I found him trying to persuade a hesitant, uncertain domestic servant that two small mousetraps, working in tandem, would easily be capable of catching one large rat. Whilst I waited for him to conclude this dubious transaction, I glanced around the shop. Besides the mousetraps, there were birdcages, shoeing-horns, lanthorns, Jews' trumps and a plethora of other items all competing to offer a bargain to prospective customers.

Davy was a small man with bluff features, and an eye for the main chance. I had first met him in the Gloucestershire market town near to my father's country estate when we had both been young lads. At the time he had already started running pack animals to and from the capital, bringing wool into the city and an assortment of foreign luxuries back to the sleepy county town, for the locals to moon and fight over. It hadn't been long before he set up base permanently in the capital and employed others to run the trade packs for him, only returning home in the holiday seasons. Davy claimed to be my distant kinsman, on my mother's side naturally, and was always friendly towards me but he insisted on treating me like a member of the aristocracy in a manner that couldn't fail to remind me that essentially we were of the same stock.

'Ah, Master John sire,' he greeted me, having sent the servant off contentedly clutching a pair of small mousetraps. 'And what can I do you for this fine morning? These fine clogs only recently arrived from the Lowlands – ideal for negotiating the snow?' Or how about this new lotion for helping the beard to grow?'

'You can tell me what you know about joint-stock companies.'

'Joint-stock companies?' he whistled dramatically. 'Well now, has the young Master finally come into some wealth, which he intends to invest? Never thought I'd see the day.'

'No such luck.'

'What do you want to know then?'

'You must have your ear to the ground here. What sort of merchant ventures are afoot?' Davy stopped rearranging items on the shelves around him and gave me a sly look.

'Why do you want to know? Seriously, are you looking to invest? Save your money and come in with me – look at all this stuff I'm getting my hands on.' In his hand he was holding what looked like a novelty German drinking tankard but the pride in his voice was palpable.

'As I said, it's nothing like that. I wish it was.' I had to admit I was flattered by his offer and tried to sound mollifying. 'No, I'm on an errand for my brother. I think he wants to know what the competition is up to.'

'I see. Well the truth is there isn't a lot happening at the moment. There's been an embargo on private enterprise since the Armada. Expect it'll be lifted soon, but in the meantime merchant ships are still confined to barracks – so to speak.'

'What about any non-sanctioned trips?'

'There I am not your man. Part of the deal with keeping a shop here is that you have to keep your nose very clean.' Davy Bennett said this with a note of regret. 'Still I know someone you could try. Kibber's your man.'

'Who is Kibber?'

'Kibber's the oracle of Paul's Walk. He has his fingers in lots of pies, including running the watermen on the East Thames. He'll know if anything unusual has been happening in the ports.'

'And I'll find him at St Paul's?'

'Never misses a day. Mention my name, he might talk to you.' A bell sounded loudly above our heads.

'Come and look at this, Lovat.' He gestured me over to the square window at the back of the shop that looked down onto the courtyard. It was quite crowded now with merchants, stockbrokers and dealers all engaged in an elaborate dance of trade. The richer men's servants had cleared most of the idlers away but a few could still be discerned in the shadows of the arcade, watching expectantly for opportunities.

Suddenly, a discordant noise could be heard. The men looked round to one of the entrances and began to scatter backwards. Into the centre of the square came a man leading a large black bear with a monkey sitting on its back, surrounded by a group of minstrels, playing a mixture of fiddles, horns and drums. The Bear-ward began announcing something over the din, which it was impossible to decipher from our lofty vantage point. The bear raised itself up on its hind legs and looked exceedingly fierce, scattering the men of commerce still further. I raised an eyebrow towards Davy.

'They're drumming up custom for the Christmas bear-baiting festival. Happens every day around this time. Priceless.'

* * *

The neighbourhood bells were sounding eleven by the time I reached the Cathedral. If the streets of London were always packed, St Paul's Churchyard was where the shoving to and fro of the narrow streets burst into a chaotic circus. Most people here were on the search for information or knowledge. The churchyard was packed with booksellers and printers, who were hawking anything from plays, poetry and political diatribes, to new translations of works that only a week earlier had arrived on one of the many boats that docked daily at London's ports. The thirst for knowledge amongst Londoners was truly insatiable.

But searching for books wasn't the only entertainment to be had here. In the yard beyond the bookstalls, an execution had just taken place and the crowd was beginning to drift away, revealing two unfortunate cutpurses swinging jerkily on a temporary gibbet erected for the purpose. The sound of their ropes squeaking eerily on the wood accompanied me as I burst into the church.

Inside, Paul's Walk was crowded with people eager, as always, to catch up on the latest news. The long nave was the centre of gossip in London and during the crisis of the last months, it had become an even more essential meeting place for keeping up to date with events. I had even been here in August with hundreds of others when the defeat of the Armada had been announced. I entered by the southern door, and, as I walked the length of the vaulted building looking for the man known as Kibber, I overheard rumours of Spanish Galleons shipwrecked on the Irish coast

After asking after him, I was eventually directed to the west end of the aisle, where advertisements for work, known as siquisses, were posted. As usual there was a cluster of unemployed gallants and servants crowding the board, perusing the notices that usually started with the Latin words si quis – 'if anyone'. Kibber was sitting in one of the adjacent pews in close consultation with a couple of young men, both with sharp eyes and hungry demeanours. Judging by the piece of paper one was holding, it looked as though they were answering an advertisement he had posted. Kibber was a lean man with a long, sallow face and bushy eyebrows. The only other hairs he had on his head were two great tufts of white thatch sticking out above each ear.

I waited patiently in the shadow of a pillar, whilst Kibber concluded his business, taking the opportunity to look at the microcosm of teeming London life that Paul's Walk afforded. Here the respectable and the disreputable rubbed shoulders daily. All manner of transactions took place, very few of which had anything to do with religion. At the far end a bishop was attempting to conduct a service but it was very hard to hear him over the general hubbub. There were lawyers conducting business with their clients, debtors collecting their dues and even prostitutes plying their trade in the deeper recesses. And all around, barely visible, the assorted cutpurses and con men, who were ready to nip and foist unsuspecting tourists, mainly countrymen up from the counties, a number of which I could see gazing about themselves in wonderment, oblivious to the threat.

The two young men stood up and departed, allowing me to slide down into the pew next to Kibber. He didn't say anything but merely looked at me morosely. I introduced myself as a friend of Davy Bennett and explained what I wanted. The man tipped his head to one side, as if sizing me up, before eventually speaking very deliberately.

'Let me see if I understand you, Master. You want to know if any merchant-adventurers have broken port lately and Davy Bennett told you I might be the man to know?'

'Correct.'

'That's all very well young man but what's in it for me?' I had anticipated something like this. It was all very well giving small change to watermen and beggars in return for help, but I imagined that Kibber would demand a good deal more than that. I sighed disappointedly, wondering what I could offer that wouldn't be too derogatory, whilst also not being a price I could ill-afford. Kibber sensed my uncertainty on the matter.

'In this town there is money, Master Lovat, but there are other rewards besides,' he said, in a sad, monotonous tone. 'Information, for example, can be of great value to a man like myself. Do you have any information we could exchange?'

'I don't know.' I remembered that Davy had said his nickname was the Oracle of Paul's Walk. 'Such as?'

'Oh, well, let's see. Perhaps you have something for me but you are not even aware of it.' He looked at me hopefully, or at least as much as his mournful face could muster up hope.

'I don't think so.'

'Well. What's this business about? Illegal voyages are a very serious matter.'

'I'm worried that a friend of mine is mixed up in something.' I lied, thinking of my brother.

'And what might that be?'

'A man has been murdered.'

'How interesting. Wouldn't happen to be a man that was fished out of the Thames would it? Hard by Cuckold's Point?'

I said nothing, dumbfounded at his knowledge. A glow seemed to form in the deadly pallor of Kibber's eyes.

'I can see from your expression that it was that very man. Who was he Master Lovat? My sources said a gentleman, possibly foreign. Can you enlighten me further?'

I had an uncomfortable feeling that I was the one being interrogated.

'How do you know these things?'

'Wouldn't be much of an oracle if I didn't now, would I? The question is what do you know about him and why are you interested in connecting the death with illegal shipping?'

'I'm sorry, Mister Kibber.'

'Just Kibber.'

'I'm sorry, Kibber. It is not meet that I can help you and it seems that you can't or are unwilling to help me?'

'Quite the contrary, Master Lovat. You have already told me quite a lot that I wasn't aware of.' I felt a horrible creeping sensation, as he said this, not having a clue what I had or hadn't given away. 'It's only fair that I should reciprocate. You asked about illegal voyages. Where do you think they have sailed from?'

'Deptford.'

'Deptford?' He weighed the word slowly for a moment. 'Interesting suggestion but sadly I must disappoint you. The only ships that have sailed from Deptford in the last month have been on domestic voyages.'

'You are sure of that?'

'Quite sure. Unless you have information to contradict that statement?'

'No,' I said firmly and stood up to leave. Kibber followed me with his sunken eyes.

'Anytime you want to share information you'll always find me here. Good day Master Lovat and commend me to your Lord, whoever that might be.'

I stumbled backwards out of the pew and left the Cathedral by the nearest door, feeling more confused than ever and with a sick feeling growing in the pit of my stomach.

* * *

At my lodgings I found an attractive woman draped across my bed, but it wasn't the one I had been expecting.

She was evidently a rich lady, elegantly dressed in a long embroidered gown, which accentuated her curves and still allowed for a low cut neckline, set off with finely trimmed lace. Adorning her arms, fingers and neck were expensive jewels and bracelets, and a large diamond pendant nestled in the cleft of her bosom. I happened to notice this before her face, because the latter was veiled with a black lace scarf, through which the shape of her high cheekbones was subtly suggested. Her disguise, however, could not hide the blueness of her eyes, nor the luxuriant, saffron coloured hair, which, tied in a plat thicker than a hangman's noose, draped over her shoulder and round her neck. It was quite a sight to come home to.

The woman barely acknowledged my entrance, only tilting her chin upwards enquiringly. In her hands she held my copy of Montaigne in French, whose pages she was nonchalantly flicking, eyes disinterestedly scanning the text. Next to her sat a maid, who had been talking to Lucius in a cooing tone just prior to my entrance and poking her fingers unwisely through his cage bars. Lucius, in return, was hopping up and down and making the occasional high-pitched squawk. The maid hastily pulled a scarf across her face but not quickly enough to prevent me from recognising her fleshy, youthful features. It was the same maid who had slammed the door in my face at my brother's house two days earlier and, therefore I reasoned, the lady spread across my bed must be the attractive, bored woman who had been attending on Anne at the same time.

'Are you Lovat?' Her voice was softer than expected, and had a seductive quality. 'I hope you don't mind. We found the door unlocked.' I wondered vaguely where Emmalina had got to and why she had left the door open to strangers, but not seriously enough to be distracted from the matter in hand.

'Don't you speak?' I realised that I was still standing awkwardly in the middle of the small room and resolved to try and handle the situation a bit better.

'John Lovat, citizen of London, at your service ma'am, and may I ask whose person I have the pleasure of addressing?' The woman sat up slowly, allowing every inch of her body to speak to me, before eyeing me coldly through the black veil. She turned to her maid.

'Leave us.' The girl hesitated for a second, wrongly suspecting that I might be any sort of match for her mistress. 'It's alright, child. I think I shall be perfectly safe with Master Lovat. Wait for me in the street downstairs – I won't be long.' The maid walked clumsily to the door, whilst another meaningful silence ensued. Lucius chose this moment to let off a longer than average screech. The woman looked at him disdainfully.

'Do we have to speak with that creature in the room?'

'It's alright. He doesn't speak English.'

'But he's a parrot isn't he? I've heard they can repeat things that they hear.'

'What of it?'

'I'd be more comfortable if he didn't overhear our conversation.' I gave her a look that suggested I thought she was making fun of me, but nevertheless deigned to move Lucius onto the landing. Whilst I did this, the lady on the bed continued to eye me up and down, though it was impossible to tell what she thought of the rough, fallen on hard times image, that I took such care in cultivating. Taking up Montaigne again, she directed a question at me.

'You like reading, Lovat?'

'Are we getting down to small talk now?'

'What I mean is: are you of a scholarly disposition? I was hoping for a man of action. Anne said I could trust you?' Despite her languid manner, it was possible to detect a hint of desperation in her voice. She was also much younger than her sophisticated appearance suggested. I found myself becoming more and more intrigued by her.

'Trust me? With what?'

'*Can* I trust you, Lovat?' For a moment all pretence of control evaporated.

'As far as anything in which Anne is concerned, you can trust me with my life.' 'Anne is not concerned in this matter.' I waved a hand as if to say that it was all the same to me. 'What I want is … I want you to find someone for me. Anne said that you were good at things like that. She also said you were discreet, trustworthy and could handle yourself. She seems to think very highly of you, although I am at a loss from your appearance to understand why.'

'Appearances aren't everything,' I said, shrugging off her slight. The compliment that Anne had paid me was more than enough to compensate. 'Whom do you want me to find?'

'An … acquaintance of mine. He has gone missing and I need to know where he is.' She stopped abruptly trying to find explanations but none, it seemed, were appropriate.

'He? I take it that your interest in this gentleman is a confidence that you would like me to respect?'

'It seems you are not as stupid as you look.' Although her words were harsh, her manner was not. She actually seemed relieved at my tact, her shoulders visibly relaxing. It occurred to me that she must be taking a huge risk in coming here and that this was far from some idle game to her.

'Well, that sounds straightforward enough. What's his name and where should I start looking for him?'

'It is anything *but* straightforward.' She stood up and handed me a piece of paper that was tucked inside the hem of her sleeve. 'I only have an address for you. I simply want you to establish whether or not he is there. You don't need to know his name and I forbid you expressly to approach him or anyone in the house. No one must know that I have visited you, or that I am looking for this man.'

'But how will I know that it is the right man? Forgive me but it all sounds a bit vague.'

'Only two men could be in that house and they are very distinct. You will understand once you have seen them. Just report what you find there. Now I have to leave before I am missed elsewhere.' She moved to the door but then paused. 'I almost forgot – this is for you.' She handed me a small purse weighted with coins, warmed from being cradled in her hands. She noticed my expression and misinterpreted it. 'There will be more for you if you find the man successfully.'

'I don't even know your name.'

'It is better that way. Just find the man and tell me where he is.'

'How? I don't even know where to find you.' Despite the sweetener she had offered, I could hear the exasperation in my voice at her haughty manner.

'I will send my maid in the next few days. I will expect you to have an answer for me by then. And Lovat … Anne is a dear friend and someone I respect highly but she is not a woman of the world like me. Don't think for a minute I will be fooled by your looks and charm. I expect you to do this task properly. Do what I ask of you and you will be properly rewarded.'

I was about to say something I would probably have regretted, when the door opened and Emmalina appeared in her hooded coat, carrying a basket of groceries in one hand and Lucius' cage in the other. She blushed as soon as she saw the lady but quickly regained her composure.

Recognising the lady's rank, she immediately curtsied. 'Forgive my intrusion Ma'am. I hope I am not interrupting something?'

'I was just leaving.' The lady and Emmalina appraised each other coldly. It was clear that both had immediately jumped to the wrong conclusion about the other as far as my involvement with either was concerned. The two of them could not have looked more different. Worldly beauty against innocent charm, expensive elegance versus thrifty panache.

After the briefest of stand-offs, the veiled lady turned her enigmatic gaze on me. 'Lovat,' she said, loading the word with meaning, and then was gone, leaving a tang of expensive perfume in the air. Emmalina took the vacated position on the bed and regarded me with an unfathomable expression on her face.

'Listen Emmalina, it isn't what it looks like. That lady is a client.' I quickly qualified that statement. 'She wants me to find someone.'

'The person you should be finding is Buck!'

'He hasn't reappeared then?' A large part of me had been hoping, suspecting even, that Buck, having cooled down, would already have returned home to make peace with his stepfather.

'No.' I suspected that Emmalina had been secretly hoping so too. 'And now I suppose you are going to give that stuck-up Aristobelle preference?'

'At least she's paying me,' I said rather unkindly, tossing the bag of coins onto the bed beside her. Emmalina emptied the coins onto the bed and started counting them.

'Who does she want you to find?'

'Her illicit lover, I suspect. She wouldn't reveal much about him.'

'First the murder to solve and now this. At least promise me that you'll make some time to find Buck.'

'I promise. First thing tomorrow I'll go to the theatre. Someone there is bound to know where he is. Don't worry.' Easier said than done.

Emmalina stopped counting coins and picked up Montaigne instead. '*Essaies de Messire Michel Seigneur de Montaigne*,' she said, reading from the cover. 'What's it about?'

'It's the philosophical musings of a French aristocrat.'

'Sounds riveting.'

'There isn't another book like it.'

'Well that's lucky then.'

She smiled at me and started to feed Lucius nuts through the cage bars. It seemed we had reached a truce.

'Come on,' I said. 'Let's *all* eat something. Matthew should be here soon and we've still got work to do tonight.'

Chapter 13

'Do not tell secrets to those whose faith and silence you have not already tested.'
(Elizabeth I)

The work that still needed to be done involved a dead of night sortie to Lion's Quay.

As distant church bells sounded three o'clock, I was perched precariously on the apex of the pitched roof of Don Alphonse's warehouse. The temperature had dropped further with the fall of darkness, and a fog had rolled in from the Essex marshes, providing perfect cover for what I had in mind. The turgid stretch of water that constituted Lion's Quay was bathed in mist, and silence, save the occasional sound of ice lapping against wooden piers and the creaks and thuds of the boats rocking in the dock.

Directly below me, clinging to the end of the wooden pier, I could see Matthew peering up from the Chancel House's slim rowing boat. His instructions were to keep lookout and be prepared, if necessary, to make a rapid escape.

An icy gust of wind blew across the harbour. I should have felt cold, but the excitement pumping through my body was doing a fine job of keeping me warm.

After my fruitless encounter with Hercules Smyth, I had come up with two separate last-ditch plans. The first – to find and talk to Simon Turney before he could set sail from London – had been achieved. The second was somewhat more prosaic – to break into Don Alphonse's warehouse.

Matthew had arrived at my lodgings earlier, frustrated at not having found the waterman. When told of my plan, he had simply nodded his head and asked when we would leave so that he could get a bit of shut eye. As I watched him gratefully accepting some beet soup, which Emmalina had brewed – she had already made a vast improvement to my eating habits, not to mention the tidiness of my lodgings – and then kicking his legs up on the bed in a no-nonsense fashion, I reflected that I was beginning to enjoy having his solid dependability for support.

While he slept, Emmalina and I sat at the small desk together, and on her instigation, and in hushed tones, discussed all of the information we had gathered so far relating to Don Alphonse's murder. Emmalina took up a quill and set out each point in neat but distinctive handwriting. After we had finished, I cast my eyes back over what she had written and added some notes of my own:

1. A Portuguese merchant, Don Alphonse de Sousa, dines with Sir Robert Rokesby and a number of other men (undisclosed) on Sunday night; the day of the Armada victory celebration to St Paul's.

2. Don Alphonse leaves the Chancel House at approximately 9pm in the company of three other men, including Simon Turney and Marmaduke Drummond. Destination unknown. ***Who is the fourth man? Can't ask Drummond for fear of upsetting my brother, and Turney wouldn't say.***

3. At dawn (7am?) the following morning (Monday), DA's corpse is dragged from the river by the Rotherhithe Watch. His body is badly beaten and he has been strangled. ***Looks as if the strangling came after the beating but need to keep an open mind.***

4. DA's body is taken back to The Chancel House by JL during which time he discovers a wedding ring and pearl pendant sewn secretly into the dead man's shirt (relevant?).

5. At a meeting between JL, Sir Robert and Sir Francis Walsingham, it is revealed that DA has a black companion – Cassangoe. Sir Robert is determined that the moor is responsible for DA's death. Turney said expressly that Cassangoe was not a servant. So what is he then?

6. Walsingham's involvement: Sir Francis suggested another possibility for DA's murder – that he had vital information for the Privy Council regarding an English traitor. ***No evidence of this at all so far***

7. Rokesby does not want to discuss the meeting or who was involved. ***Was the meeting to discuss the voyage of the Lady Merrydance? If so, then Don Alphonse must have been aware of it but Karl Würtembatter believes he wasn't involved.***

8. Cassangoe cannot be found at DA's warehouse and a neighbour at Lion's Quay, Hercules Smyth, claims to have no knowledge of either his whereabouts or DA's death. ***Smyth knows something – I'm sure of it. Lion's Quay is rundown and neglected – 'the Lepers' end of Lion's Quay', something HS said***

9. Lady Merrydance. On Tuesday afternoon, Simon Turney sets sail on a foreign voyage, funded by, amongst others, Sir Robert Rokesby. Karl Würtembatter confirms that the destination of the ship is the Baltic, but there is currently an embargo on foreign adventures (according to Davy Bennett) and Kibber confirms that only domestic bound ships have left Deptford in the last month. ***Maybe this explains my brother's reluctance to discuss the voyage in front of Walsingham?***

10. Turney denies any knowledge of DA's death but his reaction suggests that he might suspect who is responsible for it. ***He even threw suspicion on Robert by eluding to Don Alphonse's womanising – suggesting that Anne might have succumbed.***

11. Motive. Karl Würtembatter, Hercules Smyth and Turney all refer to Don Alphonse's enjoyment of cuckolding husbands. ***Brings us back to Cuckold's Point.***

It was all very well writing it down but we couldn't seem to establish any firm conclusions. The evidence did suggest, however, that my brother and Turney were involved in an illegal merchant adventure but was that enough to connect them, or anyone else involved in the voyage, with the murder? Had Don Alphonse been aware of the voyage and tried to stop it? And if so, what was he doing at the Chancel House that evening? I still thought that it was far more likely that a jealous husband had found opportunity to exact revenge.

Matthew and I had slipped outside at a time when most residents of the bridge would be asleep, and shimmied down a long narrow ladder onto one of the thick stone biers that held the arches of the bridge. We boarded the rowing boat Matthew had secured there earlier and, using the current, cast off into the centre of the wide estuary. We skirted sleeping ships as quietly as possible, and after a few minutes located the shape of Don Alphonse's warehouse, thrust out into the river at the end of Lion's Quay.

I had surmised that the stubby chimney on the end of the warehouse was likely to be its defensive weak point, and so it proved. It was a crude, wrought iron flue, about two feet high, with a coarse, turret-like motif around its top. Taking a wrench, brought expressly for the purpose, I wedged it under the base and began to coerce the vent away from its fixings. It was only loosely bolted on and, despite an alarmingly loud squeal as the metal twisted, it swung free with a sharp crack, leaving a hole a little larger than a man's head. I glanced up the wharf but there was no sign of movement – no indignant guard running, no alarums. Exhaling a large amount of pent up breath, I looked down at Matthew, who gave me a big toothy grin and jerked his thumbs upwards in encouragement.

Peering down through the hole, all was blackness, although I didn't dare light a taper until I was safely inside. I knew from my wild childhood that if a man could get his head through a hole, the rest of him would surely follow but this looked a challenge. Deciding I didn't need the extra encumbrance of either my sword or dagger, or the belts that held them, I slipped them off quietly and lowered them down softly to Matthew – dropping them carefully into his outstretched arms. All I was left with was a leather sack, brought to collect any booty.

I slid my head and one arm through the small gap, gripping onto a beam on the underside of the roof and pulling the rest of my body through behind. It was a difficult manoeuvre, and took a certain amount of wriggling to execute, but the upshot was that I was soon hanging from the ceiling and then, after a moment's pause, dropping into the unknown.

I landed awkwardly on the hard floor and clattered into some unstable objects, one of them clattering onto the floor beside me, making enough noise to wake the river Gods. Cursing, I hauled myself to my knees and, after a good deal of nervous fumbling, lit a taper. As the flame fired up, I saw that initially I had careered into a pile of boxes stacked against the wall. The top one had given way and fallen down beside me.

Don Alphonse's warehouse was a lot tidier, and spoke of much greater wealth, than Hercules Smyth's neighbouring skins and wine shack. As well as the row of boxes, there were a large number of sacks, stacked in piles all around the room. Why couldn't I have landed on one of them, I reflected ruefully, rubbing a sore ankle? A swift search of one revealed an abundance of long dried brown leaves, which, from the smell, I recognised as tobacco. In another, I found a sour-smelling dried red spice that I couldn't instantly place and, in another still, a podded seed, which this time I recognised from its distinct aroma as aniseed. Judging by the number of sacks, there was a small fortune sitting in the warehouse. There were also a dozen boxes stacked together, including the one I had knocked over, which were stamped with symbols that I didn't recognise. I tried to open one but it was nailed shut. Lifting it back into its position, all I could tell was that, whatever it contained, it was heavy.

Standing along one wall was a solid oak desk, with deep drawers on either side of a clerk's stool, and a tall back housing a dozen square compartments. I started with a ledger, which lay invitingly open on the desk's surface. It turned out to be an up-to-date record of Don Alphonse's business transactions, with dates, cargos and ship's names all clearly marked in neat black ink. I could detect at least two different hands. The last entry was dated as November 9th 1588, three weeks before the procession to St Paul's, and documented the arrival of a ship called the *Gabryell* at Lion's Quay. Next to the entry were scrawled the letters: *v, s, a,* and *t*. There were no large cargo ships in the harbour and I wondered where the *Gabryell* was now – perhaps sailing on a new assignment. The beginning of the ledger showed that it had been started in July 1586 and a further search in one of the drawers revealed a pile of similarly bound ledgers dating back over more than ten years. I took the latest one from the desk, deciding that the last two years should be enough information about Don Alphonse's activities, and put it in the bag.

I rummaged through the small drawers of the upper part of the cabinet. They mostly contained quills, inks and other stationery items. There were a few bills of sale, letters and other papers but little that I could see of interest. Nevertheless, I took a few things to peruse later.

The lower drawers contained even less of interest. String for tying sacks, bits of broken equipment, pairs of old shoes. I was about to close the second one, when it occurred to me that it was somewhat shallower than its twin on the other side. I pulled out all of the detritus it contained and examined the surface of the bottom. It appeared to be solid but tapping it gave a hollow sound. I took a quill from the desk and tried sliding it down the sides. To my satisfaction, it suddenly slipped down beside the wooden surface and the whole bottom came loose. I lifted out a thin wooden partition to reveal a hidden compartment.

The object was a velvet pouch, tied with string. I pulled it out, brushing the dust away from the soft velvet, and untied the string to find a compact leather-bound book. It was in a very poor condition, and I picked it up gingerly, being careful that it didn't disintegrate in my hands. The dark red leather had faded badly and on the front, embossed in gold, were the simple letters *R de. S.* and the date *1567.* I opened it carefully. Its edges were worn, and pages dry and fragile. In the flickering light, I squinted at the entry of the first page:

O diário de bordo da caravela portuguesa Santo Francisco, escrito pelo seu capitão D. Rodrigo de Souza em Abril de 1567. Que Deus abençoe a nossa viagem e nos traga salvos para casa.

Gently turning the pages, I saw entries at different dates suggesting some sort of log. On later pages, the neatness of the dates seemed to be abandoned giving way to densely packed pages of writing. I carefully put it back in its velvet case and, after hesitating for a moment, slipped it into the bag around my shoulder.

No sooner had I done so, there was an urgent rapping on the wall of the warehouse – Matthew's warning that danger was imminent. I hurriedly replaced the false bottom and put the rest of the implements back in the drawer, straining my ears to see if I could hear anything. After a brief pause, there came the sound of oars splashing, followed a few moments later by the banging of wood, as a boat came alongside the dock. Someone scrambled onto the jetty. I blew out the candle. Standing stock-still in the darkness, I held my breath.

Footsteps sounded on the pier, stopping directly outside the warehouse. A thin stretch of light flickered under the door. The padlock chain rattled as someone took hold of it, and then a voice said distinctly: 'break it.'

As quickly and quietly as I could, I tied the bag to my ankle, then climbed onto the boxes and stretched upwards, blood pounding in my ears. I was just able to grasp a beam and pull myself up by my fingertips. For a second, I swung wildly in space, the bag jolting clumsily about below me, but then I managed to reach an arm through the hole. I got my head in the space and desperately wriggled my way upward. For a terrifying instant, I thought I would be stuck in the hole, legs hanging downwards as the strangers broke the chain and entered, but my technique proved effective, though inelegant. After what seemed an age, and driven solely by adrenalin and fear, I finally got the bulk of my body free. Just as I pulled my legs through, I heard the sound of a large crack. As the door opened, I hauled the bag through the gap. There wasn't time to replace the chimneystack. I froze in a crouching position, thinking it was impossible that whoever was down there couldn't hear the thumping noise my heart was making.

A flare lit up the hole. On the wall I could see shadows dancing and melting together as bodies moved.

'Take everything you can, the more we've got to incriminate him, the better.' Midlands accent, blunt and to the point. Even in a low growl, the voice contained distinct power. 'Be sharp about it. We don't want to excite any drunken constables.'

Two other men wasted no time in obeying him and started loading the boat. From my vantage point, I could see the pile of sacks growing as they were thrown in. The men themselves remained in shadow. There was no sign of Matthew – after warning me, he must have slipped out of sight.

The man giving the orders walked casually into my line of vision below the hole. He stood directly beneath me, a broad-brimmed hat hiding his features. Taking a knife from his belt, he began calmly scraping his nails, all the while oblivious to my presence.

Thoughts of who they could be ran through my head. My immediate assumption was that they knew Don Alphonse was dead, but were they responsible for that too? Could I have stumbled upon the murderers by chance? If only I could identify them. I willed the man to glance up so I could at least catch a glimpse of his features but his gaze remained steadfastly low. All I could tell was that he was tall and broad shouldered. He paced slowly away to the other side of the warehouse and out of my line of vision.

The heap of sacks in the boat indicated that the warehouse must be nearly empty – it looked as though I was going to miss my chance. I strained forward to get my face level with the hole from the chimney and tried to peer, at an angle, through the gap. The man was sat at Don Alphonse's desk with his back to me, idly opening and closing drawers – just as I had done a few minutes earlier. I silently implored him to turn round and shifted my position slightly. As I did, I felt my shoulder push against something that gave way – the iron flue I had wrenched free and which had been perched precariously on the slope of the roof.

For a teasing moment, it rocked easily back and forth, and then I watched in horror as it rolled heavily down the roof and disappeared over the wooden gutter.

Chapter 14

'Fear is pain arising from the anticipation of evil.'
(Aristotle)

A boom like a drum sounded as the chimney bounced off the jetty, followed by a loud splash as it barrelled into the water beyond. One of the men swore loudly – the chimney must have almost hit him – but then came a moment of icy silence. I drew my head back from the hole, cursing my stupidity and preparing myself for escape.

Where the hell was Matthew – with both my sword and dagger? I looked around but there was no sign of him. I looked back through the hole, and there, perfectly framed, was the face of the man I had been desperate to see – short-cropped hair, hard features, eyes like a hawk's – that was all I could grasp in the shock of seeing him, but I would never forget that face – as scary as a woodkern's.

He pointed upwards and barked: 'the roof!'

I sprang from my crouching position and ran recklessly to the end of the warehouse, where the wide river was becoming clear in the first flecks of daylight. My only hope was that Matthew was waiting, but my fears were realised when all I saw was an expanse of empty river. In my haste, I almost pitched straight into the gilded, black water. Matthew and the boat were nowhere in sight.

I quickly recalculated. My only other hope was to get to the city gate of Lion's Quay and out into the maze of streets around the docks. The men had a boat full of booty and it was unlikely they would pursue me. I turned and began to run along the central arc of the roof. It was angled and damp and I slipped two or three times as I ran. I also had to negotiate the chimneys of each warehouse as I passed them. Down on the dock below I could see one of the lackeys. He strode along the dock, matching my progress on the roof. Without any of the obstacles I was forced to negotiate, he kept up with me easily. There was no chance I would beat him to the gate.

I looked back to be confronted by the other lackey about fifty yards away on the roof behind me. To the left was water, to my right the man on the dock, behind me the other man. My only hope of an escape route had already been headed off. It dawned on me that I was going to have to fight my way out of the problem.

I stopped running and stood by a one of the metal chimneys. I was about halfway along the length of the dock. My best chance of success was to engage them one at a time. The man on the roof behind me slowed when he saw me stop and then began closing in purposefully. As he did so, I saw the third man, the leader, on the dock below, carrying a pair of lit torches – one in each hand. He joined the man who had stopped a few feet ahead of me on the dock and was watching me expectantly. Both of their manners suggested an enjoyment of the chase. The leader started barking orders in his rough accent.

'Ger'up there, Grayson.' He wedged the torches in the dock and started to give the younger man a leg up. 'Let's see if we can't persuade our young friend to come down and exchange some pleasantries.'

Grayson heaved himself onto the roof below me. He was about twenty-five and was clearly employed for his muscular qualities. A mop of blond hair clouded a face whose eyes were clearly too small for it. He stood up with a slight wobble and then grinned at me disarmingly, inching up the roof at an angle designed to trap me in a pincer movement.

The man behind me on the roof was also becoming clearer. He was a good deal older than Grayson, and a good deal uglier. He had a stubbly shaven head, with a livid scar running down the left side of his face. As he got closer, I noticed with a primeval sense of dread, that the scar was only broken by a milky-white eye, which glinted when caught in the torchlight. If Grayson was on the team for his muscles, the man with scar had been chosen for his outright nastiness. He stopped one chimney away and also tried a grin, revealing a disconcerting lack of teeth.

As I contemplated my next move, Montaigne's thoughts on confrontation suddenly flashed through my brain. Should I show weakness and appeal to my assailant's mercy, or fight my way out of trouble and thereby win their respect? Judging by the look of intent on the men's faces, the latter seemed to be the only option.

Grayson was no doubt strong but his bulk suggested he was out of shape, and he was also clumsy. A couple of times he slipped onto his knees as he moved up the roof. Each time his grin became wider but the look in his piggy-sized eyes suggested that he wasn't too comfortable.

Scarface, on the other hand, appeared more than satisfied with his lot and was simply gathering his wits for the next phase – delivering me up for the 'exchange of pleasantries'. I decided Grayson was the weak link.

I knelt behind the chimney and slipped out of my bag the iron wrench that I had used earlier for breaking and entering. It felt leaden in the palm of my hand and I wondered if I had the strength and dexterity for what I intended. Grayson was coming at the chimney from an angle, up the slope. He was about four feet away. Scarface began closing in. I waited my chance.

I knew that when Grayson was close enough he would reach out for the chimney to steady himself. That would be my chance, but he had to get there before Scarface got too close. I pretended to back off, encouraging Grayson on, but as his arm shot forward, I swung my arm in an arc, only at the last second revealing the bar, which smacked resoundingly into the side of his head. He yelped with pain, lost his grip, and fell heavily onto the roof. I made to sprint past him but before I had barely made a yard, Scarface leapt forward and grabbed my ankle. I fell awkwardly away from the dock towards the oily river behind the warehouses, the bar falling from my hand and skittering ahead of me into the water. Scarface held his grip as we both rolled towards the precipice. I could hear Grayson crying out in pain on the other side of the roof and his boss exhorting him to get up and back into the fray, but the connection I had made was going to make that extremely unlikely.

I managed to grab the edge of the roof and with my free leg launched a kick at Scarface's hand that was still clutching my leg like a clam. He let go of his grip with a sharp scowl, but the extra weight of my newly free leg just served to launch me bodily towards the water. Suddenly, I was hanging on by my elbows – the water waiting to envelop me below. Scarface found his balance and stood towering above me, ruefully rubbing his knuckles. It didn't look like forgiveness was at the top of his agenda. I could see that the man was an old hand and twice as strong as me. He would simply pull me back up the roof and throw me over the other side, where the best I could hope for was a good kicking from all three of them – perhaps something a lot worse.

The dead white eye regarded me impassively. The grin widened. Huge hands reached down to grab me – inches away from the shoulders of my doublet. There was nothing for it – I let go.

As I hit the water, I thought I heard the words 'Master John'. It must have been wishful thinking – a last illusion for someone about to die a watery death. Freezing water wrapped itself around me and I began to thrash my arms around wildly, my heavy bag and boots pulling me down. Swimming had never been my strong suit, and Anne had always made fun of me on that score. Childhood summers – were they to be my last thought? Clay-filled water started choking my throat.

The next thing I knew a wooden bar was under my arm. I thought I had caught the edge of the harbour. But no – the bar was smoothly rounded and moving upwards and lifting me out of the water. I gasped for breath as I broke the surface and saw Matthew's determined face on the end of an oar. He scrambled me into the rowing boat, and with barely a thought we both started rowing for our lives. Scarface shouted and pointed and I knew the leader would be running back along the dock, but Matthew steered us away from the end of Lion's Quay and we struck out into the middle of the river – relentlessly pumping our oars, barely looking up, knowing that we had only one chance. It took us ten minutes of hard slog and we didn't let up until we reached the middle of the river.

We finally found the courage to look back, both panting heavily, lung's burning with the effort. There was no sign that we were being pursued but something else caught our attention. The fog on the north bank had given way to a different type of smoke – Lion's Quay was ablaze.

Part 2

London Suburbs

Chapter 15

'London, what are thy suburbs but licensed stews?'
(Thomas Nashe)

The Curtain, London's largest playing venue, stood in the fields hard by Norton Folgate, a stone's throw from its illustrious older cousin – known simply as The Theatre. Two days had passed since his disappearance when I finally found time to journey out there in search of Buck – the day after the fire at Lion's Quay.

On seeing the fire, Matthew and I had rowed warily back to the dock but there had been no sign of our assailants. Instead, we had helped tackle the blaze alongside a dozen other men, all alerted by the flames, and cries of 'fire' around the port. There had been no chance of saving the end warehouses, but we had managed to stop the fire spreading further into the city – starting a fire had been an incredibly reckless thing to do. It looked as though the thieves had decided to obliterate any evidence of ever having been at the warehouse.

Hercules Smyth looked as though he had enjoyed better days. I found him staring morosely at the space where his warehouse had stood, his old frame bent forward in despair. It was, by now, eight o'clock in the morning and the fire was out. Where the two end warehouses had once stood, a dozen disfigured, charred beams stuck pitifully out of the water. The substance of the buildings had collapsed and been taken away by the outgoing tide. The jetsam collectors down-stream would have a bonanza. What remained of the warehouse next to Hercules Smyth's was in the process of being pulled down by a group of tired, blackened men, amongst them Matthew. The building had been damaged beyond repair and duly condemned.

I walked up to Hercules Smyth to offer him my commiserations but he wasn't pleased to see me.

'What are you doing here, Master Lovat?'

'Trying to save your livelihood.' My sooty face and clothes were testament to that fact. 'Failing, though, I'm sorry to say.'

'Do you know anything about how the fire started? Does it have anything to do with Alphonse's death?'

'I believe the men responsible for Don Alphonse's murder may also have set fire to his warehouse, but I don't know who they are and I can't prove it.'

Hercules looked at me sadly, the weight of the disaster slowly sinking in, 'Everything gone, Master Lovat. A life's work gone up in smoke.' It was a difficult time to interrogate him but there was still the question of Cassangoe.

'Cassangoe could be in very real danger,' I began tentatively. 'These men are ruthless and will stop at nothing. Can you not tell me where he is?'

Hercules Smyth hesitated for a moment, eyeing me with his baleful gaze.

'I lied to you Master Lovat. Cassangoe was here, in my warehouse, when you called. He was hiding in the shadows behind the animal skins.'

'I don't understand,' I said, trying to keep the exasperation I felt out of my voice – it had been a very long night. 'Why did he hide and why did you lie to me?'

'Cassangoe said his life was in danger. Other men had come earlier, looking for Alphonse, and Cassangoe said they were dangerous. He had hidden from them too.'

'Dangerous? In what way?'

'I didn't ask.'

'Who were they?'

'The one who spoke was called Nicholas Ingram.' The name caused a distant echo in my mind but I couldn't place it.

'What did he look like?'

'I don't know. I'm an old man, my eyesight is poor. An unpleasant type. The other two worked for him.'

'What did he want?'

'He said he had business with Alphonse.'

'So he knew nothing of the murder then?'

'It seemed not.'

'But he could have been lying?'

'All I can say is that Cassangoe sensed danger, and we agreed it better that he hid in my warehouse until Don Alphonse returned. Up until that point we only knew that Don Alphonse was missing. His rowing boat had gone from the dock – unusual because he rarely took it out by himself – and Cassangoe hadn't heard from him for two days. We assumed he was with a woman – he often disappeared on amorous adventures – but not usually for so long and Cassangoe was worried. Then first this man Ingram arrives, looking for Alphonse, and then you with news of his death. It seems Cassangoe had a right to be cautious.'

'Of the interests that I represent, at least one of them thinks that Cassangoe most likely murdered his master.'

'That is a ridiculous suggestion. Besides theirs was not a master and servant relationship. They were as close as brothers.' Echoes of what Simon Turney had said.

'Where is Cassangoe now?' I said, trying to hide my impatience.

'I don't know. I knew you'd follow me and so I left soon after your visit to give Cassangoe a chance to get away.' So much for my great shadowing skills. 'Don Alphonse has a house somewhere in Queenhithe Ward. I have never been there and couldn't take you there if you wanted me to. Cassangoe would have avoided it whilst he thought Don Alphonse was alive, in case he disturbed one of his assignations, but I expect that is where he has gone now.'

'He definitely left? You're sure he wasn't asleep in the warehouse when it caught fire?'

'Of course not. He would have helped put the fire out. Cassangoe is not a coward – he's a good man.'

'That depends if he had been aware of it.' I looked at the blackened stumps sticking out of the water. Men were often paralysed by smoke and burnt in the flames. I doubted anyone sleeping next to the fire would have escaped. The flames had done a thorough job.

'How did Cassangoe react to the news of Don Alphonse's murder?'

'Naturally he was deeply upset. He and Don Alphonse were like brothers. I can't give you the details – long before I knew them – but they had some sort of shared history that bonded them together. Neither liked talking about it.'

'Tell me about Don Alphonse. What sort of a man was he?'

Hercules Smyth took a deep breath and thought carefully before answering.

'He was an intelligent man but a reckless one. I can't say I am altogether surprised that his life ended with violence.'

'How was he reckless?'

'He liked to upset important people. The kind of people who looked down their noses at him, and people like him – people like myself and Cassangoe, perpetual outsiders in our own homes. Oh, not just Portuguese and African. I myself was born in the Ottoman Empire, although my family is Greek. No matter how long we stay here we'll never be accepted.' The *leper's end of Lion's Quay* – now a charred wreck. 'Don Alphonse liked to celebrate his difference and never tired of reminding the people he despised, and who despised him, that an outsider could also be rich and successful.' I remembered the proud face at the procession, the defiance.

'And then there were the women,' the diminutive Hercules continued in a disapproving voice. 'Don Alphonse liked nothing more than cuckolding the great and good, and no woman could resist him, of course.'

'Do you know any of the marriages in question?'

'No,' he said, decisively. 'Although I admired Don Alphonse as a man, I didn't approve of his appetites. He respected that and didn't burden me with the knowledge.'

'Do you think it likely that one of these cuckolded husbands murdered him?'

Hercules thought for a moment, weighing the question.

'It's possible but I think it unlikely. Cuckolded husbands are common enough and they don't all go around killing their rivals.' How misleading, I wondered, was the irony that his body had washed up at Cuckold's Point?

'Besides,' Hercules Smyth continued, 'I am starting to think that there is a much darker reason for Don Alphonse's murder.'

'Go on.'

'I can't tell you the details but something happened in the last year, something that changed him. He was travelling more than usual and had a new purpose in his life. One time I overheard him and Cassangoe talking of revenge.' He looked at me, sensing that I thought it wasn't much to go on. 'I don't wish to betray Cassangoe's confidence but in Don Alphonse's absence I saw more of him – he ran the warehouse after all – and he told me a few details. There was a man, I don't know his name but a rich man and important, who Don Alphonse wanted to bring down, to 'crush into the dirt' as Cassangoe put it. When I told him of

Don Alphonse's death yesterday, he immediately exclaimed '*diabo vermelho*' under his breath. I believe this is the name they used for the man Don Alphonse was targeting, perhaps he struck first.'

'*Diabo vermelho*? What does it mean?'

'In Portuguese it means Red Devil, though who it refers to I have no idea.'

'Is there anything else you can tell me? It could help Cassangoe.'

'Nothing ... except ... I heard them mention a place called Stavening.'

'In respect of this Red Devil?'

'Perhaps. I only gleaned certain details. I really can't help you more, Master Lovat. As you can see, I have other things to worry about.' The emotion of the situation suddenly got the better of him and he turned away abruptly, cutting a forlorn figure as he wandered despondently back along what remained of the dock. I watched him go, grappling unsuccessfully with the flicker of a memory that had been sparked by something he had said.

***

Emmalina was still asleep when I arrived back at the lodgings, her rich auburn hair spread sumptuously over my straw-stuffed bolster. It was a welcome sight after the night I'd endured. I stood watching her breathe deeply for a moment, until something unconscious must have alerted her to my presence and her eyes opened. She sat up in bed when she saw me, worry clouding her pretty features.

'What happened to you?'

I laughed, realising I must look a sight, and started scrubbing my face, whilst explaining to her the events of the previous night. Wide-eyed with shock at the tale, Emmalina gently took the cloth from me and started to tend the various burns and bruises I had collected in the last few hours. They looked worse than they felt but I was glad of the attention.

When she had finished, I unpacked the spoils from Don Alphonse's warehouse and laid them out on the table. The papers were soaked from going into the water, ink running, tears appearing. They were useless. The only item that had survived more or less intact was the book wrapped in the velvet pouch. I looked at it dispiritedly before putting it on the table and turning my attentions to the small fireplace.

'*R de. S. 1567*,' Emmalina said, reading the embossed inscription.

'That book's intriguing,' I said. 'I can't tell if it's of any use but I found it in a secret compartment in Don Alphonse's desk.' Emmalina's interest was piqued and she began turning the pages.

'Careful,' I warned. 'It's very fragile. I wish Buck was here – he could have translated it for me.' In the translation house, one of Buck's areas of expertise was Portuguese. I returned to stoking the embers of the previous evening's fire.

'*The logbook of the Portuguese nao Santo Francisco, written by her Captain, Don Rodrigo de Sousa, April 1567. May God bless our voyage and bring us safely home again.*' I looked at her in surprise. Emmalina was reading from the first page of the book.

'You can close your mouth, Lovat,' she said, her eyes twinkling. 'What's a nao? And who is Rodrigo de Sousa? He sounds quite dashing.'

'A nao is a large merchant ship – mainly the preserve of Portuguese and Spanish traders. Rodrigo de Sousa must be a relation of Don Alphonse.' I took the book from her and stared at a page of incoherent, to me at least, Portuguese. 'So it's a ship's log. I wondered what all the dates meant. How on earth can you read it?'

'Buck's not the only language talent in the family, you know.'

'You read Portuguese?' I found it hard to keep a note of incredulity out of my voice.

'Read it, write it, speak it. I spent the first ten years of my life in Lisbon's foreign trading block. They're not as backward about girls learning things there,' she finished pointedly.

'Will you translate it for me? I can't explain why, but I think it may be useful. Why keep it all these years, and hide it away?'

'Maybe it's a family heirloom?'

'Perhaps, but I'd still like to know what the contents are. Call it instinct, if you like.' Emmalina regarded me for a moment before giving me the sweetest smile one could hope for.

'If you promise to go to the theatre tomorrow and look for Buck.'

'It's a deal,' I said. 'Now, move over, I need to get some sleep.'

* * *

Hence, the next morning, I found myself squeezing through Bishop's Gate alongside the usual array of pack animals, carts and people, and on towards Shoreditch, while Emmalina stayed in my lodgings, enthusiastically working on the translation.

On Bishopgate's street, just beyond the city walls, I passed a group of laughing gallants coming out of Bedlam Hospital, clearly exhilarated at having spent a morning baiting the lunatics who were incarcerated inside. The madmen were giving them a good send off with their constant cacophony of shouts and cries. You could never walk up this street without being aware of their discomforting proximity but enjoying their misfortune as a spectacle did not appeal to me.

The village of Norton Folgate lay a few hundred yards further on. I say village but slum might be a more accurate description. What had once been a pretty, well-to-do hamlet to the north of the city, inhabited by prosperous and law abiding citizens, was now a packed hothouse of immigrants, lowlifes, poets and whores, all crammed together in a tight, but rapidly expanding, space. Thefts and stabbings were as common as stepping in horse muck and a good deal more inconvenient. I kept a wary eye out as I skirted past rows of teeming tenements.

The already crowded street would become virtually impassable in a few hours' time, as a great multitude forced its way to the theatres. Aloof aristocrats carried in boxes by perfumed servants, excited apprentices given an afternoon's dispensation, adventurous maids playing truant from homes and husbands, solid tradesmen proudly shepherding their wives – all would soon be jostling their way purposefully down the street. Not all of them would make it to the theatre, some of the young men diverted by the ordinaries, gambling dens, and stews along the way, which readily touted their wares along the route. Those able to escape these temptations would make it to the large double entrance doors of the theatre, where I now stood.

The two theatres were easy to spot as soon as one set foot outside the city walls. They dwarfed the mean houses shouldering up to them, the central towers of each standing as tall as any of the dozen church spires I had passed along the way, with colourful flags adorning their roofs, and huge, cavernous bellies, flanked by wide staircases on either side. Built purposefully here, so that they were outside the jurisdiction of the city authorities, they offered the kind of entertainment district that eager citizens desired and where pretty much anything went – dramatic theatre, purses, virginities, even people's lives. The Curtain was marginally the newer of the two but both had the look and lived-in feel of buildings that often welcomed thousands of expectant people through their doors.

Despite their imposing presence, both buildings were temporary structures and could be taken down at a moment's notice if the plague, or the authorities, suddenly threatened their existence – as both did from time to time. Neither theatre had ever been deconstructed, but their impermanent nature meant that they groaned and shook as they filled up and often felt as if they would collapse under the weight of the hordes – all of which added to the tension of the spectacle, if not quite in the way that the theatre builders had originally intended.

The theatre's open pit, where the groundlings stood during the performance, was a hive of activity, with actors and stagehands all rushing to and fro in what I assumed was organised chaos. I asked one or two if they had seen Buck, or if he was at the theatre. Most shook their heads or even ignored me, finding it inconvenient to be accosted by a stranger so close to a performance, but eventually I got a reaction from a finely dressed young man who was buckling on a pair of golden shoes at the side of the stage. 'You'd better talk to the boss', he said, jerking his head in the direction of a man frantically giving orders from the centre of the stage. I elbowed my way to him, trying not to get embroiled amongst a group of actors who were rehearsing an elaborate stage fight. The young man stood up and followed me to the centre. As I reached 'the boss' he shouted over my shoulder.

'Father! This gentleman's asking about Bucklesbury.' The man immediately bore down on me threateningly.

'Bucklesbury? That useless scoundrel! What do you know about him? Where is he and don't tell me he's ill again?' Slightly taken back by this sudden questioning, I stammered my response.

'I don't know where he is. I came to ask you the same question. He wasn't at his lodgings.'

'What the devil do I care about that? I'm going to have a full house in an hour's time – all baying for blood – and he's the third actor I've had missing this week.' His aggressive manner clearly implied that I must have a cellar somewhere where I detained unsuspecting bit part players for my own nefarious ends.

'Would anyone know where he is?' I asked lamely. The man looked at me angrily.

'I doubt it and in any case, everybody's too busy to be bothered at the moment. If you don't mind leaving we can get on with the job of trying to entertain our masses.' I began to turn away when, suddenly, he seemed to have a change of heart.

'Hang on a minute. What's your name?'

'Lovat.'

'How tall are you, Lovat?'

'Six foot,' I said, perplexed.

'Size?'

'I've no idea.'

'Large, medium, small?' he barked.

'Medium?'

'You look like an intelligent lad. Can you learn lines quickly?' By this time he had taken hold of my shoulders and was spinning me round roughly. 'What do you reckon young Burbage? Can we make an actor out of him?' Young Burbage joined his father in looking me up and down like a prize horse.

'Don't see why not, father. He might even add some comedy. Better get him cribbing straight away.' Young Burbage's opinion seemed to be just the answer his father was hoping for. Keeping a firm grip on my arm, he spun around looking for someone in the pit.

'Where's Finke. Oi Finke you fat layabout,' Old Burbage bellowed across the pit to a middle-aged, tubby man who appeared to be attending to the costume needs of what looked like a beautiful young woman, but was in actual fact a pale young man in drag. Finke stopped what he was doing with a pained expression on his face and came bustling over.

'Finke. We've got a new player this afternoon. Lovat here will be taking Bucklesbury's parts – that's first Portingale, third Watchman and second Citizen. There'll also be various crowd scenes to think about. He's your responsibility, find him the relevant script pages and get him in costume – straight away.' Seeing complete bemusement on my face, he continued,

'Go with Finke, Lovat. He'll sort you out. Just learn your lines and try not to get in anyone else's way. There's two shillings and a porter of ale for you at the end of the night. Provided you don't balls up!' With that he turned back to what he'd been doing earlier, dismissing me with a wave of his arm.

I thought of protesting and making a run for it, but it occurred to me that it was the only way that I was going to get closer to the theatre company and be able to discover more about Buck. I also had to admit to some curiosity, having only ever been in the audience before. The secrets and tricks of stagecraft were something of a celebrated topic to the enthusiastic theatregoer.

These thoughts flashed through my mind as the obedient, but put upon Finke took my arm and hustled me to the back of the stage, up some stairs, and into a room of the tower where more preparations were taking place. The whole experience was akin to being press-ganged in the docks. I finally found my voice:

'But I've never done any acting in my life!'

'You'll be alright, deary. There's nothing to it – a good looking lad like you'll have them eating out of your hand – besides,' Finke said, as though he was relishing the prospect, 'there's plenty of time to get you ready. You're not on for at least an hour after we open.'

He dived into a chest, his chubby arse pointing up at me, and began digging around for something. After much cursing, he finally found what he was looking for. 'Now take a look at these scrolls and, while you're doing it, come along with me and try some frocks on.' There then followed a half hour period where I was poked, pulled and prodded into various costumes, whilst at the same time trying to learn a handful of lines and greet some fellow actors. Most of them were welcoming and the impression I got was that non-actors being pressed into service at the last minute was not an unheard of event. However, it was little comfort, and I spent the next half an hour trying to identify ways to bolt from the theatre, fear rising by the second.

After much tutting and frowning on his part, as he fussed over my costume, I eventually gleaned from Finke that the play was a revenge tragedy, set in Spain, called *Hieronimo*. I was actually relieved that I had seen it a few weeks previously, and at least had an idea of the plot. Since the defeat of the Spanish, it had been playing to packed houses, owing to its bloodthirsty portrayal of the common enemy. The thought of packed houses sent another streak of terror through me.

There were two other actors who were in all of my scenes and they made themselves known to me early on and tried to reassure me. Thomas Higges was a carpenter who had originally been employed to repair the stage before being roped into the play. He had no desire to remain an actor and was simply enjoying the ride while it lasted. Martin Skinner, on the other hand, was a starry-eyed youngster who had joined the theatre company when it passed through his hometown twelve months earlier. He was keen to graduate to playing the ladies' roles and watched the actor playing Bel-Imperia, who I had seen Finke dressing earlier, with an amusing mixture of jealousy and admiration.

Thomas and Martin took me through the scenes we were doing together and forced me to learn the lines by rote – like a pair of schoolmasters. All the time I was aware of the huge noise building up beyond the stage.

Before I knew what was happening, the performance had begun.

Chapter 16

'But wherefore stands yon silly man so mute
With mournful eyes and hands to heaven uprear'd?'
(The Spanish Tragedy; Thomas Kyd)

On reflection, my first foray onto the London stage was, broadly speaking, not a total disaster. In truth, I had very little to do and seemed to spend most of my time climbing in and out of different costumes, with the fussing Finke always close by to lend a hand. Apart from a few crowd scenes, I had three short scenes with Thomas and Martin and in each, much to the packed audience's amusement, they cleverly contrived to make me look like the stupid one out of the three of us – whether as first Portingale, third Watchman or second Citizen – so that even if I did forget a line, or said it in the wrong place, it was almost as if it was expected of me. For my part, the scenes shot by in a blur, and my overriding memory was of the sea of faces under the brown caps of the groundlings in the pit, to those of the wealthier viewers looking down on all sides – some amazed and dumbfounded, others shouting advice or abuse, all absorbed in the play.

At less frenetic moments, I was able to take up a vantage point at the side of the stage, where, like the rest of the packed audience, I could marvel at the drama unfolding in front of me and the tremendous performances that were taking place. The opening of the play was particularly striking. It started with the dead Spanish soldier, Andrea, describing his journey through the underworld before appealing to Revenge to avenge his death, and for a moment it was as though Don Alphonse himself was speaking to me from beyond the grave. But this thought was quickly swept from my mind, as the drama on stage gathered pace.

Both the theatre manager, Richard Burbage, and his son James had important roles in the play. Richard as the avenging father Hieronimo and James as the wicked nephew of the King, Lorenzo. There was also another impressive young performer playing the Portuguese Prince Balthazar and the dynamic between him and the younger Burbage, with whom he shared most scenes, was fascinating to watch, as it appeared to be based on mutual loathing and brinkmanship. Their styles were contrasting, the Younger Burbage opting for a more naturalistic approach, whilst his nemesis, whose name was Edward Alleyn, displayed a hugely powerful, but somewhat over-the-top, performance. The crowd liked it, though, and one could almost see the Younger Burbage gnashing his teeth as Alleyn stole scene after scene, whilst at the same time trampling all over his rival's performance.

I found myself drawn to this rivalry during the second half of the play when, relieved from having finished my final scene as part of the triumvirate, I was able to relax in the 'tiring house' behind the stage. As I watched, a man came to stand by my side. He was tall, with a shock of lazy hair hanging over a gaunt face that held a mixture of worry and bemusement, as though he couldn't quite come to terms with the craziness the world had to offer. Observing, too, the sparring taking place on stage he spoke to me quietly.

'So what do you think of our company's two young stars then?'

'I'd say that I hope, for Balthazar's sake, that dagger in Lorenzo's hand is a fake.'

'Yes, there's no love lost between them, that's for sure. Although rumour has it that Alleyn will be off to Henslowe at The Rose any day now. Not a moment too soon as far as our young Burbage is concerned.' He let out a wry chuckle. 'I'm Thomas Kyd by the way. I wrote this nonsense.' He offered a slim hand and I shook it gladly, telling him that I admired the play greatly, but he stopped me with a dismissive shake of his head.

'You're Lovat aren't you? Bucklesbury's friend? Any idea what's happened to him? His absence has caused a great deal of consternation amongst the powers that be.'

'I wish I knew. I came here to find out and ended up getting roped into performing.'

'And a splendid job you did too! Earned both shillings handsomely, although don't be surprised if the older Burbage docks you one for the costume hire. It's been known to happen.'

We watched on in silence for a while, as the play built up to its gruesome conclusion. Lorenzo and Balthazar were both stabbed to death with grim authenticity. Then Hieronimo bit out his own tongue in order to avoid being tortured, before killing both the Duke and himself, all of which was carried off with relish. It was hard to imagine the mild-mannered man beside me writing such strong material. Death and Revenge satisfied, a clown began leading a jig on the stage, and the crowd, who had greatly enjoyed the brutality on display, were roused into a state of near anarchy, the Curtain threatening to burst its walls. Kyd motioned me to follow him away from the clamour to the outside, where he asked me if I would like to share a pipe. Puffing companionably, I asked him if he knew Buck well.

'Quite well. We discussed writing a bit. I think he was getting fed up with the whole thing. Burbage treated him like a chattel, as he does all of the actors, worse if anything, and that was no good for Buck. He's a sensitive soul, despite the bluff. I read some of his work – definite potential – as much as some others. I'll miss him around here – someone with a brain larger than his opinion of himself. A rarity in these circles, I can assure you.' He eyed me mischievously. 'Are you planning on replacing him permanently?'

'No fear.' I realised that my whole body was still shaking from performing. 'Can you shed any light on Buck's disappearance? I knew he was unhappy with some aspects of the theatre but it hardly seems a strong enough reason to disappear completely.'

Kyd thought for a moment, his boyish face creased in a frown. Before he could speak, Finke interrupted us.

'Ah, there you are, Master Lovat. I wondered where you'd been hiding. Now come along and we'll get you undressed.' His tongue slithered across his lip as he said it.

'Hack off, Finke, and find some other victim to weasel over,' Kyd intervened on my behalf. 'Lovat and I are sharing a pipe.'

'Well I'll be damned,' Finke went bright scarlet. 'Bragging writers; think they own the place.' He trailed off in a huff of opprobrium back into the theatre and Kyd gave me a lopsided smile.

'Sorry about that but if you don't treat Finke with a firm hand at the beginning, you'll find he never stops pestering.'

'You were saying about Buck.'

'Yes. There might be a reason I can think of. Something that happened a few days ago. It's probably not the place to discuss it here. Listen, in about ten minute's time the entire company will descend on a tavern in Norton Folgate. The beer is cloudy and the pies have grit in them but it has a certain charm. You'll have to come anyway or you won't get paid. I'll tell you all about Buck when we get there.'

* * *

A few hours later, I was still squeezed into the corner of the tavern, an undistinguished coaching house on the main artery running from the Bishop's Gate to the North.

Burbage's entire theatre company had descended on the crowded inn and taken over one of the upstairs rooms, whose ancient rafters were creaking and straining at the influx. On a central bench, Edward Alleyn was holding court, basking in the success of his performance. He had been joined by a group of followers led by an extraordinary-looking gentleman wearing a bilious green doublet and hose, with long red hair greased to a point a foot or so above his head, and a similarly stiffened long beard, adorned by a single pearl hanging at its end. Robert Greene, as by now everybody in the room had learnt, had written a long ode in praise of Alleyn and was standing on the long table reciting it at high volume, much to the enjoyment of the poem's subject and his retinue.

On another table across the room, the Burbage camp was presenting an altogether more reserved front. Father and son, and a few key members of the company, had their heads close together around the table, in a manner that suggested they were hunkering down for a late evening. Occasionally, one or other would glance ruefully at the commotion taking place across the room but generally they did their best to ignore it.

Kyd had been happy to take a table with me apart from both groups. He seemed most comfortable on the fringe of things and told me at one point that he found the bickering between the factions in the company quite tiresome. He had an easy-going manner and his thin face could light up in surprising warmth at times, when he revealed some indiscretion about one of the actors, or mulled over some of the ironies of theatre life. Not long after we had both settled over a full tankard, I pressed him to continue what he had alluded to earlier about Buck. Instead, he surprised me by asking a question in a low, secretive, voice.

'Did your friend have any of the recusant tendencies about him?'

'A recusant? You mean was he a Papist?' I immediately detected a small knot of unease somewhere deep in my stomach. 'Why do you ask that?'

'Most of those inclined to Popery have been lying low recently. Understandable with the Spanish invasion looming on the horizon, and all that. As you probably know, there was a suppression during the first part of the year – all sorts of perceived undesirables and threats rounded up, and incarcerated around the various rat-infested holes in this city, politely referred to as prisons. Most of them are still in there, as far as anyone is aware, I should think – those that haven't been executed already, that is. Sources reliably inform me that at least two dozen priests and Catholic laymen have been put to death in the last three months alone.' I nodded slowly. It was well known that the relief of the Armada victory had given way to a spate of vicious bloodletting as the country took revenge for the great threat it had experienced.

'What has any of this to do with Buck?'

Kyd pulled his stool closer to the table in order to lower his voice. Despite the rowdiness going on around us, there was still a chance of someone overhearing us and conversations of this nature always had the potential to be misinterpreted. The last thing either of us wanted was to end up lounging in the Clink or Newgate over some misunderstanding. Kyd started his explanation in a roundabout way.

'The theatre's an unusual world. In many ways, it's a slice right through society and just like the rest of society it attracts its fair share of strange customers. Only you tend to notice them more in a smaller crowd, so to speak. Just look at that lot behind us.' He indicated Alleyn's table where Robert Greene was now dancing an energetic but ill-advised Galliard on the table.

'Surely you don't include Buck amongst that lot?'

There was a great roar as Greene toppled onto the table – plates, tankards and beer flying everywhere. Kyd took the opportunity to think for a moment. 'Buck is a young man in the prime of his life, having his dreams frustrated by an over-bearing theatre manager and the realisation that, despite his talent, his face doesn't quite fit.' Kyd couldn't be much older than Buck himself, but his world-weary manner made them seem a generation apart. 'Men like that are susceptible to temptation – and ideas. Especially if there is something deep inside them which makes those ideas seem attractive.'

'What exactly is it that you are getting at? What ideas?' The knot that had formed in my stomach was tightening. I had a horrible inkling of the direction the conversation was heading in.

'Buck's been keeping the wrong company. There's a man called Henry Garnet who hangs around the theatre. He hands out leaflets denouncing the plays, and theatregoing in general – *playwriting is the work of the devil* – that kind of thing. He was probably outside there this afternoon making a nuisance of himself. However, rumour has it that the whole stunt is an elaborate ruse and that he's really a recruiting officer for the Jesuits.'

'Recruiting?'

'The Spanish Armada may have united us all under the one banner of Queen and Protestantism but I can assure you that there are plenty of people in this country who still believe in the old religion and who are disappointed by the turn of events. Defeat of the Armada simply left a plague of dissatisfaction in this country, which is going to be festering for years to come. You couldn't pick a better time to start swelling the ranks of the Pope's army.'

'I still don't see what any of that has to do with Buck.'

'I lodge in Smithfield and I often walk back from the theatres across Finsbury Field. The other afternoon, after a performance, I saw Buck and another man going into a cottage there with this Garnet. It's not much to go on, I know, but there was something about the way they were behaving – something furtive – that just wasn't right. You know how it is – observant people like you and me – you get an instinct for this kind of thing.'

I sat back in my chair weighing up the information. At face value, it was evidence of very little, but the uneasy feeling I'd experienced as soon as Kyd mentioned recusancy was born out of privileged information I already knew about Buck – information that made Kyd's story all too plausible. Buck and Emmalina's natural parents had been Catholics and this was something that their Protestant stepfather had often held against them, using it as a metaphorical stick to beat them with at every available opportunity. Buck had never shown any outward signs of following his parents' faith but who knew what secret yearnings he had been harbouring in his breast.

While I was pondering this, Burbage Senior came over to the table.

Handing me a couple of coins, he put one of his large hands on my shoulder.

'You did well today, Lovat my lad. Quite the comedy turn. Fancy becoming a permanent replacement for your unreliable mate? There's nothing tomorrow but the day after that we're 'rehearsing' Greene's *Selimus*, if he's sober enough to get the final scenes to me, not to mention other performances of *Hieronimo* next week. What do you reckon, Kyd? A welcome addition to our happy nest?' This last comment was accompanied by a sly look towards Alleyn's table. I started to mumble something about how grateful and flattered I was before Kyd, sensing that acting wasn't my forte, came to the rescue.

'I rather think our Master Lovat might not survive the excitement of another performance.'

Burbage stood there sizing me up for a moment. 'Well if you change your mind you know where the theatre is. We'll be happy to accommodate you. As for you Kyd, where's that other revenge play you promised me. Hamnet wasn't it?'

'*Hamlet* actually and all in good time.' Although not arrogant, Kyd was clearly aware of the acclaim that a success like *The Spanish Tragedy* had given him. How galling it must have been for Buck, I thought, to witness the kind of ease with which Kyd dealt with Burbage.

'Well, see that I get it soon. Audiences are a fickle bunch – Hieronimo won't satisfy them forever. In the meantime, there's a drink for you both on the house.' With that he returned to his son's table and I turned back to Kyd.

'Where's this cottage you mentioned?'

'Finsbury Fields. I'll take you there if you like.'

'And this other man that was with him? What did he look like?'

'Remember it was dark and so I couldn't see them that clearly. Tall, short beard, finely dressed. I've seen him at the theatre before. His name's Montague or something similar.'

'Mortimer?'

'That's it. Funny how the mind alters these things. Greville Mortimer. You know him?'

'I've met him.' Greville was Buck's old friend, whom I had met for the first time at the Queen's Procession. Could his return to London, and Buck's disappearance, have something in common? It seemed all too likely.

By now the tables around us were getting even rowdier. After speaking to us, Burbage Senior had departed, taking his son with him, and following that the divided tables had broadly come together in what seemed to be some sort of drunken truce. Someone spotted Kyd and decided it was time to celebrate his role as the writer of the great success they had just been part of. Kyd was dragged reluctantly to the middle of the room and for a few minutes was held as the centre of attention. I concentrated on my drink, trying to make sense of what he had told me about Buck. Not for long, however. I was soon spotted and dragged into the fun as the company's newest member. Fun which involved having to down a succession of tankards and join in some boisterous singing. It looked like it would be a long night.

Sometime later, after I had lost count of the number of ales we had downed, Kyd and I were ensconced in a dark corner and, with a loosened tongue, I was spilling out the entire story of Don Alphonse's murder.

'So what's your theory as to who did the Portingale in?' Kyd asked, when I reached an opportune moment. By way of answer, I went into more detail about the meeting my brother had held the night before and about Cassangoe.

'Don Alphonse left the meeting with three other men – Simon Turney, who has since sailed to the Baltic, Marmaduke Drummond, who I can't question because he is a confidant of my brother, and someone else whose name I haven't got hold of yet.'

'Drummond? The poet? Who writes the worst doggerel in the entire Kingdom?'

'The very same. He's my brother's protégé. As far as I can tell, neither Drummond nor Turney had any reason to murder Don Alphonse, although there was another man in the shadows that evening who argued with Don Alphonse, possibly about a woman.'

'And who was that?'

'That's another thing that I don't know.' I sighed in frustration. 'There's no doubt though that Don Alphonse was a womaniser with a history of seducing other men's wives. The richer or more powerful the husband, the better, so I am told.' I paused to take a draught of ale, while Kyd nodded thoughtfully. 'Anyway, Turney claims that Don Alphonse was unmolested by the time they left him. Unless I can locate the boatman who rowed him on, I've got no idea where he was heading.'

'Well, it sounds like you've got your work cut out. Still, you never know, his background might have something to do with it. I did some study of the Portuguese when I was writing *The Spanish Tragedy*, to give it its proper title, and went out of my way to find the real thing. You know that there are very few Portuguese in London and most of those are *Marranos*.'

'*Marranos*? What the hell does that mean?'

'It *means* swine in Spanish. But it's also the word used by the Spanish and the Portuguese to describe *Conversos*.' Seeing incomprehension spreading on my face, Kyd continued: '*Conversos* – secret Jews!'

'I didn't think there were any Jews in England,' I said, ironically. Although Jews were legally barred from the country, everyone knew that there were small pockets scattered throughout the city – tolerated, provided that they were outwardly Christian. Still, I had no idea that the Portuguese community were predominantly Jewish. I thought about Don Alphonse and suddenly remembered something.

'Jewish men … they get their you-know-what's snipped, don't they?' I said, indicating my nether regions. Kyd laughed at my manner.

'Are you trying to say that they have their cock's circumcised? The oldest known surgical operation in the world, as far as I'm aware. Didn't realise you were such a prude, Lovat.' But I ignored this, my mind focusing on the image of the naked body I had cast my eyes over in my brother's cellar. It occurred to me after all that there was a good chance Don Alphonse had indeed been Jewish. Not just a leper of Lion's Quay – but an illegal leper at that.By now, there was a raucous cacophony all around us and I suddenly felt emboldened by the ale flooding through my veins.

'You said you would take me to the cottage where you saw Buck and Mortimer. Where did you say this Henry Garnet lives?'

'Close to Finsbury Fields.'

'Come on then,' I said. 'Let's go and see if we can find him.'

Chapter 17

'A gem cannot be polished without friction, nor a man perfected without trials.'
(Seneca)

Cold flecks of snow stung our faces, as Kyd and I turned down Hogge Lane, which led to Finsbury Fields beyond. The lane was infamous as a meeting place for duellists and often crowds gathered here to enjoy the unlicensed sport of plaintiffs settling their differences outside legal boundaries. By night-time it reverted to a desolate track, bordered by a row of rundown houses, broken occasionally by stretches of desolate fields. There was no one about in the cold, and Kyd and I passed unchallenged as we picked our way along the uneven track formed of frozen mud.

Soon, even the track itself petered out into a forlorn stretch of patchy scrub, which undulated for another half a mile through the Moorfields, before abruptly hitting the stretch of wall either side of the ancient Roman postern, Moor Gate. Somehow, the wall here had managed to stem the tide of London spilling inexorably into the open countryside. During the warmer months, these fields were awash with the colours of damp linen, and also home to mayings, trainbands, and a variety of more wholesome sports than were enjoyed in Hogge Lane. In the winter, though, it became a drab, bleak space, used far less frequently and, on cold nights like this, deserted. The frequent howls of icy wind around our ears, combined with the vastness of the distant city, wrapped us in isolation as we trudged across the broken turf.

After a stretch of marching in silence, Kyd began outlining a plan for tackling Henry Garnet, should we find him at home.

'We can't very well go in there demanding to know what he's done with your friend, can we? He'll clam up like … well, a clam … and we won't get a thing out of him.'

This had occurred to me too. 'What do you suggest?'

'I thought it would be a good idea if we pretended to be fencing for the other team. If you understand me?'

'I think I do. Go on.'

'Well, let's assume that this Garnet is recruiting for the Jesuits: why not give the impression that we, too, are a pair of dissolute and disaffected young men who are rather fond of the relics and superstition of the old religion and would be happy to betray our Queen and country in exchange for the joy of seeing a few puritans strung up outside the Tower?'

'It's a risky strategy. What if the authorities find out? And what if Garnet asks us to prove our credentials?'

'I thought of that too,' he said, pulling something out from under his cloak. After leaving the tavern, Kyd had insisted on a quick return to the Curtain. Ostensibly, it had been to pick up one of Garnet's leaflets denouncing the theatre. Now, however, he produced something else he had collected – a string of wooden balls that he was cradling in his hands. 'Rosary beads,' he volunteered, by way of explanation. 'I liberated them from Finke's prop box.'

'I know what they are. What do you intend doing with them?'

'Nothing. Just thought they added a bit of authenticity, that's all,' he said, with a boyish grin. 'Don't worry,' he added. Seeing my bemused expression. 'I'll keep them more or less hidden but with a small section surreptitiously sticking out of my doublet. Credentials taken care of.' I sincerely doubted the veracity of that statement but didn't have time to argue, as we were approaching our destination.

The cottage was a poor dwelling amongst a row of ancient buildings that had all seen better days. Formerly part of a prosperous farmstead, they were now on the outskirts of the new developments north of the city, and homes for the poorest type of citizen who is neither living off the land, nor part of the teeming madness creeping up on him. The houses looked as though they were waiting for some ruthless property speculator to declare them unfit for habitation, before evicting their inhabitants and replacing them with brash new tenements of the sort now ruining the view from my brother's bedroom window.

There was no one about outside, the cold had seen to that. I tried to imagine the crammed, dirty interiors, where drunkenness, disease and depression huddled around airless, pathetic fireplaces.

Kyd, busy tucking the rosary beads down his doublet, pointed out the cottage we were seeking and I noticed a feeble streak of wispy grey smoke struggling out of the chimney. There were holes in the roof where slates had fallen away, and rotten posts tentatively supporting the structure. On the door was daubed a faded blue cross – a sign that a plague victim had died there in the past – though there hadn't been a bad bout of disease in London for a while. No doubt this morbid reminder had been left to deter unwanted visitors.

Kyd and I looked at each other, forming a silent bond of courage, before I took the plunge and knocked.

After a brief moment, the flimsy wooden door was pulled open by a stocky old woman wearing an apron. She looked from one of us to the other with a wily gaze but didn't say anything.

'Reverend Garnet?' I asked.

'Follow me.'

She led us through a small parlour into a dining room beyond. The room was dark and damp, with a low ceiling that bowed disconcertingly in the middle. At the far end was a heat-less, smoking fire where an impish looking man sat, with a dark, full beard and a completely hairless head. He looked to be in his mid-thirties and reminded me of a painting of the hermit St Jerome that my father had brought back from a venture to Italy. He stood up enquiringly as we entered.

'I am Henry Garnet. How can I help you?'

Neither Kyd nor I said anything, but I quickly stepped forward, indicating the leaflet, which Garnet took from me. He perused it for a moment and then invited us to sit on an ornate wooden bench, which looked as though it had once belonged to a parish church. Kyd and I huddled together like a couple of eager schoolboys, whilst Garnet crouched opposite us, all of the time eyeing us calmly.

'The scourge of plays and players,' he said, reading aloud from the pamphlet. 'Plays are not tolerable nor sufferable in any common weal.' He looked up at us. 'I take it that you two gentleman are connected with the theatre?'

Neither of us said anything. He smiled and indicated a metal bowl suspended over the fire, which, from the smell of it, contained some kind of broth.

'Some sustenance, my sons?'

'Actually, the kind of nourishment we seek is of a more spiritual kind.' I said, spotting an opening and finding my tongue.

'Ah, I see. A man can survive without food or water for many a day, but without spiritual guidance he is as good as dead. Do you not agree?' Aimed directly at Kyd, this statement seemed to flummox him. I noticed that with one hand he was playing nervously with the row of exposed rosary beads. I thought I had better take the initiative.

'We believe you might be in a position to help us undertake the journey we seek to make.'

Henry Garnet turned his level gaze on me, his grey eyes appearing to pierce my pretence. 'And what journey might that be?'

'We wish to join our brothers and learn the true ways.' I was trying to keep my remarks as vague as possible but Garnet's silence suggested he was going to make me spell it out. 'So that we can ourselves spread the word,' I concluded, lamely.

'And what makes you think I can help?'

'A friend who visited you recently. We wish to make contact with him.'

'What is your friend's name?'

'Harry Bucklesbury.' Up to this point, Garnet had given very little understanding that he knew what I was talking about. I desperately hoped that mentioning Buck's name would be the catalyst for a more relaxed conversation. Instead, it seemed to have the opposite effect.

'Bucklesbury? I'm not sure the name is familiar to me. I'm sorry, I don't believe I can help you.' He stood, as if he wanted us to leave.

I gulped down a breath and plunged onwards. 'He visited you with another friend, Greville Mortimer, about a week ago. What they were doing is no concern of ours, we simply want to make contact with them.'

Garnet thought for a moment, eyeing us up and down. Eventually he seemed to accept that we presented no threat. 'That won't be possible, they have gone abroad.' So my fears were confirmed, the pair of them were in this together.

'Where have they gone?'

'To France. Rheims.' He underlined the French town with meaning, which wasn't lost on me. Rheims was the location of the seminary in France where disaffected young Englishmen were trained as priests.

Garnet was still standing. 'Is there anything else I can help you with?'

'Can you get a message to our friends?'

'I would advise against it.'

There seemed nothing for it but to leave. I had discovered pretty much what I had suspected. Buck and Greville were on their way to France to join the English seminary in Rheims, presumably to take instructions as Catholic priests and to return to England at some stage to preach the Old Religion. My only concern was how I could save my friend from becoming a traitor in the eyes of Queen and country, and returning to what I felt sure would be certain execution.

As we reached the door, Garnet drew me to one side and looked down meaningfully at my boots.

'Master Bucklesbury did mention one of his friends. A certain John Lovat, whose boots he had decided to borrow for the long march ahead. Perhaps if you know Master Lovat you will pass on Master Bucklesbury's gratitude. He said it was comforting to undertake his journey in the boots of a dear friend.' With that he closed the rickety door firmly behind us.

Outside the snow had stopped but there was little activity amongst the cottages. A solitary man stood drinking a pipe about three houses down the street. He appeared more interested in the stars than he did in us.

'Get what you came for Lovat?' Kyd stamped his feet in the cold, looking relieved to be out of the cottage.

'Yes. Thanks for bringing me here. At least we know what's happened to Buck.'

'What do you intend to do?'

'Truthfully, I don't know.' Buck and Greville had two day's head start on me and even if I did have time to chase and catch him, what strategy would I employ to stay their course?

We shook hands warmly, arranging to meet the next day after I had returned from Walsingham's. He took off towards Smithfield and I watched his lanky frame for a moment, with a warm feeling of friendship, until he passed out of sight.

The pipe-drinker had disappeared; the run-down street was empty.

* * *

I stumped up the stairs of my lodging to be met at the top by a reception committee. Looking from face to face, it was all I could do, as I recognised the awkwardness between them all, not to stifle a laugh. The only one doing any talking was Lucius, the parrot, who was chirping enquiringly at the assorted bunch. Emmalina, sitting on the bed, knees drawn up to her chest, and Matthew, hunched on Karl Würtembatter's trunk, were both welcome and expected, a third crouching in the doorway, was Pinchkin Junior, no doubt come to collect the Rotherhithe Watch's reward. However, I dealt with the fourth, and most unwelcome first, Nesbitt.

Dressed in his habitual black cloak, he leapt up from the stool as I entered and wasted no time getting to the point. Waiting for me had clearly been an ordeal.

'Progress, Master John? His Lordship wants to know if you have found the black-a-moor yet. He also wants a report on everything else you've been doing for the past three days.'

I knew I had to tell Nesbitt something, to keep my brother off my back. The question was how much? I still couldn't be sure to what extent Robert was involved in Don Alphonse's death. I decided to stick to the Cassangoe angle and say nothing at all of what I had learned about the voyage of the Lady Merrydance.

'Cassangoe has gone to ground and someone has burnt Don Alphonse's warehouse down, making it unlikely that Cassangoe will return there. That only leaves Don Alphonse's house and I've yet to find anyone who knows where that is, other than that it is somewhere in the vicinity of Queenhithe.'

'Is that all?' Nesbitt's tone implied that he knew there was a lot more. 'His Lordship also wants to know precisely what you will be telling Sir Francis, when you visit him on the morrow.' So that was Robert's concern – that I would tell Walsingham something that I wouldn't tell him.

'You can assure Robert that I will tell Walsingham exactly what I have told you.' I didn't add that I would probably tell him a lot more besides. It seemed unlikely that Walsingham himself was a suspect and he was the one person who might be able to make sense of all of the information I had gathered.

Nesbitt nodded in a way that suggested he was far from satisfied but it would have to do. He made to leave but, as he reached the doorway, I remembered the question that I had been meaning to ask him.

'Nesbitt, before you go, does the name Nicholas Ingram mean anything to you?'

'Nicholas Ingram. Yes. At least, I believe he is known to your brother.'

'Of course.' The niggling question that had been in the back of my mind, ever since Hercules Smyth had mentioned the name, suddenly cleared. 'What is his connection with Robert?'

'I believe he was in service to the Earl of Leicester, who died a few weeks ago.'

'I'm aware of that Nesbitt.' The whole country knew that – the Queen had reportedly been in mourning for weeks at the death of her favourite, causing delays to the Armada celebration.

'Ingram, having become masterless, approached your brother looking for a position in the household. I believe your brother has yet to make a decision on the matter.'

Nesbitt stooped mournfully in the doorway for a moment, the very harbinger of doom.

'Don't forget, Master Lovat, like myself, your brother's protection is the one privilege you enjoy in this world. It would be a disaster to lose it.'

'Is that a threat, Nesbitt?'

'*A contrario*, think of it as some well-meant advice. The same can be said for you, Master Jordan.' And, with that parting shot, he was gone.

Evidently relieved to see the back of him, Emmalina jumped off the bed and wrapped her arms around my neck in a welcoming hug.

'That man scares me. There's something unnatural about him.' She then went on to explain how Nesbitt had barged in and immediately taken her for a whore keeping the bed warm for my return. 'Who is he anyway, with his deathly clothes and hunched back?'

'He works for my brother. He's alright really, just takes his job a little too seriously.'

'He was trying to get information out of Matthew, but Matthew's far too wily for him.' The admiration in her voice suggested that the two of them had already struck up a firm friendship.

'Told him I was just rowing you here and there and anythin' to be said was better comin' from you.' Matthew grinned at me, and winked at Emmalina for good measure.

'Don't pay any attention to his threats. My brother won't punish you for my mistakes.'

'What about my brother?' Emmalina said. 'Did you discover anything at the theatre?'

'I did, but let me deal with this young chap first.' I indicated Pinchkin Junior, who had been waiting patiently since my return, looking as frightened and vulnerable as ever. 'Have you come for your reward?'

'Yes Master. Father sent me.' I reached for the bag that the mysterious woman had given me, and extracted a few coins for the Watch. 'Are you hungry, lad? What have we got for him Emmalina?' Ever since entering, I had been aware of a delicious aroma in the air. Coming home to fresh cooking was something I could certainly get used to.

'Scallion soup. There's plenty to go round.' She took a bowl, and while she dished up some soup for the younger Pinchkin, I took the opportunity to speak to Matthew, who had been itching to tell me something ever since I had arrived.

After leaving Lion's Quay, Matthew had taken some rest before returning to the docks to see if he could find any information about the thieves that we had encountered. My hunch was that they would simply have removed Don Alphonse's goods to another warehouse close by and it seemed that Matthew had found information to support this theory. I let him enjoy telling me the story in his deliberate manner.

'Highly Master, it took a good while. I went to all of the *divers* quays round Billingsgate like you asked me to, but at the first two or three no one had anythin' unusual to report. I didn't have any trouble with the warehouse porters. Most of them were happy to talk, once I'd taken them into my confidence, but a few of the night shift men had already gone away to their beds.' Emmalina handed him soup and he paused to raise the bowl to his lips. From his manner, I could tell that he had enjoyed the task and was taking further pleasure in drawing out the tale.

'It weren't until I had the idea of goin' to some of the older docks at Queenhithe that I struck the bull's-eye. Although they're a bit ramshackle, a number of larger houses still store their goods there – it's always been easier for the up-river trade and the Strand.' Matthew paused for another draft of soup. 'Highly Mistress Emma, that's a fine brew, and no mistake.'

'Next to Brooke's Wharf is Abbey Wharf. As all of Queenhithe, there's mainly grain stored there nowadays, but there are one or two privy warehouses. I had a word with the old porter and, would you believe, he had a rum story to relate. The man came on duty at six o'clock in the mornin'. Then, he reckons it were about an half hour later, a boat oared by three men snuck into the dock. He didn't know the men, but one of them had a seal showing he had the authority to visit a warehouse along the wharf. Only unusual thing was that one of the men had a fresh injury to his face and was muttering about a broken cheekbone and missing teeth.' Matthew grinned at me suddenly. 'I reckon you must have dealt him a good blow, Master.'

'Never mind that. Whose warehouse did they take the goods to?' It was hard to keep the edginess out of my voice but I already feared I knew the answer. Matthew saw that I had worked it out.

'Highly Master John, you've got it. No doubts at all – it was one of your brother's warehouses.'

'And my brother's seal.'

'The very same.'

'You're certain? The porter couldn't have got it wrong?'

'Unfortunately not. He's a companionable chap – even helped them unload.'

'Did any of the men make themselves known to him?'

'Yes, he wrote the leader's name down in the register.'

'What was it?'

'Well, that's the best bit. None other than Nicholas Ingram, the very man you were just askin' Nesbitt about.'

'There seems no doubt that they were the same men.'

'Ingram opened one of the bags and made a small gift of its contents. It were tobacco. The porter was nigh grateful for it – he doesn't partake himself but said he could exchange it for some whittles. When he commented on the quality, the men told him that they had just exchanged the tobacco for wool with a Dutch trader who had come in that mornin'. There was a bit of a wink and a nudge about it as if they had been involved in something illicit and after that the porter thought he'd better leave them to it.'

'Interesting that they felt the need to lie to the porter. Nice touch, though, making it sound like an illegal trading deal. A good way of throwing the scent off if anyone starts snooping.' I stared morosely at nothing in particular for a few seconds. I was starting to get a very uneasy feeling about what was going on. Firstly Don Alphonse was strangled with my brother's gift and now the stolen goods had ended up in his warehouse. The clues were all pointing in one definite direction.

Pinchkin Junior had been listening to our conversation. Now that he had finished his soup he piped up with some information of his own.

'A man with a scar came to Cuckold's Point. Livid it was, all down the side of his face.'

'When was this?'

'Day after you came. Three of 'em in total. They was askin' about the man we fished out the drink.'

'I described in as much details as I could the thieves who had come to the warehouse, although leaving Grayson's face in its pristine condition before our encounter. When I finished, Pinchkin Junior nodded emphatically and Matthew also agreed.

'Highly Master, sounds like the same three – first on the river, then at Don Alphonse's warehouse and finally at your brother's.'

'This man Nicholas Ingram and his two henchmen. Dangerous men. We should be on our guard.'

I packed Pinchkin Junior off into the night with an extra reward and Matthew volunteered to walk with him along the south bank until he knew he was on safe ground. Emmalina and I were left alone in the garret, which would have suddenly felt empty if it wasn't for Lucius' constant attempts at conversation.

I took the opportunity to explain to Emmalina everything that Thomas Kyd and I had discovered about Buck, giving her the details of what Kyd and I had learnt from Henry Garnet. She found the whole idea of Buck's recusancy deeply upsetting. When I finished her face was a mixture of heart-broken sorrow, and fear.

'But what if he comes back to preach? He'll be executed as a traitor! Hung, drawn and quartered like an animal.'

'It won't come to that,' I reassured her, speaking with more confidence than I felt.

'Greville's responsible, isn't he?' She suddenly said bitterly, tears starting in her eyes. 'He was always a bad influence. I knew it was dangerous that Buck was so enthralled by him.' I nodded thoughtfully. I had been thinking along the same lines but I knew that Buck was headstrong too.

'Tell me about Greville,' I asked her gently, when she had wiped away the involuntary tears. 'I only met him once – at the Procession.'

'Buck and he were at school together. Greville was always the leader. Buck trailed along in his wake. A few years ago, Greville left London. We hadn't seen him for ages.'

'Did it ever occur to you that Buck might be sympathetic to the Pope's cause?'

'Buck and I grew up as Catholics in Portugal. It was second nature then, but we haven't discussed it for years. We had to adapt to our … new circumstances.'

'He never talked to me about it either. Let's hope it was a sudden decision born out of frustration with his progress at the theatre and the malign influence of an old friend. Hopefully we can persuade him to reconsider when we get the chance.' Despite my efforts at cheering Emmalina, I felt little hope. I had failed to discover the depths of my friend's disillusionment and he hadn't chosen to confide in me. The only thing he had wanted from me was my boots.

To take Emmalina's mind off her brother, I took out the parchment that we had made our notes on concerning the case, and began adding the information I had gathered since then. Emmalina sat at the desk and I sat next to her on Karl Würtembatter's box. Lucius jumped around in his cage, trying to get a better view of what we were doing.

As before, Emmalina wrote the facts and I added some thoughts afterwards:

12. Don Alphonse: HS thinks that DA and Cassangoe were on some kind of revenge mission. There is a man that they called the Red Devil. DA travelled more often, possible as part of the plot. HS also confirmed that Don Alphonse liked upsetting people, the more important the better; his favourite method was by sleeping with their wives. He was also very likely a Jew. ***Where did DA travel to?***

13. Cassangoe feared for his life before he heard of DA's death and was hiding in HS's warehouse when I visited. He has gone to ground – probably in DA's house at a secret location.

14. DA's warehouse was full of goods – tobacco, aniseed, other spices (possibly sumac? – Emmalina's suggestion), *heavy boxes – these were taken from the warehouse by Nicholas Ingram and removed to my brother's warehouse in Queenhithe. Ingram wants to be in my brother's service. Is he doing this work to impress my brother?*

Satisfied with what we had written, and feeling at last that we were getting somewhere, I, somewhat belatedly, remembered to ask Emmalina how she had got on translating the book. I hadn't expected her to get far and was not at all sure that it would be of any use. Emmalina lifted the cover of the bed, to reveal the book itself, and a large handful of parchment.

'I've made a good start with it. It makes fascinating reading, all about an adventure at sea over twenty years ago. I'll carry on with it now.' She smiled at the expression of pleasant surprise on my face, and moved closer to the candlelight on the table.

I was tired and had little enthusiasm for the task but Emmalina's words had intrigued me and besides I didn't want to disappoint her. I shifted to the comfort of the bed, lit another taper, and started to read.

Chapter 18

"A man that studieth revenge keeps his own wounds green, which otherwise would heal and do well."
(Sir Francis Bacon)

The logbook of the Portuguese caravel Santo Francisco, written by her Captain, Don Rodrigo de Sousa, April 1567. May God bless our voyage and bring us safely home again.

October 21st, 1567
After a month of waiting in Lisbon harbour for favourable winds, we are finally able to set sail for the Indian Ocean. The banks of the Tagus river have been our home for six ponderous months and we shall not think of them again until our return in a year from now. Following extensive damage in the Turkish wars, the Santo Francisco has been lying in harbour for repairs. She is now fully seaworthy, her hull careened and her crew refreshed.

In total our fleet is seven strong, boasting four caravels and three naus. Amongst those accompanying the Santo Francisco on its voyage are the ships Chagras, captained by my cousin Pero da Cuhna and the Mossem Gaspard, captained by my old friend and leader of our fleet, Joam Vaz Teixeira. The Chagras is a caravel like the Santo Francisco with a crew of 80 but the Mossem Gaspard is a large nau with a crew of over 150 men and 32 guns on board.

The crew of the Santo Francisco numbers amongst it many men that I have had the privilege of captaining before. There is also one very special personal addition to our fleet. My fifteen year old son Alphonse joins me on a voyage for the first time.

October 27th, 1567
After a week of uneventful sailing, we have docked on the island of Porto Santo, to take on fresh supplies, as well as goods for trading along the route. These new items, which will supplement the textiles, glass beads, brandy and firearms we have brought with us from Portugal, will be essential on our journey to the Governorship of Goa on the Indian Ocean. We will trade them for valuable cargo to bring back to Portugal: spices, such as pepper, ginger, and saffron from Malabar; mace and nutmeg from the Banda

Islands; cloves from the Moluccas, cinnamon from Ceylon; horses from Arabia; and many other precious commodities.

I am proud that we will be sailing in the wake of many of our illustrious countrymen – Bartolomeo Diaz, Pedro Cabral and Vasco da Gama – who have carved their names in history in the last hundred years, forging trading routes around the Orbis Christianus and making Portugal the great nation that it is today. I hope they will look down on us with benevolence in their hearts.

The weather has been good, the winds favourable and as we move southwards the seas have gradually warmed. Our crews are in high spirits. Despite this, I must admit to some apprehension. French corsairs have long threatened the African colonies, and there are even reports that ships carrying English ensigns have for the first time been espied by our trading posts along the coasts.

November 1st 1567
This afternoon I taught Alphonse how to determine latitude using an astrolabe and also how to read the Portolan charts. He is a quick learner and has already plotted our course from Cape Bojador to Arguin Bay, and the Capo Verde islands beyond. I feel sure his future as a seaman is assured. There is a modest library in my quarters and this evening as I write Alphonse is deep in the travels of Jean de Mandeville. He has already read Jordanus's account of Prester John and the chronicles of Marco Polo's journey's to the East. His enthusiasm for adventure knows no bounds.

The ocean remains friendly and we are making good headway.

November 9th, 1567
Canary Islands
We have made port in the Spanish controlled city of Los Palmas on the island of Gran Canaria. Although our ships are welcome with the Spanish authorities there is tension in the port as we find ourselves berthed alongside English ships. The Spanish tolerate the English for trade reasons, although their presence causes much consternation among the islanders. There are even reports of atrocities to Roman churches by the heathens on remote parts of the islands.

The English visit the Canary Islands to trade for Malmsey wine, which the whole nation doth get drunk upon. Their ships are poorly equipped, their captains no sailors and their seamen ill-nourished and downtrodden but they never lose an opportunity to bate our crew or to heap indignities upon us. Yesterday a fight broke out in the harbour and a crew member of the Chagras was badly clubbed. I have forbidden my crew from leaving the ship whilst we lie in port, which serves only to dampen morale and raise feverish passions.

This evening I dined aboard the Mossem Gaspard with all of the ship's captains and officers, and we agreed to weigh anchor sooner than planned in order to leave the contentious English pirates behind.

November 12th, 1567
A minor disaster has struck. At sunset on the afternoon of the 10th, not long after we had made sail from Las Palmas, the winds turned and a violent stormed overcame us. Two of our ships, the Madre Teresa and the Nossa Senhora de Rosario have been blown off course and separated from the remainder of the fleet. This morning, with the seas finally calmed, there was no sign of them on the horizon. In the day and a half that the storm lasted they could have been blown over one hundred miles off course. We attached chains between the Santo Francisco and Chagras and were spared the same fate. I fear, though, we may have many repairs to make to the Santo Francisco as the storm has probed some of the weaknesses already inherent in the ship. Even as I write, my midshipman, Joam Tumao, has reported a new leak in the hold.

November 13th, 1567
There is still no sign of either the NS de Rosario or the Madre Teresa and we have decided to continue onwards in the hope that we will meet them again when we put into shore at the Capo
Verde islands.

November 19th, 1567
Santiago, Capo Verde Islands.
After six further days of sailing, we have made port at Santiago where we are able to make necessary repairs to the ships, whilst stocking up on supplies for the final stretch of water to the African coast. Neither of the two missing ships are in port but we pray they will have time to catch us. We will lie in dock here for at least one week.

A MURDEROUS AFFAIR

November 20th 1567

Today the governor of the islands has given us a tour of the slave prisons. Here are stationed hundreds of miserable souls who have been taken captive along the shores of Africa, before being transported across the Atlantic to the sugar plantations and factories of the new colonies. They appeared very well built, exceedingly black, and all clothed in white cotton shirts; some of them wore small white caps on their heads, very like the German style, except that on each side they had a white ring with a feather in the middle of the cap. It was a piteous sight to behold, for some kept their heads low and their faces bathed in tears. Others lay on the ground groaning very dolorously at the fate that had befallen them. Still more fixed their eyes upon the heavens shouting loudly to some unseen God, while the remainder struck their faces with the palms of their hands, throwing themselves at full length upon the ground. Alphonse was particularly moved by their plight.

The governor had an ulterior motive for this expedition to the slave camps. This valuable cargo is increasingly threatened. He explained to us the recent problems he has been experiencing with English pirates. All along the coast of Africa our slave ships are attacked and their cargoes plundered. At other times, they lie in wait on the shipping paths a few miles off the Capo Verde islands, laying traps for the Portuguese caravels. Once they have stolen the slaves, they sail across the Atlantic and sell them to the colonists, who, although expressly forbidden to trade with the heathen English, are sometimes forced to do so at the end of the canon and harquebus. The governor has appealed to us to help stop these pirates by finding and attacking their ships along the coast.

November 24th, 1567

Today we rejoiced as the two missing ships finally joined us at Santiago. Both were blown into harbour on the island of Tenerife and have experienced little damage. The Santo Francisco is also less damaged than was first feared and has been patched up well.

A decision has been taken. We will delay our planned voyage to the East Indies to root out pirates along the African coast and protect our valuable property. We leave the Capo Verde islands tomorrow.

November 29th, 1567

As soon as we came in sight of the African shores, we wasted no time in engaging the pirates and have spent the last two days pursuing ships along the Guinean coast. Only two hours after we had sighted land, we encountered three French corsairs and immediately gave pursuit. We caught one ship, dispersing the other two into the open seas. After a brief skirmish, control was taken of the ship and we discovered ivory, wax and many other goods all stolen from Portuguese traders. There were no slaves on board, however. The ship has been transferred into my command and I have put a fledgling crew aboard.

We have shown no quarter to the French pirates who have all been hung as a warning to others.

December 3rd, 1567
Bezeguiche Fort, Guinea
We arrived this afternoon at the Portuguese feitoria on the island of Bezeguiche nestled into the bay of the Green Cape. The feitoria is the northern holding post for slaves to be taken to Capo Verde and is heavily fortified. We were welcomed by the governor, Jorge da Verlascus, who is relieved that we have come to support efforts to rid the coastline of pirates. He says that the pirates would never dare attack Bezeguiche as it is too well fortified but that reports have come in of an English fleet, seven ships strong, which has been harassing our crews and stealing goods further south along the Guinean coast. There is also disturbing news that the feitoria of Cacheu on the Santo Domingo river, less well fortified than Bezeguiche, has been razed to the ground by the English.

December 8th, 1567
We have continued our journey south along the African coast and arrived at the peninsula of Serra de Leão. The flat coastline and mangrove swamps, which we have followed for the last hundred miles, have vanished, to be replaced by peaked mountains, cut with many estuaries and sandy beaches.

Our fleet is now nine strong, having been joined by the Portuguese man-of-war, Christavaldes, which was lying in harbour in Bezeguiche. The Christavaldes is captained by Blasius d'Aragon, a proud and foolhardy captain, who I have known since the Mediterranean wars. He regards the English as no threat.

Pilot ships that were dispatched up the Santo Domingo river have returned to report great destruction at Cacheu, although there are many stories of heroism and bravery on the part of the Portuguese colonists. The English pirates have moved on and there is no sign of them.

December 10th, 1567
We know that the enemy we seek is near. Yesterday we encountered a French trading ship that had been attacked by the English fleet and was severely damaged. The ship was limping on the ocean and taking on water. Many of its crew had been killed in the fighting and its cargo stolen. We were told many tales of savagery on account of the English sailors. We will weigh anchor at Cape Tagrin and send pilot ships up the Mitomba river, where many of our slave barracoons are in operation, to reconnoitre the situation and report back to us.

December 11th, 1567
We remain anchored in the mouth of the Mitomba river awaiting news from upstream. The heat is quite unlike any I have experienced, even in the height of the Mediterranean summer. Most of the time it sits oppressively upon us, with no relief from the breeze. Strong men that I have known deal with great hardships become listless and tired, and disease is ever present.

There are many great beasts along the riverbanks and in the water itself. A small pilot ship exploring the interior of a river estuary was attacked by a river horse. It did much damage and the twenty men aboard were pleased to escape with their lives.

December 12th, 1567
This morning I was awoken early to be informed that ten ships have entered the river mouth. They sit about half a mile from us across the wide bay. Confirmation that they were the English ships, that have been causing great destruction upon the colonies, was immediate. No sooner had they arrived than a small pinnace, flying flags of peace, came towards our ships and a delegation of men came aboard. They said that they want no fight with us but only wish to trade. I and the other captains have been invited to dine on their flagship this evening with their captain. To show their goodwill the men brought us yards of Rouen cloth and other gifts from their stores. We agreed that we would go aboard their ship and have only lately returned.

The English flagship is called the Jesus of Lübeck and is a mighty warship. It was agreed that Blasius d'Aragon, Pero da Cuhna, Alphonse and myself would dine with the English. I was reluctant to include d'Aragon in the party, knowing his manner to be rude and confrontational, but was overruled by Pero who gives far too much respect to his position as captain of a man-of-war. The English were nothing like we have been led to expect. They welcomed us aboard with great ceremony and treated us to a feast the likes of which we have only dreamt of for the last month. They were also pleased to give us further gifts of cloth, food and other victuals. Despite these gifts, we were at pains to impress upon the English that they are forbidden to trade on our lands and that our ships are there with express orders to prevent them.

At the centre of all negotiation is their captain, a stout man of thirty with ruddy cheeks, sharp black eyes and the reddest hair I have ever seen upon a man, from the hair on the top of his head to the whiskers on his chin. Alphonse immediately christened him Diabo Vermehlo, the red devil. His God-given name is Christopher Hardwick.

Sir Christopher Hardwick, Diabo Vermehlo. A frisson of excitement coursed my spine. Suddenly here it was, in Emmalina's neat, girlish handwriting – a clue as solid as the candlestick holder on my table. Hardwick's name was familiar to me, as it was to anyone in the realm. He was a war hero and erstwhile favourite of Elizabeth, and many tales were told of his heroism on the high seas. In recent years, his star had waned somewhat but he was still held in high regard by many in the land.

And in a remote river bay of the swamp infested shores of Africa, some twenty years ago, he had come face to face with none other than Don Rodrigo de Sousa and his fifteen year old son Alphonse.

It was also the same Christopher Hardwick whose son had commissioned Buck to write an impresa – the one that I had found him struggling over on the morning of the Queen's procession. The presentation to the Queen would have taken place the next day and I had no doubt that the father would have been there to enjoy his son's moment of glory. I nudged Emmalina gently, who had taken my place on the bed some time earlier and was dozing peacefully.

'The commission that Buck had for the impresa – was it collected do you know? The name was Hardwick.'

The sleepy confusion in her face gradually cleared. 'Yes. A servant collected it not long after you had left for the procession. There was a Hardwick mentioned in the document, wasn't there? Are they related?

'Father and son.'

'Interesting.' The word petered out as she fell asleep again, her long hair, darker in the candlelight, flowing wildly across her face. It was tempting to stroke it away gently from her cheek.

Instead, I reached for my father's eyeglass, pointing it at the heavens through a small gap in the window. The night sky was clear and a rich dark blue in colour, the moon as flat and round as a silver coin. I idly studied the mysterious shadows on its surface, my mind full of sailing ships, exotic shores and rich treasures. I had only been to sea twice in my life, a short trip to the Low Countries and back, and remembered being terrified the ship would sink on both occasions. The thought of sailing halfway around the globe in one of those leaky, disease-ridden tubs was not an appealing one.

Both my candle and the fire had burnt low. I busied myself stoking the grate and throwing an extra rug over Emmalina, before lighting a new taper and continuing to read. The next two entries in the log described an awkward stand-off that took place between the English and Portuguese ships over the following days, and then the start of a battle. I stifled a yawn and wondered if I should call it a night. It was the following entry that made me sit up sharply. There was no date:

This is the ship's log of the Portuguese caravel Santo Francisco, captained by Don Roderigo de Sousa. Just writing those words I feel my hand tremble and bitter tears start in my eyes, for the Santo Francisco is no longer a Portuguese ship and her captain no longer alive – murdered most cruelly by vicious English pirates.

Where shall I begin my tale? What chance is there that anyone will ever read it? Nevertheless, I shall write it, in order that I may record the indignities and privations I have suffered. Perhaps I should start by describing the situation that I find myself in as a result of my misfortune. I write this from the damp and heat of an African prison, where I am incarcerated with other slaves and treated as a curiosity by my capturers. Occasionally, I am pulled out by my gaoler to be shown off as an exotic item but most of the time I am left to rot with my fellow prisoners. There are six of them in all, who ignore and avoid me to a man as though my presence here is an unlucky talisman. It matters not – we cannot communicate with each other in any case and there is no comfort they could bring me.

JONATHAN DIGBY

The only comfort I have is this book, which I have kept hidden about my person for two whole months. For all that time I have lived in fear of having my clothes torn from me and being left as naked as the other prisoners, the book and pencil discovered. I feel it is a miracle that I have managed to hide them, the only things I have left of my father's, from the different gaolers that I have passed between, and now, having removed them from their hiding place for the first time, I am fearful that my present captors will discover me writing or one of the others in my prison will sound the alarm in an effort to buy their freedom. Fortunately, the midday sun makes everyone lethargic and sleepy; each lies in a state of torpor, oblivious to the insects that feed upon their naked torsos.

So where to begin? My misfortune began when we came upon English ships at the mouth of a large river on the coast of Guinea. To that point I can never remember a time of greater happiness, saving when my mother was alive. I had spent two delightful months at the helm of my father's ship – it was the longest time I had ever spent in his company and we were to sail together to India and the port of Goa, and to see many wonders, discover many exotic places and peoples.

At first the English talked only of peaceful trade. We were equal with them in arms and men and there was nothing to be gained from a battle – besides we had nothing aboard that interested them. It was human cargo that they were after. The trouble started when barracoons carrying hundreds of slaves appeared from upriver. Despite the protection we afforded them, the English knew this was far too good an opportunity to pass up. We awoke the next morning to the sound of cannon fire and the sight of the English ships bearing down on us. A fearful battle ensued which continued into the afternoon and the following night, although no darkness descended as the bright fire of burning ships illuminated the whole bay. By morning, we had sunk one English vessel and another was taking in water. For their part the English had taken one of our ships but it looked as though their gamble would be in vain.

It was just at the moment when success seemed assured, that the tide turned in their favour. The English ships had made to withdraw, as though they realised they could not win and would settle for the spoils of one ship, when one of ours broke ranks to pursue them – the captain a rash, witless fool called Blasius d'Aragon. His ship, which had more firepower than all of the others but was clumsy in comparison to the more nimble ships of our enemy, was quickly surrounded and boarded and its guns turned on us. We fought bravely to a man deep into the next night but it was all in vain. Our ship was the last to be boarded by the Englishmen wielding clubs and halberds. They spared few – many were pitched directly overboard, others beaten so hard all sense was lost to them, the officers imprisoned and humiliated.

I struggle to recall what happened next – not from any loss of memory but from the pain that these images cause my troubled soul. My father and I had been taken separately and I was incarcerated below decks with the men of the ship – because of my youth the English had taken me for a cabin boy. My father had been made prisoner in his own quarters and I was denied any access to him. I had been entrusted the log only the day before, otherwise the means I have now of recording this, my one comfort, would have been denied me. After two days in captivity, we were taken on deck to learn of our fate and the fate of our captain. We all believed to a man that we would be set free, that the English would be satisfied with their loot and leave us to make our own way home, that their blood lust had been assuaged now that the heat of battle had died down. But we reckoned without the cruelty of our chief captor.

When we came on deck we found all of the surviving captains together – Joam Vaz Teixeira, my father and that scoundrel Blasius d'Aragon. My kinsman Pero da Cuhna, amongst others, had been killed in the fray. The captains had been tortured using ropes – the English trying to discover where other riches could be found – and were in a pitiful state, the ropes now loosely held around their necks. I felt compelled to appeal to my father but he was ready for this and stopped me with a look. A look which spoke of anger and despair. A look I shall never forget. He must have guessed already what was about to happen. The Englishman with the red hair, the one who will always be the devil to me, made a speech. It contained much ill feeling towards the Roman church and the greed of the Portuguese. He said how their intentions had been only to trade peacefully but we had forced them into an act of war with our intransigence. He then began to rant against the Jewish faith and it was at that point that my blood froze because there, exposed on my father's naked chest, was the Star of David necklace that he always wore hidden beneath his shirt. The voice of the Englishman was replaced by blood thumping in my ears – I only caught snatches – but watched in horror as … as … oh my heart breaks to write this … they were all hung, not just my father.

The prison I am in is about ten feet square and built of wooden posts hammered deep into the ground. There is no roof – only unforgiving sun moving slowly across the gap between the sharpened stakes. The posts afford a gap of a few inches through which I can see glimpses of the town my captors inhabit. I find myself staring at it trying to piece together the broken images – I have time enough. The town's streets are laid out neatly and the low wooden houses are spaced comfortably apart. It is a marked contrast to the rat-infested, open sewer that constitutes modern Lisbon and quite different to how the savages of my imagination lived. But there is no doubt they are savages – I have witnessed great cruelty amongst the people and even, after great battles, have I witnessed the victors eat their vanquished foes, as though the victory is not complete until they totally possess their victims. But are they any more savage than the men I have left behind? The men who abandoned me to my fate.

Following the execution (I don't know what else to call it) of my father, the rest of the crew that remained were pitched unceremoniously overboard. Those of us that could swim did what we could to help the others but at least two men drowned before we could reach the riverbank. Another was taken by a crocodile – one that had failed to gorge on the numerous dead bodies floating around the river mouth.

As our sodden troupe regrouped amongst the mangrove trees, I became quickly aware of a growing animosity towards me. No doubt many of the men were shocked to learn that my father and I were Jewish and without him there, I was to become the sole focus of their anger. I was blamed for all of the woes that had befallen us. Former comrades, who only a day earlier had fought alongside me, set upon me. I was badly beaten and left to die in the jungle. I surely would have perished had it not been for a group of natives who carried me away with them. They must have been watching from the safety of the jungle as I was attacked, and had waited for my tormentors to leave me, before coming forward to investigate. I was tied to a wooden pole and carried through the jungle like a swine on a spit.

We walked for many days. I grew ill with fever and, with no relief from my captors, many moments on the journey I thought were my last and my final sensation would be the view of the jungle towering over me and the strange sounds and laughter of the natives who held me. On two occasions, I was sold to other tribes before finally being brought to the town where I am now held captive. Some bargain was struck for me and I was unceremoniously dumped in the enclosure from where I now write.

I have a new gaol companion – a tall, young African who is about the same age as me. Late last night, the rough door to my prison was wrenched open and the terrified boy was thrown in beside me. For the first night we eyed each other suspiciously from the opposite corners of the cell. Neither of us daring to speak. But this morning a miracle happened – the boy opened his mouth and spoke to me in Portuguese.

* * *

The boy's name is Cassangoe and we have been speaking. He tells me that he comes from an African Kingdom, which is many days from here, situated on the West bank of a river which the Portuguese call Niger. Now that he has found his tongue he talks incessantly, all-be-it in a low rumbling whisper. He tells me he is a prince in his country, which is called Nri, and that he is a missionary, the word he used was mbùríchi, whose role it is to spread the word of the Kingdom. His people are called the Igbo. He tells me it is a very great kingdom where nobody is poor and all slaves are freed. He learnt his Portuguese along the coast when trying to convert other tribes, who trade slaves with us, to the philosophy of the Nri people. When I told him that I too was the son of a nobleman he fixed me with a deep stare before grasping my shoulders and hugging me to him. 'We are noble brothers, Alphonse. The great God Chineke has brought us together and together we will find Anyanwu, the Light'. His words were a great comfort to me.

For the first time in months my spirit has lifted and I no longer yearn for death.

Chapter 19

'There is less danger in fearing too much than too little.'
(Sir Francis Walsingham)

The following morning I hired a horse from a tavern in Southwark and rode to Walsingham's country house west of the city. It was a long way to expect Matthew to row, which probably meant I would end up doing a lot of the work with him, and besides, after his success at uncovering the events at Abbey Wharf, he had recovered some enthusiasm for the task of finding the boatman, whose continuing elusiveness was leaving a big hole in our investigation.

Before leaving the city, I paid another visit to Davy Bennett at Gresham's Exchange, hoping he could give me some information on certain people whose names had recently come up. I found him in discussion with another trader complaining about inflation – a common gripe in the city – but we were soon left alone, and over a mug of hot perry, our native Gloucestershire brew, I was able to put my questions to him.

'Nicholas Ingram, now there's a name I haven't heard in a while,' he said, after I had made my first prompting. 'A nasty piece of work. I had some trade with the Earl of Leicester's estate a couple of years ago. Ingram was in his service then. He was a fixer for Leicester – knows his way in and out of the law – but I also heard that he had a reputation for being a loan shark. The type who lends money with nasty sub-clauses. When the unsuspecting dupe comes to pay the money back, Ingram is nowhere to be found so the poor buggers end up forfeiting the deal and having to pay back three times as much. That's one way these people operate anyway – there are lots of other scams on the go. Never borrow money if you can help it, Lovat my lad, it'll come back to haunt you.' Bennett was barely a month older than me, but he always managed to make me feel like his baby brother.

'Was Ingram in service to Leicester up to his death?'

'As far as I know, but a man like Ingram would be looking for a new patron pretty quickly. He wouldn't want the grass to grow under his feet.'

'That would explain why he recently approached my brother.'

'Possibly but …', Davy looked doubtful, 'no disrespect, Lovat, but from

Leicester to your brother is a bit of a step down the ladder. I would expect him to try and ingratiate himself with the Cecils or Hatton. Much more in his league, and, what's more, should be easy for someone who's had access to Leicester's secrets.' I nodded thoughtfully. There was certainly something in that, but, if true, then what was Ingram up to?

Next, I turned the conversation to Sir Christopher Hardwick. There, Davey Bennett could only offer me confirmation of what I'd already heard. He did help me make one very important connection though, something that I knew would stand me in good stead when I reported to Walsingham.

* * *

The Half Moon Inn, a short walk from the bridge, marked the border between town and country and was somewhere that I often slipped off to for a quiet jar when time allowed. The landlord was a ruddy faced giant called Peblow, who knew me well. He offered me a friendly welcome, a warm fire and a meal of honey-coated pancakes followed by pippin, with a dish of carroways and leather oats, while the young ostler brought my horse for the day. My mount was a spritely grey gelding called George who seemed delighted, despite the cold, to be spending a day in the countryside.

A hazy sun was slowly reaching the top of its arc, as I kicked George into a trot along Stane Street, which legend claimed was as ancient as the Romans that once inhabited the land. The weather had temporarily cleared and there was a wintery crispness in the air. Stretched out beyond the hedgerows on either side of the track were wetlands and fields covered in a veneer of white, powdery snow. As I rode, I passed fowlers carrying bundles of game birds for city taverns, pleachers laying hedges for the Spring and barrel-laden carts bringing goods from the South. There were also a range of itinerants and masterless men, reminding me to keep watchful. I kept my satchel tied closely to my waist and kicked George into a canter to avoid becoming easy prey. At times, though, the countryside became quite devoid of people, and my only company was the wildlife darting in and out of the hedgerows.

Walsingham's country house, Barn Elms, was on a broad, sweeping stretch of the Surrey bank, not far north of the village of Putney. At around noon, George and I trotted through a grand set of gates from which a low, ramshackle manor was clearly visible in the distance.

I had expected the ailing Walsingham to be tucked up in front of a fire with a rug over knees, sipping on his green medicine and avoiding the cold like the London plague. So I was surprised to be informed, whilst dismounting, that Walsingham was hawking and expecting me in the garden beyond the house.

I skirted around the wing to see a wide stretch of lawn running down to a row of thick hawthorn scrub set against the backdrop of a calm Thames. I found Walsingham, a thick Russian fur about his shoulders, with a group of servants and several large birds of prey. As I crossed the grass towards them, a man, whom Walsingham had been talking to, broke away from him and walked in my direction. As we met, he pulled a pipe out of his coat pocket and raised it to his lips. His eyes caught mine and a surreptitious smile played across his face. I had the distinct impression I had seen him somewhere before, quite recently, although I couldn't immediately call to mind where.

'Stand perfectly still, Master Lovat.' Walsingham was holding his left arm out with a leather glove strapped onto it. I stood still as ordered and felt the wind as a magnificent blur of white and brown flashed past my head, the tip of a wing clipping my ear, and swooped onto Walsingham's outstretched arm. It was a peregrine falcon, which came to rest and dropped its prey, a small mammal of some kind, into Walsingham's other palm. As I bowed low and greeted Walsingham with words 'at your service, sire', the thought that crossed my mind was whether or not the falcon had just deposited my lunch.

'You have experience of falconry, Master Lovat.' It was more of statement than a question and left me wondering as before how much Walsingham really knew about me. Hawking had been a large part of my childhood, like any boy growing up on a country estate. 'A fine specimen, don't you think?'

Walsingham attached one of its legs to the jesses and invited me to admire the bird at close quarters. I made some suitably complementary noises about its weight and plumage, whilst Walsingham nodded indulgently.

'A most noble creature. The fastest of all my birds and an audacious hunter. This winter alone she has caught over a hundred creatures, nearly all of which have graced our table.' He gently stroked the breast of the bird, showing an unexpected affection. 'A most solitary creature – she hunts alone. Only this week I have heard of a species of hawk in America that hunts in packs – like the Catholic wolves surrounding this isle.' Walsingham fixed his gaze upon me and, as before in my brother's hall, I could sense a great intelligence behind those dark eyes. He indicated the bird on his arm. 'Care to show me your skill, Master Lovat?'

He signalled to a servant who stepped forward. Attached to his midriff was a bar supporting three more birds of prey. The servant handed me a glove and Walsingham invited me to take my pick. I chose a small, brown sparrowhawk, which had always been my favourite hunting bird when hawking with my father. I gently released the bird's jesses and removed its hood. Fierce eyes immediately began taking in their surroundings – a sense of impending action palpable. The powerful bird seemed remarkably relaxed on the arm of a stranger but nevertheless I took great care, knowing how dangerous these creatures could be when startled. In a slow, but deliberate, movement, I stretched out my arm and the bird took flight – immediately finding a vantage point in a tall elm tree standing by the side of the house. Surveying the scene below from this elevated position, the sparrowhawk soon launched itself again and began circling high over the surrounding fields along the river.

Walsingham seemed delighted to be in the presence of a fellow enthusiast and we began swapping hawking stories. Over half an hour passed before he signalled an end to proceedings and asked me to accompany him to the riverbank, where he invited me to divulge all of the information I had gathered in the last few days. I fished the notes that Emmalina and I had made out of my tunic and which I intended to use as a guide. Whilst I spoke, Walsingham leant on his walking stick, his head slightly inclined towards me, his breathing barely perceptible. I had the sense that he wasn't so much listening as absorbing my words through his very skin.

I picked those words carefully. I told him about my failure to find Cassangoe, the events at Lion's Quay and my interviews with Turney and Hercules Smyth. I also told him that I could identify Nicholas Ingram as the man who had stolen the goods from Don Alphonse's warehouse. I omitted to tell him, however, that the stolen goods had ended up in Robert's wharf. Finally, I revealed what I considered to be my trump card – the discovery of the ship's log and the link it gave between Don Alphonse and Sir Christopher Hardwick.

After I had finished, Walsingham paused for a moment before asking.

'Sir Christopher Hardwick you say was responsible for Don Alphonse's father's death?'

'Indeed, sire.'

'You are absolutely certain on this point?'

'It is plainly written in the ship's log. Could he be the high level traitor that Don Alphonse referred to you when he visited you before?'

'Perhaps. We shall see.' With that, he turned suddenly on his heel and walked with surprising sprightliness towards the house, calling over his shoulder: 'Come Master Lovat, let's get out of this incessant cold.'

Taken by surprise, I jogged to catch him up and we entered the house.

* * *

Dinner was a relatively modest affair, with Walsingham sitting at the head of a table that included family, staff and servants. The meal consisted of a mixture of wild game, home cooked bread and meats, and small beer, Walsingham forbidding any wines or spirits to be drunk under his roof during the hours of daylight. Despite its modest nature, though, everything was exquisitely prepared and cooked. Next to Walsingham sat his wife Ursula. She wore a long black dress, with a gold trim, square black cap, and a fine cambric ruff, and presented an admirable, if rather austere version, of the good Protestant wife. She had, however, a kindly face and manner, and Walsingham appeared to dote on her.

I was placed at the opposite end of the table next to one of Walsingham's secretaries, a man named Nicholas Faunt, who spent the entire meal interrogating me good-naturedly on every aspect of my life. How was life in my brother's service, what religion did the family follow, what was my landlord Charles like and did the bridge present suitable lodgings for a citizen of the town and so on and so forth? At first, I tried to deflect his questions, but he asked them in such a charming manner and not wishing to seem rude, I soon found myself talking about the old grievances with being my brother's dogsbody, and how my place in his household was somewhat lower than that of any of the useful animals in his service.

Dinner complete, Walsingham asked me to follow him to a small, wood-panelled chamber at the back of the house, with a fireplace set-off by rows and rows of books. We were joined by Faunt, who shut the door firmly behind him before taking a seat. Although the atmosphere had turned more business-like since lunch, I was still taken aback by Walsingham's opening question.

'Tell me about your father's religious persuasion.'

'My father?' I was immediately on my guard.

'Yes, not in his early years, before you were born, I know all about that. No, later in life when you lived with him in Gloucestershire, what were his leanings at that time?'

'I'm sorry, your lordship, but I'm not at all sure what you are getting at.' Walsingham sighed, in the manner of a schoolteacher disappointed with his student's ineptitude on a particularly easy subject.

'Well then, let me explain. When the Catholic Queen Mary came to the throne in 1553, a decade before you were born, many of her subjects, who were persuaded that our country's future lay not with the old religion, went to live abroad – myself among them. Your father did not, choosing instead to take up a high-ranking position in her government. Whilst I was continuing my studies in Padua and travelling in Switzerland, your father was a member of a council that presided over the deaths of many of those that shared my religious beliefs. Naturally, that didn't make him too popular on the death of Queen Mary and despite his converting to the Protestant faith on the ascension of Queen Elizabeth, as I believe he had done before at the time of her father Henry, his position in government was untenable. An intelligent man, he quickly realised it was in everyone's best interests if he retired to his Gloucestershire estate to concentrate on farm rents, and farm maidens, if you will forgive me for saying so.'

I felt my face burn fiercely at this last remark, but said nothing.

'Ah come, Master Lovat, just my little joke, the circumstances of your birth are not the subject at issue here. What I am interested in is whether or not your father, who, let it be said, changed his religion as often as his shirts, was persuaded in one particular direction and merely wore the clothes of the other, if you will allow me to continue the metaphor, for convenience sake.'

I looked steadily at Walsingham and thought how best to answer him, whilst weighing up what he had said. The black stain on my father's character had been an open secret but never discussed. It did explain, though, why my brother was so vehemently and outwardly Protestant, and surrounded himself with men like Nesbitt. To some extent, it was to curry favour with the Queen and grease the wheels of his political career, but banishing the memories of a disgraced father was also a contributing factor.

The truth was that neither of us had been brought up as true Protestants. My father had been a very superstitious man and whilst he had recognised the way the world was moving under the reign of Elizabeth, and had ensured that our tutors had educated us accordingly, he had always been reluctant to part with the rituals and comforts of the old religion. The fact that he had professed a change of allegiance to suit his political career did not necessarily surprise me – my father had always been expedient in these matters – but I believed that, while outwardly he made little practise towards it, his soul had always been with the Roman Church. How much of a subversive that made him I wasn't sure but I decided to preserve his memory and shield the facts from Walsingham, who after all, was being far too free with insinuations about my parentage.

'My father is not here to answer for himself but during my time with him I certainly witnessed him observing the rites of the Church of England. If he did change his allegiance at times in the past then it seems, from what you are saying, that he only did so in order that he might better serve his country.'

'Or himself.' A trace of anger marked Walsingham's words, but it quickly subsided. 'No matter, let us move on. The question, Master Lovat, is where your father's, shall we say, fickle relationship with religion has left you and your brother? Is there to be any doubt about your allegiance to the Church of England?'

'I'm surprised that you question my brother's commitment to the Protestant Church. Surely there can be no question where that is concerned?'

Walsingham gave me the full gaze of his black eyes: 'So there *can* be a question in your case then, Master Lovat?'

Chapter 20

'The public weal requires that men should betray, and lie, and massacre.'
(Michel de Montaigne)

Despite the well-stocked log fire, a sudden chill descended on the room. The air became completely still and I became aware of flecks of dust caught by the low winter sun piercing through the diamond shaped patterns of the window.

Too late I realised the trap that had been sprung. Not only that, I was on very shaky ground. To be a Catholic was one thing but there were still plenty of them about and they were largely tolerated as long as they put patriotism before faith. To believe in nothing, on the other hand, as was increasingly becoming my tendency, was another thing altogether. Atheists were the enemies of everyone and nothing was as likely to bring Catholics and Protestants together as the opportunity of roasting a non-believer over the proverbial fires of hell.

What was more, I hadn't been to church lately to give myself cover. Attending church at least once a month was compulsory across the country, and the little church of St Magnus the Martyr at the end of the bridge was where I was expected to be of a Sunday morning along with the rest of the Bridge Within Ward. But in the last few weeks I had found one excuse after another for not attending and hadn't missed the experience in the least. With these thoughts flashing through my mind, I was about to start defending myself when Walsingham gave me a get out route – of a fashion.

'Faunt, please read to Master Lovat the intelligence that was divulged to us earlier, concerning his visit to a certain cottage hard by Finsbury Fields.' I felt a sudden sinking in my stomach as Faunt pulled open a thin notebook, found a page and started to read.

'Two evenings ago, close to the hour of ten, Master Lovat was seen leaving the house of the recusant priest known in familiar circles as the 'Reverend' Henry Garnet, a recruiter of Catholic sympathisers for the seminary in Rheims. Lovat was in the company of one Thomas Kyd, poet and playwright. The two parted company on exiting the house and our informer, recognising the poet but not the other gentleman, decided to follow Master Lovat, unobserved, to his lodgings on London Bridge, where he was able to ascertain Master Lovat's name from a neighbour.'

During this rather pedantic, though disconcertingly accurate statement, it had gradually dawned on me where I had seen the man with the pipe and arrogant sneer, who I had passed on arriving at the house. He was the same man who had been standing nonchalantly in the road outside Garnet's house as Kyd and I were leaving. Had he been following me in the first place, though, or was it purely coincidence that he had been watching the house that we visited on Walsingham's orders? Walsingham set me straight on this point immediately.

'Garnet's safe house for priests has been known to us for some time and is being watched. It is by fortune alone that your presence at the house was brought to my notice this morning. The only question is: what were you doing there? Given your background, your father's attitude to religion and your own base birth, there is every reason that one might suppose you to be a disillusioned young man who seeks solace in rebelling against the true faith and laws of his country. Or was there some other purpose to your visit?'

'Some other purpose.' I said, with a mixture of meekness and stubbornness.

'Well then let's have it.'

'It was an adventure.' Here we go, I thought, do or die time.

'An adventure?'

'Suggested by Mr Kyd but instigated by myself.'

'And what was the purpose of this … adventure.'

'Research, sir, for Mr Kyd's new play.' It was a barefaced lie, of course, but the last thing I wanted to do was put Walsingham and his 'informers' on to Buck and Greville. It was bad enough that I had been seen.

Walsingham's black eyes bore into me silently and I felt a need to embellish my explanation. 'I have recently embarked upon a career in the theatre – to supplement the income my brother affords me. I made the acquaintance of Mr Kyd and during discussions about his new play, we decided to go to Mr Garnet's house to gather information.'

'And what is the subject of Mr Kyd's new play?' I secretly thanked Kyd under my breath, as I recounted what he had told me of his play.

'It is about the war between the Christians and the Turks in Rhodes.

The 'Reverend' was said to be an expert on such matters.'

'A most suitable theme for our theatres. Did your visit prove fruitful for the poet?' Walsingham was struggling to hide the scepticism in his voice.

'Not really. Henry Garnet was not forthcoming on such matters. We only spent a matter of minutes with him.'

Walsingham glanced at Faunt as if for validation of this statement and received a short nod in return. I was grateful that we hadn't lingered at the cottage. 'Whatever your reasons for visiting Garnet, I am sure that I hardly need to stress the seriousness of your position. Consorting with known Catholic troublemakers is an offence punishable by the most extreme measures.' I felt beads of sweat break out on my brow. Was this to be the shortest-lived career in the service of Elizabeth's spymaster? My heart felt heavy, as if it was being weighed down by Foxe's Book of Martyrs. 'For the time being, I will accept the view that you are not a Catholic sympathiser or recusant but I want you to be sure exactly how I view the Catholic threat.' Walsingham sat back in his chair and fixed me with his black eyes.

'Sixteen years ago, when you were only a small boy running around carefree on your father's estate, I was the English ambassador to Paris. One August at Midnight, a bell rang out across the city signalling the start of bloody genocide. For seven consecutive days I was barricaded into the embassy house, along with my wife and four year old daughter, as well as other English men and women seeking refuge, while organised bloodshed and mayhem continued unabated outside. Some who were unable to reach the embassy in time were not so lucky – at least three Englishmen were killed on that first night alone, alongside thousands of Huguenots.

'A baying mob spent the week outside the house calling for our blood. When, after a week of confinement, I was able to emerge under armed protection I could see for myself the congealing blood on the streets and smell the fires of burning bodies across the city, all the while being continually abused and insulted by Catholic gangs, not yet satiated in their desire for Protestant blood. That experience has haunted me ever since and has taught me one very valuable lesson, Master Lovat, that I want you to remember well – that we can never trust any member of that bloody and treacherous religion. In the future, I will be taking a keen interest in the behaviour of yourself and Mr Kyd, and the company you keep. Now to this other business.'

The matter seemed closed and I breathed a huge sigh of relief, although Walsingham's words had had the desired effect on me. I knew that I was going to have to be very careful in the future.

'When Don Alphonse wrote to me earlier this year, he talked of a traitor at the highest level of our government – someone who had access to the Queen herself. There are only two men mentioned in this affair who could vaguely fit that description. One is Sir Christopher Hardwick and the other, as you no doubt realise, is your brother, Sir Robert Rokesby. Faunt here has been undertaking some investigations along those lines. Perhaps you would lay before us the case as you see it?'

'Certainly your Lordship.' Faunt once again referred to his notebook, a habit that could easily get on my nerves. 'On the face of it, the case against Rokesby would appear difficult to make. He has been a member of her Majesty's privy council for nigh on two years. In that time, he has proved to be an able minister and has offered most valuable advice and support to her Majesty, particularly during the time of our most recent crisis. Your Lordship already alluded to the black marks against Rokesby's father, but these seem not to have hindered Lord Robert's career in any way, no doubt in large part to his staunch support of the Church of England. If he is involved in some plot then it has been most carefully concealed.'

Faunt paused for breath and Walsingham took over the narrative. He cleared his throat with a short barking cough and then proceeded.

'Your brother's implication in the death of de Sousa, on the other hand, is much easier to surmise. According to what you have told us, Lovat, De Sousa was known to have dined with your brother, Rokesby, and certain other gentlemen on the night of the murder. There were reports of a disagreement in the garden just before Don Alphonse was seen leaving in the company of two members of Rokesby's household, the poet Marmaduke Drummond and the adventurer Simon Turney, as well as a fourth man, who you surmise may have been Nicholas Ingram, formerly in the service of the Earl of Leicester, and whom it is believed is hoping for a place in your brother's household. It would seem mostly likely, therefore, that the man disagreeing with Don Alphonse was your brother himself, as hinted at by Turney, and that the subject of the dispute was your sister-in-law, Anne. Correct so far?'

'The only fact I would dispute is the argument. There is no proof that it was my brother arguing with Don Alphonse. Turney could have insinuated this to put me off the scent.'

'Perhaps, but let me continue. At this point, the trail on the night in question goes cold but, on the evidence we have, these were the last people seen with Don Alphonse whilst he was alive. Added to that the fact that Don Alphonse was strangled with a chain, which was a gift given to him by your brother, and that your brother was so keen to point to Cassangoe's guilt, then there is no doubt that a circumstantial case can be made for Sir Robert's involvement at the very least. There is of course one other thing.' Here he paused, eyeing me with a somewhat embarrassed expression. 'Go on, Faunt.'

Faunt cleared his throat administratively and took up the narrative.

'Well, there is also the matter that Ingram was later seen removing Don Alphonse's goods from his warehouse, as attested to by Master Lovat, and witnessed removing them to the wharf where Rokesby has a warehouse, as attested to by a, um, third-party.' Seeing me start, he glanced at me but said nothing. Walsingham filled the void.

'It was noble of you to try and protect your brother in this matter but you will start to realise that very little escapes my notice. Munday, the man who saw you at Garnet's cottage and was here earlier, has taken an interest in the case and wished to bring that detail to my notice.'

The waters around me were appearing to get murkier and murkier. I had noticed on our first meeting that Walsingham had been very reserved towards Robert and now it appeared that he had been looking to make a case against him all of the time. But it wasn't a strong case. I had listened patiently to both of them but now felt it was time to speak out.

'Robert may be worried about something but I don't believe he ordered Don Alphonse's death. There is no evidence of a motive and no evidence of a plot. I believe that if there was an argument between Don Alphonse and Robert, which is not confirmed, then it took place in the heat of the moment. Robert had no time to subsequently arrange Don Alphonse's death. It doesn't make sense. Besides Turney was adamant that all of them, including the fourth man, disembarked on the south bank, leaving Don Alphonse alone in the boat. The only man who can dispute this is the lighterman and finding him is proving difficult.' I realised that I had been raising my voice impassionedly and decided to rein myself in a bit.

'No, it seems to me that Robert is simply worried that Don Alphonse's death is being laid at his door – it is the rumours and insinuations in court that he most fears. And then there is the matter of the Lady Merrydance. That is where Robert's guilt lies, if anywhere at all.'

'Yes, this mysterious ship that sailed from Deptford. We have yet to discuss that in detail. What do you believe it portends?'

I thought carefully before answering. 'Truthfully I don't know. There is something strange about the voyage. I have heard conflicting accounts about its destination.' I thought of Würtembatter's belief that it was bound for the Baltic and Kibber's assertion that only ships bound for domestic ports had embarked from Deptford. 'But Robert's secrecy in the matter suggests that he at least believes he is guilty of something.'

'Well then,' Walsingham demanded, issuing me a challenge, 'if not Robert, can you make a better case for Sir Christopher Hardwick? He's the only other senior figure implicated in this business.'

'There may be little evidence linking Hardwick to the actual murder but there is another link between Don Alphonse and Hardwick, and I think I can make a stab at suggesting a motive.'

'Go on then.'

'From the ship's log I found, we know that Hardwick was directly responsible for the death of Don Alphonse's father and that Don Alphonse had vowed to be avenged. I think that this revenge is something that he has been dwelling on, nurturing in his breast, and plotting with great devotion and fidelity for the past twenty years. Now, I can't prove it as yet, but I believe the man he wanted to betray to you, when he wrote to you before the Armada, was Hardwick.' I thought about what Hercules Smyth had told me as well as the connection that Davy Bennett had made.

'One thing I discovered is that Don Alphonse was overheard discussing a place called Stavening with Cassangoe, and Stavening is the country estate of Sir Christopher Hardwick.' I glanced up, noticing that I now had their full attention. This was the nugget of information that Davy

Bennett had given to me. 'Suppose that, after twenty years of patiently waiting, an opportunity for revenge finally presents itself. Perhaps Hardwick has been compromised through some of his trading connections and Don Alphonse wants to use it to implicate him in a plot against the Queen. It is pure conjecture at this stage but something like that is not beyond the bounds of possibility.' I began warming to my theme.

'We have evidence that Don Alphonse's neighbour at Lion's Quay overheard talk of a plot and revenge – there is no doubt that he and Cassangoe were cooking something up – and the evidence of the ship's log, as well as the fact that Stavening is mentioned, makes it very likely that Hardwick was the target. What better way to get revenge than by discrediting him in the eyes of the state with every possibility that he might be executed, his family left in disgrace, his estates confiscated? Don Alphonse comes to you with a story. He doesn't name Hardwick but says that there is talk of treason. Someone at the highest level is implicated. Possibly at this stage, he thinks he can get Hardwick without you knowing the full facts. However, rather than listening to gossip, you demand evidence and Don Alphonse leaves. He goes away to make his own enquiries.'

'Then why is it Don Alphonse who ends up in the river?' Faunt interjected 'None of this explains why he was killed.' He spread his hands out by way of demonstrating to Walsingham that he wasn't buying it. Nevertheless I ploughed on.

'Maybe Hardwick discovered Don Alphonse's intentions? He certainly strikes me as a man who would act quickly to wipe out a perceived threat.'

'I congratulate you on your logic and clarity, Master Lovat, but do you have any evidence to support your theory?' Walsingham sounded less sceptical than earlier, but nor did he sound convinced. 'And can you explain why the circumstantial evidence points so strongly towards your brother?'

'I don't know. I have an idea about that but …'

'You don't wish to say before you have had a chance to make further enquiries?'

'I would be grateful for that opportunity, sire.'

'Well, Master Lovat, I am going to give you that opportunity. There may be something in your story and I feel it is only fair to let you try to prove it.' Walsingham paused for a moment. 'You have never met Sir Christopher Hardwick, have you?'

'No, your Lordship.'

'Good. Then he won't recognise you. Because I want you to infiltrate his household.'

Chapter 21

'Goodness is beauty in the best estate.'
(Christopher Marlowe)

Darkness was beginning to fall when I rode between the stone gates of Walsingham's country park and headed swiftly back towards the restless chaos of the city. There were equally restless thoughts going round my mind, as I kicked George into a gallop and guided him down the darkening lanes and hedgerows.

Once I had seen George safely home to a deserved feed in a warm stable at the Half Moon, I hustled my way hastily to the Chancel House. Robert wasn't at home but in a downstairs chamber I found the odious Marmaduke Drummond, composing one of his obsequious hack jobs, his portly frame enveloping the writing desk. He put down his quill as I entered and gave me his usual condescending look.

'Look what the c-cat dragged in. A rat running onto a sinking ship. How original.'

'What's that supposed to mean?'

'Don't you know little J-Jack? Not being k-kept up to date? Of course, I forget that you're a few steps below the hired help. Her majesty's a little tired of her favourite,' he said, twirling one of his perfumed fingers in a circle to indicate Robert's property, 'rumour has it that he's finished. Don't want to tempt fate and all that, but my c-c-c-current composition could be his final ode.' He chuckled unpleasantly and went back to his scroll.

Not for the first time, I wondered why my brother had allowed this ridiculous fop to darken his corridors. I felt a strong urge to evict him there and then but thought better of it – unbelievably, writers of doggerel like Drummond had plenty more rights in society than bastards did. Instead, I decided to channel my anger into interrogating him.

'What do you know about the Portuguese merchant, Don Alphonse? You were here the evening he was killed. You left with him didn't you? You must know my brother wasn't involved.'

'You and I might think we know that but others b-beg to differ. How do we know dear Robert didn't pay someone else to do the dirty deed?

There was some unpleasantness that evening, if I recall.'

'Unpleasantness about what?'

'I c-couldn't possibly say.'

'Was it to do with a woman?'

'What would I know about women? V-vulgar creatures, the lot of them.'

'I suspect they feel the same way about you.'

'Careful, J-Jackie boy.' Drummond's eyes narrowed nastily but I pressed on regardless.

'What was the meeting about that night? Have you also invested in this overseas venture?' It was a complete stab in the dark but I could tell immediately that I had scored a hit.

'I don't know anything about that,' Drummond said, unconvincingly. It was too late for denials. I had already seen the surprise in his face at my mentioning it. I immediately tried another tack.

'What about later that night? I only have your word that you didn't stay on the boat with Don Alphonse and murder him yourself.' It was a desperate attempt but Drummond, perhaps surprisingly, seemed eager to defend himself.

'What possible reason c-could I have? Besides, everyone on that b-boat will testify to the fact that I disembarked at the P-P-Paris Gardens.'

'And no doubt half the molly houses in Southwark will vouch for your custom that evening?'

I left him smarting at that remark and went further into the bowels of the house.

In a room on the first floor, I was surprised to find Anne. She was wearing travelling clothes and must have only returned that afternoon from the country. On seeing me, she dismissed her maids and beckoned me to enter. I was immediately struck by the strain showing on her face. Her fine cheekbones had a gauntness about them, and the skin had sunk in slightly around her blue eyes.

'What's happening, Anne? I've just seen that coxcomb Drummond downstairs. He says Robert's in some kind of trouble. What's he talking about?'

If I was expecting anything at all from Anne, it certainly wasn't anger. As soon as I had closed the door behind me, she started berating me. 'In the Lord's name, John, where have you been? Robert trusts you with this one, very important task and what do you do? Disappear for days on end like an irresponsible child – getting drunk, frolicking at the theatre.' I stood awkwardly in the centre of the room, taken aback by her manner towards me. 'Yes, I know all about that. And so does Robert. Honestly, John, what were you thinking? Don't you realise that we are all in this together.'

'Anne, I don't know what you have or haven't heard but I don't intend to defend myself here and now. Will you please tell me what Drummond is talking about?'

'Robert has been denounced in Court. He went straight to see the Queen and he is at Greenwich now, defending himself.'

'Who denounced him?' Walsingham had already told me something of this before I had departed, but I decided to let Anne tell me in her own words, mindful that in serving two masters there was every chance I would look disloyal in her eyes.

'We don't know. An anonymous bill was posted at Court accusing a member of the privy council of divers crimes – the death of a foreign guest in this country being one of them and illegal venturing another. It doesn't take much reading between the lines to know that the member in question is Robert – there are some obvious hints. It is pernicious and false but Robert has no choice but to try and quell the rumours at once, otherwise goodness knows what will happen.' A faint quivering in her voice was the only clue to the fear she must be feeling.

I sat down next to her, despite her not offering, and tried to convince her that things were not as black as they appeared. 'For what it's worth, I don't believe that Robert had anything to do with Don Alphonse's death. The evidence is purely circumstantial.' Whether I whole-heartedly believed that or not, I knew that I desperately wanted to for Anne's sake. 'As for the voyage, well, that's a strange business, but Robert seems to have got himself mixed up in something. And he hasn't helped himself by being so hugger-mugger about it. What do you know about it Anne?'

'What voyage?' I explained to her about the Lady Merrydance. When I had finished, Anne looked at me with a worried expression. She had clearly known nothing about it.

'So, there is some truth in that accusation after all?'

'In the part about the venture, perhaps, but the ship has sailed – I witnessed that myself – though where it has actually gone to is anybody's guess.' I explained about the conflicting testimonies of Karl Würtembatter and Kibber. 'The problem is that Robert believes he has done something wrong. I hope he doesn't incriminate himself at Court.'

'If he is found guilty, everything will be gone. There is even talk of imprisonment.' Imprisonment could be the least of Robert's worries, but I didn't think it appropriate to mention that.

'The charges will have to be proved first.'

'The bill talked of unearthing proof.'

'At the moment, the only 'proof' of Robert's guilt is circumstantial and, in any case, I am convinced that it has been manufactured.'

'Manufactured?'

I took a deep breath. 'It's only a theory that I am working on, but I believe that someone is deliberately trying to discredit Robert at Court. And this anonymous bill only adds to my suspicions. The murder of Don Alphonse has simply helped to muddy the waters.'

'But who?' And then a more anguished, 'Why?'

'Well, the question is who benefits from the demise of the house of Rokesby? If we can answer that question then we might have a better idea.' I looked at Anne intensely for a moment, her anger had subsided and been replaced with a terse sense of fear. It was time to try winning her over. 'You may think that I've been idle, Anne, and, God knows, I've not been the most enthusiastic of servants, but in this matter, I can assure you, I have not rested this past week. I have discovered a great deal but there are still holes in my knowledge. What I really need to know is: what happened in this house the night that Don Alphonse was murdered? Robert was very coy about the whole affair, especially in front of Walsingham. What was the reason for the meeting here that night?'

'I was only at the dinner beforehand and not at the actual meeting itself but from what you have just told me I can only assume that it was to do with this sea venture.'

'So Robert and Don Alphonse were present. And who else? Turney, and that fool Drummond. Was Nesbitt there too?'

'I don't know. He was in attendance at dinner but after that I don't know.'

'And there was someone else too? Was it a man called Nicholas Ingram?'

'Yes. Ingram was here that evening. It was the first time I had met him. Robert was considering offering him patronage.'

'Alright, well let's make some assumptions. Supposing Robert was to finance this sea venture and Turney to captain it. Where did the others fit in?'

'I don't know.'

'Nor do I, but let's make an educated guess. Don Alphonse had ships, maybe he provided the Lady Merrydance and as for Ingram, well … '

'He wanted to prove himself in the household, so perhaps he helped to organise the venture.'

'Possibly, from what I know of him he is certainly a capable individual. And, besides their specific tasks, all of them may have provided financial support in a so-called joint-stock company,' I paused to think for a moment. 'What strikes me is that I have been in and out of this house for two years now and these men – Turney, Ingram, Don Alphonse – I've never come across any of them. That in itself strikes me as strange.'

'Robert has been keen to develop new connections.' Anne looked uncertain as she said it. 'They are up and coming men. That is how Robert sees it.'

'I can just hear him saying that. What can you tell me about any of them? Ingram, for example?'

A cloud immediately passed across Anne's face. 'I know nothing about him. What I saw of him I didn't like. He was all about money and profit by any means – an unsavoury character. There was something about him I didn't trust.'

'And what about Don Alphonse, himself? I have heard a lot of differing things about him. What did you think of him? I've heard he was considered attractive to the fairer sex?' I asked this question gingerly bearing in mind the insinuation that Turney had laid at Anne's door. Anne's answer was immediately reassuring.

'He was very handsome, certainly … but always the perfect gentleman.' She thought carefully for a few seconds. 'No doubt he broke a few hearts but I think his reputation was also something that he played upon. There was something altogether too serious about him to think that trifling with ladies' affections was his raison d'être.'

'That night, I believe that Don Alphonse argued with Robert in the garden. That's the rumour I've heard and Drummond more or less confirmed it just now. Do you know what that was about?'

'What argument? That doesn't sound likely. Robert was in good humour that evening.' She held a diaphanous white hand out as if to prevent further comment. 'Drummond must be mistaken.'

I shook my head. Nothing was making sense. Don Alphonse had argued with someone but who?

There was one more name to throw into the mix and Anne's reaction surprised me. 'Sir Christopher Hardwick?'

'Yes. I forgot about him.'

'Forgot about him how?'

'He was also here that night. Not at the dinner. He came later.'

'So he was also present at the meeting?'

'Yes.' Hardwick – present in this house on the night of the murder and plotting a sea venture with Robert, Turney, Drummond, Ingram and Don Alphonse. The links were gradually becoming clearer but the reasons behind them were still obscure. I thought for a moment. There were only four men on the boat that departed, prompting another question.

'Did Hardwick stay in the house that night?'

'Yes, he was our guest.' Anne sensed the note of tension in my voice that mention of Hardwick had caused. 'What is it John?'

I ignored her question, another thought occurring to me.

'The afternoon that I brought Don Alphonse's dead body here, there was a lady with you. Who was that?'

Anne didn't speak for a moment.

'Anne?' I pressed gently.

Eventually she said: 'She came to see you then? I told her you would help her. I thought you could use the extra money. Did I do the right thing?'

'Yes of course. I'm grateful. But who was she?'

'To tell you would betray a confidence. You're clever enough. You'll work it out.'

'I think I know who she is. I just wanted you to confirm it. More importantly do you have any idea who the man she is seeking is?'

'There I can't help you.'

I stood up to leave. Anne had regained her composure and the moment of intimacy we had shared earlier had evaporated.

'I'm glad I saw you Anne. I'm going away for a while. I can't tell you where but I'm doing it for Robert. To find the proof I talked about.' I paused. 'I just wanted you to know.''John.' I stood in the doorway – a shadow framed by the ornate woodwork. 'I know things haven't been easy for you. Especially in this house, with Robert the way he is. We have no right to expect your help but if there is anything you can do, anything at all to clear Robert's name and solve the mystery of Alphonse's murder …' her words trailed off hopelessly.

There was nothing I could say, other than bid her farewell and close the door behind me

Chapter 22

'I am a human being; nothing human can be alien to me.'
(Publius Terentius Afer)

I found Matthew in the room he shared above one of the stables. He had returned from a fruitless day on the river searching for the lighterman, and was now listening listlessly to two other servants, who were anxiously discussing the events taking place at court and how they might affect their job prospects.

He jumped up eagerly when I asked him to row me to Queenhithe, his natural good nature getting the better of any fatigue he might still be feeling from his ordeal at the warehouse two night's previously. I was glad of the company, as the task I had in mind involved visiting some unknown back streets in darkness and I didn't much fancy the prospect of exploring them on my own. Matthew said little as he got into the rhythm of rowing, choosing instead to grunt in acknowledgement occasionally as I told him about my visit to Walsingham's and what had transpired there. He looked concerned when I told him that Walsingham wanted me to infiltrate Hardwick's household and paused his rowing, the boat bobbing gently on the ice-cold water.

'How are you going to accomplish that, Master? You can't simply walk in and ask for a job.'

'Walsingham has given me a letter of introduction. I'm to play the part of his kinsman back in the country after a tour of the Low Countries and Armada glory, and eager to learn the vagaries of trade.'

'Sounds dangerous to me. What if he suspects something?'

'Let's hope he doesn't. And, by the way, don't breathe a word of it to anyone in the Chancel House. I don't want my brother getting an inkling of what I am doing.'

'Naturally, Master.'

Matthew gripped the oars again and began rowing with powerful strokes through the river traffic along the north bank.

Queenhithe had once been the hub of all Thames trade, when the drawbridge still operated, allowing traffic to come up the river beyond the great bridge. Since the drawbridge had decayed and seized up, the larger cargo ships had begun docking at Billingsgate. However Queenhithe was still a bustling port in late summer and autumn with many boats, barges and lighters crammed into its water gate. All of the grain barges coming from farms upriver docked here and the port was known as the 'breadbasket' of the city. In winter, the port was much quieter and a graveyard in the evenings, with the only life in the ward inhabiting the inns and taverns in streets which had gone to seed. As Matthew and I walked across the dock, the silhouette of two giant cranes used for lifting wheat bales from the barges loomed over us ominously. There was no one about and an eerie silence was only broken by the occasional roar from one of the inns as a door opened to admit or expel customers.

Walsingham had given me until the next morning to prepare myself for the trip to Hardwick's estate in Sussex, which meant that I had one night to solve the mystery the beautiful friend of Anne's had set me, and collect the second part of my reward. I was only partly doing it for the money, however. Anne had more or less confirmed to me who she was, which had given me a clue as to how the matter might have a bearing on the wider case of Don Alphonse's death.

The veiled lady had given me an address in an area amongst tightly knit streets between the port and St Paul's. I removed the paper she had given me from the pocket in my sleeve to remind myself where we were heading by the light of a tavern window:

Cokeash Yard, Trinity Street, The Queen's Hythe

Neither Matthew nor I knew this part of the city well and we moved cautiously through the streets. The few people we passed stared at us sullenly, or with open threat in their faces, as though questioning our very right to be venturing into their territory. The usual smells of the city – smoke, rotting waste, faeces – seemed heightened by the cold and hung around us stiffly as we trod a careful path, keeping to the wall as much as possible.

The streets narrowed and gables hung directly overhead as though they were closing in some ancient secret known only to them. The snow here had solidified into a series of small shiny pools that reflected the dark sky. The only sound was the cracking of ice underfoot as we trod gingerly on the treacherous, frozen mud.

The district appeared to be very run down and dilapidated. A number of houses and even churches looked as though they might be about to crumble into a cloud of dust. It was not the kind of area I had expected at all for the assignations of a rich lady. On Knightrider's street, next to a Church dedicated to the Holy Trinity, which was propped up with stilts to stop it falling down, I came across a small curiosity shop still open despite the lack of passing trade. I asked within if they knew where Cokeash Yard was, while Matthew stood outside, stamping his feet in the cold.

An old man, who was half hidden under a moth eaten woollen cap, was manning the cramped, dusty counter. 'You're almost there, young man,' he said, after eyeing me suspiciously for what seemed an eternity. 'Go back out the door and turn up Trinity Street on the right, just past the church. You'll find Cokeash Yard on the Eastern side, opposite the old Paintstainers Hall.'

I thanked him and beckoned Matthew to follow. We walked back past the crumbling stone church and after a few moments found ourselves standing outside another large decrepit building. It announced itself as the Paintstainers Hall on a sign that was hanging by one nail and looked as though it was only waiting for a sudden gust of wind to consign it to the mud in the doorway. The whole building was falling dangerously forward as though it wished to rest on its neighbour across the street. I peered through a window and could see from the lack of furniture and the dust collected in every corner that the house was derelict. Pain-staining had evidently gone out of fashion, along with the paintstainers themselves.

At first glance, it looked as though there was no street or yard to speak of opposite the old Hall. Matthew and I wandered a little further up the street, peering curiously from side to side. The street curved away in the distance and was quite empty. As we stood there, a freezing mist began to gather around us. Both of us shuddered and pulled our cloaks tightly about our necks.

We were on the point of letting the cold win and giving up the search, when a cat suddenly darted out of a gap between two houses of no more than two feet wide. On closer inspection, that gap was revealed as a dark passageway leading through to a yard beyond, signified by a dim rectangle of light at the far end.

We edged quietly through the tight passageway. The alley was dark, damp and smelled of mould. Twice I tripped on debris lying in the path and cursed as Matthew pulled me up by the shoulder.

The passageway broadened out and suddenly in front of us stood a well-proportioned but rather plain looking timber-frame house. In the gloom, it was possible to make out a set of square black posts supporting two wide gables on either side of a central door. The tops of the gables were lost in the gloom and it was impossible to make out the chimneys. Each window was made up of small, symmetrical squares of glass, but there were no fancy details. The building was in much better condition than any that surrounded it, but the whole effect was one of unprepossessing modesty, quite unlike the gauche displays of wealth that were common amongst rich merchants in other parts of town. On each side of the yard were the back walls of adjacent houses but no doors or over-looking windows. There was a cobble path leading diagonally up to the front door and the rest of the yard was paved with stone, bare and exposed, just as I felt standing in the entrance to the courtyard.

I studied the house carefully deciding what to do. All of the windows were dark, and there was nothing to suggest that the house was occupied. The facade seemed to return my gaze with a bland expression of anonymity. The house was giving nothing away.

Leaving Matthew at the entrance to the passageway with instructions to alert me if anyone came, I walked over to the front door and thinking about it for a second, decided the best thing was to knock. Although the mysterious woman had expressly forbidden me to approach the man she was looking for, I didn't intend to hang around in the cold for a long time waiting for him to enter or exit. Hopefully a servant would answer and I could ask if his master was at home before scarpering.

The door was made of plain, solid oak and there was a heavy iron doorknob hanging at its centre in the shape of a lion's head. I took hold of it and gave three loud, equally spaced raps, stepped back and waited for a response. Each knock echoed round the yard but nothing stirred inside the house. If anything, the stillness inside seemed to solidify. Once the echoes had died out, the yard returned to complete tranquillity again.

The mist, which seemed to have followed us down the passageway, spread slowly around me, obscuring Matthew from sight.

I jumped as I felt something brush my legs. Looking down, I noticed the cat had followed me into the yard and was trying to get my attention. It was a grey tabby with a blaze of white on its chest, a white nose and four long white socks. I bent down to stroke it. The cat meowed softly and hopped onto one of the window ledges expectantly. No one came to the door.

I peered through windows but shutters on the inside prevented me from seeing into the first three. At the fourth, however, the shutters were slightly ajar, though I could make out nothing in the gloom beyond the gap. I tried the window but it was tightly locked. The cat had leapt from the window ledge and was sidling over towards me. I wondered if it was connected to the house and bent down to stroke it again.

'Where's the spare key kitty?' I asked hopelessly. The cat merely rubbed against my legs and purred in response.

Gradually getting bolder, I tried the door but it was firmly locked. Then, without thinking much, I kicked out a heavy round pebble from the path and with a careful, quick movement smashed through the small square pane of glass closest to the handle of the window with the open shutter. The glass clattered on the floor but nothing stirred in the house.

My course now thoroughly determined, I quickly reached in and undid the catch, letting the window fall open towards me. With one quick movement, I hoisted myself over the ledge and, pushing the shutters back gently, dropped quietly onto the floor. Before I could stop it, the cat followed me in. I decided not to object and pulled the window shut behind us.

Once my eyes adjusted to the darkness, I saw I was standing in a small parlour with a stone oven, basin, and numerous household implements such as buckets, brooms and bowls. I took a taper from my pocket and lit it. The oven was about a foot wide and there was a small arched gap beneath for putting the ashes in. The fire looked as though it hadn't been used in a while.

The cat, which had been watching me with interest, now began pawing at my sleeve suggestively. There were a few cupboards and I opened one to find a few scraps of meat and bone. The cat had obviously been here before. I offered it some rather stale looking meat, which it immediately turned its nose up at.

A doorway led into a well-proportioned hall adjacent to the front door. My fears were raised for a moment when I saw that the bolts on the front door were drawn shut and a key was in the lock but an inspection of the back door revealed it to be locked with no sign of a key. I surmised that any inhabitant must have left by that exit. Still, it was very unusual for a house of this size to have no servants at home at all – there was just an eerie silence.

The room opposite the parlour turned out to be a long storage room with boxes and sacks, very similar to the ones I had seen stored in Don Alphonse's warehouse. I had a quick look in one and the contents seemed very similar too. I closed the door gently. Apart from the outside doors, there were no other exits. There was nothing for it but to look upstairs.

The cat skipped ahead of me and I followed it into the main hall of the house, which ran the length of the building. It was a pleasant and prettily laid out room. Equally perfect for entertaining guests or relaxing in private. The wooden panelled walls were adorned with rich tapestries and there were ornamental vases positioned in each corner, with the same blue pattern. At one end of the room was a fireplace and next to it there was a richly carved four-poster bed, with its curtains drawn. Was this where her beau had entertained the beautiful veiled lady?

Throughout the room there were a range of upholstered chairs and down the middle a long oak table that supported on its polished surface many fine ornaments, including books and maps, as well as scientific instruments. The centrepiece of the table was a wooden globe, about a foot in height and mounted on a cast iron stand. Pushing it around gently my eyes were immediately drawn to the coast of West Africa and the places that I had read about in Don Alphonse's journal.

I suddenly became fully aware of a low hissing noise coming from the end of the room. I walked towards the noise and saw that it was coming from the fireplace. Bending forward I touched a blackened log. It was damp. Too late I realised that a lit fire had moments earlier been doused with water. Out of the corner of my eye I saw the curtains of the bed pulled a part and a huge arm swinging out of the darkness with a long object attached to it. I swivelled as sharply as I could to remove my head from the weapon's trajectory, at the same time uttering the only word I thought would save me from a braining.

'Cassangoe!'

The arm seemed to hesitate momentarily before continuing its path, connecting squarely with the part of my back between my shoulder blades, knocking the wind out of my lungs as I fell into the fireplace. Cursing myself for leaving Matthew outside, I braced myself for further blows but nothing came. I swung round to face my assailant, who I had guessed correctly was Don Alphonse's friend and confidante.

Cassangoe would have been very hard to miss in a crowd even if the colour of his skin hadn't marked him out as exotic on these shores. He was well over a head taller than most men and clearly didn't need a weapon, which I now saw was a metal poker from the fireside, to get the better of me, as he could easily have broken my neck with his bare hands. But more than that, it was the strangeness of the man's head and face that struck me. His head was like some classical statue with broad cheekbones in perfect symmetry and a fine aquiline nose but what stood out most was the livid scarring pattern all across one side of his forehead and across both cheeks. Dressed in richly coloured Italian style clothes, similar to those of Don Alphonse, he cut an impressive figure, a view only heightened by bright gold hoped earrings that dangled from his ear lobes and a head shaven to the skin. He stood in the middle of the room, weapon raised, wide eyes as white as marble, clearly undecided whether or not to finish me off or flee for his life.

I tried to push myself up from my knees but I was still reeling from the blow and knew I was still at his mercy. It was time to talk fast.

'Cassangoe.' I croaked, the word barely leaving my lips. I could hardly breathe let alone speak. 'I'm a friend. I don't want to hurt you. Or you to hurt me for that matter.' I made an attempt at a smile as if I was trying to appease a rabid dog. Bad move.

'How do you know my name, devil?' His voice had a deep, bassy resonance, which seemed out of place in this refined setting, and a marked accent. He took a step forward, weapon poised. I found myself recoiling into the fireplace, arms instinctively covering my face.

'Please, listen to me Cassangoe. I can help you … protect you.' Some chance, I could barely protect myself, 'I don't believe you killed Don

Alphonse.'

Cassangoe moved closer to me, teeth bared, the mention of his dead friend had clearly touched a nerve.

'Devil,' the word was hissed between his teeth. 'What do you know about the death of my friend?'

'I've been asked by Walsingham to investigate his death. I know you had nothing to do with it and I think I can prove who did. I've talked to Hercules Smyth – he'll vouch for me. Please you have to trust me.'

'How did you know where to find me? Not even Hercules knows this place.' The distrust in his face and voice was all too clear.

'A woman, a lady rather, she gave me this address. She used to meet her lover here – Don Alphonse, I presume – she was worried about him.' The tension in Cassangoe's body loosened a fraction. The weapon in his hand lowered.

'What lady? Describe her?'

'Voice of a siren, eyes like deep wells, an abundance of chestnut hair. "Beware, danger!" written all over her.'

Cassangoe fixed me with his eyes for a split second before throwing back his head and letting out a huge laugh. 'I believe you, devil, I believe you. You describe her well! Know who she is?'

I thought I did: 'Lady Leticia Hardwick? Wife of Sir Christopher?'

'That's right, devil. You know.'

'So Don Alphonse *was* cuckolding him. That's a motive for murder right there.'

'Is that what you think, devil? Is that what you think?' Disconcertingly, he let out another huge laugh, which reverberated around the room.

'Stands to reason. Leticia Hardwick asks me to find her lover and gives me the location for their secret meetings. The location just happens to be Don Alphonse's London house. Don Alphonse wants revenge for his father's death and takes her as a lover. Perhaps he even wanted Hardwick to know. A dangerous game but one he might consider playing. In any case, Hardwick finds out and takes action, or at least gets one of his henchmen to do it.'

'I like your reasoning. Ha ha, you know, devil, you know. Only one problem with your deduction, devil. You got the wrong man. The Don wasn't Leticia's lover. Her lover still very much alive,' he held me in that statue like stare, challenging my brain to do the calculation. 'Her lover is me.'

And with that, he let out another huge guffaw, which I thought was going to shatter the windowpanes.

Chapter 23

'Let us celebrate the occasion with wine and sweet words.'
(Titus Maccius Plautus)

'Don Alphonse was a great, great man. A legend of a man and a great friend. Come, devil, let us raise a toast to the great Don. You would have loved him. Ha ha! The stories I could tell you. *Devil.* You are a *devil* – a clever *devil* – a bad *devil* – a bastard *devil*! Ha ha ha! Come a toast – to great men and bastards, and the bastards of great men!'

We were sitting at the long oak table, crystal glasses in hand, the tapestries on the wall dancing to the shadows of a newly lit fire and making strange patterns with the scarring on the black man's face. Once I had managed to convince Cassangoe that I posed no threat, he proved to be a surprisingly genial host. A bottle of Sicilian wine had been produced from 'Don Alphonse's supplies' and every amenity made for my comfort, including a rub down for my sore back, which I was reliably informed looked 'as ravished as a priest's arse'. At least the poker had been put to its proper use and we were sitting in relative warmth.

I had started questioning Cassangoe warily but having got him talking it was hard to get a word in edgeways. The man had been cooped up for too long and once the smooth red wine had loosened the sides of his tongue it wouldn't stop wagging. He told me how he and Hercules Smyth had been worried that Don Alphonse was missing, and how he had been hiding when the first men came to the warehouse and was still in hiding when I arrived some time later. He had heard of Don Alphonse's death from behind the skins. 'I could have ripped those skins apart with the swelling in my bosom.' After I left, he had agreed with Hercules that he would hide out in the house and Hercules left on purpose in the hope that I would follow him – a plan that had worked as smartly as they hoped. After which, he had stolen away into the heart of the city and the safety of the hidden house. I thought of telling him that the warehouse had been destroyed in the fire but decided against it, fearing that his rage would get the better of him, and instead prompted him to tell me more about the secretive house we were now sitting in and where he had sought refuge.

The invitation to talk about the house prompted a narrative digression on the secret trysts it was often used for and in particular the arrangement he had with Leticia Hardwick. It seemed that they had a coded message system for arranging their meetings and that Don Alphonse, who had access to the Hardwick household through business dealings, had been the go-between – a role I assumed he must have relished performing with the thought that his father's murderer was being cuckolded by the huge, affable moor.

I had told Cassangoe early on about my discovery of Don Alphonse's diaries and of reading about their great adventure across the African continent, which revelation set Cassangoe off on a whole other tangent of reminiscing. Listening to Cassangoe speak, I found it hard to reconcile the innocent young African missionary or mbùríchi that Don Alphonse had described in his diaries with the urbane, garrulous sophisticate that now sat before me offering cynicism and wit on everything from the Queen's wardrobe to the perils of non-licensed bear-baiting (apparently Russian bears were to be avoided at all costs). Cassangoe may have suffered many hardships in Africa as a young man but it seemed that nothing could have changed the man as much as his exposure to London society. He seemed to worship and despise it in equal measures and was full of stories about how he and Don Alphonse had manipulated the system to their advantage. Cassangoe's narrative ranged from love of his friend, to tears and anger at his death, to his own personal deprivations in such quick succession that it was hard to keep up. Every story he told was punctuated with love, sadness, laughter and despair.

'I've been here for three whole days, devil. Three whole days without vixen or victuals. You understand devil? I know you do ha ha ha! I'm thirsty devil. Thirsty.' Followed by a huge glug on his glass. 'No one else know where I am devil?' The cat, whose name was Andromeda, was now sitting on Cassangoe's lap enjoying being stroked by his enormous hand.

'No.' I reassured him. 'Only Hercules Smyth and he doesn't know where the house is.'

'I know they going to rope me up for the Don's death, if they catch me, devil, they'll rope me up good and true. Though I as innocent as the Virgin Queen herself, the Lord bless her cruel soul. Those bastards make me the goat that scapes. Bastards, I spit on them.' Followed by the action into the fireplace, just missing my cloak, 'No offence devil, ha ha ha! There's bastards and bastards! Ha ha ha! But I tell you if I get that particular bastard's neck between my hands, that bastard who killed the Don, I tell you, I'll squeeze and squeeze till that blackguard's neck be wrung like a spring chicken. You mark my speech.' I felt my own neck constrict at the thought.

He paused again to take a huge draught on his glass and I managed to fire a question in.

'What was Don Alphonse's plan for destroying Hardwick?' Cassangoe gave me a suspicious look as though this sudden change of track was both surprising and unwelcome. 'I know from the ship's log or diaries that Hardwick murdered his father and Hercules told me that Don Alphonse was planning some sort of revenge. What was it? Was it to do with their business dealings?'

'I want that diary back, you hear me. You bring it back to me. That's the Don's property and mine now. It's the only memories I got.'

'Of course, I will bring it to you next time I visit.'

'See you do.' Cassangoe looked satisfied. 'I'll tell you about the Don. Always he talked of revenge. Always the same, over and over again. It eat him up inside, so it did, that he grew so lean on it. I told him many times to forget it. Move on I said, life too short I said, we having too much fun, but every time he brought me back to Africa and the time we were captives together – that's when he swore on his life and soul that he would avenge his father and nothing I could say would shake him.' As he spoke these heartfelt words, I ran my mind over the ship's log and Don Alphonse's own expression on the subject. The two accounts tallied.

'What was the plan with Hardwick?'

'I don't know exactly. He was very secretive about it. Told me he didn't want me to be involved. All I know is that it was something to do with smuggling.'

'Smuggling?'

'I don't know the full details but I think the Don was trying to get Hardwick into some racket so that he could then expose him.'

'That sounds extremely risky. How was he to avoid being exposed himself?

'The Don cared not about himself.'

'What was the cargo?'

'That I don't know.'

'Could it be tobacco? There was tobacco in the warehouse and a red spice.' I remembered Emmalina's suggestion. 'Was it Sumac?'

'Sumac, that's right. Alphonse had a license for that and the tobacco, but that doesn't mean to say he didn't encourage Hardwick to smuggle them.'

'Who else was involved?'

'There was a group of them. I don't know their names. Some Lord or other was at the head of it – he provided the legitimacy at least.'

I sat and thought for a moment, allowing this information to sink in and connect with everything else I had learned in the case so far. Involvement in smuggling was not something I had expected but I had to admit it implied a certain logic. The 'Lord' providing legitimacy to the operation might well be my brother and it would neatly explain why he was reluctant for me to visit Simon Turney and the Lady Merrydance, which I was almost certain now had been chartered for illicit trading activities. It would also tie in the merchandise that I found in Don Alphonse's warehouse and which had seemingly now been transferred to my brother's wharf. So far so good. But what it certainly didn't explain was Walsingham's interest in the case. The only thing the spymaster usually concerned himself with were plots against Queen or country. I could hardly imagine him being concerned with a two-bit smuggling operation. Something didn't add up.

I was about to explore some of these concerns with the talkative Cassangoe when there was a sudden noise on the staircase outside. Cassangoe froze before reaching for the poker, the cat shooting out of his lap. 'Who is it devil? Who followed you here?' He hissed in a low growl. He picked up the wine and was about to fling it on to the fire again.

'For goodness sake be calm,' I told him, holding a hand up to stop him. The wine was far too good to waste. I moved stealthily onto my feet and took up a position behind the door. Cassangoe on the far side of the room was looking wild eyed and terrified. Footsteps stopped outside the door and then it began to open slowly with an inquisitive creak. I braced myself ready to pounce.

A grey hatless head appeared around the edge of the door.

'Master?'

'God's teeth, Matthew, you frightened the sodding life out of us. It's all right', I said to Cassangoe, breathing an audible sigh of relief. 'It's just my man. I left him waiting outside.' This remark was made rather pointedly, as my heartbeat was only just starting to subside.

'I wondered what had become of you, Master.' Matthew looked at me with a mixture of apology and indignation on his face. He had obviously got bored of waiting and followed me in through the parlour window.

'Come in man, for goodness sake.'

The look on Matthew's face on first encountering Cassangoe was a joy to see, and made me wonder if my own reaction had been similar. His jaw dropped open in an expression of outright shock and his eyes were a mixture of dumb incomprehension and fear. At the same time, his arm involuntarily went over the top of his head and started a low rubbing motion on the thin strands of grey hair, which made him look a little like a monkey. It was as if his brain couldn't quite let him believe what his eyes were seeing.

'What's the matter, old man?' Cassangoe, who must have been used to this kind of reaction, showed no sign of anger, only bemusement. 'Haven't you ever seen a blackie before?' He then let out one of his huge barking laughs, which all of London must have heard, and which made me wonder how he could possibly have remained hidden without giving himself away. Matthew's mouth shut and then opened again but no response came out. He continued to stare until I told him to take a seat and asked him if he wanted a drink. He accepted, never once taking his eyes off Cassangoe.

* * *

It was some time after the bells of St Paul's had struck midnight that Matthew and I stole away from the house, leaving Cassangoe to his wine and introspection. I had pressed him hard for any more information he could give me about Don Alphonse's murder, the smuggling or anything else that could shed some light on the mystery but he had insisted he could help no further with the matter and, as the wine took hold, had gradually become less and less coherent, continually asking Matthew and

I to raise our glasses to the 'great Don'. I asked him if there was anything we could get for him and promised him I would return with the diary and any news as soon as I had it, but in truth it was a relief to get away from his morbid and frenetic company. To some degree, I actually feared for the man's mind, holed up in the house with only Andromeda the cat and his thoughts for company.

On returning to my lodgings on London Bridge, Matthew and I were greeted by laughter as we climbed the narrow stairs. At first I assumed that Fat Hugh, my downstairs neighbour, had got himself a goose for the night from Bankside but entering my room I found Emmalina bent closely over a manuscript in the company of none other than Thomas Kyd, their heads almost touching. They broke apart as we entered and I experienced a strange sensation as though I had just swallowed nugget of lead. Kyd looked suitably sheepish.

'There you are Lovat, old chap, and who's this bluff fellow?' He jumped up from the astronomical clock he had been perched on, and shook Matthew warmly by the hand, sensing, perhaps, a certain stiffness in my demeanour. 'We were wondering what had happened to you both, weren't we Emmy?' Kyd glanced at Emmalina but it was hard to tell what she was wondering. She was looking down at the manuscript, her face covered by her rich hair – glistening strands, luxurious as an Ottoman's silks.

'Emmy's been showing me her wonderful job of translation.' Kyd lifted up the manuscript and waved it at me. 'It's all in there – and a wonderful tail of derring-do it is too. When you're done with it I thought I might steal it for a plot.'

'Is it finished?' I had meant to sound casual, but the words came out rather more tersely than expected. Fortunately, Emmalina didn't seem to notice. She gave me a beaming smile, pleased at Kyd's praise of her work.

'It's not quite finished yet. I have a sheaf of about ten pages to go.'

'It's already been most useful.' I assured her. I wanted to say more than that but somehow couldn't. There was a slight awkwardness, on my part at least, but this was quickly dissipated by Kyd, who started telling me how he had been admiring my eyeglass and astronomical clock and how he would welcome an evening's stargazing at some point.

The irrational pang of emotion I had felt on seeing Kyd and Emmalina so intimate together quickly passed, and a few moments later the four of us sat in a huddle, while I relayed both my visits to Walsingham and the Chancel House, and the discovery of the hidden dwelling where Matthew and I had discovered Cassangoe. Matthew interjected his own observations on the latter. 'Man's as black as coal and as mad as a March hare if you ask me. Wouldn't surprise me at all if he had done the Portingale in and convinced himself it was someone else.'

Kyd and Emmalina were suitably shocked that a black African had cuckolded the great Sir Christopher Hardwick.

'So it wasn't Don Alphonse playing fast and loose with Lady Hardwick after all?'

'It would appear not.'

'And so it should have been Cassangoe's body washed up at Cuckold's Point?' Kyd was enjoying the irony of that point.

'You have a macabre sense of poetic justice. But yes, it would appear that the coincidence relating to where Don Alphonse's body was found was misleading. Unless, of course, he had encouraged Cassangoe in the matter, which seems likely.'

I explained to them the mission that Walsingham had given me, and how it meant I would be leaving for the Sussex coast the next morning. Kyd immediately surprised me.

'I'll go with you.'

'Don't be foolish. I only have an introduction to the household for myself.'

'Not to the house. I'll hole up in an inn in Rye. You'll need someone on the outside, to pass messages to and the like, and anyway', Kyd gave me the full benefit of his guileless grin, 'someone as reckless as you needs someone as resourceful as me to watch his back.' I thought about it for a moment. It was certainly an appealing suggestion and for one reason in particular that I didn't care to dwell on. I looked at the others.

'It's a good idea master,' Matthew reasoned slowly, 'if anything happens to you, Master Kyd here can send for the troops so to speak.'

'Emmalina? Will you be all right if I leave you alone here for a few days. There is still the matter of your stepfather.'

'I feel safe here. Besides, Matthew can look after me.' She looked at Matthew enquiringly and he nodded assuredly. 'It makes sense to have the pair of you go.'

'Well Kyd, I don't want to involve you in any danger but I can't see what harm could come of it and it would certainly be good to have the company.'

'There – it's settled then.' Kyd beamed with happiness, Matthew nodded sagely and Emmalina looked … well, enigmatic.

We conspired for another twenty minutes, agreeing that Matthew would continue his vigil at the docks, whilst making contact with Emmalina at the lodging at least twice a day to see if there was any news from Kyd, and to protect her in case her stepfather came looking for her. Emmalina said she would finish translating Don Alphonse's journal. She sounded determined and enthralled with the task and I realised that it had provided her with a welcome distraction from thoughts of Buck's disappearance, her stepfather and the odious Shuttleworth.

We resolved to all be together again soon and not long after Matthew left for his bed at the Chancel House. There was little point Kyd going back to his own lodgings, and so the three of us bedded down for what was, in my case, a restless night's sleep. Emmalina slept on the bed, Kyd on the truckle, and me, ever mindful of my gentlemanly upbringing, on a sack on the floor.

I lay awake for a long time, listening to their mingled breathing, and, under the indolent gaze of the young man in the portrait, tried to imagine what lay in store in the days ahead.

Part 3

Sussex

December 1588

Chapter 24

'See and keep silent.'
(Sir Francis Walsingham)

The road from London to the south coast was little better than a dirt track, made practically impassable at times by a mixture of recent damage caused by the weather and the general wear and tear of traffic going to and from the coast. It had snowed during the night and now a powder thin white layer disguised the potholes and crevices of the highway, making it even more treacherous.

But the snow brought some joys, at least aesthetically. For, after an hour's hard riding, as we reached the summit of the North Downs just past the village of Sevenoaks, the whole countryside lay before us like an unblemished bridle sheet. Ahead of us we could see the white-capped treetops of the forests of the Weald and beyond that the sharp rise of the South Downs indicating where our final destination lay. Kyd and I breathed in the view before us, as well as the cold air, before kicking our mounts on and riding at pace into the valley.

Once again I was united with the gallant George, who I had asked for especially on this occasion. As with the previous day, he appeared to welcome the chance for some fresh country air and galloped on gamely, picking his way carefully along the slippery and uneven surface. Beside me, on an ungainly roan, 'rode' Kyd who looked about as comfortable on a horse as a dog on ice skates at a winter fair (something that I had actually witnessed the previous winter). No matter how he tried, he couldn't get into any rhythm with the horse and would always be going down as the horse went up and vice versa. Neither did he have any control of the beast, choosing to point the animal at the nearest wide tree whenever we needed to stop to consult the map – a major hazard when we were in open pasture. Despite these inconveniences, the man's spirit could not be dimmed and his ridiculous grin stayed in place for almost the entire journey, apart from on one occasion when the roan decided to stop prematurely and deposited Kyd in a frozen ditch. I laughed unkindly before helping him back into the saddle.

* * *

Conversation was difficult as we rode, which suited me fine as I had a number of things swirling around my mind – not least the task that awaited me. The day before, having coerced me into infiltrating Hardwick's household, Walsingham had finally revealed his hand. In front of his books and the ever present Faunt, he had spelled out his suspicions against both my brother and Hardwick and made it clear that I only had one chance to prove the former's innocence and the latter's guilt.

'Let us put aside the murder of Don Alphonse for one moment. Let us leave talk of revenge and suggestions of infidelities, however much truth there may be in them, and concentrate on some of the broader implications of this mystery. Your brother is an ambitious man, Master Lovat, is he not, like many of the moths that flutter around the bright court of her majesty? But unlike their forefathers who sought advancement through glory in war and the protection of their estates, today's courtier, more often than not, seeks advancement through the more rewarding, and no doubt quicker and safer route, of riches through trade. No, don't misunderstand me. I merely pass comment not judgement. It is not only a desire on their part but also a necessity. Believe me I understand this only too well.' As Walsingham spoke, he lulled both Faunt and I into the same sense of enchantment that I had witnessed in my brother's hall one week previously.

'Take your brother's case for instance. The war with Spain and the closing of the Dutch ports has impinged heavily on the sales of the wool, produced so abundantly on his Cotswold estate, and the debilitating price inflations we endure on everything else bite hard on the gut. These deprivations place great burdens on a man of responsibility like Sir Robert. You agree?'

'Yes, Sire.'

'In their desire for wealth, the younger generation of moths, by which I refer to your brother and his contemporaries, look for their example to an older generation of adventurers and merchants, amongst whom there are few with such a glorious reputation as Sir Christopher Hardwick. You have already alluded to his African voyages and their unfortunate consequences for the late Don Alphonse and his father. What perhaps you are not aware of is the great wealth that these voyagers brought Hardwick? A triangular trade of wools and copper to the African shores, Africans slaves to meet the growing burdens of the Spanish colonies, and pearls and gold from those shores to ours. The way in which much of this business was conducted was no doubt questionable – Don Alphonse's own account sheds interesting new light to that effect – but there was one very important factor about these voyages and that is that they were sanctioned, and indeed part financed, by the Queen. The question I pose is do all of today's proposed adventures have such Royal blessing, as indeed they must? This is not merely a question of regal prejudice. Quite the contrary, whilst we welcome trade and advancement for the country as a whole, we must ensure that the very trade we conduct in order to give our nation strength does not at the same time give succour to our enemies. Faunt, a glass.' Walsingham paused for a moment, whilst Faunt brought him a glass and filled it with wine. Walsingham then intimated that he could do the same for both members of his audience.

'Let us not dwell too much on the maybes but get down to the hard facts. Before and during the war with Spain, all ships were confined to English ports and that embargo remains in place. There are still reports of Spanish aggressors harassing these shores and the threat, although reduced, remains. However, I learn that a trading adventure is afoot to which your brother has put his name. You yourself saw the ship disembark from Deptford. I can categorically state that this is not a voyage that has Royal blessing. That is one black mark against your brother. Of course your brother, either naive or reckless, has taken a gamble. The Spanish imperialist is wounded; there are opportunities to be had. Besides, many unsanctioned voyages have taken place before. The fleets return, bounties are offered to the Queen, assurances are given that it was in the interest of Queen and Country that such a voyage was taken, promises are made that it won't happen again, few get punished, even fewer lose favour. The Queen, in all honesty, is more likely to banish a courtier that makes an unfavourable marriage, than one who is reckless in the pursuit of wealth, provided she shares that wealth. Who cares that these are dangerous times with the Spanish aggression only newly defeated, and that restrictions are at their height. Your brother, and his co-conspirators, for he is only the figurehead for a group, naively or recklessly as I say, seize their opportunity to fill the void left by Spain and gamble that they will come out victorious. Do you follow my reasoning so far?'

I nodded my agreement, anxious not to interrupt his flow.

'There is one snag however, that tears the cloth. In this instance, the ship does not slip out of harbour quietly, away from prying eyes and jealous informers. On the contrary, this very morning the Lady Merry-dance's departure is proclaimed on a bill posted at court by someone who wishes to serve her Majesty. An anonymous someone, who has got wind of the expedition and wishes to make plain the treachery of your brother. The question I ask myself is: who will gain from such a denouncement? Not the denouncer, he wishes to remain in the shadows. Then who?' This was the information that had caused me to rush straight to the Chancel House, where I had been able to witness the effects of the denouncement on Anne first hand.

'Now let us consider Hardwick. We already have a sketch of him. In his youth, ruthless adventurer and opportunist – a man able to seize the initiative and turn it to his advantage. Now in comfortable middle age a peer of the realm, holder of high office and confidante of her majesty. This much you know, Master Lovat. Now let us colour in this sketch and perhaps it may reveal an altogether different picture. Consider if you will for a moment what favours, bargains, bribes and so on it takes to mount an operation on the scale of Hardwick's slaving adventures and consider also with whom these trysts are made. Well there are few Protestants in the lands beyond these shores and even fewer Englishmen – Spaniards, French, Portingales and each and every one of them Catholics. These are the cogs that need oiling for such an expedition to succeed. Naturally there is little evidence of these bargains taking place but there is rumour and hearsay aplenty. I have even heard it said that Hardwick, to all outward appearances a follower of our own true faith, took Mass on the island of Madeira. And moreover, not only was Hardwick supported by this network of undesirables twenty years ago but enjoys their continued support even up to the last months. How else can we explain his burgeoning wealth and success at a time when the seas are closed to our ships and our merchants are barred from trade? His country estate, Staven-ing, which you so cleverly discovered through your enquiries, is situated near the port of Rye, a port that he holds great influence over, and from which ships are arriving and leaving at frequent intervals. My hypothesis, and one supported very much by the evidence of Don Alphonse, is thus: Hardwick created a network of undesirable partners in the late 1560s and he continues to enjoy the support of those relationships today.' Walsingham paused to take a sip of wine and both Faunt and I, who had yet to touch our lips to our glasses, did likewise.

'Well so what, I hear you say? What harm does it do us that Hardwick trades with the enemy? Well, let us see. We might ask where the loyalties of such a man may lie? When Spanish invaders make inroads into our countryside and towns, can we rely on such a man to protect his country or to join with the invader? You see my interest perhaps, Master Lovat, do you not? These were the suspicions brought to me by Don Alphonse. Hardwick is a member of the Privy Council and an advisor to the admiralty, amongst other things. As it happens the Spaniards did not land and Hardwick's loyalty was not tested but there is still the nagging doubt that we cradle a traitor in our bosom.' He arched his fingers together in his characteristic manner.

'So there is general suspicion, let us say, now let us explore specific accusations. You will recall the Babington Plot that I exposed that led to the execution of the Pretender Mary last February?'

'I do remember it. I witnessed her execution.' Walsingham's words had transported me back to a cold February night the previous year, when my brother had summoned me late to the Chancel House. News had come to London that after many years of rumour, Mary had finally been found guilty of treason and was to be executed the next morning. My brother could not attend but was determined that a member of his household should bear witness to the event.

I had left the walls of London at dusk and ridden relentlessly through the night, arriving at Fotheringhay, Mary's final prison, at dawn, only minutes before the appointed hour. I recalled how she kept us waiting, her noble speech in the face of death, the farce of the executioners and administrators, the utter distress of her maids and pages as they were ushered away from her headless body, and then the long, slow, leisurely ride back to London where I conversed with other witnesses to the execution, and marvelled at the great event we had been party to.

Walsingham had paused in his long speech for a second, whilst these memories had played in my mind, but now he continued in his slow, deliberate manner:

'Well, indeed, you were at the execution, Master Lovat, I recall your brother telling me proudly that he had sent someone to attend. However, I don't expect you to know the ins and outs of the plot itself and I don't intend to explore them here. What I will say though is that Babington and his co-conspirators were, quite rightly as it turned out, never sure of their success and were constantly searching for an escape route. Babington himself applied to me on a number of occasions for a permit to travel, though each time I refused him. Immediately the plot was exposed a warning was sent out to all of the ports. Babington escaped to Uxendon in Harrow, where he was eventually apprehended. During his interrogation, he revealed that a means of escape from the country had been proposed to him but he was not sure of its author. The only clue he was able to give us was that the escape was to be made from the port of Rye. It may be circumstantial perhaps but once again we are brought close to the realm of Hardwick – a man who has many undesirable connections and trades with them openly, who is suspected of recusancy, and who has now been brought to my attention as a potential traitor to this country.' Walsingham paused for dramatic effect before continuing.

'Now, suppose such a traitor is aware he is suspected and sees an opportunity to both deflect attention from himself and bring down one of his younger rivals in the bargain? A seed is planted in the mind of the ambitious young courtier, who after all needs the riches such an expedition will bring. A group of men, ostensibly friends of your brother's, for it is he who I allude to, rally to the cause but only under the banner of your brother's patronage. And Hardwick stays in the shadows, perhaps he has given some investment, some encouragement, no doubt many contacts – for these are the key – but he is old and established, let your brother take the glory for the first expedition since the Armada that will bring back untold riches. Then once the plans are made and the ships ready to sail, he denounces, through an anonymous third party, the expedition as treasonous. The group of investors melts away, leaving only your brother to carry the blame. On the ship, perhaps, will be found Catholic traitors making passage to France, incriminating letters of introduction, or inflammatory pamphlets perhaps. The charge of treason will be firmly pointed at a new target and, although it does not completely deflect the attention from Hardwick, it certainly gives those of us that guard the security of this country extra food for thought. Perhaps further witnesses will be produced in the future denouncing your brother. Men like Drummond, who have nestled in your brother's bosom, might suddenly discover a 'conscience' which forces them to tell tales of your brother's conduct. Perhaps, if all goes to plan, Hardwick will eventually reveal himself as the proud patriot who was architect of your brother's downfall?'

Walsingham paused for breath to reach for his green medicine, which he added to the wine before swigging it back. 'The only thing that went wrong, as far as Hardwick is concerned, is that I allowed the ship to sail. But no matter, if Turney is Hardwick's man, as I suspect him to be, he will simply take the ships to safe harbour and lie low for a while. As for the others, Ingram was in the service of Leicester and having made overtures to your brother will no doubt end up in the service of Hardwick, having been his pawn in this matter. Drummond will also find a new patron for his doggerel – no doubt Hardwick as well. Turney will be reprimanded but he will plead innocence and be protected by his benefactor – Hardwick. All of the strings tie together. A neat plot I think you will agree, Master Lovat?'

I had to admit there was a horrible truth at the core of what Walsingham was saying. I thought for a moment of the men surrounding my brother, the men that had been with him on the night of Don Alphonse's murder. Ingram, Drummond, Turney – they were none of them true friends of my brother. But what of Don Alphonse – he appeared to be the odd one out? I put this thought from my mind as Walsingham's voice again seared into my consciousness.

'I see in you the burning eyes of the convert, Master Lovat. For too long you have drifted aimlessly, a waste both to yourself and to your country, and to a Queen who needs able men like you to shoulder their share of the burden. The opportunity to discover the facts surrounding Don Alphonse's death has changed all that. I see that you are now driven with a purpose and, if I may say so, it shows an admirable quality in you. However, the fact that your brother got you involved in the mystery of Don Alphonse's death has been fortunate for me too. And I mean to make use of that fortune. You are unknown to Hardwick and he to you.

I want you to infiltrate his household at Stavening and find the evidence that will both prove he is a traitor, whilst at the same time sparing your brother the loss of his reputation and standing. Serve me well in this, and you shall not find me ungrateful, nor her majesty.' He paused for a moment, giving me a sideways glance. 'Know you also that an illegitimate birth can only be made legitimate by Royal Decree.'

'Where does Don Alphonse fit in to all of this?' I asked, careful to ignore this carrot, which had been so tantalisingly dangled. 'His death can't be explained as neatly as the rest of the matter.' This indeed was the one element that was troubling me in all that had been said. Walsingham paused for a moment, weighing his words before answering me.

'Alphonse's death does indeed cause me some perturbation. I believe that you are close to the mark with your assessment that Hardwick is responsible for it. Certainly Alphonse had his own reasons for being involved. He had many of the same connections as Hardwick, and he was able to move freely in the same circles. I am only glad that he came to me with his suspicions and I can only assume that Hardwick discovered this and dealt with him. Let us make a bargain here and now – bring me my traitor, Master Lovat, and I feel certain you shall have your murderer, and perhaps much else besides.'

* * *

The letter of introduction Walsingham had given me supported my cover as the son of one of Walsingham's kinsmen, recently returned from a trip abroad, who was looking for suitable employment in the household of a wealthy merchant. Whether or not Hardwick had such a post, it was unlikely that he would refuse a request from Walsingham before trying to find alternative solutions and this would give me a window of opportunity to discover any evidence that may point to Hardwick's guilt in Don Alphonse's death, as well as explain his involvement in the trading scandal that was engulfing my brother. This of course was the hard part. Gaining access to the house was one thing but access to Hardwick's private papers and affairs? Who knew what hurdles would need to be overcome, or more specifically locks picking, before I could obtain such jewels. I felt forlorn at the prospect.

The other niggling thorn that had kept me awake, and which now continued to poison my thoughts as we galloped through the snow, was the strong reaction I had felt on seeing Kyd and Emmalina enjoying each other's company the previous evening. If the prospect of success at Hardwick's was enough to make me turn round and give it up as a hopeless case, then it was that leaden feeling in the pit of my stomach that urged me recklessly on, come what may, to oblivion if necessary. But what was that feeling – envy of an intimate touch, jealousy of a prized possession, the seeds of love even? I kept going over in my mind what Emmalina had always been to me – Buck's irritating younger sister, a gawky girl who used to moon at me over the counter of her stepfather's shop, a jest, a plaything. Not anymore – I had to admit that my feelings had deepened considerably. But while she was under my protection I knew that I had no right to take advantage of her and in any case I could no longer tell if she reciprocated my feelings. These barbed thoughts and others plagued me as we galloped onwards across the white hillsides and down into the darkened forest.

We passed few other travellers on our journey, stopping only once at an inn at the centre of a meagre village, deep in the heart of the Weald, where we warmed ourselves by the fire, and took ale and food. The only other patrons were a squalid bunch of woodsmen and charcoal burners, who eyed us suspiciously as we entered but soon returned to their glasses and mumbling, in deference to our rank. A half hour later we were back in the saddle, Kyd complaining of a sore arse, and wending our way along a winding woodland track.

After another hour, we stopped at the summit of a small hill, whilst Kyd dismounted and ran to a tree to relieve himself of the ale we had drunk. As I sat quietly on George, holding the reins of Kyd's roan, I suddenly heard the dashing of hooves and the crunch of wheels. Looking back the way we had just come, a fine, modern coach pulled by six horses was coming towards me rapidly up the hill. The driver on the box seat bellowed to me to make way. I kicked George and yanked the roan in a flustered manner allowing the coach to pass, catching a glimpse of its occupants as it rumbled past – a finely dressed lady with a wealth of blond hair. She didn't deign to notice me and soon all I could see was the back of the coach as it disappeared over the next ridge.

'Who was that?' Kyd asked, buttoning his breeches as he ambled back from the shrubs.

'Whoever it was, they were in a hurry.'

'And I thought the countryside was all about the slow pace of life?'

'No, that's just a cliché that you poets persist with.'

'Sorry, Lovat old chap, I forget you're still a country clod at heart.'

'I'll clod you in a minute if you don't hurry up and mount.'

'Perhaps I should walk for a while. There doesn't appear to be any sensation in my nether regions.'

'That will be a permanent handicap if you don't get a move on.'

'Alright, alright.' Kyd mounted grudgingly but it was hard to escape from his irrepressible good humour. We both found ourselves laughing as we set off in the wake of the carriage.

* * *

An hour later Kyd left me at the gates of Stavening. We agreed that he would continue the further half dozen miles to Rye and find suitable lodgings. I would visit Rye on some pretence in the next few days and seek him out. If Kyd had not heard from me within a week, he was to find some excuse for visiting the house.

Kyd tried to explain his plan to me as to which tavern I would find him lodging in.

'I'll go to the first inn I find whose name includes something with legs – you know the Horse and Cart, or The Dragon. However, I'll start with the least number of legs – so it will be the Pheasant, or the Green Man, for example. If that inn isn't suitable, I will carry on to next one whose name also has legs and so on – gradually increasing the number of legs until I find somewhere suitable. You follow? All you have to do is use the same system and you'll find me soon enough.'

'But what if it's got the same number of legs? Why am I even having this conversation?'

'Good point. If it has the same number of legs then we need to work on a system that takes into account animal hierarchy – horse above cow, cow above pig and so on.'

'Have you ever stayed in an inn called the Coach and Chickens?'

'Not that I recall but what's that got to do with it? All you have to do is follow the system and you're sure to find me.'

'All I have to do is ask at any inn whether or not they've had a great coxcomb ask for lodgings in the last few days. That way I'll find you a lot quicker.'

'You are unkind Lovat. You'll never make a great leader if you dampen subordinate initiative.'

'Get going you fool and look after yourself.' We shook hands warmly and parted company.

I entered through a grand gatehouse and began to pass through the dozens of acres that surrounded Hardwick's house. The outer land was given to deer and hunting parks, where the dark shapes of animals could be seen huddling against the edges of the forest for warmth. As the house came closer, the landscape became more civilised with rows of orchards followed by a great garden, which contained all manner of shaped hedges and blue and white striped poles supporting wooden carvings of heraldic creatures; amongst others I espied a luzern and a griffin. To the west of the house there were a number of raised banks, where in the summer guests could sit and admire the intricate knot patterns and parterres laid out around the house. To the east lay an ornamental maze and beyond that the spire of a small church could be seen just above a thicket of trees. Behind the house, the garden undulated down and then up again in a gentle valley that eventually gave way to trees that marked the beginning of the Weald and higher ground. However, in its formality, the garden as a whole was a far cry from the wild rolling countryside around my father's Cotswold estate and seemed to have been designed with an eye towards entertaining prestigious guests, including, no doubt, Royalty.

There were a number of men working in the gardens, despite the cold weather, tidying the hedges and the beds, pruning back the apple and medlar trees, and I imagined that in the warmer months these gardens would be teeming with hundreds of workers, all doing their master's bidding. Many of those braving the cold glanced up at me suspiciously as I rode by, as if they wondered what sort of fool would be riding out in this weather, making me feel all the more exposed in the wide open landscape.

The house itself was a huge affair – part castle, part country home.

There was a medieval hall surrounded by towers with ramparts, as well as a whole new extension, in the Italianate style which, by the look of the scaffolding supporting it, was still in the process of being built, although the builders had wisely retired for the winter. This new building design was a style that I knew my brother to covet and one he would happily raze the Chancel House to the ground for, if he had the funds. Perhaps it was this sort of aspiration that had fuelled his unwise involvement in the shipping adventure.

I rode straight up to the front door, passing as I did the very same carriage that had overtaken us earlier on the road. Now disgorged of its passengers, it was presumably on its way to the stables. The driver doffed his cap to me as I came alongside him. Heart in mouth I dismounted with the help of a servant and strode cautiously into the bowels of the great house. The front door opened onto a wide hallway with a high ceiling. I had barely taken two steps forward and was still trying to adjust my eyes to the change in light, when I heard a shrill shriek. Looking sideways I saw coming down a grand staircase to the side of the hall the very same lady who I had seen with Anne, and who had later visited me in my lodgings, surrounded by four ladies-in-waiting, all of whom were gaping at her wondering what had made her shout out. Leticia Hardwick, for now I was convinced that it was she, had her eyes fixed on me. As I returned her gaze, her hand flew to her mouth, and she turned as white as the virgin snow I had seen that morning, collapsing in a dramatic faint.

The four ladies-in-waiting all turned their eyes towards me, their expressions holding a mixture of shock and, dare I say it, admiration.

Chapter 25

"Things forbidden have a secret charm."
(Publius Cornelius Tacitus)

'So you're a sort of nephew of Walsingham's are you? Well, what the hell does he expect me to do with you? Who does Walsingham think he is? What does he think I run here, for that matter, some sort of alms-house? Why can't he take you in? What the hell's wrong with you that he won't own up to, eh?'

My first meeting with Hardwick had not got off to the most auspicious of starts. It looked as though he was going to turn me out on my ear before I'd even had a tour of the house. To say the very least, his manner was hostile. Thank goodness that he had no idea of the impact that my arrival had just had on his wife. My first impression of him was that he was capable of anything, including setting up my brother and murdering Don Alphonse.

At least he was buying the cover story – only too well as it happened.

'Do you have any idea Lovat how many hangers-on I already have about this place? An entire army of them – sons, brothers and nephews of the great and good in London. I've got a bellyful of them. All sent here by the likes of Walsingham, who aren't inclined to look after their own. All wanting to advance their prospects at my expense. All useless to a man.'

Hardwick was nothing like I had imagined. I had pictured a wizened old seadog with a certain amount of charm and dash about him. What I found instead was a squat bull of man, less than five feet tall, with a large round head rather like the ball that Drake had been rumoured to have been bowling at Plymouth Hoe, as the Spanish Armada appeared on the horizon. On his shiny head there was no sign of the wild red hair that had prompted Don Alphonse and his father to christen him the 'red devil'. His ample frame was stuffed into a threadbare doublet of a style at least two decades out of date, and which looked very much as though it may have been the same one that he wore on his maiden sea voyage. There was no sign from his appearance that he was one of the wealthiest and most influential men in England.

Standing to one side, and watching me closely with a cold impassive eye, was a wiry, grey-haired Scotsman with a face like granite, who had been introduced simply as Dakers. He had been in consultation with Hardwick when my arrival had been announced and Hardwick had bade him stay to hear what I wanted. He said very little throughout the meeting but kept his cold eyes trained on me as if, whatever Hardwick thought, he didn't believe a word of anything I said. The interaction between them gradually led me to understand that Dakers was in charge of many of Hardwick's day-to-day affairs, a bit like Nesbitt to my brother.

To avoid the discomfort of the Scotsman's penetrative stare, as much as to look as nonchalant as possible, I found my eyes wandering around the room. The state of the study gave an insight, of a sort, into the man who inhabited it – namely that he wasn't very tidy. Piles of paper stood on every conceivable surface, some over a foot high, which, when combined with the height of the desk, had the unintentionally amusing effect at times of completely obscuring Hardwick. I groaned inwardly – it was one thing to search for secret papers, but quite another to take the risk of sifting through endless dusty piles in the hope of finding something incriminating. Unlike Walsingham's study, there were few books to be seen, just endless sheathes of parchment crammed into shelves, interspersed with unusual and strange ornaments that might have been souvenirs of Hardwick's travels. Hanging on a nail I noticed a seal on a chain very similar to the one that Don Alphonse had been strangled with but my eye was then drawn by another ornament, which was striking – and revolting – in equal measure. It looked like the shrunken head of a Negro. A macabre souvenir from his travels, no doubt.

'Well don't just stand there gawping Lovat, what skills do you possess?'

'Er... commercial skills, bookkeeping, translation sire.'

'Languages?'

'French, Latin, Italian, a little German.'

'I see. So fancies himself as a bit of a linguist, eh Dakers?'

Dakers said in a rich highland brogue: 'So it would appear, sire.' His eyes, on the other hand, boring into my skull, said: 'I don't believe a word of it'.

'Fancy yourself as a bit of linguist do you Lovat?'

'Not exactly sir.'

'Know any Flemish?'

'I'm afraid not sir.'

'Useless, what did I tell you? It just so happens I've got a consignment of Florentine Majolica just arrived from Antwerp – all the paperwork written in that interminable language and not one dolt in the entire household who can understand a word of it. Too much to hope that Lovat would be that man, eh Dakers?'

Dakers said nothing, his eyes merely confirming that it was too much to expect anything at all from this worthless specimen.

'Perhaps my rudimentary German may be of some use?'

'May it, by God? Though why anyone would want to learn such an ugly language is beyond me. Don't care for Germans. Don't care much for the Flemish, for that matter. Arrogant lot! What commercial skills?'

'Keeping ledgers, checking invoices, filing – that kind of thing.' Here I was on shaky ground, but Faunt had suggested a good way of getting close to Hardwick's dealings was to pass myself off as a bookkeeper.

'So, are you a bugger Lovat? The only good bookkeepers I ever knew were buggers or Lutherans. Which do you own up to?'

'Neither, I must profess, sire?'

'Neither, ay? Well, we could always do with someone keeping records who isn't a complete idiot. What do you say Dakers?'

Dakers' mouth said: 'As you wish, your lordship.' His eyes said: 'I wouldn't trust this imbecile as far as I could spit.'

Hardwick disappeared behind a pile of papers as he gave some thought to the matter. All I could see was the top of his shiny head. 'All right, Lovat, you can have a berth for the night, at least. If I can't find anything for you here, I'll find you something down at the port. Get Champernowne to show you to your quarters. Work hard, keep your mouth shut, and all will be well. No one stays in this house without earning their bread. You understand me, Lovat? See that you do and we'll get along just fine'.

I said I understood whilst bowing low, and then retreated from the room. Just as I reached the doorway, and just out of sight of Hardwick, who had returned to some papers on the desk, Dakers caught my arm, his unflinching gaze drilled into me.

'Lovat's an interesting name. Where does it come from?'

'As for the name, I have no idea, but as for myself from Gloucestershire.'

'Gloucestershire? Doesn't the honourable Lord Rokesby have an estate in Gloucestershire?'

My blood froze in my veins at the mention of my brother. 'I wouldn't know. I'm from more humble stock, sir.'

'Are you indeed?' He stared at me for fully ten seconds without blinking, his hand still gripping my arm.

'Dakers, have you got that shipment order?' Hardwick called impatiently from somewhere behind his desk. Dakers kept both his grip and eyes fixed for a full five seconds more before releasing me. Shaken, I moved quickly out of the room.

* * *

Ever since Walsingham had voiced his desire for me to infiltrate Hardwick's household, I had known that bumping into Leticia Hardwick was a distinct possibility, but I hadn't expected it to happen the moment I had walked through the front entrance. The commotion that followed had been right out of a mystery play farce. The four ladies-in-waiting, one of whom I recognised as the maid that had accompanied her to my lodgings, their attention on me and not their mistress, had barely noticed her beginning to fall down the stairs. Without thinking, I had leapt forward, bounded up three or four steps at a time and caught the lady in my arms, just as her head was about to hit a hard stone step. What made it all the more surreal was that as I carried Leticia Hardwick down the stairs to place her on a long couch in the hallway, she had opened one eye and winked at me.

The butler of the house, a very old man with long, ragged grey hair and a crooked back, who I now knew by the name of Champernowne, had heard the commotion and produced a pouch of smelling salts, which he proceeded to wave under her ladyship's nose. However, he must have been so short sighted that he proceeded to drop most of it over her ruff and into the cleavage of her dress, which meant that she had to act very hard to pretend that she was still in a faint, whilst trying not to choke. I almost laughed but by this time I had been pushed out of the way by the four maids who had belatedly woken up to the fact that their mistress was in some kind of distress.

Champernowne had soon been pushed out of the way too and I took the opportunity to ask him where I could find Hardwick. Champernowne had walked me along corridors, upstairs, and around various rooms of state, all at a snail's pace, until we had arrived at Hardwick's study and my first encounter had taken place with the shiny-headed entrepreneur and his sinister aide.

After Hardwick had dismissed me, I was looking for Champernowne when I was accosted by the same maid that had accompanied Lady Hardwick to my lodgings. She spoke to me in a hushed whisper.

'Master Lovat, my lady wishes to see you in her private rooms.'

'Now?'

'Yes sir.'

'She has quite recovered from her faint, then?'

'Oh quite recovered, Master.' I couldn't detect any irony in her voice. The maid led the way along another maze of corridors, stairs and rooms until we arrived at Leticia Hardwick's private boudoir, which amounted to a suite of four light and airy rooms at the opposite end of the house from Hardwick's study.

'You gave me quite a shock earlier, Master Lovat.' Leticia Hardwick had dispensed with the services of her maids and was reclining on a huge four-poster bed. She dismissed the remaining maid with a wave of her hand, and motioned for me to stop stooping in front of her and come and sit on a chair by her bedside. There was no veil this time and I was able to appreciate the full beauty of her features without hindrance. Her pale face could not quite hide the pink flush of youth in her cheeks, nor the rubicund colour of her delicate lips, which were permanently set in a sardonic, slightly crooked smile. As well as beauty, there was something else described on the features of Leticia's face – insolence, defiance, a world-weariness even. The loveliness of her face was set off by wild, rich hair, which she had attempted to tame with a loose plait.

'I beg your pardon, your Ladyship. I didn't wish to give you a shock. Though not such a shock I believe as your Ladyship is unable to stand.'

'I felt it expedient earlier to pretend that I wasn't feeling well. Not that it worked of course – my ladies all think that I fainted at the sight of your good looks. I'd be careful if I was you. The story will spread around the house like wildfire and my husband is prone to jealousy.' I took a seat next to her bedside. 'But what are you doing in this house, Master Lovat? I thought our agreement was that I would seek you out. In fact I even tried to do so this morning, to discover from the pretty young girl … what's her name? Emma something? … that you had left London. If I had known you were coming here, I would have saved myself the trouble.'

I thought for a moment how to explain my presence in the house: 'I am here on another matter – one that is only loosely connected with the matter between us and concerns your husband rather than yourself.'

'My husband?' There was a brief pause while she took this in. 'I am not interested in the affairs of that … pigmy.' The word was spat out with a level of contempt that was as venomous as it was unexpected. 'Aside from that, do you have any news for me?'

'I do your ladyship. I have found the gentleman you sought, safe and well, and in the house where you suggested I should look.'

'God be praised. I am so relieved. I had heard a rumour that he was dead.'

'Very much alive and in rude health, I am pleased to report.'

'Then I believe I owe you further recompense.' She swept elegantly off the bed and began to reach into the drawer of a bedside cabinet. Taking into account her opinion of her husband, I decided to try my luck.

'Perhaps, madam, you would honour me with some information, rather than a financial reward?'

'Information? Of what kind?' She tilted her perfectly smooth, white neck and fixed me with her sparkling sapphire eyes. I felt immediately that I may have overstepped the mark but soldiered on gamely.

'Information about the affairs of this house … your husband.'

'You may have some considerable charm, but don't assume that, simply because he is an uneducated oaf, I will readily betray him.' She reached into the closet and pulled out a similar bag to the one she had produced in my lodgings. 'Here. You had better take this and we'll say no more about it.'

She handed me the bag. It felt quite heavy, which was some consolation for the reproach I felt. I thought I had better cut my losses and simply said: 'I beg your pardon your ladyship. I didn't mean to be impertinent.'

'Think nothing of it, Lovat. I like a man who tries his luck. Whilst you are in this house you will find no enemy here. In fact be prepared, I may require your services again.'

* * *

My first few days at Stavening were relatively uneventful. I spent them ingratiating myself into the household and trying to think of ways of getting the evidence I needed to prove that my brother had been set up and that Hardwick was guilty of treason. On the first, I felt sure that Walsingham was right. Hardwick had used my brother's vanity to set him up, and eventually bring him crashing down. I wasn't sure I would find the proof but, even so, I somehow knew this to be true in my bones. The attitudes of Drummond and Turney, the conniving of Ingram and his cronies, the fear that I had sensed in my brother – the only thing I needed to do was connect Hardwick to the plot.

On the second point, though, I felt very unsure. Nothing about Hardwick, or his household, suggested treasonous behaviour. The whole estate was geared towards the business of trade and making as much wealth as possible. There barely seemed time for anything else, least of all overturning the country. The only person guilty of treasonous behaviour, as far as I could tell, was Hardwick's wife, who had betrayed their marriage bed. I began to wonder if Walsingham was either mistaken or pursuing some private vendetta against Hardwick for reasons unfathomable to me. The thought made me feel very uneasy.

I was given a room in the attic of the house, that I was to share with a young clerk called Tichborne, and put to work on translating Latin legal documents into English. Sadly, there was nothing in the least controversial about them and all I could do was knuckle down to the tasks Hardwick set me, whilst gradually developing my cover and gaining his trust.

I was placed in an office outside Hardwick's inner sanctum, where I was subject to the constant observation of Dakers, who had his desk not three feet away from mine. Apart from Tichborne and myself, there was one other man, an aloof Frenchman with a gaunt face called Vaillons, who came and went regularly and seemed to have responsibilities at the port of Rye. Vaillons and Dakers were the only two ever admitted to Hardwick's study and Tichborne, who had only been there himself for two months, and myself, were very much made to feel the junior employees. At times when Dakers and Vaillons were in our bureau, the atmosphere was like a morgue with no one saying a word for hours. In their absence, Tichborne and I relieved the stolid atmosphere, as well as our boredom, by indulging in idle chatter or playing improvised games of shove ha'penny across the tops of our desks.

I didn't see Leticia Hardwick at all during the hours of daytime – the only time that the whole household came together was for dinner. Tichborne and I took our lunch together, either at our desks or kicking our feet through the winter landscape in the garden, whilst admiring the craftwork of the gardeners and carpenters.

During one of our excursions around the snowy wastes of the garden, I managed to engineer our path so that we were walking along the back of the house close to the exterior of Hardwick's study. Since arriving, I had been giving a lot of thought as to how I was going to get into Hardwick's inner sanctum without being caught. On one occasion I had waited as late as possible before going to the office on a pretext that I needed some advice on a paper I was translating. I had found Hardwick, Dakers and Vaillons bent over Hardwick's desk in close conference. They had all looked at me in an unfriendly manner and I had made my excuses and left. At night Tichborne and I were kicked out of our side office and the whole end of the building was locked.

The outside proved just as unpromising for a spot of breaking and entering. Hardwick's offices were on the first floor of the building in an old, fortified part of the house. The windows were barred and below them was a straight drop to the terrace. It was also a side of the house that was exposed to the whole garden – any attempt at scaling the wall and breaking in would be extremely risky. I dropped the idea then and there.

Tichborne was a pleasant lad of twenty, with fresh, innocent looks and unassuming manner. He wore round eyeglasses that gave him a studious air and, like Pinchkin Junior, had a tuft of blond hair on his head that refused to lie down whatever pressure he brought to bear on it. The room in the attic was awash with lotions and waxes of every kind, none of which proved in the least effective.

Fortunately, Tichborne saw no danger in chatting amiably to me. He told me that he was a distant cousin of Hardwick's and had been sent here by his guardian after he had come down from Cambridge the previous summer. His family were Catholic and the most exciting thing that had happened in the family in the previous years had been the execution of another of his distant cousins, Chidiock Tichborne, for his part in the Babington plot that Walsingham had discussed with me only the previous week. I wanted to tell him that I had witnessed the Pretender Mary's execution myself but thought better of it as it didn't fit with my cover story, and in any case might not fall that sympathetically on Catholic ears. Instead, I jokingly asked him what sort of name Chidiock was. He laughed, before telling me with a straight face that his cousin was named after a village in Dorset. In the meantime, I reflected with some relief, there was at least one link in the Hardwick household to that treasonous event, however tenuous.

Tichborne was able to tell me what little he knew about Dakers and Vaillons. Vaillons was in charge of all of Hardwick's French trade, the bulk of his business dealings, and was constantly going backwards and forwards across the channel on a variety of ships. He was also a Catholic and Tichborne suggested that he tried to be in France every Sunday so that he could say Mass in safety. I wondered mischievously to myself where he took Mass when he was stuck in England, and whether or not Hardwick joined him. Tichborne told me that the Frenchman kept himself to himself most of the time and seemed to regard his English counterparts, with the exception of Hardwick and Dakers, with disdain. Hardwick also had an office in Rye and there were two or three other clerks working there, and Tichborne said that Vaillons treated this office as his own private fiefdom.

Unlike Vaillons, Dakers was a Scottish Protestant, who was known to preach the righteousness of the new religion, which didn't seem to fit at all with the idea of Hardwick as a secret Catholic. Dakers had been in service to Hardwick for many years, had served with him at sea, and was known for being a hard taskmaster. Tichborne told me of another clerk who had been driven out of the house only a week ago because his work hadn't met Dakers' approval.

I was careful not to ask Tichborne too many questions as I didn't want to rouse his suspicions, but he did offer one tantalising piece of information without much prompting. It was a day when heavy sleet was adding to the overnight snow and we were crouching round the small fireplace in our office, both of us tucking into a small plate of roast meats that had been brought by Champernowne. Dakers and Vaillons were in with Hardwick and the rest of the house felt deserted.

'It's much quieter around here now than it was a month ago.'

'What do you mean?'

'Well a month ago you could barely move around here for bumping into somebody. People coming and going, meetings taking place.'

'Who was here?' I said out of the side of my mouth, as I chewed on a piece of gristle, trying to make myself sound disinterested as possible. 'Anyone of renown?'

'No, quite the opposite. The sort of men who stay in the shadows if you understand me?'

'You mean the type that don't like to draw attention to themselves.'

'Yes. A rough lot.'

'What were they doing here?'

'Good question. They didn't seem to do much work. One of them spent a lot of time in Hardwick's office, with Vaillons and Dakers, whilst his two henchmen sat around here making impolite remarks about those like myself who were of a bookish persuasion.' A man with two henchmen – could this be Ingram, Grayson and Scarface? Linking them to the house would go a long way to supporting Walsingham's assertions of the plot against my brother. I thought about how to play it.

'You see a lot of groups like that in London. One organ-grinder and a couple of monkeys. The monkeys usually wear their scars quite openly. Gives the organ-grinder a bit of kudos.'

'Funny you should say that. One of this lot had a scar on his face – livid it was, running right down his cheek,' Tichborne shuddered, 'nasty piece of work.'

I said nothing, choosing instead to concentrate on the gristle, but taking some satisfaction in the knowledge that Ingram had been plotting in this house not more than a month ago.

Chapter 26

'A wife, a spaniel, a walnut tree:
The more you beat them, the better they be.'
(Elizabethan Proverb)

There was little to do at Stavening in the evenings and I spent the time on my attic mattress, reading Don Alphonse's manuscript. I waited until Tichborne was asleep before producing it from my bag, because although he seemed harmless enough, I thought it prudent not to rouse any suspicion.

Reading the manuscript was comforting for a number of reasons. It was pleasant in this unfamiliar environment to have a physical connection to my life in London, not to mention the bewitching girl whose work I was holding, but, having discovered Don Alphonse's connection to Hardwick in the document, I also still held strong hope that there would be other useful clues forthcoming.

Most importantly, though, reading the manuscript gave me some relief from the anxiety I felt in this foreboding house, and gave me respite from the unpleasant suspicions swirling around my head. I had gone out on a limb for Walsingham but why? Because I wanted to impress him? Because I wanted to finally escape the drudgery of my brother's household? Because I wanted to advance myself?

And what was the truth of my mission at Stavening? Don Alphonse had been murdered, that much was beyond dispute but, despite any suspicions I might have, by whom, and why, seemed further from my grasp than ever before. Instead, I had allowed the fervour I felt in wanting to unmask the killer of a stranger to pull me into an altogether different, more dangerous and complex affair, working for men whose motives I didn't trust and whose machinations I didn't understand. The manuscript in its simplicity of authorship and its epic narrative was a welcome distraction.

* * *

Many months have passed and much has happened since I last had the opportunity of making an entry in these pages. After many weeks of hardship at the hands of our captives, Cassangoe and I have finally managed to escape their clutches. The idea had come to us both separately but one night we fell to discussing it and found that our plots were of one mind. With each new day that our captors took us out into the jungle, where we forced to dig for yamyams – a tubular vegetable with rough skin that grows in very hard ground – they appeared to become less and less concerned that we would try to escape. Cassangoe and I decided to enforce that idea by acting as weak and docile as possible. It meant we were forced to take increased beatings as our cruel masters upped their means of encouragement, but it also ensured that they were far from ready when we sprang our surprise.

On the day we escaped, about twenty other slaves and only half a dozen guards had accompanied us into the jungle. Most of the guards took the opportunity to sit around talking and smoking qat, a strong narcotic that the natives in these parts partake of in abundance. Occasionally one would get up to shout at us, seemingly made madder by the effects of the tobacco, but it generally rendered them lethargic and sleepy. As we worked we watched them secretly, waiting for the moment we knew would come when one or two were sleeping, the flies playing around their faces.

Instead of digging I spent the morning hours hacking at the manacles around our legs with the small metal tool I had been given. Cassangoe worked doubly hard making the amount of vegetables dug up look like the work of two. Finally I broke through the chain and signalled to Cassangoe. We then signalled to the nearest guard, as was common, that we wanted to take a break in the bushes. He pushed us on in his usual lazy manner, not suspecting that both of us were now free to move easily. Once we were out of sight of the others Cassangoe struck. He lifted the chains that we had been dragging and with a sudden movement wrapped them around the neck of our captor and pulled viciously. There was no sound and in a few tense moments the deed was done. Cassangoe left him to slump in a heap and we both ran for our lives into the jungle.

I have never run so hard or fast in my life. We kept on until my heart was pounding so greatly that I thought it was going to burst through my chest. Every time I fell over a branch, or collapsed for want of breath, Cassangoe would haul me to my feet and pull me onwards. His strength seemed inexhaustible. We continued deep into the thickest part of the forest, away from the village of our captors, through rivers and swamps, and thickets and trees; ripping our skin on branches and stones, stubbing our bare feet on rocks and stumps, tearing our muscles as we climbed over fallen trees, or beat our way through the raging force of rivers.

After it seemed that we had been running for a lifetime, Cassangoe deemed it safe for us to pause and assess our situation. We had reached a rocky outcrop on the edge of a wide river and we climbed to the top before collapsing in exhaustion. Colourful birds soared over our heads, monkeys howled in the trees, water crashed into the river from a tributary – but there was no sound of our tormentors chasing us, no shouts of discovery or whistle of spears. Perhaps they had given up or never even tried to recapture us. Instinctively we knew we were free. I wanted to roll back on the rock and laugh the laugh of a madman but Cassangoe stayed my mouth with a large, black hand. After resting for a few minutes he motioned me onwards.

We walk for days like two spirits of the forest, not seeing another soul save the animals and birds that populate the jungle. When we encounter villages deep in the jungle we wait until nightfall and then skirt round them, loath as we are to put our faith in the humanity of anyone we encounter. The forest changes shape and is never still. At times it is swampy and in the waters lie great crocodiles that can easily overturn our makeshift canoes. In these God forsaken places there are also thousands of insects that continually harry and attack our flesh. At other times the forest is like a limitless cathedral, with thick brown-and-white columns stretching as far as the eye can see, enclosed by a ceiling of rainy mist and with only the occasional large fern as decoration. In other parts, the terrain becomes rougher and thicker in foliage, where endless thorny ropes hang down from the forest canopy and we are forced to crawl under great fallen trees that block our route. It rains relentlessly and we are always soaked but every evening before sunset the rain always stops and the mists clear and we are able to take some respite. Mostly though I believe all manner of burdens have been sent to test us by the cruel Gods that have taken ownership of our souls.

There is no doubt that I would be dead already had it not been for Cassangoe. He has an inexhaustible knowledge of plants and found us herbs to eat, or to press on our wounds. He taught me which flowers collected rain within their leaves and how to make clothes and shoes from bark and reeds. The only knowledge I could offer was my under-

standing of the sun and its rotation, learnt on a ship's deck, and on the few occasions that the sun shone I was able to keep us moving northwards, away from the coast where I had been abandoned for dead, and away from the towns and villages where we had been caged for so long. In my mind, I tried to envisage a map of Africa that my father had proudly displayed in his cabin and tried to picture where we were but it was a forlorn hope that anything remembered would be useful. All I knew from the map was that if we kept going north we would eventually arrive at the Mediterranean Sea and beyond that the civilisation that I knew. When I told Cassangoe this he laughed. He says that he wants to see the sort of civilisation that causes brutal wars all along his coastal homeland and can enslave whole populations. Stung by this criticism, and the truth of his words, I told him of many wondrous things to be found there too – some I knew first hand, others I had only read of – the port at Lisbon where thousands of huge ships can nestle side by side, cities such as Venice and Krakow, where wealth, beauty and learning jostle together, the glittering court of the virgin Queen Elizabeth in England, where it is said all the colours of the spectrum can be seen amongst one meeting of the court. I have promised myself that I will visit many of the earth's wonders if we survive.

At times, our journey north seemed to be endless and fruitless. Many times I sat in despair upon the damp earth professing my reluctance to continue but each time Cassangoe encouraged and cajoled me onwards. On one particularly desperate day, when I felt as though my legs and heart would both give out, he sat beside me and taught me a song from his native lands:

Calm down, little brother,
Time heals all wounds,
No matter how much one is weeping,
The moon always follows the sun

Eat your bananas and fresh leaves,
And don't cry anymore,
Because forever and ever,
The moon will follow the sun.

Now every time I start to feel the weight of hopelessness upon me, we strike up this song in tandem and it gives me the strength to match his. These days in the jungle will stay with me always, and always with that simple tune.

After countless days, the jungle slowly began to turn to scrub, and the scrub slowly became savannah. We were more exposed but there were fewer dangers too. The land was wild with few inhabitants save herds of creatures that I had only read of before but never dreamed of seeing in the flesh. The land steadily rose until we were walking on high cliff tops, overlooking spoon-shaped valleys and wide rivers. The only humans we encountered were shepherds most of whom were too frightened by our appearance to approach us. Eventually though our trust in and need for human company was returning. We tentatively approached a remote village that we found perched high on the edge of a cliff and we discovered the people to be inquisitive but friendly. To me, their language was beyond even the most rudimentary understanding I had picked up in captivity but Cassangoe was able to find common ground with them. They told him of trading routes that went to the north and great cities at the end of them. We resolved to find them and after a few days of the villagers' hospitality, Cassangoe and I set out, re-clothed and refreshed, and with generous provisions bestowed upon us; a new sense of purpose in our strides. A guide led us out of the village and pointed us on the route we should take.

After a further week's travel we came to a mountain ridge where, some miles ahead in the valley below us, we could see the flowing, dusty train of a caravan snaking its way slowly northwards. We knew we must have discovered the trading route we had been told of. After a day of trailing them we caught up with the train of carts and asked for passage in return for offering our services, howsoever they might be used. The leader of the caravan, a jovial man called Assam, accepted our offer and it is from the back of one of the stage-wagons that I now write these passages as we make our way slowly and deliberately northwards. The caravan has a rich cargo of gold, iron, ivory, wood and kola nuts. There are also black slaves and in order to allay suspicion, Cassangoe has taken the role of my servant. Assam spends much of his leisure tormenting these poor brutes and offering them to me. It will be a wonder if we reach our destination without Cassangoe killing him.

Our destination lies four days hence – Assam continually tells us of a great city in the desert where every manner of commodity can be found and bought. It is called Timbuktu.

* * *

Despite the presence of his luxurious wife, dinner in the Hardwick household was a grim affair. This was not a reflection on the food, which proved to be far richer and fancier than anything I had previously experienced, even in my brother's household. It also made Walsingham's simple lunch look positively frugal, but there was none of the erudite discussion and worldly interest that I had experienced there. Instead, the diners had to sit through a constant diatribe from Hardwick, the theme of which was generally along the lines of 'nobody knows how to do anything except me' and 'if I was running this country' and so on. There was little evidence of the array of 'useless' hangers-on amongst those eating, unless Hardwick was referring to his kinsmen. Apart from Dakers, Vaillons, Tichborne and myself, they appeared mostly to be a ragged assortment of ageing relatives, who, judging by the cowed manner in which they put their heads down and got on with the business of supping, were well used to listening to Hardwick holding forth. When Hardwick wasn't giving his tiresome opinions about the state of the country, the economy or the government, he turned his attention to one or other of the relatives and their various failings and inadequacies.

The only brightness in the gloomy dining hall emanated from Leticia Hardwick, who sat serenely at the opposite end of the table from Hardwick and deflected all of his barbed comments, which seemed to be particularly vicious as far as she was concerned, with a patient smile or change of topic. In the presence of her husband, her youthfulness seemed even more at odds with her situation, and it was difficult to imagine a less well-suited couple. Where he was narrow-minded and gruff, she was expansive and radiant; where he was charmless and self-obsessed, she was luminous and attentive; where he was obdurate and rude, she was witty, amenable and refined. Her clever combating of Hardwick's various vulgarities would result in a bout of pocket-sized grunting, followed by an attack on his food with gusto for a few moments before the launch of another offensive.

It was only a matter of time before his attention focused on me and on my fourth dinner in the household I had to endure a sustained period of being held up as the 'feckless' youth of today that was the cause of all of the country's problems. The fact that I didn't rise to the bait seemed only to spur Hardwick on and in the end it was Leticia Hardwick, who made an ill-fated attempt to come to my rescue.

'I beg your pardon, my dear husband, but if it wasn't for the bravery of young men such as Lovat here, we would have had a much harder time repelling the Spanish invasion. It might even be some Spaniard sitting where you are now.'

'Absolute balderdash! It was the superiority of our ships that made the difference. What does a woman know about it anyway? Needlework, that's what you know about, needlework and sitting on your pampered arse all day.'

'And who do you think was manning those ships, dear husband?' The sarcasm of that 'dear' could be cut with a knife. 'Young men like Lovat. Not old farts like yourself, that's for certain.' She said it with a slight laugh in her voice but there was no doubting that she really meant it.

'Old fart ay? I might be an old fart to you, my dear, but just remember which old fart keeps you in the manner to which you have become oh-so-well accustomed and which I doubt any other of your young men would be able to provide.' He looked at her pointedly with this remark, but his wife said nothing, spurring him on to further insults. 'Besides, if it were a Spaniard sitting here I have no doubt that you would feel perfectly well accommodated.'

Silence descended on the table. Assorted relatives and staff halted in mid chew; eyes fixed ahead on anything but the two protagonists. I glanced at Lady Hardwick – her face had turned a bright pink but apart from that she showed admirable composure. The look in her eyes would have reduced many men to a charred heap, but not Hardwick, who stared back through hard, narrow eyes and dared her to speak. After the most excruciating of silences, Lady Hardwick rose stiffly but elegantly from her chair, causing the whole table to rise with her – except for Hardwick, who sat triumphantly in his seat, gnawing malevolently on a chicken leg.

'I think I'll take the rest of my dinner in my private rooms. I feel a slight chill.'

'As you wish *my dear*. I'm sure the rest of us can manage without you.' And with this final riposte ringing in her ears, Leticia Hardwick swept from the dining room, followed by an entourage of maids.

* * *

After dinner I was in the room I shared with Tichborne, listening to him snoring and perusing Don Alphonse's story, when there was a slight tap on the door and a small piece of paper was pushed under it. Intrigued, I reached for the paper, which was a folded note with the single word *Lovat* writ large on one side. I opened it out – in Lady Hardwick's hand it asked me to pay a visit to her quarters at once.

I took the candle and crept quietly through the corridors of the sleeping house. There were many unfamiliar stairs and passageways to negotiate and I wanted to make the journey without attracting anyone's attention. I could hear the sounds of servants somewhere in the bowels of the house, presumably preparing the table for the morning, but I met no one along the corridors.

On reaching her door, I knocked quietly and heard the command 'enter'.

I entered and went through the usual rigmarole of bowing low to my betters.

'Your ladyship.'

Unlike before, Lady Hardwick was not draped elegantly across her bed but sitting at a writing desk to one side of the room, surrounded by an array of candlelit lamps and writing a letter in rounded handwriting. She had switched the elaborate dress she had worn at dinner for a long, patterned gown that made her look even younger and a lot more vulnerable than usual.

'Lovat.' She continued writing without glancing at me.

'How can I be of service to you, your Ladyship?'

'You can't. I sent you that note because I wish to be of service to you.'

'Your ladyship?' I was in very real peril of misunderstanding her and kept looking at the ground. Without looking at me, she must have sensed what I was thinking.

'Don't flatter yourself, Lovat. I may think you handsome but my heart is beholden elsewhere.'

I began to blush, stammering that I had no idea what she meant. Leticia Hardwick finally looked at me.

'You can stop calling my 'your ladyship'. Leticia or Letty will do. Now, bolt the door and sit down, for goodness sake. Standing there, you look like an overgrown schoolboy.' She indicated a chair at the desk. 'A few days ago you asked me for information but I wasn't inclined to humour your request. However, you heard how my husband spoke to me this evening. What is it you want to know? I find that I am suddenly only too happy to be of assistance.'

She was so direct that it took me a moment to order my thoughts. I looked at her face, which was wide-eyed and earnest.

'What if your husband should chance upon us?'

'There is no danger of that happening. The last time my husband visited me in the night was two years ago – and he found the door locked. Well?'

'There are a number of things, your Ladyship.' She looked at me sharply. 'Leticia. Do you remember that morning when you first saw me at the Chancel House? When Anne pointed me out to you and said I would help you.'

'Yes. I remember.' She stopped writing and tilted her delicate chin towards me. Even in this light I could see that her cerulean eyes held something other than the usual mixture of beauty and disdain but I couldn't quite pinpoint the emotion. What was it? Revenge? Regret? Anger? Whatever was causing it, there was a new fire burning in her that only served to make her more beautiful. 'How could I forget that day – it was that very night that Alphonse disappeared.'

I remembered that Don Alphonse had been the go-between twixt her and Cassangoe and realised that they must also have been close, although the way she said it one could have been forgiven for thinking that Don Alphonse was also her lover. I felt another irrational pang of jealousy.

'That day, you came to the Chancel House with your husband?'

'That's right. He took me to London for the Queen's parade and then had business at the house. I spent the evening and the next day with Anne. He went to the Ascension Day tilts, where his son was presented at court. A son by a previous marriage I should add.' Whilst being in the house I had wondered where Hardwick's son, Richard, was but had learnt from Tichborne that he had lodgings in London, was concentrating on soldiery and had very little dealings with his father's business. I wondered if Hardwick was keeping him away from his nefarious businesses on purpose.

'Had your husband had dealings with …', I stopped myself saying 'my brother'. I had no idea what Anne had told Leticia about me. If she didn't know I was Robert's brother then it seemed prudent not to tell her in case it became common knowledge throughout the house. Once again I was reminded of the dangerous game I was playing '…Sir Robert Rokesby beforehand.'

'No. And I must say it surprised me that he did.'

'Wherefore?'

'Because my husband despises Robert and all of the similar young upstarts, as he puts it, that hover about court and gain the ear of the Queen. It is common knowledge in this house and surely must be obvious to you after suffering only a handful of dinners.'

I changed tack. 'But, in this case, Don Alphonse was a connection?'

'Alphonse visits the country houses of Britain with impunity, although he certainly has business with my husband and I believe he has business dealings with Sir Robert also.' Whenever she spoke of Don Alphonse she couldn't keep a note of admiration out of her voice. Her use of the present tense made it suddenly occur to me that she had no idea that he was dead. I decided it was better not to tell her.

'Do you know what your husband and Don Alphonse are involved in with Lord Rokesby?'

'An adventure by sea I believe. They are always planning such schemes.'

'Don Alphonse planned it?'

'Yes. What is this Lovat? I thought you were interested in my husband.'

'I am, only, Anne is worried about her husband's latest venture and I thought I could help her in some way.' I decided to leave that particular line of questioning and return to Hardwick. Not before thinking, however, how the fact that Don Alphonse had been involved in planning the shipping adventure was of the highest interest. I started to ponder Don Alphonse in a new light. Was he simply one of Robert's silent partners or was he more immediately involved in the whole planning of the adventure as Leticia Hardwick thought, perhaps on Hardwick's behalf? Another motive for murder raised its ugly head.

Returning to the subject of Hardwick was difficult as, despite her seeming willingness to help, I didn't dare ask her if her husband was guilty of treason, or, for that matter, if she would help me break into his study.

However, prompted by memories of my meeting with Cassangoe, my brain had finally come up with a less contentious angle that I could try.

'Would you be aware of your husband's involvement at all in smuggling?'

'Smuggling.' Leticia made the word sound like 'a-ha' as she curled her feet coquettishly under her body and gave me a conspiratorial smile. 'So that's why you're snooping around here, is it? I wondered what it might be. Well I might just know something about that. Is her Majesty worried about her coffers?'

'Is your husband involved in smuggling?'

'Yes. I rather think he might be.' She let out a short, musical laugh.

'Could you elaborate at all?' Rather than answering me, Leticia stood up and moved gracefully to the wide four-poster bed that took up a large part of the room. She sat down and patted a spot next to her.

'Indulge me, Lovat. No. I can't keep calling you "Lovat". What's your first name?'

I moved tentatively beside her, still nervous, despite her assurances, that her husband might come barging through the door at any moment. 'John'.

'Well John. Isn't this fun?'

'Smuggling is a serious offence.'

'Oh don't be stuffy. Half the country is at it. I'm surprised that my husband should be singled out. Although I imagine he is one of the most notorious.'

'What can you tell me about his... er... activities?'

'Oh don't sound so serious or I will start calling you Lovat again. I don't know exactly how it works but I can offer a theory.'

'Go on.' At this proximity, her beauty was intoxicating. I tried not to think of Cassangoe's huge hands caressing that transparent, white skin.

'I should say it is all about ships that pass in the night.' Followed by that same musical giggle. 'My husband owns or leases a whole fleet of ships. A few operate legally bringing their wares into ports like Rye where they can be checked by the authorities but, from what I have heard, my husband also has a number of ships lying off port that either bring the goods or collect them from other ships. The goods are then rowed ashore, stored somewhere along the coast, before being taken to London across the Weald. Sometimes they are even brought to the house in the dead of night. Before anyone is the wiser they are on the market in London and a rather large amount of money has come back the other way. There are also goods going in the other direction – to France – that is the Vaillons connection.'

'How do you know all this?'

'I have my spies. But I don't really *know* it – not the details at least.'

'Who is the London connection?'

She shook her head. 'I don't really know.'

I thought of Walsingham's suspicion that Hardwick had been prepared to smuggle the Babington conspirators out of England. 'Is it only goods that get smuggled or people as well?'

There was hesitation before Leticia spoke.

'I don't know ... possibly, there have been some strange goings on in this house ... I do know a way of possibly finding out.'

'How?'

'By breaking into my husband's study of course.'

'I don't think that's possible – I've already considered all of the options.' The matter-of-fact cynicism in my voice came out all too plainly.

'Yes, my dear John, but, in your ignorance, you are not in possession of all of the facts.'

'Such as?'

'Who knows this house better than anyone? I do. I spent a large part of my childhood here as a ward to the previous owner. When Hardwick bought the house he practically bought me with it. I was already here.' Despite her flirtatiousness she could not disguise a note of bitterness. 'The beauty of it is that I know this house and its secrets far better than my husband does and I have one secret in particular that I think you would be very interested in.'

She came close to me and for the first time I was aware of the gentle scent of her skin. It was far from the alternatively sweet or stale stench, or both, of the women in London I was used to – the pomaded ladies, the sweating stall keepers, the perfumed whores. I was suddenly reminded of Mostellaria's words as quoted by Montaigne: *mulier tum bene olet, ubi nihilo let – A woman smells most perfectly when she does not smell at all.* For the first time I understood the meaning of those words.

'Well, do you want to know my secret?'

I let out a short chuckle to release the tension I was feeling – she was enjoying teasing me so much that it was infectious. 'And what might that be?'

She moved in close until her lips brushed the hairs of my ear, causing darts of lightening all down my spine, and whispered:

'Why, the secret passageway that leads right into his office, of course!'

Chapter 27

"I find my lust less depraved than my reason."
(Michel de Montaigne)

'Wait here.'

The bewitching Leticia Hardwick broke away from me and disappeared into a side chamber. I waited without moving, still savouring the scent of her skin, and the soft heat of her breathe that had coursed so enticingly into my ear.

A few moments later she returned, wearing her third outfit of the evening. The white lace dress had been replaced by leather boots, brown breeches and a black doublet that was buttoned tightly over her shapely figure. Despite being dressed as a man, the effect was just as arresting as the previous outfit and did little to cool my arousal.

'Come on, John. What are you sitting there for? Grab some spare candles and that lantern and follow me.' I did as I was told and followed her through the door and down a narrow set of wooden stairs that led down from her quarters.

Such was her enthusiasm for the task in hand that I practically had to run to keep up with her. This led to me tripping over a couple of steps and making a huge din, which in turn led to a huge, stage-like 'Shhhhhhhhh' coming back up the stairs. I cursed under my breath and picked myself up.

She led me downstairs to a side entrance that I hadn't used before. Yanking it open we were immediately hit by a blast of cold air. The white garden stretched out in front of us, lit by a discursive moonlight.

'Where in God's name are you taking me?'

'You'll see. Now cover the lantern while we're outside. We needn't worry about our footprints in the snow. People have been trampling around here all day. Another pair won't be noticed.'

She struck out ahead down a slight incline, towards the shadow of a low slung building, huddled in charcoal grey trees. I glanced around but the garden appeared deserted and hopefully anyone awake inside would be safely behind thick, closed curtains.

Slowly getting my bearings, I realised that the building ahead of us must be the small church that I had seen on my first arrival. As we approached, its low, arched bell-tower gradually became separated from the shadow of the trees and the church appeared numinously out of the gloom. It was short in length and looked more like the kind of chapel that a hermit from one of the King Arthur legends would live in.

The church had a simple porch to one side that protected the entrance to a panelled door with a point shaped like the ace of a playing card. As we reached it, I turned to check that no one had seen or followed us when I suddenly froze. To the side of the house, in the direction of the long entrance road, I could see a light. I motioned to Leticia and we both crouched in the porch watching the light swaying to and fro as it came closer to the house. After a moment, it split and became two lights, surrounded by a cluster of shadows.

'A bit late for visitors, isn't it? Is this a regular occurrence?'

'Probably a servant returning from Rye.'

'Servants don't usually drag goods around in the middle of the night.' The shadows had now split out into separate forms, one lighting the way, another two pulling what looked like a cart, the rumble of whose wheels was now quite clear across the still night.

'There's always something happening in this house. Come on, we had better get moving.' I hesitated for a moment; eyes fixed on the small group that was now only a hundred yards from the house. In the gloom, it appeared that the cart was carrying what looked like two separate sacks. Then one of the sacks moved its head towards the other – not sacks, people.

'John! Come on!'

The door to the church was unlocked and opened smoothly. We found ourselves in a small, uncluttered nave, with a stone aisle flanked on either side by a range of smooth wooden pews. At the end of the aisle, Leticia led me past a small stone alter to the left of which was a concealed flight of stairs going down via a half landing into the depths. At the bottom, the space opened out to reveal a wide room with a vaulted ceiling running the length of the church. It was full of headstones and tombs all piled up on top of one another with no apparent deferment to the dead their inscriptions commemorated.

'The crypt,' Leticia said unnecessarily. 'All of the headstones and tombs were dumped in here when my barbarian of a husband had the garden extended. Hence the mess.'

There were other remnants of the old graveyard too. All around the walls on wooden shelves were rows and rows of bones and skulls, far more than could be expected from the size of the Stavening estate. Many of the shelves had been broken by the influx of tombs and consequently the ground was littered with shattered bones.

'Victims of the Black Death. There used to be quite a substantial village here – a thousand people or more but no longer. The remains of the houses were destroyed when the manor was built. There's nothing left of the village now apart from this church.'

She asked me to hold her lantern, whilst she clambered over the pile of gravestones, then leant forward to take them both from me as I followed. After doing this a couple more times we made it to the far end, Leticia surveying an area at the back of the crypt.

'I haven't done this for a while. Let's hope the entrance hasn't been blocked in.'

Alarm bells went off in my head. 'When did you last use the tunnel?'

'When I was a girl – ten years ago or more.' 'Dammit!'

'Stop blaspheming and help me shift these.' She indicated a row of headstones that had been piled up against the wall. With grave misgivings, I began to heave them one by one to a spot on the side, trying to make as little noise as possible, whilst also not breaking my back. There was little room for manoeuvre and Leticia and I were continually bumping into one another, she cursing my clumsiness, I quite enjoying the proximity. Eventually, a space had been cleared to her satisfaction. Leticia knelt in the gap that we had created next to the wall.

'There, you see?' She indicated two dusty wooden panels set at a 45 degree angle between the floor and wall, looking rather like the street entrance to an inn cellar, where the barrels get dropped in. She got her fingers under one of them but it didn't shift an inch. For a moment her confidence waned.

'It's been nailed shut.'

'Out of the way. Let me try.' I took hold of a length of bone – a rib, I think – and wedged it into the gap between the two planks. One hard jerk and it shattered. I groped around and found another bone – possibly a jaw – it too shattered. A third attempt, this time with a femur from what was presumably a well-built villager, was more successful. Three good jerks and the wood fractured into a hundred rotten fragments, most of which fell into a yawning black gap below. I stood back wielding the thighbone, admiring my handiwork.

Leticia had been watching this performance with a laconical expression on her face. 'Good job, Atlas. We won't be able to put that back then. Never mind a little finesse, when you can rely on brute strength eh?!'

'Is that all the thanks I get?'

'What would you like? A kiss?' Followed by the musical giggle that, despite its charm, I could imagine getting on my nerves, particularly if it continued to accompany such teasing. 'You might as well finish the job. Get all of those shards out of the way. I don't want to tear my beautiful doublet.'

Once this was accomplished, it left a gap two feet wide. I lowered a lamp into the darkness. Shadows loomed beyond the bloom of the lantern – it was impossible to see the floor below.

'How far down does it go?

'You'll see. Follow me.'

'Are you sure it's safe?'

'No – but it's an adventure.'

She turned round and let her legs dangle into the void, her elbows holding onto the sides of the gap. All I could see of her was her face surrounded by a cloud of wild, golden hair. She smiled at me and then dropped out of sight.

I heard her hit the ground and shone the lantern back in the hole. She was about four feet below me, reaching up with her hands.

'Pass me the lanterns and hurry up.' I did as bidden and followed her into the hollow, wondering as I did so how we were ever going to get out again.

If there was a time for calling a halt to the adventure this was it – I let go of the sides and dropped into the void.

I landed awkwardly but no damage was done. Leticia was waiting for me on all fours, her backside wedged into a small hole to one side that looked as though it was just about big enough for a fox.

'You're joking?'

'It's only this narrow for a few feet – come on.'

She crawled backwards on all fours, smiling at me the entire time, until she had disappeared completely into the hole. 'Here goes nothing', I thought, and followed headfirst. The tunnel pressed in tightly around my shoulders and I began to feel a panic rising from the pit of my stomach, which I struggled to control. Thoughts of being stuck underground tormented me as I inched forwards, encouraged only by Leticia's voice ahead of me in the dark. Much to my relief, though, the hole gradually widened. I joined my tormentor at the top of a staircase, where we were both able to stand, all-be-it hunched over in my case.

'This is the original entrance, I think, but at some time in the past it was blocked off. I don't know who dug the tunnel from the church but no one knows about it anymore – apart from me, of course. I used to play here as a child.'

'What fun you must have had.'

I counted a dozen steps before the ground levelled out and the tunnel took a sharp turn to the left. Despite clearly not having been used in years, the tunnel was surprisingly intact. There were lots of cobwebs and the walls were damp, but sturdy.

'Built to last.' Leticia said, as if reading my mind. 'This tunnel will be here long after we are gone.'

'A comforting thought.'

Raising my lantern to the ceiling, I could see that, although the body of the tunnel had been dug through a mixture of clay and chalk, there was a stone ceiling, which had been built by craftsman but in a very archaic style. Continuing her theme, Leticia began giving me a guided tour.

'Years and years ago, a long time before the village and the Black Death, there used to be a religious meeting place here where people worshipped the pagan Gods. Rumour has it that this is where the Hyperboreans came down to worship.'

'Hyper-whats?'

'Ancient Britons. They probably made sacrifices of virgins and that kind of thing.'

'Another comforting thought.'

'Don't worry. I don't think either of us are in danger – unless you've been living a rather more sheltered life than you've been letting on.'

'I'm not going to dignify that remark with a reply.'

'Then I'll just assume that you're chaste!'

'Shut up!'

'Have I touched a nerve? Better watch your back for those Celtic druids.'

'Just move.'

The tunnel was not straight but meandered left and right, presumably following a contour that the builders had found easiest to dig. The shadows from our lanterns played along all around us. We were alone with only the amplified sound of our crunching footsteps and the musty, dry smell of the chalk. I had lost all perspective with the land above and had no idea where we were in relation to the house.

The passageway suddenly took a sharp turn to the left and then back to right. A few feet further and the tunnel opened out into a circular pit, where the floor gave way to a gaping hole, around which there was only the width of a row of bricks. Running about eight feet up from the floor was a rotten wooden ladder, from which half the rungs were missing.

'This is it.'

'Where are we?'

'This is an old well shaft – there's still water down there.' She kicked a pebble into the void and two seconds later we heard a hollow slap as it hit the water below. 'It used to go straight up into the kitchen but got closed off when the house was re-built. The study is just above us.

'Where in Hardwick's study is the entrance?'

'This ladder leads to the back of a false panel. It's the one to the left of the window behind the desk.'

'Have you been in your husband's office lately? I think he might have added shelves to that panel. Shelves that are covered in all manner of crud.'

'Stop being such a sceptic. Do you want to find out what he's up to or not?'

'Of course.'

'Well come on then.'

'This ladder's not going to hold both of us. I'll go first this time.'

'No, I'll go first. You won't know how to open it.' She didn't give me time to argue and shimmied silkily up the ladder. I watched her move a board above her head before disappearing nimbly out of view. I was left standing in the pit for what seemed like an age whilst all sorts of paranoid thoughts started crowding into my head. How well did I actually know this beguiling woman? Had I been foolish to trust her? What if this was some elaborate ploy to prove beyond doubt that I was a spy? Was the room empty up there or were Hardwick, Dakers and Vaillons sitting by a cosy fire waiting for me to pop my head out of a cupboard? A head that would soon be looking through a noose if Hardwick dragged me into Rye as a traitor.

'John, what are you doing down there?' Leticia's smiling face was filling the hole in the ceiling. 'Come up. I'm in.' 'This is it – now or never' I thought.

I moved gingerly up the ladder, whose remaining rungs were threatening to give way at any minute and cautiously poked my head through the gap at the top. The ladder led to a small platform that stretched along the length of the wall, where some ingenious architect had built the panelling of the office about a foot away from the stone wall. From the inside it would be impossible to tell that there was a gap.

Leticia was waiting for me in a rectangular space made by pushing a panel out into the room. The gap behind the panel that the ladder went in to was tiny and she had to put an arm under my shoulder to help me through. After much pulling and tugging we ended up in a heap together half in and half out of Hardwick's study, our heads roughly where he had been standing when I first met him a few days earlier. Leticia, who was hugging me tightly, couldn't stop giggling, which I put down to a mixture of nerves and triumph, and buried her head in my chest. I was simply relieved to find the room empty. Eventually she managed to stop laughing long enough to speak.

'You see. We did it!' She leant forward and kissed me fully on the lips. After a stunned moment, I kissed her back whole-heartedly. She pushed me away, laughing again, and began looking around.

All around us were papers and books that must have fallen when she forced the panel out. 'I had to make a bit of a mess but it shouldn't be too hard to fix it before we leave. We had better get searching. Where do you want to start?'

Still reeling from the kiss, it took a moment for my brain to click into action. I had been thinking about this for a few days now – where I would search for incriminating evidence in the mess that was Hardwick's filing system.

'See if you can find a private safe or chest anywhere? I don't hold out much hope for all of the bundles of paper on the shelves.'

'I see what you mean. My husband could really do with a spring clean in here.'

It was easy to find potential hiding places for sensitive items. There were two chests and a tall Flemish cabinet but both the chests were locked and the cabinet proved to be another repository for bills and accounts.

'See if you can find a set of keys anywhere. In the meantime, I'll see if I can accomplish the feat of picking these locks.'

'A man of hidden talents.'

'We'll see about that.' I set to working on the first chest, while Leticia started rummaging through the numerous drawers in his desk. I watched for a moment and smiled – she was evidently enjoying herself thoroughly and her delight was infectious. She caught my eye and smiled back at me. The adrenaline built up in the tunnel coupled with the desire I felt for that woman made my whole body feel light.

I had been taught the black arts of lock-picking by an old tinker who used to peddle his tins and cups in the village where my mother grew up. It had come in useful when I had wanted to break into my brother's secret chests and cupboards as a boy. As with everything that wasn't strictly ethical, my father had delighted in my newfound occupation. He encouraged my skills whole-heartedly and used to buy boxes purely to set me the task of opening them without the key.

Hardwick's chests were of a sophisticated kind and I was handicapped by the fact that I didn't have any of my tools with me, other than a thin sliver of metal that I always had tucked in the pocket of my sleeve. Fortunately this proved adequate and after playing with the lock of the first chest for five minutes it clicked open. Leticia had stopped looking for keys and instead was kneeling by my side watching me avidly.

'I am the very *stand* to your *charm*.' She said, using the street terms for a lock-picker and his watcher. 'Can you pick hearts as you do these locks?'

'I fear I lack the requisite tools.' I said with a deprecatory smile, angling for a compliment that was not forthcoming.

The chest was not full of incriminating letters as I had hoped but gold coins. More gold coins than I had ever seen in my life. Leticia's eyes opened wide and she reached into the box. I caught her hand.

'Don't worry, John. Just taking my dues and my fee for employing you.' She took two large handfuls and put one in each pocket of the doublet she was wearing. 'I don't think he'll miss it, do you?'

'Probably not.'

'Why don't you help yourself?' I had to admit it was tempting but I wanted to get the other chest open before dawn.

The second chest proved more problematic. The lock was new and of a kind that I hadn't encountered before. I struggled with it for about twenty minutes, getting ever more heated and frustrated, before finally succeeding.

But this time it proved to be more than worth the effort.

Concealed within the chest were three smaller boxes, none of which were locked and all of which contained letters. This time Leticia didn't reach in at all but sat back with a suddenly serious expression on her face, as though she had just realised what we had both done.

'Have you found what you sought?'

'I don't know. Hopefully. I think you should start putting those papers back on the shelves whilst I search. It'll be dawn soon.' To my relief Leticia didn't object. I was worried that we had very little time left but I also didn't want her to see exactly which letters I was interested in.

There were too many letters to search them all thoroughly so I concentrated on reading the signatures. Within minutes I had a pile of letters written by some very interesting people, that I thought would prove fruitful. The rest I put back in the boxes as I had found them, hoping that Hardwick wouldn't notice a few gaps. I planned to take the interesting letters with me to peruse them at my leisure, before hopefully being able to return them at a later date.

'Let's leave.' I said, when I was satisfied that I had got enough material. I had a pile of around a dozen letters, which I tied in a bundle using some loose ribbon found on Hardwick's desk.

I clicked the locks of the chests back into place and then helped Leticia replace the remaining books and papers on shelves. Faint sounds in the distance told us that the house was beginning to stir and a glance through the window showed the dawn beginning to creep in. The servants would be re-lighting fires around the house and beginning to prepare breakfast in the kitchen. I paused briefly only to examine the seal and chain that I had seen hanging in the study the first time I had entered it, and then followed Leticia.

We squeezed backwards into the hole in the wall and gently pulled the panel back in place behind us, being careful not to disturb the shelves more than we had to. It was quite a feat in that small space, juggling lanterns, bundles and each other. Eventually we were as satisfied as we could be that our breaking and entering would pass unnoticed. Leticia slipped first down the ladder and I followed.

We had wound our way back along the passage and up the tight tunnel, and I had given Leticia a leg up out of the pit and into the crypt, when I came to a decision that had been brewing in my mind for some time.

'Listen, Letty. Find a way to get Tichborne to tell Hardwick that I'm ill in bed and I'm not able to work today. I think we can trust him – at least to not ask too many questions – he's a straightforward enough lad. Maybe get one of your maids to give the impression that I'm bed with you or something.'

'You'd love him to think that wouldn't you, John?' The earlier kiss was still with me. I felt a deep longing.

'That's a disgraceful suggestion.'

'Anymore disgraceful than you suggesting it in the first place? What do you intend doing?'

'I'm going to go back and spend the day behind the panel and glean whatever I can from Hardwick's business dealings. You had better push a couple of gravestones back over the hole.'

'How will you get out?'

'I should be able to manage it?' Looking up at her framed by the hole above, I wasn't quite sure how, and was relieved when she said:

'I'll come back later anyway. I might have a bout of religious fervour and spend the evening in the church. Just throw a stone up into the crypt a few times when you are ready. I should hear it and I'll help you out.'

'You're incredible.' If she hadn't been out of reach, I might have taken her in my arms and recklessly kissed again. And more besides!

'Stop twinkling your eyes at me Lovat and get back down that hole where you belong. I'll see you tonight.' And with that she was gone.

Chapter 28

"A mouse does not rely on just one hole."
(Plautus)

Hiding in secret behind the panel proved to be a stroke of genius, though not for any reason I had anticipated.

I had been squeezed into that damp, cramped space for about half an hour when I became aware of the first sounds of activity in Hardwick's study. I quickly snuffed out the candle I'd been using to scan through the letters taken from the box, whilst trying my best not to set fire to them in that hampered space. I hadn't got very far but I'd already discovered some interesting titbits, whetting my appetite for further study – creaking floorboards a few feet away told me that now was not the moment.

I sat in the darkness as still as possible, hardly daring to breathe. The blackness was total, which allowed me to concentrate solely on listening. Hardwick shuffled about the room – scraping chairs, shifting papers, humming to himself. I prayed that his first task of the day would not involve the casket full of letters – some of which I was now holding in my hand – or that he wouldn't notice the rearranged bundles and sheaf's on the wall behind his desk.

Any worries I had that the sound of voices would be too muffled to decipher were quickly dispelled as I heard Hardwick bellow out a greeting to Dakers who entered a few minutes later. The greeting was typical Hardwick – gruff and to the point.

'Morning Jock! Any news in the night?'

It was as though he was standing just above me, which he literally was with only a thin wooden partition between us. The partition even wobbled when he stood close to it, letting in flecks of light. There was no response to his question, but I judged by the impatient sigh that Hardwick let out that Dakers had answered with a shake of the head.

Hardwick settled down to the day's work. For the most part he worked in silence, occasionally barking out an instruction, or making some observation on what he was reading. I began to think that spying on him could prove to be an enormous waste of time.

Time passed for what seemed like an eternity with only the occasional brief exchange of conversation. At one point, I heard Tichborne enter and report my 'indisposition'. Hardwick muttered that I was a lazy swine but other than that the news went unremarked. My body became stiff and began to ache in various places and I cursed my inability to move in even the slightest manner. Fatigue also gripped me, along with the very real fear of falling asleep. Anxiety, an aching body and a curious mouse, that had popped out of a hole nearby and was wondering if my intentions were honourable, whilst wandering maddeningly up and down my leg, kept me awake. Still, I knew that if I stayed like this for too long my invented illness would surely become a reality.

Time lingered inexorably.

The luck I craved came in the form of the old butler, Champernowne, at what I assumed to be about mid-way through the morning – although by now I had lost all track of time and was becoming almost delirious in the darkness. He knocked on the door and announced that a messenger had come from the nearby harbour of Rye.

'Well show him in Champernowne.' A few seconds later an unfamiliar, youthful voice spoke out.

'Begging your pardon m'lord but I have news from Monsieur Vaillons at the port.'

'Well, spit it out lad.'

'He says to inform you that the Lady Merrydance docked in the night, sir, and to tell you that the ship's cargo has been delivered safely to the house. You wouldn't be aware of it m'lord, it happened in the early hours. He and Master Turney send their compliments and await your instruction or if you please to visit him on the deck of the Lady Merrydance.'

'Very good. Get back to Rye and inform Vaillons and Turney they can expect me this evening around seven. That's all.'

The Lady Merrydance and Turney in Rye harbour! If the information that the overweight German, Karl Würtembatter, had indiscreetly fed me on the tilt boat to Deptford was right, the ship should by now be somewhere off the Flemish coast sailing north to the Baltic. Not nestling in Rye harbour less than two weeks after setting sail. At last, here was incontrovertible proof that linked Hardwick to the ship my brother had chartered. Walsingham's hunch had been eerily correct.

I made the connection with the cart that Leticia and I had witnessed drawing up to the house in the dark. I hadn't seen any evidence of goods but at that distance in the dark I could easily have missed something.

The euphoria of this realisation was interrupted by a conversation that had struck up in the room following the delivery of the message. It was Dakers who was speaking.

'The cargo can be moved tonight. I'll get a message to … (the name was garbled but sounded like *Harbury*) and his crew that we're ready to move the other goods.'

'Yes, move them tonight. This is the last time that I want that particular cargo anywhere near the house – it's becoming far too risky. And I don't want any nonsense from … (more clear this time – Carberry). He'll stick to the price we agreed or there will be consequences. Make sure he understands. Is the other cargo ready?'

'Naturally, sire. We can load the ship tonight!'

'I'm glad to hear it. Turney has made exceptionally good time and I don't want the Lady Merrydance in the harbour any longer than she needs to be. The good burghers of Rye might start asking questions. Ingram arrives today. He can help you as necessary.'

I felt the hairs on the back of my neck stand up in terror. Ingram coming to Stavening. Would he leave Grayson and Scarface at home? I sincerely doubted it. This was an unwelcome development.

'If everything goes to plan, Vaillons can set sail for France in the morning. No need for him to return here first. Let's keep things as simple as possible.'

'Very well.'

'I'll be very glad when this affair with Rokesby is finished and we can get back to business as usual. The whole thing has been a complete pain in the backside to be honest.'

'Yes. But it has been politically expedient. Don Alphonse was no fool after all.'

'Yes. Got to hand it to him – the randy little Dego!'

By now my mind was racing. My brother, the ships, Turney. Ingram and Don Alphonse all being mentioned in the same conversation was more than I could ever have hoped for but I still felt clueless as to how to bring the whole mystery together. The next part of the conversation confused me even more.

'Still no word from him?'

'No. Ingram should have news of him today.'

'Well if we never hear from him again, so much the better.'

The room lapsed into silence. I could almost hear my brain clanking into action. The implications of what had just been said went against everything I had assumed about Don Alphonse's death. I suddenly had the greatest desire on earth to get out of that tight space and find room to think. This was impossible of course. I knew that I had to sit there until the room behind the panel was empty. Moving any earlier was far too risky. The cold and darkness closed in around me.

I calculated that another hour had come and gone before Hardwick finally vacated the room on the announcement from Champernowne that lunch was served and Master Ingram had arrived. I scuttled out of my hiding place thinking that this was last thing I wanted to hear.

* * *

Riding at high speed in darkness, on unfamiliar roads, is never the best of ideas. When that road consists of mudded ruts, frozen hard as rock, and covered in a treacherous layer of snow and ice, it is even less ingenious.

On two or three occasions George slipped and stumbled, nearly pitching me into one of the roadside ditches. Fortunately, each time he recovered niftily and I was able to cling on but his snorted disapproval told me that I was sorely trying his patience. As with the previous evening, there was at least a hint of moonlight and after ten minutes riding I could see faint lights in the distance and better still smell the sea, which was enough to guide us onward. George cocked his head at this new sensation and forgot his worries about the road.

As soon as I'd heard that the Lady Merrydance had docked at Rye Harbour, I had immediately decided to pay her a visit, at the very least to satisfy my curiosity about what she was being used to smuggle – if indeed she was. Darkness had come just after four o'clock and my plan was to get to Rye and the ship before Hardwick's appointment with Turney and Dakers three hours later.

Leticia Hardwick had been as good as her word. When I reached the chamber below the church I had thrown up a pebble and immediately in response a length of rope had unravelled into the hole. I had pulled myself up to find the rope attached to a set of gravestones and Leticia calmly sitting beside it eating an apple, one of a number she had brought for me.

'My husband thinks that I'm out riding,' she said, as if reading my mind. 'What with you being 'indisposed' all day and me being 'out', I can only hope that his mind is racked with jealousy.'

'You like playing with fire don't you?'

'Yes. It brightens this deathly place up no end.'

'Well, I'm sorry to have to tell you that your husband has other things on his mind.' I explained to her about the arrival of the Lady Merry-dance.

'That's not surprising. He was always more interested in business than in me. I was business.'

'What shall I do with these?' The bundle of letters I had stolen was resting on my knees. It was bulky and I didn't fancy lugging it around with me.

'Let's stash them here,' Leticia said, noticing my preoccupation. 'You can pick them up before you leave.'

'Good idea.' I pushed the bundle out of sight before covering the hiding place with some bones. A thought occurred to me: 'I may have to make a quick exit. Do you think you could bring my other belongings down here; in case I don't get a chance to retrieve them?' I was thinking chiefly of Don Alphonse's manuscript, which was in the bag in my room.

'You don't ask much of a girl, do you John?' She thought for a moment. 'I should think I can manage and I'll put a letter in there myself for you to deliver.' Her mouth curved into a delicious smile. Lucky Cassangoe, I thought.

I decided to change the subject. 'I overheard Vaillons mentioning a cargo being brought in the night? Could that have been the lights we saw?'

'I suppose so. As I said before, there are a lot of comings and goings at night. I always felt it prudent to stay out of the way.'

'Very wise. I wish I could do the same – but no such luck. Where in the house would your husband hide cargo?' I had been racking my brains to think of a storage area in the actual house itself, which is definitely where the cart had been heading, but couldn't think of anywhere.

'It doesn't really make sense. The only places I can think of are the stables or the barns. Nowhere in the house itself.'

'Talking of stables I need to find my horse and get to Rye.'

'Come on then.'

Leticia showed me a back way to the stables and without ceremony I had saddled and set off for Rye, only pausing to tell her that I would be back later that evening and that this would in all probability be my last night in the house. If I had expected her to look a little disappointed at the news, she didn't show it. There was to be no repeat of the passionate kiss.

Once again I found myself galloping dangerously on horseback with my mind preoccupied with a woman.

* * *

I had another problem to negotiate once I reached the town. On our way to the stables, Leticia told me that due to fighting amongst ships crews a curfew had been imposed, which meant that all the townspeople and sailors had to be indoors or onboard by nightfall. Anyone found out after this time was likely to get a nasty hiding from the watch and either thrown into prison, if they were a sailor, or thrown onto a ship if they weren't. Strangers riding into town after nightfall were likely to get the full treatment.

I had thought of telling the gatekeepers that I was on business of Hardwick's. There seemed no doubt his name would carry weight in the town. But without any documentation, and knowing he would be following close behind, it might pose an awkward situation if they mentioned my arrival. Better to enter the town incognito, but how?

Once again the resourceful-as-she-was-beautiful Leticia Hardwick had come to my aid. On our way to the stables she described a section of the walls where it was possible to gain access and the guards were unlikely to be too alert. When I asked her how she knew this, she simply gave me a delicious wink and tapped her nose coquettishly. The only problem now in the darkness was finding it without blundering about too much. I almost wished I had asked Leticia to accompany me and judging by the excitement in her eyes I think she might have accepted.

About half a mile from the town I slowed George to a trot and struck off across a field running adjacent to the town. Slowly circumventing the walls from a safe distance I eventually spotted the area where they had fallen into disrepair. I found a disused shed nearby, where I could tether my feverish mount in relative warmth, and set off to negotiate the rubble.

* * *

For the most part the town was quiet and bathed in shadow. Only the inns showed any signs of life. The odd lamp burnt at intervals but it was easy to remain in darkness as I picked my way carefully along the cobbled streets trying to avoid the Watch.

My first plan was to find Kyd. After searching haplessly in and out of various taverns, whose names all described creatures with various numbers of legs, which was not only frustrating but extremely dangerous because of the attention it attracted, I was eventually annoyed, but relieved, to find him supping in the comfort and warmth of a tavern called The Mermaid. When I pointed out to him that mermaids didn't have legs, he looked at me as if I had just landed from the moon.

'What happened to your code for helping me find you? Inns with number of legs, diminishing etc etc. I've been in every inn in town looking for you!'

'Well then you will know that this is far and away the best in terms of comfort. Naturally, you wouldn't have expected me to bunk down in the squalor the alternatives afforded. Use your brain old boy.'

'You said… ' I gritted my teeth. 'Oh never mind. Shut up and listen for a bit.'

I apprised Kyd of the situation and told him what I needed him to do.

'I hope you've been discreet.'

'The very model of discretion. I've spent most of the time holed up here trying to avoid the press gangs. You were lucky to find me. I only dare venture downstairs after the curfew, when all of the sailors should be safely confined to their ships.'

'No one would be foolish enough to try and turn you into a sailor. Might as well try teaching a cow to sing.'

'You've never heard Moll at the Three Cranes Tavern then?'

I smothered a laugh by sticking my face in a tankard of beer. I didn't want him to know yet that I had forgiven him. 'You can't have found out much if you've been skulking in here all day,' I said, trying but failing to sound reproachful.

'Au contraire, mon ami. Betty, the landlady over there', he indicated the cheerful, comfortable looking lady, who had served us earlier, 'has been keeping me abreast of all the gossip. Some strange goings on in this town, I must say.'

'Strange how?'

'Oh people in the night who aren't supposed to be there – that kind of thing.'

'What people? Make some sense will you?'

'If you believe Betty,' he gave the blowsy woman, who was out of ear-shot, a wink across the bar, which was returned with a knowing grin, 'they're not people at all but ghosts; spirits of the night. Simple soul but does a rare beef dinner. Betty my love,' he raised his voice and waved his glass in the air, 'fill these up for us would you?'

'Spirits of the night?'

'Don't worry Lovat. They're not ghosts. Do spirits ride in a cart, I ask you?'

'A cart? Pulled by man or beast?'

'Man. I saw them myself last night. A small parade through the town in the wee hours. People coming from the harbour and heading in the direction of the gatehouse by torchlight.'

'And I think I know where they were heading. How on earth did you know when to look?'

'Let's just say that Betty was conveniently close by at the time and she has a remarkable ear for these things. I would guess at a handful of locals and at least two strangers.'

'Foreigners?'

'No not foreigners but not exactly local types either – the two in the cart. Perhaps of a religious persuasion. Mind you it was just an impression; it was pretty dark.'

'A religious persuasion? Do you mean Catholics? Were they prisoners?'

'Not prisoners exactly but they looked as though they were being kept close, if you know what I mean?'

'A bit like Betty.'

Kyd gave me a sheepish grin. 'You could say that.'

At that moment, Betty herself arrived with our refills and didn't waste any time disabusing me of any lingering doubt I might have had concerning Kyd's conduct by pinching his cheek between chubby fingers and ruffling his hair so that it stood up in a sandy quiff. Betty had that proprietary air of a lady used to running her own establishment. Up close, she was a plump woman of about thirty, with a clump of black curls framing a corpulent, if pretty face, and a broad, guileless smile, showing a gap in her front teeth between which you could have stuck two shillings.

'Aren't you going to introduce me to your friend, Master Thomas? A handsome stranger arriving in the dead of night.' She eyed me with faux suspicion. 'What will the neighbours think?'

'I have it on good authority, my dear Betty, that the neighbours couldn't think any worse of this den of iniquity than they already do.'

'Ooh, Master Thomas, don't be a tease. You know perfectly well I run a model establishment.' She gave me a wink as she said it. 'I don't suppose you'll be wanting a bed for the night deary? Only, we're a bit full up at the moment.'

'This is Master Lamb from Hastings.' Kyd said, inventing a code name for me out of nowhere. 'And no he won't be wanting a bed, he's like the Devil – he never sleeps. Now give us some space Betty darling, Master Lamb and I need to discuss some business.'

* * *

I followed Kyd's directions to the harbour. The town was thick with mist and only once did I espy a man walking ahead of me. Sensibly assuming him to be a member of the Watch, I let him move on at a safe distance before slipping down the road he had just come from. To the most part, though, the streets were deserted. The cold temperature had ensured that most of the nightly guardsmen had been dissuaded from bothering to patrol outside.

Any worries I had about finding the Lady Merrydance quickly dissipated. Although there were numerous ships in the dock, there was only one of her size and it wasn't long before I found her at the furthest point from the low lying, sleepy houses of the town, towering over her neighbours in the dock. A light flickered in the wide stern window, which overhung the water at the end of the jetty, and which I took to be the captain's quarters. I assumed that Turney and Vaillons were waiting up there in the warmth for Hardwick's arrival.

Just as I was debating the best approach for boarding her, I heard the sound of footsteps. I shrank into the misty gloom just in time to avoid being seen by a group of men who were striding purposefully towards the ship, their collective breath creating a cloud around them. And at the centre of them none other than Hardwick. The bell had only just struck six after I had left Kyd at the Crown. I cursed under my breath – he had come early.

There were four men with him. Dakers' loping gait was easy to make out but I didn't at first recognise the others, until it struck me whose arrival had been announced that afternoon. One of them stepped forward and the light caught the line of the scar running down from his forehead, across his eye and over the curve of his cheek. The other two needed no further investigation – Grayson with his muscles and mop of blonde hair and between them, with his set jaw and his hawk's eyes, Nicholas Ingram.

I shivered, but this time not from the cold but fear. It was the second time I had been in close proximity to that man; without doubt the most dangerous I had met in my life.

Chapter 29

"A person's fears are lighter when the danger is at hand."
(Lucius Annaeus Seneca)

As I shrank back into the shadows, keeping a fixed eye on the group of men on the dock, a dozen sailors appeared on the deck of the Lady Merrydance. Dakers began to issue them with instructions and the men started carrying sacks from the Lady Merrydance and depositing them onto a smaller ship that was moored alongside. Having discarded one cargo, they collected another from the smaller ship and carried it back to the Lady Merrydance. While this was happening, Hardwick, Ingram and his two lackeys boarded the ship.

The men on the dock went about their work efficiently. Very little was said, just the occasional grunt of acknowledgement, as each made frequent trips back and forth between the two boats. Only once was there a break in the rhythm when two men collided. A sack destined for the smaller ship fell open on the dock and its contents scattered – exotic leaves with a distinct smell that quickly filled the cold air – tobacco. That answered one question of what Hardwick was smuggling into the country, but what was in the sacks going the other way?

I had backed away, until I was hidden from view between a couple of large crates. Pressed against the edge of the dock, I could see icy sheets on the surface of the water lapping against the wooden supports. I watched closely, waiting for an opportunity. Eventually it came.

Dakers, satisfied that everything was running smoothly, went to join the others in the warmth of the galley. I unbuckled my belt, slipped off my doublet, so that I was only wearing a shirt like most of the sailors, pulled my cap low down over my eyes and moved stealthily into the line to collect a sack from the smaller boat. There was enough commotion on the dock to conceal where I had come from and none of the men seemed to notice an interloper sidling in amongst them.

I reached out for a sack, heaved the heavy weight onto my shoulder to hide my face, and set off after the man in front. Before I knew it, I was up on the deck of the Lady Merrydance, brushing closely past Scarface and Grayson, before clambering heavily into the depths of the ship, where I simply followed the man in front and dumped the sack onto a pile. There were no further goods to take up, so I gave the man I'd been following a few seconds to get ahead of me and then scrambled across the sacks to the other end, where I was hidden again. So far so good.

I had tried to time my move to coincide with the end of the unloading and luckily this proved to be the case. After a few more sacks were dumped on the pile, the deliveries stopped coming and I was left alone with only a low, yellow torchlight for company and the leisurely creaking of the ship's timbers as she lolled gently in the harbour.

I quickly opened one of the sacks with my knife and was intrigued to discover a stash of wool. I sat back on my heels, thinking about this discovery. There were very strict laws governing the export of woollen cloths. In particular, it was illegal to adulterate wool with lesser materials, which reduced the quality of the cloth and caused the clothes they were fashioned into to shrink when washed – the usual suspects were either chalk, hair or yarn. The authorities were particularly keen on protecting the wool trade from complaints from abroad, which could potentially damage the English market. If Hardwick was smuggling inferior wool across the channel, and what other explanation could there be for this late night activity, it was a serious crime. Tobacco coming in and wool going out. It appeared as though Hardwick and his associates had a very lucrative operation running.

I examined the cloths closely. It was hard to tell in the dim light, but a vague knowledge of wool – my father's estate had survived on sheep after all – combined with a gut feeling, left me feeling fairly certain that these were of an inferior quality. I cut into more sacks until I found what I was looking for – sleeveless woollen jackets. I slipped one on – at least I would be able to get this examined in London, and for the time being I was glad of the warmth.

***

The cargo hold was towards the bow of the ship, three flights of stairs below the main deck. I moved to the back of the cramped space and began cautiously to search out the stern of the ship. I wanted to get as close as possible to the captain's deck and the meeting that was taking place there.

The only sailors I encountered on the lower levels were either asleep in bunks or hunched over cards and dice, although I could also hear the muffled sound of someone strangling a violin. There was barely any light on the lower desks and it was easy, although nerve-racking, to pass unnoticed. Nobody spoke to me or challenged me, and I had the curious sensation of being a ghost.

I eased out of the hatchway onto the main deck and was relieved to see no sign of Grayson or Scarface. At the very rear of the ship, I could hear voices coming from the captain's quarters. I stepped through a small curved doorway into the narrow atrium. There was light spilling out beneath the door and I carefully put my eye to the keyhole.

I could just about gauge the situation in the room. On one side, Hardwick was pacing up and down. At the end of the table, facing towards me and with his back to the wide galley window, sat Simon Turney. He looked somewhat beleaguered, his head resting on his hands. Just behind him stood Dakers, watching the proceedings with a cold impartiality. Although, I couldn't see him, Ingram must have been sitting to the left of the table because Hardwick was addressing him. It took me a while to understand the gist of the conversation before I realised with a start that they were talking about me.

'This man was at De Sousa's warehouse. What the hell was he doing there?'

'Sticking his nose in where it wasn't wanted.'

'And you let him escape?' More of an accusation than a question. 'If I ever catch some busybody meddling in my affairs he will rue the day he was born.'

'He had help,' Ingram said, sounding defensive. 'A boat was waiting for him behind the dock. There was nothing my men could do once he had gone into the river.'

'Shame he didn't drown. Whose idea was it to go the warehouse in the first place?'

'Our man in the house suggested it. He knew of Don Alphonse's death and thought it a good way of loading more suspicion on Rokesby.'

'Turney, tell us again about the man who came to the ship before you departed.' Dakers spoke from his position in the corner, his voice sounding like a cat purring. Turney turned to him with a pained expression on his face.

'I told you. The German, Würtembatter, ran frantically on board to tell me that an agent of Walsingham was approaching but, after all that, he didn't seem to be interested in the ship. He was just asking questions about De Sousa – that was all. There was nothing I could help him with. I didn't even know Don Alphonse was dead, God rest his soul.'

'And you're sure he was an agent of Walsingham?'

'He said he was, and Würtembatter said he produced a letter from Walsingham when they were on the tilt boat together. That's why I sailed.' A thought suddenly struck him. 'That's right, I remember now, he also said he was Rokesby's brother and he was investigating Don Alphonse's murder.'

'Rokesby's brother?' Hardwick sounded as though he was likely to lose his temper at any moment.

'Yes. Frankly, I barely gave it another thought – there didn't seem to be a connection.'

'Of course there's a connection, you damned fool.' Hardwick's fuse had finally been lit.

'What I want to know is the name of this man who interrogated you on the ship.' Dakers was remaining far calmer than the others.

'He didn't tell me his name.'

'And you didn't think to ask him?' Hardwick was rapidly losing all sense of perspective.

'Who was it who murdered Don Alphonse? Someone who had a very good reason, I should say.' Turney had finally risen to the bait and made this point markedly at Hardwick.

'Damn your eyes man, what are you suggesting?' Hardwick moved threateningly towards Turney, who started to back off. It looked as though it was going to turn ugly. I had to repress a chuckle.

Dakers stepped forward in a calming manner. 'Let's not change the subject. Can you at least describe him, Turney?'

'Youngish – early twenties, brown, curly hair, not much of a beard to speak of.'

'Ingram, does that description match?'

'It could be the same man who was on the roof of the warehouse.'

'And it could also be the same man who has been working as our clerk for the last few days – supposedly a kinsman of Walsingham's.'

It took a moment, but Hardwick suddenly grasped what Dakers was getting at.

'What are you saying Dakers? That Walsingham has sent a spy to my house? He wouldn't dare.'

'I am merely trying to ascertain the facts, my Lord. If Lovat is the same man who went aboard this ship in Deptford before she sailed, and was also at the warehouse, then it is more than a coincidence that he has turned up at Stavening.

'What are you saying? That young upstart was at the warehouse and at Deptford? I don't believe it.' But he sounded as if he was certainly coming round to that point of view.

'It is a possibility that we can't ignore. *If* Lovat is the same man, and *if* he is working for Walsingham, then he has got a damn sight closer to us than I for one feel comfortable with.'

'He won't know anything about the cargo. He can't.' Hardwick sounded as though he was trying to convince himself.

'We need to find out.'

'Ingram. Take your men and get back to Stavening. Rouse Lovat and bring him to my study. We'll follow on directly. If he's been making a monkey out of me then he will sorely regret it.'

'Right away, your Lordship.' As he said this, I heard the sound of Ingram's chair scraping backwards as he stood up. I moved swiftly out of the corridor and back along the deck. To my dismay, I could see the shadows of two men about ten feet away leaning over the deck of the boat with their backs to me – Grayson and Scarface. I heard the cabin door open behind me. My only escape was the same staircase I had come up from, leading to below decks. There was no choice. Just as Ingram's feet appeared on the deck, my head was disappearing through the hatch beneath them.

I crouched in a dark corner and heard Ingram call out to his men. A few seconds later, to my dismay, I heard footsteps approaching the stairs and saw a shadow filling the entrance. There was nothing for it but to creep further down into the bowels if the ship.

After groping in a panic down another set of stairs, my eyes became adjusted to a low light along a passageway ahead. I was in a different part of the ship than before. All I could hear was the rumbling of low voices speaking quietly in the distance. I stood transfixed, pondering my next move, when a hand suddenly shot out and grabbed my arm.

'Herr Lovat? Herr Lovat, mein Gott I must be seeing things. Can it really be you?' The hand that had grabbed me was flabby and damp and belonged to none other than Karl Würtembatter. He had been lying prone on a bunk in a cramped section, that he seemed to have all to himself, but now he pushed himself upright and gripped me by the shoulders. He still wore the same flamboyant clothes but they appeared to have endured some severe wear and tear since the last time we had met. There was no sign of the feathered hat.

'Herr Lovat! I am overjoyed to see you. You must helfen me. I am a prisoner on this ship. We all are.' Raising his voice in his excitement, Würtembatter, looking as excited as a child that had just discovered marzipan, couldn't help spluttering in my face as he spoke. His features were still as fleshy as before but in the dim light of the deck I could sense a new seediness about them, which hadn't been there that day on the Thames.

'For goodness sake, quieten down man,' I whispered, releasing myself from his grip and wiping a hand across my face. His breath no longer smelt of sour damsons – now it was something far, far worse. 'No one must know I'm on board.' I put my finger to my lips and opened my eyes wide as I said it, to exaggerate the notion of secrecy. The idea seemed to slowly dawn on Würtembatter, who nodded at me uncertainly.

'You come to rescue us, yah?'

I took a moment to look along the clammy corridor of the deck. Voices were still murmuring in the distance and no one seemed to have been alarmed by Würtembatter's outburst. I motioned him to lie back and I slipped under his hammock, so that the corridor was free if anyone wanted to pass. Propping myself up, so our heads were as close as possible, I began whispering questions to him.

'Tell me all you can about the voyage but keep your voice down.' Würtembatter turned so that he could whisper down to me, his large frame rocking the canopy so that the ropes holding it groaned worryingly. 'I have been tricked, Herr Lovat. We sailed to France as planned but then everything changed. We stayed in dock for three days and weren't allowed to leave the harbour. Sometimes they kept us prisoner below decks. It was disgraceful.'

'Alright. Try not to get excited. What happened in France? Did you take on any goods or passengers.'

'Yah. Wie viele goods. I was forced to carry some of them. They didn't want a factor at all – I have been pressganged me into becoming a slave. All day long they make me work, work, work. Me and the others.'

'What others?'

'There are young men aboard who wanted to travel to France. All of them have been tricked like me.'

'Alright, never mind that for now. Which French port did you dock in?

'I'm not sure. Not a large one – Boulogne, vielleicht. No distance from London.'

'And you say that they kept you below decks at times. Any idea why?'

'I think they bring on some secret cargo that they don't want us to see.'

'Do you know what it was?'

'No,' Würtembatter rolled around as he thought for a moment, 'something small I think. Small enough to keep in the captain's quarters.'

'What happened next?'

'We sailed here – but where is here? They haven't allowed me on deck yet?'

'The port of Rye on the South coast of England.'

'England, thank Gott. I can go back to London. You will take me with you, Herr Lovat, right?

I thought for a moment how I could sweeten the bitter pill I had to administer. 'Listen Karl, I can't take you with me now. It's too dangerous. There are men guarding the ship. Here's what I want you to do,' I continued quickly, brushing away his attempt at remonstration. 'Stay on the ship and gather as much information as you can about what is going on, I give you my word that Walsingham will reward you well.'

'You can't leave me in this cess pool. Please, Herr Lovat.'

'It's the only way Karl,' by now I had stood up beside him and was busy unclasping his fingers that were fixed to my new woollen jacket. 'You have a very important job to do. I won't forget you, don't worry.'

The message appeared to be getting through. Würtembatter slumped back heavily on the couch but then a thought occurred to him.

'My belongings, Herr Lovat, and my bird Lucius? What has become of them?'

'Lucius is safely ensconced in my lodgings; fortunately Emmalina took a shine to him, though I can't think why. Some of your more valuable items are there too, the rest are in a tavern in Deptford. You can repay me the debt once we get you out of here.'

Würtembatter grasped my hand again. 'Thank you, Herr Lovat. You are a good man. I know you will come back for me.' His words sounded confident but the look in his eyes was more pleading than anything else. I patted his hand, put my finger to my lips, and moved away from him with exaggerated stealth.

I began grouping down an unfamiliar corridor, when it suddenly occurred to me that the encounter with Würtembatter had made me somewhat disorientated. I paused for a moment, trying to work out the best way back up to the bow end of the deck, which I reckoned was the best escape route.

As I stood in the shadows, I became aware of a low murmur of voices only a few feet away from me and there was something about one of the voices that caught my attention. I peered round a beam to have a look at the group.

In an open half cabin sat a group of three men playing a game of cards under smoky candlelight. Beyond them I could just make out lines of bunks slung between the rafters with men sleeping. But it was the group that interested me, and one man in particular. Although the sound of his voice had piqued my interest, it was the unusual way that he held his playing cards which really got my attention. Instead of holding them in a fan like most players, he held them in both hands in a straight line so that rather than being able to take one with the spare hand and place it on the table, he was forced to move both hands over the playing area and drop a card, a move he made with great speed and skill, so that the card always fell face up. It was a technique that I had witnessed numerous times under low candlelight in my lodgings during our late night games. I moved as close as I dared to make sure my eyes weren't deceiving me, but there was no doubting it – the man was Buck.

Buck, who had run away to France; Buck, who by now should be playing cards opposite a cardinal at a seminary in Rheims.

I stood for a moment wondering what to do, when footsteps alerted me to someone coming into the corridor. I slipped to my knees and rolled under a nearby bunk. He walked past me into the room and began speaking to Buck's group. I was torn but I knew it was my only opportunity to escape.

Out on the deck the coast was clear. Ingram and his men must have set off to Stavening by now where they would be surprised to find my bed empty. I glided over the ship's railing and down the ladder as quickly as I could. After retrieving my doublet from the dock, I crept back to the safety of Kyd's tavern.

* * *

'All I can prove is that Hardwick is smuggling wool, probably adulterated, and tobacco. That's all there was in the hold. But I'm sure there is something else – both he and Würtembatter talked of a specific cargo as if it was something other than the goods – something more important, more dangerous.'

'And then there were the men in the night.'

'Yes but that's what I don't get – they didn't have anything with them. None of this makes any sense.'

'It seems to me, my dear fellow, that solving mysteries is a bit like doing a puzzle. There's no point starting until you have all of the pieces. Seems that you are missing some vital information – otherwise why wouldn't it make sense? Ergo sum and all that.'

I looked at Kyd to see if he was being serious – it seemed that he was. It was hard to believe that anything sensible could come from such a carefree face.

'The strangest thing is that Hardwick doesn't appear to be involved at all in Don Alphonse's death.'

'What about this Dakers? He sounds like a cold fish.'

'I doubt he would baulk at murder but only under Hardwick's bidding.'

Kyd thought for a moment whilst chewing 'Then that only leaves Ingram and Drummond. At least from the list of suspects we have.'

'I still don't fancy Drummond as our man. He wouldn't be capable. Ingram on the other hand, or one of his henchmen, most certainly is but from what I heard Ingram is Hardwick's man too. There's something else.

It looks as though Don Alphonse was also involved in the plot to discredit Robert. He was on the same side as Hardwick all of the time.'

'That's hard to believe given their history.'

'There's another thing you won't believe.'

'What's that?'

'I saw Buck on the boat. Under decks, playing cards with a couple of old sea dogs.'

'You don't say. Theatre's great loss has ended up a sailor.'

'I want you to go to that ship before you leave and see if you can get a message to him.'

'Steady Lovat, old boy, I don't want to get pressed.'

'I rather fear that that is exactly what has happened to Buck. Tell him that Emmalina is worried about him and that if he's in trouble we'll help him out.'

'How do you expect me to do that?'

'You're the playwright. You'll think of something. I have to go.'

'What are you going to do?'

'Get back to Stavening. Collect the papers I stole and scarper.' I had been regretting the decision to leave the letters in the church but there was nothing I could do about it now. The little that I had read told me that they very likely held those missing pieces of the puzzle that Kyd was referring to. Hopefully I could get back to the church under cover of night, retrieve the papers and leave again without anyone being the wiser. Kyd did nothing to support this view.

'Why the hell didn't you bring them with you? If you get caught they'll lynch you.'

'Let's just say a beguiling woman led me astray. Once you've delivered the message to Buck, you should leave here. I suggest we meet in the inn where we stopped on the way down and return to London together.'

'Right-o.'

Little did either of us know that Kyd was going to have a long wait.

***

The grand house was quiet. Its endless black windows reflecting the pale moon. I rode as close to it as I dared before dismounting and leaving

George tethered to one of the inner gates. An owl screeched somewhere in the distance.

All I had to do was reach the church, collect the bag of letters and disappear. On paper it seemed relatively simple. Simple, except that I had to pass close to the house to reach the church. I struck off to one side of the entrance path and began cautiously sidling through the garden. Strange shapes loomed at me out of the darkness – mystical figures on poles, strangely cut hedges – Hardwick's fanciful garden ornaments, pretty in the daylight but damn right eerie at night. Two or three times a figure looked as though it was moving and I had to tell myself to take a deep breath and calm down. I edged forward, the crunch of icy snow beneath my feet.

Then I saw him.

At first just a shadow, then clearly the shape of a man – a big man, possibly Grayson, closing in on me from behind. I heard a whistle, followed by sounds of footsteps and the dancing shadows of torchlight. I darted behind one of the sculptured hedges and began moving swiftly towards where I thought the church to be. I had no choice but to continue blindly on.

There was no chance of seeing the church in the dark and I simply had to trust my judgement as to where it was. My judgement proved to be poor. I had gradually been following the line of a path between two hedges, but, at a sharp turn, I now realised I had run into a section of the ornamental maze. The hedges, over six feet high, reared up on either side of me. I didn't know how far in I had gone but there was nothing for it but to turn back.

I spun round but the flare of a light blocked my path. Turning, I ran desperately towards the centre of the maze. The voices had turned to shouts – 'the maze, he's in the maze, we've got him' – their quarry was trapped and they were moving in for the kill.

I stumbled around square corners, turning back on myself, hearing feet scuttling along adjacent paths. Suddenly I found myself in a square box, hedges on every side. I scrambled at the hedge, trying to climb it and would almost have made it but for rough hands grabbing my legs and pulling my hard backwards. I landed awkwardly and a torch was blazed into my face.

Scarface was standing over me, his milky eye thrust forward. Behind him stood Grayson holding the torch. They didn't say anything – just grinned.

Chapter 30

Why dost thou then, ô Man, ô Hunter me pursue,
With cry of hounds, with blast of horne, with hallow, and with hue?
Or why dost thou deuise, such nets and instruments,
Such toyles & toyes, as hunters vse, to bring me to their bents?
(George Turberville: The Wofull wordes of the Hart to the Hunter)

The cabal stood in a line in front of me – Grayson and Scarface, ugly brutes cracking their knuckles, looking as though they would like to set to work beating the living daylights out of me as soon as possible; Dakers, altogether more refined, looking as though he was planning a crueller, but ever-so-entertaining, form of torture; Ingram, hawk-like eyes fixed on me, comfortably settling back to enjoy the show; and finally Hardwick himself, red-faced, murderous, and looking as though he might ruin everyone's fun by tearing me apart then and there with his bare hands.

I had been dragged unceremoniously to Hardwick's study and thrown into a chair by the fireplace – I didn't think I would be sitting comfortably for long. I'd expected to be taken to a shed or stable but I supposed there wasn't anywhere more private in the entire residence. Private for what, was the question. I looked closely at the chests that I had been rummaging through only a day ago, but there appeared to be no sign that Hardwick was aware of the fact. Despite capturing me, he must still assume that his study was impregnable.

It was obvious to me that my arrival had been expected and I had wondered painfully if the beautiful Leticia had betrayed me. I needn't have doubted her though. A terrified Tichborne was cowering in a corner of Hardwick's study. He was wearing his nightgown and a reddening eye told me that his awakening had likely been a rude one.

'Sorry Lovat. I saw you leave,' was all he could get out before Hardwick slapped him hard in the mouth.

'Get out Tichborne. I'll deal with you later.' Tichborne simpered his way out of the door, which was shut and bolted behind him. Hardwick was gradually gaining control of his anger.

'Well now, Master Lovat.' He pulled up a chair and sat in front of me, his livid face inches from mine. 'Or should I call you Robert Rokesby's little bastard brother? How did Walsingham get his claws into you? And what are you really doing in my house?'

I decided to try ignorance as a first form of defence. 'I beg your pardon, sire, but you know perfectly well that Walsingham sent me here to learn my trade as a clerk.'

'Is that so? Are you sure it isn't some other trade he wants you to learn?'

'Such as what?'

'Are you going to be tiresome Lovat? Ingram, have your men soften him up.'

Violence is a reality; violence is a way of life. From the vicious schoolmasters with their canes, to the stupid husbandry men that batter their wives, to the soldiers, thieves and vagabonds in the perilous London streets. I was used to violence. These and other fanciful thoughts mixed with the stars in my brain as Grayson and Scarface set about 'softening me up.' I was kicked off the chair, hauled up, one behind holding in my arms, one in front, thumped down again, blows to the face and stomach. 'This is in return for the night at the warehouse', muttered Grayson into my ear before one particularly well-targeted blow to the eye.

There was no fighting back – this was a professional beating. They took it in turns to pin my arms, whilst the other took free hits – a distinct crack told of a fractured rib. When Hardwick stopped the first round, I was badly winded and on my knees.

Just batter me over to the left next time, I thought, just a little further to the left.

I was hauled back into the chair.

'Feel like talking? Or should I let them continue? What were you doing here Lovat?'

'I spat some blood from my mouth: 'Ok, I'll come clean. Walsingham's taken an interest in gardening. He thinks you've got one of the finest gardens in England – he wanted me to steal some ideas.'

'Grayson.' The blow landed on my ear, knocking me to floor on the right – to the left next time, I willed – before receiving a kick in the ribs. The hollow pain in my side increased markedly.

'We've got all night Lovat. And by the end of it I can promise you that you'll be telling me everything I want to know and a damn sight more that I don't. What does Walsingham want?' I shook my head, barely able to speak even if I had wanted to. 'Alright, we'll leave that for a moment and try something else. What's your connection with De Sousa? What were you doing at the warehouse?'

'Fixing the chimney.'

'Dammit! Grayson make him speak.'

To the left, I thought, just hit me to the left.

Grayson stepped forward and I stood, stumbling, as if to get away, but making sure that I made him an offer of my right cheek. He didn't waste the opportunity. As the blow came in, I flung myself in time with it to the space behind Hardwick's desk – at the panel that I knew to be there – at the wall that I prayed would give way.

My prayers were answered. I smashed through the wooden panelling, bringing the shelves down above me, and before Grayson or anyone else could react, I was through the trapdoor and falling headfirst down the ladder into the secret tunnel. My last vision of them was of gaping-mouthed silence at this completely unexpected turn of events.

I landed awkwardly, severely twisting one of my arms, but wasted no time wrenching the ladder from its fixings. It was a matter of rotten wood and disintegrated easily. I looked up just in time to see a figure flinging itself down on top of me. Grayson evidently didn't need the ladder.

In the quickest move I have ever made in my life, I bent forward, stuck out a shoulder, and, on impact, catapulted the unsuspecting thug into the vicinity of the well.

My luck held. Grayson landed half-in and half-out of the disused well head. An accurately aimed punch to his groin and I tipped the scales in favour of gravity. Grayson plunged downwards. I heard the desperate scraping of his fingers along the inner bricks before the inevitable splash of water.

'Grayson! Grayson! Have you got him?' A light appeared in the space above but I was too deep in the gloom for anyone to spot me. I scrambled into the tunnel to the church, leaving the sound of Ingram's increasingly futile cries. 'Grayson! Where the hell are you?'

I don't remember my escape down the tunnel. My mind was already ahead of my feet – would the rope still be there to get me out, would the bag with the letters be in its hiding place? Could I make it to the entrance of the church and beyond before anyone spotted me?

The rope was still there – I clambered up it. I dug the bag out of its hiding place – bulky weight, but sod it – had to be done – bless you Leticia for remembering to bring it from my room. Up the stone steps three at a time – ribs, arms in agony – a quick glance at the door – dawn breaking over the fields to the East, giving the snow a pink tinge – maybe an hour more of darkness if I was lucky. Would they have followed me into the tunnel or be looking for me outside? No way of knowing, simply had to chance it. The next beating would end in my death.

I didn't run – at first. Quietly round to the back of the church, carefully into the trees and now – thanks be to God the bastards didn't break my legs – ran for my life.

***

It was about an hour later when I first heard the dogs.

Not the bass-level grunt of mastiffs, nor the high-pitched yapping of alaunts but, much more disconcertingly, the collective howling of a pack of running-hounds – the sort usually employed to track and corner harts or boar, although I had no doubt in this instance that I was their quarry.

I had reached the fringes of open ground and was taking shelter in an untidy thicket, beyond which lay the forest of the Weald. The ground had been steadily rising and the house and gardens were now somewhere below me in the valley beyond the grey dawn, obscured by a thick mist that had enveloped the entire length of the valley. The snow had thinned out in the last hundred yards before I reached the scattered blackthorn and hawthorn bushes, which guarded the entrance to the wilder woods. Now I found myself on rough turf, broken by the ravages of the cold but at least no longer leaving an easy trail of footprints for anyone to follow – not that the dogs would need those to track me.

I was grateful to the dawn, which had been creeping in so slowly, as though it could barely be bothered to start a new day. Even now, as the mist began to clear slightly, grey clouds overhead were stalling the onset of day. Had anyone in the house been alert to the direction I had taken, they would not have been able to see me, despite the openness of the terrain.

I calculated that it would have taken at least a quarter of an hour for anyone to have been lowered into the well pit below Hardwick's study and discover the passageway, and another ten minutes to reach the church and discover the secret entrance, from which I had conveniently removed the rope. There was also the time taken to fish Grayson out of the well – assuming anyone had bothered. All-in-all the best part of an hour must have passed before they would have discovered that the church had been my means of escape, by which time I had been well away across the fields.

I bent double with my hands on my knees, watching the warm breath bursting painfully out of my screaming lungs, contemplating the next problem that now presented itself. Should I stay in the open where I was easy prey but could move quickly, or dive into the forest, where the dogs would have no trouble following me, but I might at least find means of outwitting them and be able to put some obstacles between myself and the horses that the followers would no doubt be riding? I chose the forest. My legs were exhausted from the climb, my lungs bursting and my ribs and arm aching, but there was no time to think about any of that. The ground that had taken me an hour to cover would be gained in less than half the time by the dogs.

I had no choice but to keep moving.

Before taking refuge in the woods, I ran up and down, and around the thicket, knowing that the best way to slow the dogs would be to confuse them as much as possible. I also tore up my undershirt, shoving part of it as far as possible down a nearby rabbit hole with the help of a thick wooden stick, and throwing other parts on the tops of the tallest bushes I could find. It all added up to what was, most likely, a futile attempt at deception.

The prickly bushes soon gave way to more substantial woodlands of broad oak and wand-like straight ashes. The first part of it was still very much part of the estate, with rows of coppiced and pollarded trees, and piles of stakes that had been cut from them and stored for the winter under cover. Quickly, though, the managed part of the forest gave way to thicker, more impenetrable terrain. I ran on as fast as the uneven ground would allow me, pausing only occasionally to catch my breath and listen for my pursuers.

Each time I wished I hadn't – the cries and whines of the dogs grew ever nearer, urged on by the trill of hunting horns. I thought of my own experiences of hunting – if Hardwick, the hunting enthusiast, was doing things properly there would be a pack of around forty hounds, followed by a handful of armed men on horseback, and a further group of men on foot leading mastiffs and greyhounds. I judged that they were already halfway between the house and the scrub and closing rapidly. The only thing for it was to keep pressing further and further into the forest.

It was hard to tell if my delaying tactics were successful at all, but if they were, they only bought me a little time. It wasn't long before, with a feeling of dismay, I could hear the sound of the hounds closing in from behind.

I tripped over roots and stones, pitched into bogs and ditches, clambered up banks, caught my clothing and skin on sharp branches and thorns. As I ran, panting loudly, I thought with irony of Don Alphonse's flight through the African jungle and how history was now repeating itself. The only advice I could glean from Don Alphonse's document was to run and run but, I thought grimly, he hadn't being pursued by dogs with every instinct to kill.

The ground, which had continued to rise in the forest, now suddenly plunged downwards. Glad, at first, of the change in gradient, I charged headlong down the slope, but soon found myself hemmed into a ravine, high, rocky banks on either side, with only one choice of direction. If the hounds followed me in here, I was easy prey. Behind me I could now hear their whimpering, as they relayed the message of my scent, as well as the thump of hooves and the cries of the men in pursuit.

After a drop of around fifty feet, I stopped momentarily and turned. My heart sank as above me I saw the hounds starting to pour into the ravine and then almost stopped as I saw a man on horseback pull his mount sharply up behind them, judging correctly that the ravine was too steep for the horse. I couldn't tell which of my pursuers it was but he had clearly spotted me. As I stared at him, I felt a flutter of air across my cheek and heard the thud of a crossbow bolt penetrating a tree only inches from my head. I didn't wait to give him a second shot.

With heavy legs and a heart threatening to burst through my chest, I pressed onwards. The ravine twisted and turned down the hillside, surrounded by trees on every side. At some places it closed in tightly, which I prayed would slow down the dogs. I knew I had momentarily lost the horsemen but the dogs were still in hot pursuit. Perhaps unsettled by the loss of their commander, the hounds seemed momentarily to falter and I was able to gain some ground on them.

At the bottom of the ravine was a stream. I plunged into its icy waters, only knee deep, but hopefully enough to cause some disguising of my scent. I ran down the stream as far as I dared in the open before darting back off into the forest.

The ground, now thick and muddy, rose away from the stream. I clambered my way upwards, catching at roots and stones. The next time I stopped for a breather, I looked back to see the hounds running, confusedly, down both sides of the bank. They turned in circles and barked at one another – my trick had worked temporarily. Hidden among the trees, and slowly recovering my breath, I watched transfixed until two or three of the horsemen caught up with the dogs. One leapt from his horse and started shouting for the footmen – it was Ingram.

After a moment, a man arrived with another dog on a lead – I recognised it from its white skin with large brown spots as a Lymerhound, the breed that my father and I had used to pick up the scent of boars when hunting on the Gloucestershire estate. The Lymers had a keen nose for individual scents, and were used for picking up the trail of a quarry once the hounds had lost it. The man held a fragment of my torn shirt to the hound's nose. I knew it was only a matter of minutes before they were pursuing me again. Only partly recovered I fled again into the forest. My only hope, a forlorn one, was to try and out run the dogs.

I don't know for how much longer I had been running, stumbling, limping, when I next heard the dogs on my trail. I had reached a part of the forest where the ground had levelled out and there was only the cover of trees, neatly spaced around me. There was nowhere to hide, nowhere to take refuge. The dogs were gaining fast – maybe twenty, fifteen yards behind me.

Fearing that this was the end, I burst suddenly from the shade of the trees into a wide clearing, where only a few tree stumps stood covered in a thin veil of snow that smoothly caressed the mossy ground. Standing majestically in the centre of this Arcadian setting was a hart – a proud red stag, fully mature and the largest I had ever seen.

A warrantable hart of ten with magnificent antlers.

I had come upon it so fast that it had barely had time to react. We both stood frozen to the spot, each eyeing the other with the haunted look of the hunted. The hart twitched nervously and let out a plume of steamy air from its nostrils.

At the echo of the hounds crashing through the bedraggled trees, the hart lifted its head. Time seemed to choke to a standstill. I heard the slow beat of my heart, saw the recognition of danger flash in the stag's black eyes, watched helplessly as it turned gracefully on its heels and kicked its hind legs backwards.

Leave me to die. That's the sensible thing to do, I thought.

As the stag turned, the loll-tongued hounds tumbled out of the trees, I braced myself for the impact of their bodies, the tearing of their teeth. Would Hardwick and Ingram and Dakers get to me before I was torn to pieces? Would it be better for me if they didn't? These and other unavailing thoughts had all the time in the world to torment my mournful soul. The hounds closed in and I began to let out a roar of anguish.

When I tell this tale in the future I will call it The Miracle of the Red Hart.

The hart had turned fully and was gracefully loping towards the safety of its own secret forest. The hounds, perhaps momentarily disconnected by this sudden sight of movement, alighted on a new quarry. They tore past me on either side as I stood stock still, their warm, sweaty flanks brushing the tears in my breeches and stockings. I felt the hairs on my leg tingle with the sensation of fur. And then they were gone into the trees beyond and I stood alone in the clearing, trying to grasp what had just happened.

I had seconds to take cover before the first of the horsemen came crashing into the clearing. Shimmying high into an ash tree, I watched as the horsemen gathered, detected the direction of the hounds from their cries and then galloped off in their wake. Ingram, Dakers, Hardwick himself, among servants I didn't recognise. I waited, clinging to the trunk of the tree as the footmen, with their dogs and weapons, ran on behind. The Lymerhound momentarily paused and twitched its nostrils in my direction but he was pulled on impatiently by his handler – who I noticed with a start was Scarface. Soon all of them had disappeared into the trees beyond and an eerie silence descended on the clearing.

I clung to the branches and wept silently with relief.

Chapter 31

What is the way to London town?
One foot up, the other foot down,
That is the way to London town.
(Traditional 16th century song)

Darkness fell as I trudged forlornly through the forest. And with the darkness came an uncheery quilt of cold. For the first hours after my escape, I had been kept warm by excitement and fear but the cold was seeping into my bones. Although I was grateful for the extra warmth afforded me by the woollen coat I had taken from the ship, I still needed to find shelter quickly.

I had heard nothing more of the hunt. How long the stag had run on with hounds and men in pursuit I had no way of telling. I only knew that the noble beast had saved my life. I vowed the foregoing of venison for good, if I ever returned safely to London.

Walking was becoming increasingly problematic in the dusk and after another half an hour had passed I was relieved to stumble across a pathway. I decided to follow it until I found some sort of shelter. I was still deep in the forest and didn't expect to encounter anyone. Like all well brought up children, I had been regaled many times with tales of bandits and outlaws that lived in the woods, and it was true that recent wars and changes in the countryside had left many people homeless and living rough, but I was hopeful that any self-respecting robber would be snuggled up in warmth somewhere, rather than hanging around profitless paths in the forest.

I had not been on the track for long when I chanced upon a small clearing containing three pointed shapes against the outline of the starless sky. For a horrible moment I thought I was back in Hardwick's garden, encountering more strange topiary, but investigation showed them to be three abandoned charcoal-burner's huts, with high triangular roofs built of turf – ideal as a place of shelter. I prudently made sure that they were all empty, before picking the one that had the best-preserved roof and setting about making myself comfortable.

To begin with, this involved a tortuous search for kindling and wood.

My first task was to find a birch tree, knowing that birch bark will light even when damp – not the easiest thing to do in the dark. Fortunately, they were relatively plentiful in the wood and it didn't take me too long to find a small copse of the thin white trees. The second task, though, was obtaining enough bark to start a fire. Hardwick had taken my knife, so I used the buckle of my bag to scrape as much bark as I could – resulting in the buckle snapping after only a few strips had been harvested. In the end I settled for less than I wanted and decided to substitute the bark with bombast, the stuffing used for puffing out clothing, which was already sticking out of various holes in my ripped doublet. The final task was finding a flint from which I could get a spark using the broken buckle. I managed to get a small part of the kindling burning and then spent a good fifteen minutes coaxing it into flames. After what seemed an inordinate struggle, I finally created enough fire and started to relax.

One thing I wasn't short of for my impromptu camping trip was reading material. The bag had come through the ordeal unscathed – that is at least until I broke the buckle – and the letters I had stolen, along with Don Alphonse's manuscript, were all present and correct.

I began sifting through the letters one by one under the firelight, sorting them by signatures and dates, and, in particular, looking for the ones that I had already noted were interesting. I had twenty-seven letters in total. All of them were addressed to Hardwick apart from four that were addressed to Dakers. There were three from Ingram, written in an illiterate scrawl, five from my brother, one from Marmaduke Drummond, one from Walsingham, and two from Don Alphonse. The rest were from unknowns, at least to me, but chosen because they were from interesting places such as France and the Canary Islands.

I read through my brother's letters first – they set out in excruciating, and characteristically pompous, detail the plans for the phantom 'expedition' that he clearly believed in all too well. He had been only too willing to place himself at the head of the operation and he talked at endless length about the riches and fame that would be forthcoming. I found myself laughing out loud at some of his preposterous optimism, although I acknowledged to myself that hindsight was a great gift. It was difficult having only one side of the correspondence but the impression I got was that Hardwick had been weaving a clever web – encouraging Robert to assume command, whilst committing nothing himself. Robert's last two letters were amongst those addressed to Dakers, suggesting that Hardwick had eventually managed to submerge himself completely into the background as far as the plans were concerned.

Ingram's letters were more informative and I understood fully for the first time his role in the affair. His earliest letter was a speculative plea for future employment. He explained that since his patron, the Earl of Leicester, had recently died he was looking for a new position in service. He listed a number of skills, but as handwriting didn't appear to be amongst them, I found it hard to decipher a lot of what he wrote. The skills I could discern though mostly seemed to revolve around conning people, all-be-it technically by legal means. His second letter was briefer but confirmed that Ingram had embarked upon the task that Hardwick had set him, presumably as some sort of test, a task which involved my brother and Don Alphonse, and could only be the setting up of the expedition that my brother was so keen on being a figurehead for.

I thought about this for a moment. Leicester had died at the beginning of September, about a month after the Armada had been repelled. Ingram's second letter was dated midway through September, showing that he hadn't wasted any time getting involved in the plot. From what I could glean, his role had been to offer himself in service to Robert, and in particular bring his business acumen to the expedition. Leicester had been no stranger to investment and trade, and having someone of Ingram's calibre involved must have been very attractive for Robert. Some of this was guess work on my part but I felt pretty sure I was right.

Marmaduke Drummond's letter had been tied together with one of Ingram's and in it he also offered himself in service to Hardwick – using the device of a sycophantic poem that made me cringe. Drummond appeared to be acquainted with Ingram and must have somehow got wind of the plot and seen an opportunity to obtain a new patron. I thought about meeting him on the day after Don Alphonse's death – he knew then precisely what was going on but was still playing the dutiful servant to my brother. I hoped I would get the opportunity of confronting him with the letter.

Opening Drummond's letter out fully, another page slipped out. I looked at it casually and then felt my jaw drop. As an example of disloyalty, it took some beating.

The letter from Don Alphonse to Hardwick was dated much earlier than the others – almost a year before his death. As I huddled close to my makeshift fire the letter by turns made me gape in admiration, tense with anger and laugh out loud at the final outrageousness of it all. I had only glanced at Walsingham's letter but now I looked at it afresh and saw in there everything I needed to confirm what I now knew. Don Alphonse – Catholic and Jew, patriot and traitor, cuckolder, adventurer, merchant, friend to the rich and famous, as well as to the Lion's Quay lepers, and finally the master of a clever revenge plot. The only thing I still couldn't fathom was who had killed him – and why.

I silently doffed my hat to him in the firelight and picked up the manuscript Emmalina had translated – wanting more than ever to understand all I could about this man.

October 1569 – Timbuktu

After many weeks of travelling, we have finally reached the city of Timbuktu, the great city that Gbère has repeatedly spoken of. Our journey has taken us through many Kingdoms, through magnificent valleys, and along great rivers. In every kingdom we encountered, we have been received by the king whom Gbère paid tribute so that we were allowed to pass through unmolested and with the goods of the caravan intact. The people we have met have been for the most part friendly to us, although they fight constantly amongst themselves, but my white skin has been a perpetual source of wonderment to them. Some think I am a God, others an evil spirit. In every village I would be surrounded by a horde of natives, all wanting to touch my hands and face, and stare at me for hours. I am glad that we have finally reached a large city where I can be somewhat anonymous. Cassangoe is also relieved to be away from the caravan. For much of the journey he was afraid to speak, lest his native tongue should mark him out as different from the people we met, who are far more vicious to their own kind than they are to strangers from afar. Cassangoe also suffered many iniquities as my pretend slave, particularly from Gbèré, who offered to buy Cassangoe from me on many occasions and add him to the party of slaves he was bringing to the city to sell.

Gbèré was right to describe Timbuktu as a great city. As we approached, we could see its golden towers rising high above the fortified city wall, built of sun-baked clay, and once inside we could not fail to be impressed by the buildings, many of whose roofs were tiled with gold, and the great multitude of peoples of all kinds. On venturing into the vast markets, we found Songhai, Wangara, Fulani, Tuareg and Arabs all rubbing shoulders, and dealing with one another over the array of goods that seemed to pour into the city from all directions. Gbèré told me proudly that gold came from the south, salt from the north and Divine knowledge itself, from Timbuktu. The city is the capital of the Songhai Empire and the King has his palace at its centre. On certain days he rides abroad in the streets accompanied by a great entourage. The King possesses no less than 3000 foot soldiers armed with poisoned arrows and all those refusing to pay appropriate homage are executed. Also, at the heart of the city is a great mosque, where adherents to the Mohammedan faith, who vastly out number all other religious persuasions, go to worship. There are also many libraries in the city that hold hundreds of thousands of manuscripts, and many scholars travel here to study the Islamic faith in preparation for the Hajj. Even though we are considered infidels, we are encouraged to visit the libraries but there is very little there that I can read or understand, besides I am busy learning the ropes of trade from Gbèré.

We have taken lodgings in the city, but I spend my days accompanying Gbèré as his aide, whilst he buys goods in the market and begins to organise a train that will carry us across the desert to the north and to the Mediterranean Sea beyond. When not speaking of his home city, or stuffing his mouth with kola nuts, Gbèré spent much of the journey from the South discussing his plans with me for trade between Africa and Europe. His vision is that on returning me to my homeland, we will work together to create a trading empire that reaches to all the known corners of the world. I spent most of my time laughing at his plans – I don't even know where my homeland is now anyway – but gradually he has worn me down and I must admit that the thought of having vast wealth is an appealing one.

Cassangoe, who haunts my side for fear of being enslaved, disagrees with me. He tells me that in his tribe, individual wealth is taken as a sin against the many and all must be shared for the good of the whole. It is true that the relationship between Gbèré and myself has caused there to be some disagreement between Cassangoe and myself, but I have become a prize asset to the trader and he insists on taking me under his wing and parading me about the town. And anyway, I am convinced the friendship, the bond, that Cassangoe and I hold, will survive the present. We are blood brothers and he knows I would lay down my life for him.

One last thing – as the top of this page reveals, I have discovered the Christian date finally. It is nearly two years since I set off from Lisbon with my father. Two years of captivity and deprivation, of adventure. I left Lisbon a boy, now I am a young man.

Chapter 32

'.... they do come into the [Realm] by secret Creeks, and Landing Places, disguised, both in their Names and Persons.'
(Queen Elizabeth 1)

I woke with a start like a hunted animal, Don Alphonse's manuscript falling from my chest, where it had lain through the night, onto the earthen floor I had been sleeping on.

At first, I wondered what had woken me but then heard a rumbling noise coming along the path outside the huts. A quick glance through the smoke-hole in the ceiling told me that dawn was just breaking. The fire had burned out and there was no giveaway smoke rising through the hole.

I roused myself quickly and positioned myself by the entrance, ready to make a run for it, although the prospect held no joy considering the pain in my stiffened ribs and arm. The trundling sound of heavy wooden wheels came closer. It didn't slow down as it reached the huts but continued on in the same slow manner. Just after it passed, I risked glancing from the doorway, and saw a low wooden cart being pulled along the track by two men, a third man walking beside. On the cart itself sat two further men, both huddled up – one seemingly asleep, the other glancing into the forest. I quickly gathered the letters and manuscript into my bag, waited until the cart was out of sight, and then set off cautiously in pursuit.

It was a beautiful morning. The rising sun was just beginning to filter through the trees, sending shafts of light dancing into the forest, and the air tasted fresh and light, unlike the heavy dampness of the day before. The night must have been above freezing, as most of the snow was now gone.

It quickly became apparent that the huts I had discovered were situated close to the edge of the forest. The sun became ever stronger as the trees thinned out and after only a short while, the cart had reached an area that was far more open but still populated by trees. I followed along at a safe distance enjoying the fresh breeze, the birdsong, and a general sense of freedom, and, despite the aches from various injuries and a gnawing hunger in my belly, I felt a sensation of light-heartedness that I hadn't experienced for a good many days.

The cart rumbled doggedly ahead along the winding track. I followed – skipping into and then out of the trees – constantly glancing backwards to make sure that I too wasn't being followed. There was no need to worry though. Apart from the cart and myself, we were alone in the world.

The group ahead had now reached an escarpment that ran along the edge of the forest. The track was high up and from this vantage point there was a view across a far ranging valley. I watched as they slowed to a halt and the two men doing the pulling relaxed to take some refreshment and enjoy the view. I crouched in a ditch and watched enviously as they drank and ate victuals from the cart.

Sensing from their demeanour that they were planning to rest there for a while I decided to get as close as possible to see if I could hear any of their conversation. I circled round through the wood, making sure to tread carefully, and managed to reach a point where I was about twenty yards away from them but hidden in the foliage of the forest. The two men pulling, and the one who had been walking along beside, were sitting some distance from the cart, and talking easily amongst themselves, whilst passing round a flagon of beer.

'Well Carb! That were some commotion at the big 'ouse yesterday, weren't it? What were all the fuss about?' I couldn't see the speaker, who spoke with a broad Sussex accent, but he must have been one of the two who had been doing the pulling because the man Carb he addressed his question to was clearly in my vision and had been the man walking beside the cart.

'The servant's reckon as there was a thief in the 'ouse. Stole som'at the master's gold, or so I heard.'

'It weren't nothin' more serious then, eh? Nothin' to do wit what we're carrying?'

'If it were, then no one's told me.'

'Got the 'ole 'unt out after him, so he did.' The third man joined with a voice that was a funny high-pitched squeak. 'Chasin' all day they were. Not that they caught 'im mind.'

'You don't need to tell me that. Dakers were in a right foul mood when I went to get our money last night. Threat'ned to reduce the amount, he did. Until it was that I pointed out how there's many in aut'ority who'd like very much to 'ear about the little cargos we been atrundling all over the county – and beyond.'

'God Carb! You don wanna be doin' that with Dakers. He could tear the skin off your back with just a look 'e could.' The high-pitched squeal and stage whisper combined to sound as though Dakers had already got his hands around the man's throat.

'Ah quit your whinnying Morris. I got Dakers just where I wan' him. Besides, my nose tells me there won't be too many more of these jobs. *Cut rye while the sun's high*. That's what my ol' man used to say to me. An' Solomon Carberry knew a devil's trick or two.'

'He taught the devil a few an' all.' They all laughed at this and then sank into silence, apart from slurping and munching sounds, with the odd belch thrown in for good measure. After a while Morris squeaked up again. 'Reckon if that thief escaped he won't survive long in these 'ere woods.' Neither of the other two bothered to comment on this statement, choosing instead to concentrate on their meal.

So I had been reduced to the status of a common thief. Well I suppose there are worse things to be called – a spy, for instance – but it was informative that Hardwick and Dakers hadn't wanted it to become common knowledge that there was a spy in the house, at least not to these men who were running secretive errands for them. Carberry, who appeared to be the leader, although I doubted there was much hierarchy amongst them, was the same man that I had overheard Hardwick and Vaillons discussing disparagingly in the study. He didn't strike me at all like the kind of man that Hardwick would be used to employing.

The intriguing question involved the two men in the cart. I could see them through the trees, heads close together, talking earnestly, with frequent looks to the others, as though they were anxious to get moving again. They were little older than a pair of boys, both beardless with a hint of neatly cut hair peeping out from under hooded cloaks. They couldn't have contrasted more greatly with the three men escorting them. Whereas the other three seemed totally at home in this wild, winter landscape, the two in the cart couldn't have stood out more incongruously.

I was working on the theory that they were the same men that Kyd had seen at night in the streets of Rye and that Leticia and I had seen entering the gates of Stavening as we slipped into the church. The logical extrapolation of this thinking was that they had originally been onboard The Lady Merrydance. But who were they? As I watched them from under the cover of fern and bracken it suddenly dawned on me exactly who they might be.

My attention was drawn back to the group of three. Carberry had stood up and was relieving himself by the side of the path. I was grateful that he wasn't the kind of man likely to seek privacy in the woods.

'Right, come on. We got to get 'is lordship's little servants to Chillenham before dark.' Carb glanced at the sky as he said this as if assessing the weather, 'Don't want to end up spending the night in the forest. I doubt those sensitive little souls could stan' it.'

'At least they got the Lord on their side.'

'An' we got the devil. Come on.' The other two men started moving, one of them flinging a half-eaten chicken leg to within a yard of where I was sitting. I waited till they were out of sight and then gratefully cleaned the scraps of meat off the bone.

* * *

The rest of the morning and early afternoon proved for the most part to be an enjoyable trot through the wilds of the English countryside. Carberry and his crew wound their way down tracks, through groves, over ridges and along stretches of forest. It was clear to me that they knew the tracks intimately and were taking a route that meant they avoided meeting anyone else. On a number of occasions we reached forks where a much more civilised path presented itself and each time the cart was drawn along a more obstinate route. It involved some heavy pulling but Carberry, Morris and the third man, whose name I didn't know, seemed well able to manoeuvre the cart, and, even when they were slogging up hills through deep mud, declined any offers of help from their young charges.

The men stopped for a couple more rests along the way but on both of these occasions I decided to stay well out of sight in the forest and waited patiently for the heavy wheels to start rolling, a sign that I could start following.

About two hours into the afternoon, when the sun was just starting to dip below the tree line, the cart began a long descent from the ridge we had been following. Shadows lengthened across the pathway as the cart rattled ever lower down the hillside. The terrain gradually became less wild, and gates and fences indicated that we were now entering farmland. We came to an open field, and I had to hang back while the cart trundled across it, before disappearing into a copse on the other side.

I ran across the field so that they couldn't get too far ahead and almost tripped over them. They had parked the cart to the side of the track and Carberry had gone on ahead. I quickly retreated, berating myself silently for becoming too complacent.

I could smell smoke drifting above the treeline, suggesting that we were close to habitation. Carberry was gone for about a quarter of an hour and when he returned they started moving again.

After only a short while they reached a wall with a ha-ha and two huge pillars either side of an ornate gateway. It looked like the back entrance to an estate – perhaps the place called Chillenham that had been mentioned earlier.

At the gate stood a reception committee of about ten people, a group of well-to-do gentlemen and ladies. At the head of them was a well-dressed man of about fifty. I crept as close as I dared and watched as this new man greeted the two youngsters in the cart. It was an interesting performance – he had two servants offer them help from the cart and then knelt before them, kissing both of their hands in turn. This was followed by the rest of the party kneeling on the gravel pathway, each of them with their heads bowed. The young men walked among them offering their hands to be kissed.

They had thrown off the rough hooded garments they had worn for warmth and secrecy in the cart and now stood proudly like ravens in the black robes of their chosen vocation. I was gratified to see the proof that my theory about them had been correct.

Chapter 33

'I never come back home with the same moral character I went out with.'
(Lucius Annaeus Seneca)

There is, to my eyes at least, no finer sight than the elongated roof of St Paul's, rising imperiously above the smoking city. Even the squat remains of the spire, burnt down on account, some say, of the negligence of a plumber, years before I was born, didn't matter and I doubt that even the sight of that elegant needle, purportedly rising 500 ft above the nave, could have made my heart feel any gladder than it did on that chilled December morning. I stood on the brow of a hill, about five miles south of the river – my home – and took in the sights and sounds before me. It was a Sunday and bells were ringing out in a dissonant harmony all across the city in the hundreds of towers and spires, which more than made up for the missing one. I even flattered myself that the bells were heralding my return.

It was more than two weeks since I had last set foot in the city, and four miserable days since I had witnessed Carberry and his men secretly deliver their precious cargo to the back gates of Chillenham Manor. Ever since slipping away from the curious meeting I had witnessed, I had spent most of the last leg of my journey regretting the fact that I hadn't taken a good handful of Hardwick's gold when I'd had the opportunity. I had managed to keep a small amount of the reward that Leticia had given me for finding Cassangoe, but much of it had been lost in the forest when I'd been running from the hounds, falling out of various tears in my attire. What little I had left I put to buying food, but there wasn't enough for lodging too, meaning that I had spent three further nights trying to sleep in different, but equally uninviting, forests. When the money had run out I had even had to barter using my only surviving earring, a pearl stud that had been a gift from Anne. The other member of the pair was also somewhere in the forest.

I knew that I looked in a dreadful state too – torn clothes, face and arms smeared in dirt, bruises and bloodstains, bedraggled hair. Whenever I encountered anyone they looked at me strangely, and in one village I was even chased out by a group of children throwing bricks and stones, who rightly assumed I was a vagabond. Despite their countless dangers, the woods held more comforts and I tried to avoid civilisation wherever I could. At least I was beginning to get the hang of surviving in the wild.

Nights in the forest – once a suitable bedding area had been found, and a fire taken care of – were lonely affairs, with just the moon and the howling of wolves for comfort. But there was plenty of time to think – I thought about Hardwick and Ingram, and Dakers and Vaillons, about the crooked schemes they were involved in, which they had tried to pass on to my brother, and which, with any luck, I would soon be bringing to an end.

I thought about Emmalina, and how I was going to break the news to her that her brother was on a ship bound for France or God knows where – possibly a priest in the making, possibly a pressganged sailor. I also thought about poor Karl Würtembatter rotting away on the same ship, not knowing when his ordeal would end.

I thought about Kyd and Matthew and the loyalty they had both shown me over the previous days, loyalty that was as welcome as it was unexpected, I thought about Leticia and smiled, and then chuckled, and then laughed out loud – before stopping and telling myself not to behave as if I was going insane.

I thought about Walsingham and shuddered in the dark. Above all I thought about Don Alphonse and the dangerous games he had been playing, and how in death he had unwittingly pulled me into them. I read his manuscript again, in Emmalina's neat handwriting, and thought about the mangled body washed up under the monument to cuckolded husbands. I realised now that I had been right all along and that his death did have an ironic sense of justice, however undeserved.

Now it was daybreak, all thoughts and fears from the nights banished, and the city of London lay spread before me. As I reached the main thoroughfare to the Southwark end of the Bridge I gradually began to feel like less of an outcast. People stopped taking any notice of me after a while, and, by the time I reached the Bridge, in many people's eyes I had just become another anonymous member of the city's poor and deprived. Even the boiled heads on traitor's gate appeared welcoming.

The downstairs workshop was closed; Charles and his family were probably at the Huguenot Church in Spitalfields to the East of the city.

I climbed wearily up the stairs to my lodgings, half expecting to find it empty, but the incongruous heavy door was slightly ajar and from within I could hear heated voices. I froze on the stairwell, fearing that Hardwick might have caught up with me, but after a moment's intense listening, realised I recognised both of the voices within. I pushed the door open.

'I'm telling you I don't know where he is. No one has heard from him for days'. Emmalina was sitting on the bed, knees up to her chest, the same pose she had adopted on the previous occasion when this particular visitor had come calling. Her long auburn hair was tied back but two wavy tresses fell onto her shoulders on either side. Her soft brown eyes were fixed ahead and her delicate chin was stuck out in a manner of defiance. The visitor, Nesbitt, was standing in the centre of the room, towering over her in the cramped space, his curved back bending forwards like a harbinger of doom – as usual I couldn't help imagining him with a scythe. They both turned their heads towards me as I entered.

'Did anybody miss me?' I said, trying on a crooked smile for size.

'John!' Emmalina was the first to react. She jumped from the bed and put her arms around me and then, sensing me wince on contact, coaxed me gently to a seat on the bed. 'My goodness, what happened to you? Thank heavens you're alive.'

Nesbitt's reaction to my arrival was somewhat less sympathetic. 'Lovat. What on earth do you mean by this? Look at the state of you. Where the hell have you been, your brother is going frantic.' He didn't add 'with worry' but then I hardly expected him to.

I chose to ignore this outburst. Dredging up my strength I stared fixedly at a knot in the wooden floorboards.

'Is Marmaduke Drummond still at the Chancel House?'

'What?'

'Drummond. Is he still in my brother's service?'

'Yes but … '

'Good. Then listen. Go back to the house immediately, find Drummond and detain him. I don't care what you tell him or my brother, but get him under lock and key. Then, when you've got him secure, send a message to Walsingham to come to the Chancel House – as quickly as he can.'

'Lovat. In the Lord's name. How dare you come here issuing me orders?'

'Nesbitt. Go. Now. If you care anything for my brother's wellbeing, or for your position for that matter. Believe me, there isn't a moment to lose'. The thickness of intent in my voice and the unblinking gaze that I had turned on Nesbitt seemed to do the trick. He started to move towards the door, then hesitated.

'How do you know Walsingham will come?'

'He'll come all right but you can make sure if you like. Tell him that I've returned and I've finished Don Alphonse's work.'

'Don Alphonse? So you know who murdered him?

'Just do what I've asked you to as quickly as you can. I'll be at the Chancel House in three hours. That should give Walsingham enough time to get there. In the meantime I intend to clean myself up and have something to eat – something other than roots and scraps.'

'I hope you know what you're doing Lovat.' It was a parting shot that told me he would do my bidding, however reluctantly. He closed the door behind him and I sank backwards onto the bed.

'John? Tell me? What happened to you?' Emmalina's pretty face was a picture of concern. She took the earthenware jug from the desk and began pouring water into a small ceramic bowl before taking a cloth and dabbing gently at a cut on my forehead.

'Where are Matthew and Kyd?'

'Matthew's down at the dock. He goes there every day looking for the Lighterman. I told him it was hopeless – like looking for a needle in a haystack – but he says he owes it to you not to rest until he finds him. Especially after Master Thomas told us about what you were doing.'

'So you've seen Kyd?'

'He came back from the coast two days ago. He says the last thing he knew was that you were going back to Hardwick's house to collect something. That was days ago – we've been worried sick about you.'

'Where's Kyd now?'

'He's gone to the theatre – said he had to talk to someone called Henslowe about an idea for a new play, but he'll be coming back here soon.'

'So he's been staying here since he got back?' I tried to keep my voice neutral.

'Yes. On the truckle. He only wanted to be close by in case you returned.' I took a deep breath and thought about how to phrase what I had to tell her.

'Emmalina. I saw Buck.'

'Saw him? Where?' It was clear from her reaction that Kyd hadn't broken the news to her. 'Did you speak to him?'

'No I … he was on a boat bound for France. It was very dangerous for me at the time – I wanted to speak to him but ... it was impossible.' My excuses sounded lame under her intense scrutiny.

'But you saw him, then why didn't you … ?' She let the question trail off.

'I had to make a quick decision. You would have understood if you'd been there.' I took her hands, and tried to give her my most comforting demeanour. 'I only saw him briefly but he seemed well – he was playing cards with some sailors. Once this business with Walsingham is finished I promise that I'll go to France and find him – at least I have an idea of where he is now.'

'I'll come with you.'

'We'll see about that when the time comes.' I said this thinking that I would dissuade her in the future, but the zealous look in her eyes told me that I would have my work cut out.

'Emmalina?'

'Yes.'

'The translation you were doing of Don Alphonse's diary. Did you finish it?'

'Yes. It's all here.' She reached inside the lid of the old school desk and pulled out a sheath of papers. 'Has it been useful?'

'In more ways than you could possibly imagine.' I thought of the bleak nights huddled around a makeshift fire in the woods hunched over the manuscript, twitching at every sound in the darkness. 'It has not only been a great comfort to me but I think it has also solved the mystery of Don Alphonse's death.'

Emmalina was about to ask me what I meant when heavy footsteps were heard clumping up the stairs and Matthew came bustling into the room. He was overjoyed to see me and gave me a huge bear hug. I didn't have the heart to tell him how much it hurt. But his joy was twofold and after exclaiming over me for some moments he could contain himself no longer.

'Master John, I've news.' He stood there with a big stupid grin on his face. 'Well ain't you gonna ask me?'

'What news, Matthew?'

'I've only gone and found him, Master.' He sensed I was being a little slow on the take up. 'The lighterman, Master John. The one who rowed the men from the Chancel House the night that the Portingale was murdered. I knew how I'd find him and I've only bleedin' gone and done it! I was lucky mind – I'd been told that there was a group of lightermen that hang around the grand houses at night, waitin' for fares, but I was havin' that much trouble catchin' up with them I don't mind tellin' you and … ' he suddenly broke off. 'But master, here am I a-rabbiting on and you in that state. What must you think of me?'

'You've done a fine job Matthew. Don't worry about me – I'll be as right as rain in no time. When can we meet this lighterman of yours?'

'Tonight master. He'll be in a tavern on the Southwark shore before beginnin' a night shift on the river.'

'So, we will go and find him straight after our visit to the Chancel House and you can explain to me how you came to find him on the way.' Matthew beamed and I explained to both him and Emmalina what I intended to do at my brother's house. Matthew agreed to row me as soon as I was refreshed and presentable.

The next three hours were amongst the most pleasurable I could remember. The three of us chatted like old friends, whilst Emmalina dressed my wounds and cooked a delicious broth on the small fireplace, and after a short while we were even joined by Kyd, whose delight at seeing me, if anything, topped the other two. Kyd told us the remarkable story about how, after waiting two days and fearing for my safety when I failed to make our rendezvous, he had gone to Hardwick's house, Stavening, on the pretence of wanting to look at the gardens, whilst secretly hoping to discover my whereabouts. He had been met by a flustered Champernowne, who had told him that the whole household was out hunting and had been for three days in a row.

'When I asked him what the quarry was he said that he didn't know but it must be a difficult catch. I had no idea it was you Lovat, old boy. I assumed that you had gone along for the ride. I then had to put up with an hour of the old boy showing me round the garden, boring on about box hedges, terraces and pergolas.'

'Tell us about your new play, Thomas.' I was eager to change the subject, that particular garden holding no happy memories for me.

'It's a love story called Soliman and Perseda. It's the one set in Rhodes that I told you about. I started writing it in Rye. You'll be amazed what sea air and a bit of solitude does for the imagination.' And the attentions of an adoring landlady, I was tempted to add, but didn't feel it fair to mention it in front of Emmalina.

'Talking of new manuscripts, I need to get on with this one,' I said, indicating the translation of Don Alphonse's diary. Emmalina, Matthew and Kyd spoke quietly together, whilst I caught up on the latest instalment of Don Alphonse's past.

Chapter 34

'He who establishes his argument by noise and command shows that his reason is weak.'
(Michel de Montaigne)

The scene was far from set when Kyd, Matthew and I entered the long, panelled hall on the first floor of the Chancel House. I had hoped that Nesbitt had performed my wish of locking up Marmaduke Drummond until I arrived, but I was dismayed to find him very much at liberty, and holding forth in the room. He made a beeline for me as soon as I entered, his chubby face creased with strong (if insincere to my mind) outrage, and started demanding stutteringly who the hell I thought I was ordering his detainment and besmirching his good name. I was relieved that Nesbitt stepped in quickly and reminded him who was present in the room.

Walsingham had arrived only minutes before me and was sitting beside Robert in the same seat by the fireside as on the night when we had first met. I hadn't seen Robert for over two weeks and he looked drawn and pale, as though recent events had been weighing heavily upon him. Nevertheless, he was turned out as sprucely as always, as though his clothes and finery would be able to carry him through these difficult times. He also had further support on this occasion in the form of Anne, who gave me a look of encouragement as I entered.

Walsingham, dressed as always in black, looked his usual sickly self, with only his quick eyes belying his spider-like intelligence. He had brought Faunt with him, who was standing respectfully behind Walsingham's chair pretending not to notice that relationships were strained between his master, on the one hand, and the Lord and Lady of the house, on the other.

Skirting round Drummond's obese frame, I bowed low before all three of them, wincing from the pain in my ribs as I did so, but taking care, for once, to show my brother the full respect his position warranted – the last thing I wanted was for a fit of pique to spoil my plan. From what Nesbitt had told me earlier, I expected him to be at his most difficult, and, despite Anne's restraining presence, I was not disappointed.

'I hope you have a good explanation for this, Lovat. I do not expect to be ordered about by a servant in my own house and I am sure that Sir Francis doesn't appreciate being dragged out of his home on a Sunday for no good reason.'

'No matter, Lord Robert, I am very interested to hear what Master Lovat has to say.' Walsingham's words helped to diffuse the situation but there was still a note of warning in his tone.

Taking up a central position with my back to the fireplace, I began to appeal to my brother. 'With your permission, I would like to put some questions to Drummond? I believe that the answers will be of some interest to you.'

Drummond, who had been listening eagerly, pounced at this.

'Lord Robert, that is a c-complete impertinence. Are you going to let this w-whipjack, this knave, this … this illegitimate stable b-boy slander me in your household?'

Again Walsingham calmed the situation: 'Master Drummond, please be seated. I am sure there will be ample time for you to refute any allegations. If, indeed, Master Lovat intends to make any.' Drummond remained standing, his indignance etched all too clearly on the pudgy canvas of his face.

'I merely wish, Sir Francis, to pose some questions concerning Sir Christopher Hardwick. The man whose household, you will recall, I have been visiting of late.'

'Quite so, Master Lovat.' The warning note in Walsingham's voice had intensified a notch.

'What's that? Visiting Hardwick?' My brother, a distinct wildness in his eyes, looked from Walsingham to me and back again. 'I thought this was to do with the murder of Don Alphonse De Sousa? What has Hardwick to do with it?'

I looked at Walsingham, wondering how far I could go. 'With respect, Sir Francis, I humbly submit that my brother has a right to know the details of where I have been for the last fortnight because of the bearing it has on his own fortunes.'

'I have no objection, providing it is made clear that your visit to Stavening was something you felt you had to undertake under your own initiative in defence of your brother. I merely gave you my blessing in the adventure.' So that was how the land lay – I had suspected as much. I glanced enquiringly at Faunt but he was suddenly studying the ornate stucco of the ceiling with great interest.

'What about Hardwick?' Drummond spat into the pause in conversation. 'I've only ever m-met the man once.'

'The night of the Armada parade, when he and his wife dined in this house – of that I actually have no doubt. It seems he was reluctant to meet you at any other time, despite your advances. You have though, correct me if I am wrong, had correspondence with him.'

'Utter n-nonsense. Lord Robert, am I to be questioned like a c-common thief?'

'Get to the point, Lovat, for goodness sake.' Robert was making it absolutely clear that his protégée had his full support, and I was grateful to see Anne laying a calming hand on his arm.

'As you wish brother. Drummond certainly has had correspondence with Hardwick. In fact, I have evidence that he has offered himself in service and asked for Hardwick's patronage.'

'That is absurd.' Drummond was still forceful, perhaps feeling that with Robert on his side he was untouchable. 'The stable boy is b-bluffing.'

'Quite the contrary. Perhaps I should refresh your memory. Let me see, how did it go now,' I assumed the pose of a gallant about to serenade his lady love '... *with this poor ode I crave your wish/to wait upon your mastered bliss* ... not your finest line I admit but undeniably a 'Drummond', or this ... *to thee most illustrious Lord, whom'st I would serve/this rhyme I give to reap the prize it may deserve* ... a personal favourite of mine.'

The amusing thing was that, even as he tried to deny it, I could sense that Drummond was proud of his doggerel. It was all he could do not to lay claim to the lines, whilst appealing to my brother.

'Your unc-couth, illegitimate s-sibling is making m-mischief at my expense. I n-never heard those lines before in my life and certainly c-cannot take c-c-credit for their c-composition.' His stutter was becoming increasingly affected as he blustered his innocence.

'Is that so?' I produced the letter from my bag and handed it to my brother. 'Robert, I believe you will confirm for Sir Francis that this is Drummond's handwriting. You will notice underlined the lines I spoke just now. Perhaps you will also notice the addressee – Sir Christopher Hardwick.'

'Where did you get that?' Drummond's face became a brighter shade of scarlet, his porcine chin trembling. 'I d-demand to know.'

'So you don't deny that you wrote it?'

'I'm n-not staying to listen to this.' Drummond started for the door but found his way blocked by Matthew.

'Sit down Drummond. It appears that you have a case to answer.' My brother passed the letter reluctantly to Walsingham. His voice sounded thin and breathless in the large room, but his words had the desired effect. Drummond looked around, realising that to leave at that moment would be tantamount to admitting guilt, and sat down heavily in a chair. I watched him closely, thinking about my next move.

'Go on, brother,' Robert prompted.

'The letters are dated September of this year, some three months ago. Would you kindly explain to their Lordships why you decided that a change of patron would be expedient at that time?'

Drummond started to squirm unattractively in his chair but he still wasn't going to capitulate that easily, and certainly not to me. 'What do you m-mean?'

'The letter I produced shows clear evidence that you were seeking a new patron. Why? Why then?'

'With d-deepest respect, your Lordship,' Drummond decided that a direct appeal to Robert was his best defence. 'Whilst I am grateful for the p-patronage you have shown me, I felt that my artistic muse was being somewhat stifled in this house and that a change of p-patron might be b-beneficial. Perhaps it has something to do with the low c-company that is admitted.' He accompanied this last remark with a pointed look in my direction. I brushed it aside.

'So it had nothing to do with a certain plot to discredit this house? A plot which you knew about and sought to take advantage of?'

Drummond didn't say anything. For the first time I sensed his fear. He studied my face with a nervous expression, obviously wondering exactly how much I knew.

'We're waiting Drummond.' My brother also had a worried expression on his face, but combined with a look of stoical determination, as if he expected the worst and now just wanted to hear it.

'Let the b-bastard speak. If he has accusations to make, let him m-make them.'

'Drummond, how dare you?' It was the first time Anne had spoken and there was a genuine shock in her tone.

'It's of no consequence, Lady Anne. My parentage may be in question but I hope to show that my loyalty to this house is beyond reproach. Drummond invites me to make accusations. Very well – let me delay no further.' I gathered myself together to lay the facts before them. The heat of the fire was making me feel far too soporific.

'Brother, the knowledge has come into my possession that you have been the victim of a base fraud. A fraud perpetrated by this man here and others who professed friendship towards you – namely Nicholas Ingram, Simon Turney and Don Alphonse de Sousa – men who were acting under the authority of another. They dazzled you with the promise of great riches and, like many before you, you were seduced. The joint-stock company that you agreed upon together, probably in this very room, and that you agreed to be the figurehead for, is nothing more than vapour, the ships you chartered mirages, the whole enterprise a smoke screen.'

The pallor of my brother's skin had lightened a couple of notches but he maintained his reticent demeanour. 'Go on,' he said.

'The scheme was instigated by a man both jealous of your success at Court and eager to deflect scrutiny of his own illicit practises. None other than Sir Christopher Hardwick.'

'Hardwick.' It was less of a question – more of an affirmation of something already known on some unfathomable, subconscious level.

'I have in my possession letters, which, pieced together, confirm the entire plot. It went something like this: Ingram, recently made masterless following the death of the Earl of Leicester, came to Hardwick offering his services. I don't have Hardwick's side of the conversation but it seems that he invited Ingram to first prove his worth. He was told to offer himself to this house in service and to bring the idea of the joint-stock company as a sweetener. You are probably in a better position than I am to give a full account of how it started.' I paused for a moment to see if my brother would confirm or deny any of what I had said. He glanced sideways at Walsingham.

'Lord Robert, let us assume for the moment that anything said here today will remain between these four walls.'

There was an audible sigh in Robert's voice as he spoke: 'In that case, what my brother says is true. Ingram did offer himself to me in service. He told me about an adventure that Dudley had been planning and a week later brought Alphonse, who was already known to me, and Turney. Alphonse was to charter the ships, and he and Turney would pilot them, I would provide the finance. Drummond got involved later.'

'What was his role? To write a poem to bless the voyage?' I said, for once struggling to hide my bitterness. It may have been an ill-advised plot but there was a strong part of me that would like to have been invited.

'Also financial.' Robert said tersely.

'Except that none of the partners were what they seemed. Ingram, De Sousa and Turney were all in league with Hardwick and at some point even Drummond got whiff of the plot and saw an opportunity of both leaving the service of a man who was about to be disgraced, and advancing himself at the same time. What was it you said to me the last time I came to this house, Drummond – "*A rat running onto a sinking ship*"? The denouncement at Court had just been made but my brother wasn't mentioned by name and only someone with inside knowledge of the plot could have known what deep trouble he was in. The problem for you is that Hardwick didn't really want you. Not that I blame him. Anyone can see, if they can get past your sycophantic scribblings, that your letter is little more than an attempt to blackmail him into becoming your patron.'

'I protest. This is outrageous.'

'Save your protestations till later, Drummond.' Robert's words cut through the air like a whip-crack. He was finally finding some anger. 'Continue, brother.'

'Let us move forward to the night when Don Alphonse was murdered, the night before I became involved. A meeting took place in this house – one that you, Robert, were reluctant to speak of in front of Sir Francis because you knew, forgive me for saying so, that your venture would be frowned upon at Court. Present at this meeting were yourself, Don Alphonse, Ingram, Drummond, Turney and, most interestingly, Hardwick. Hardwick has remained in the shadows throughout the plot but he has given encouragement, perhaps he even recommended Don Alphonse to the party.' I glanced at Walsingham as I said this, but his face was inscrutable. 'At the meeting you hand out your gift of a chain holding your seal to each of the members of the company, so-to-speak. The gift is a form of bond, binding each member to the cause. Hardwick's was hanging on a peg in his study – confirmation that he was also part of the venture.'

'The 'ships' were to set sail the next morning and so you made final plans, perhaps you drank a toast to your impending success. You probably speculated on the illicit nature of your adventure and discussed again how you hoped that Her Majesty would forgive you if you were able to furnish her with riches, perhaps some Spanish treasure, on the ships' return. Sometime after darkness the four – Ingram, Don Alphonse, Drummond and Turney leave together from the river gate. The night is still young and they intend to have some fun at the Southwark Fair before they all, Drummond excepted, 'depart' in the morning. Hardwick, who was a guest in the house along with his wife, stays. How is that for speculation Robert?'

'If I didn't know better, I could almost swear that you were here that evening.'

'Thank you. Except that, apart from Turney, who was only sailing around the coast, none of them were going anywhere. The thing that interests me is Hardwick's presence. He was here ostensibly as your guest – he was not part of the adventure. True he had given some moral support but he had made sure his hands were clean. However, his son was to be presented at Court the next day and so it was convenient to be in London. One conclusion is that he came here to make sure nothing went wrong at the last minute. Another is that he was simply here to gloat.'

Stillness had descended in the room, whilst I had been speaking. Kyd and Matthew still stood close to the shadows of the doorway; Nesbitt was standing behind Drummond, who had suddenly become very preoccupied with his nails. Faunt stood quietly behind Walsingham, his eyes still on the ceiling but his ear tilted towards me. Robert was sitting upright and rigid in his chair, his eyes fixed on some indiscernible spot in his imagination. Anne, her arm still on Robert's, was watching his face anxiously. Only Walsingham, slumped down in his chair, kept his eyes rigidly fixed on me. Might well he wonder what I was going to say next.

'Now things become a little more complicated. The conspirator's plan is for an anonymous source to post a bill at Court denouncing the voyage, with the expectation that an order will be given to search the 'ships'. I say 'ships' in that manner because there is only one ship – The Lady Merrydance – no doubt moored in Deptford in case my brother should choose to inspect his investment. However, as the 'ships' will have sailed already, a search will be futile – but an air of suspicion will pervade over my brother. Witnesses will be called forward to confirm that the 'ships' were prepared for a long voyage and have departed, until they return again, Robert will be in disgrace for sanctioning the voyage. Of course they will never return – lost at sea, or some such explanation. Thus Robert loses not only his position at Court but his investment as well. All this can be gleaned from the letters. Everyone else concerned – Ingram, Don Alphonse and Turney – are, as far as anyone suspects, on the boats, so they can't be questioned. No doubt they will keep a low profile for a time. Drummond will not mind the disgrace. He can hide in Robert's shadow and, in any case, he already has his escape plan mapped out.'

'However, something happens that the plotters don't foresee – Don Alphonse is murdered and fished out of the river near Rotherhithe. I am immediately asked to investigate his death – my brother, realising the threat that the death poses in highlighting the venture, hopes that I will, with his prompting, come to the swift conclusion that Cassangoe is guilty.' My brother gave me a hard stare at these words and I saw in his face a mixture of defiance, and sadness. There was nothing for it but to press on.

'I'm afraid that I am too bloody-minded. Despite my brother's protestations to the contrary, I immediately suspect the men from the previous evening of being involved. I rush to Deptford to interview Turney before the 'ships' sail. He, thinking that I am a government agent sent by Walsingham, whose badge I am carrying, believes that something has gone wrong with the plot – the voyage has been denounced too early – and expects me to search the ship. He immediately orders the departure of The Lady Merrydance, so that I have to be put ashore, although imagine both his relief and confusion when I tell him that I am simply interested in Don Alphonse's death. Interestingly, he takes the opportunity to throw suspicion for the death of Don Alphonse on Robert, on the grounds, I beg your forgiveness Lady Anne, that he is a cuckold. To do this, he alludes to an argument that took place in the garden that night, which he hints was between Robert and Don Alphonse. Turney is trying to reflect suspicion away from the man he knows to be the real cuckold – Sir Christopher Hardwick himself, who has no doubt expressed his desire to see the demise of Don Alphonse during one of his darker moods.' I paused for breath, suddenly feeling a debilitating weariness.

'I digress. The denouncement is duly posted two days later and Robert is summoned to Court. I haven't been party to developments in the last two weeks but I should imagine that Robert is very close to being disgraced at Court. Am I correct Sir Francis?'

Walsingham stirred himself. 'The matter is out of my hands I am afraid, but I have heard rumours to that extent. Can you prove all of this Lovat?'

'I have the letters from Ingram, Drummond and Don Alphonse. They are pretty conclusive.' I thought it prudent not to mention the letters that my brother had sent Hardwick. I would have to find a quiet time to return those to him, though I doubted he would thank me for it.

'Good. It would seem on the evidence that, despite being guilty of a certain rash foolishness not to mention greed, no ships have actually sailed forth in Sir Robert's name and hence your brother has no case to answer. I will inform the interested parties at Court of this forthwith.'

I looked at my brother. His expression was a mixture of shame and relief. I had no doubt that he would bounce back strongly, but for the time being it looked as though a period of reflection was in store. 'What about the murder of Don Alphonse,' he said weakly?

'If you mean that suspicion might fall on you because Don Alphonse was part of the plot to defraud you, then I think it is plain that you had no idea of his intentions. You considered him a friend right up to the moment that news of his death was brought here. Besides, I think it can be shown pretty clearly that you had neither cause, nor opportunity. His death was the last thing you wanted, as I've already established. I for one don't believe that you had anything to do with it. Do you agree Sir Francis?'

'Agreed. In the matter of Don Alphonse's death I am satisfied for the time being that your brother has no case to answer. Perhaps you will shed further light on that in due course.' Perhaps not, I thought, but held my tongue.

'Drummond. It seems to me that you have been guilty of gross treachery towards your patron and master.' Walsingham was suddenly taking charge of events. 'However, as you appear to have only been a minor player, I think Robert might be persuaded to act leniently were you to give a full and frank account of your actions and the plot you were involved in. Is that right Lord Robert?' My brother nodded stiffly. 'Nesbitt, will you be kind enough to escort Drummond to another room, where Faunt can take a full statement from him. I warn you Drummond, leave nothing out – men have been hung for far less. For the time being you will remain in this house until such time as you will be called to give further evidence.' Drummond had visibly shrunk in the last half an hour but the news that he was to be treated leniently appeared to perk him up again.

'N-naturally, Sir Francis, I will humbly do everything I can to help and if you ever n-need my services again, please don't h-hesitate to ask.'

Listening to this exchange I had slumped wearily in a chair. I suddenly felt a huge lethargy taking hold of me and my battered body had begun throbbing anew. Despite this, I held up my hand to halt Drummond's departure.

'Forgive me, your Lordships, there is one further twist to this plot that I have yet to reveal and I would be grateful if Drummond would stay to hear it.'

'Very well, speak.'

'I think I have shown conclusively that Drummond only had a small part in the plot – a side act, if you will. He had no knowledge of what I was doing, nor of Don Alphonse's death – Robert swore all of us to secrecy. How was it then, I asked myself, that information was reaching the likes of Ingram? He knew that Don Alphonse had been killed and that I was investigating the death. From that knowledge it was only a short stretch to connect my visit to the Lady Merrydance in Deptford, my presence at the warehouse, as well as my infiltration of Hardwick's household – information that very nearly got me killed.'

'There was also the episode of Don Alphonse's goods being removed from his warehouse, by Ingram, and taken to one of Robert's. This was an opportunist act designed to increase the pressure on Robert by tying him more closely to Don Alphonse's murder. In the denouncement, the allusion to the murder was almost tacked on as an afterthought and it occurred to me that an astute intelligence had very quickly seen the way to turn Don Alphonse's death to the plotter's advantage. But who? It must have been someone with knowledge both of Don Alphonse's death and the plot, and who also knew where Robert's warehouses were situated. Matthew, who spoke to the porter, discovered that Ingram had never been there before but that he had Robert's written permission to enter the dock. Had you given him that permission Robert.'

'No.'

'So who gave it to him? And, lastly, who was it that posted the denouncement at Court. Possibly Drummond, possibly Ingram, but more likely someone who goes to Court every day, in the shadow of his master, and understands the workings of that institution.'

Whilst speaking, I had been looking from one set of eyes to the next, but now I settled on just one person. He was standing in his usual diffident manner – fading into the background and almost invisible amongst the company.

'I knew that there was only one person who fitted as an answer to all of these questions, and who I didn't wholly trust, but I had no way of proving it. He was also someone who was present at the meeting in the house, although his presence then, like now, was barely discernible – I even neglected to mention his name. Moreover he had license to visit me, find out what I was doing and report back – to Ingram and Hardwick, rather than his true master.'

By now, my sole attention on one person had become apparent to the others who turned to look at the hunched, moribund figure in black, who stared back at me with an unfathomable expression in his eyes. The reason that I had asked Drummond to remain in the room was simply so his escort would have to remain too – my nemesis and the arch-traitor in my brother's household – Nesbitt.

Chapter 35

'If a man will begin with certainties, he shall end in doubts; but if he will be content to begin with doubts, he shall end in certainties.'
(Sir Francis Bacon)

As everybody turned towards him, Nesbitt stood stock still in a corner of the room. The usual obsequious expression on his face had been replaced by something that wasn't immediately easy to interpret – equivocation perhaps, possibly defiance.

It appeared that he wasn't about to say anything to either confirm or deny my accusation and it was only when Robert prompted him that he began to speak. His usual deliberate manner was in evidence, but there was something added to his words – the legal tone that had been his education before going into service. Apart from the odd Latin flourish, I had never heard him speaking in this way before and it added a, hitherto only briefly glimpsed, obduracy to his bent frame.

'Master Drummond's already rather weak performance has shown that there is little point in my arguing with any points made by Rokesby's illegitimate sibling. He seems to have done a thorough job in this matter – and one that I certainly expected to be far beyond his capabilities. I congratulate him. However, what I should like to know is: what exactly am I being accused of? As Master Lovat has already made abundantly clear, there was a plan made in this house to launch an illegal adventure overseas. In going along with that plot, I was only doing the duty expected of me in this house, but was I content in that duty? Could I in all honesty say that my conscience was clear? And if not, and I felt it expedient to speak to others about my concerns, then can I be blamed?'

He paused for a moment and then gave me his best lawyer's smile.

'I see Master Lovat waving a letter that he believes will confirm my guilt but I say: *ei incumbit probatio qui dicit* - proof lies on him that asserts and not on he who denies. If it is the letter that I expect it to be, you will find nothing in there to reproach me with. I do not deny writing it – only that it proves my guilt, beyond anything other than being a concerned citizen.'

Nesbitt was right. The letter he had written to Hardwick, which I had discovered amongst the others and was brandishing, only proved that they had been in contact. That had been enough for me to string the rest of the facts together, but Nesbitt had been careful not to display any disloyalty to my brother. He had talked in terms of 'being of service' and 'friendship' but these were hardly enough to convict.

'If Lord Robert wishes to press claims that I have been disloyal to this household, then it is natural that those who judge me should be abreast of all of the facts of what service in this household consists of.'

As threats go, it was mildly put – but the inference was clear.

'However, I accept that my position in this household has now become untenable. I am sensitive to the knowledge that where doubt and mistrust exists, there can be no harmony between master and servant. Naturally I leave *sub silentio*.' As he finished speaking, he began to shuffle his crooked frame towards the door, slowly at first, as if wary that someone might stop him and then with more confident strides. I looked at Robert's face – it was a mixture of anger, despair, hatred, embarrassment even, but, nevertheless, he clearly felt unable to stop Nesbitt from leaving. Walsingham also looked as though he didn't want to get involved. It was left for me to stop Nesbitt in the doorway and give him the only parting shot I was capable of.

'You may not find the conditions in this household acceptable, but I should be very wary of accepting an offer of service from Hardwick. The goings on in his household may be too much for your conscience to bear.' As I spoke, a bitterness that I had barely been aware of forced itself into my voice, to the point where I almost spat out the last part. For a moment, Nesbitt looked at me as though he might respond in kind, but he thought better of it.

'Thank you for your good advice, Master Lovat,' he simply said in the mildest of tones, 'You can be sure I will heed it.' And with that he was gone, leaving a room full of dismay and bafflement.

* * *

'Master Lovat, you mentioned that part of Hardwick's plan was to divert attention away from his own illicit practises. Do you have more light to shed on those?'

Walsingham and I were alone in the hall. Following Nesbitt's exit, I had half expected Drummond to announce loudly that he wouldn't hang around either and follow Nesbitt's bent shape out of the door. However, he stayed meekly and allowed Faunt to escort him into an adjoining chamber. After a brief discussion with my brother, Walsingham requested a word in private with me, and the others withdrew, all-be-it reluctantly in Robert's case – perhaps fearing further embarrassing revelations.

I got straight to the point with Walsingham: 'I suggest you send a guard immediately to Chillenham Manor in Sussex. It is the home of Lord and Lady Asthor, both staunch Catholics and frequently fined for recusancy. Tell your men that their orders are to find two priests that have lately been delivered to the house. Once you have those priests, I suggest you question them as to how they came into this country.'

'Explain?'

'They arrived on the Lady Merrydance, the same ship that my brother thought was going to increase his fortune. The priests stayed one night at Stavening and then were taken via a rather backwards route to Chillenham Manor. I know this because I was able to follow them. At the Manor they were received by a small welcoming committee, which I believe included the Lord and Lady of the house. My enquiries in the vicinity told me who they were.'

'So this ship, the Lady Merrydance?'

'Owned by Hardwick. It runs frequent trips to and from France, always captained by Turney and I suspect always carrying divers illicit goods, including the human cargo. Docking the ship in Deptford was part of the plot to discredit Robert and proved quite an inconvenience for Hardwick. He was pleased to get the ship back running its usual errands. After leaving Deptford it went to France, picked up the priests and a consignment of tobacco, and returned to Rye, where it took on a cargo of, what I suspect are, adulterated woollen cloths and garments.' I handed the coat, which I had been grateful for during my travails in the forest, to Walsingham. 'I took this from the ship's hold, just after it had been loaded. I suggest you get it tested.'

'I see. Adulterated woollen exports – a serious matter but not as serious as the priests. Do you think he was involved in the Babington plot?'

'It seems very likely that he would have offered the conspirators safe passage – for a fee of course. I only have circumstantial evidence but there is a young clerk in his household who is related to Chidiock Tichborne.'

'One of the conspirators.'

'He also is a distant kinsman of Hardwick's. I should hasten to add that he knows nothing of Hardwick's activities.'

'And Hardwick himself? Is he a Catholic?'

'I can't give you any further evidence as to Hardwick's own religious sympathies. His house was one of the most Godless places I ever visited. There's a small church in the grounds, which is largely unused. All Hardwick is interested in is money and,' I said, thinking of the chest full of coins I had opened in his study, 'I can assure you that he is getting paid handsomely for his various activities. The operation is run from his estate near Rye by a Frenchman called Vaillons and a Scotsman called Dakers. Vaillons recently sailed for France but Hardwick and Dakers should still be at Stavening. Ingram was also there a few days ago with at least one of his henchmen – the second might also be there depending on whether or not he survived our last encounter. I'm afraid I didn't stay around to find out.'

'And you can testify to all that you have told me?

'Yes. I have a number of other revealing letters and also the men I brought with me can give their accounts, should it be necessary.'

'Excellent work, Master Lovat. When Faunt returns from his interrogation of Drummond, I will order him to put in motion the necessary plans for Hardwick and his associates arrest.'

'Very good, sire.'

'Those letters that have come into your possession. Far be it for me to question the means by which you obtained them – I can only say that you seem to be a most resourceful fellow. However, I would be interested to know if there were any others that you have so far failed to mention.'

'There are one or two that you might be interested in Sir Francis.' I reached into my bag and brought out two closely tied bundles. 'I didn't think you would appreciate my mentioning them in front of my brother.'

'May I have them, please?' I passed them to him reluctantly. He took them, glanced at them briefly, and then tucked them into a pocket on the inside of his coat. I thought that was to be the end of the matter but it seemed Walsingham was prepared to give me some credit, or at least enough rope so that I would hang myself. 'And what do these letters tell you?'

I chose my words carefully. 'The first, in your hand, is a letter of recommendation concerning Don Alphonse. The second, in Don Alphonse's, tells me that the whole idea of defrauding Robert came, not from Hardwick, but from Don Alphonse. He designed the plot, suggested it to Hardwick and put much of it into action. The idea was to get Hardwick looking one way, whilst all of the time entrapping him in his own plot. Don Alphonse was working for you all of the time wasn't he?'

'A moot point. I believe if you asked him that same question he would have said he was working for himself. I merely provided the means to facilitate his own plan. Of course, it certainly suited my intentions. Let's just say that Don Alphonse and I had the same objective.'

'To see Hardwick exposed. That was the plan all along but unfortunately Don Alphonse didn't live to see it through. That's why you needed me, wasn't it – to finish what he had started?'

'If it's any consolation, you achieved in a matter of days something that Don Alphonse failed to achieve in a year – absolute proof of Hardwick's treacherous behaviour. Ever since the Babington plot I had my suspicions about him but there was no way of finding proof without somebody infiltrating his household. Unfortunately, as you have discovered, Don Alphonse had his own motives. I think that Don Alphonse was certainly capable of bringing me the proof I needed but he was, how shall I put it, having far too much fun at Hardwick's expense.'

'He was also involved in the smuggling. I saw the same bags of tobacco in his warehouse as the ones that were being loaded onto Hardwick's ship. And he was an enthusiastic member of the group out to defraud my brother. Did Don Alphonse have anything against Robert specifically?'

'Purely coincidental, I'm afraid. Robert was simply an obvious target for the fraud – mind you, I understand that it wasn't hard to persuade him to get involved. Hopefully he will learn from his errors – he still has a promising future but pride and ambition have been the downfall of many a man.'

'I think he has learnt his lesson.'

'There is still the business of Don Alphonse's murder. Did your time in the Hardwick household unearth any information to do with that?'

'I don't believe that Hardwick, or any of them had anything to do with it. No one had discovered he was working for you. I believe that I was erroneous, before, in assuming Hardwick's guilt.'

'There is of course the question of the wife. A beauty by all accounts?' Walsingham let his words hang as a question but I refused to oblige him, forcing him to ask directly. 'Do you think the wife was involved?'

'Not directly.' I answered, a little evasively, before adding. 'Hardwick was aware he was being cuckolded but, although it made him angry, other matters were more important. Money and privilege, those were his interests. His wife was well … an adjunct to his property.'

'It sounds as though you came to know the relationship intimately. And you never found Don Alphonse's manservant? The black-a-moor.'

'No,' I lied, without hesitation and then added, 'and he wasn't Don Alphonse's servant. A friend and business partner would be a more accurate description.'

'Well, well. So who did kill Don Alphonse?'

'Perhaps it was simply a random act of violence. They are common in the city after all.'

'Perhaps. Well Master Lovat, I think that satisfactorily concludes our business for the time being. But what of your future? I invite you to visit me in a day or two's time. Perhaps you would enjoy a day's hawking and I have another proposal of work that I would like you to consider.' Sensing that I was about to dismiss this suggestion off the cuff, he raised a hand. 'Please. Don't give me an answer now. Naturally you need to think about it, to recuperate from your ordeal – yes, your bruises and evident discomfort have not escaped my notice – but at the very least come and visit me for your reward.'

'I have to travel to France.'

'Not more research for the theatre with your friend Kyd, I hope?' Although Walsingham was not smiling, there was the slightest glint in his eyes, which suggested he wasn't entirely serious.

'No, not that. I have to go to the aid of a friend.'

'Well, how perfectly convenient. France is just the place I had in mind for you. It is vital at this time of upheaval that we come to the aid of Henri of Navarre, the one beacon of light in that land of heathens. I understand that you speak excellent French and of course you will need a permit to travel.' The glint in the eyes had gone. He nodded to me and departed.

* * *

Matthew rowed Kyd and myself solemnly across the Thames to the South bank. Even Kyd was silent for once. Faunt, at Walsingham's bidding, had asked them both to corroborate what they knew about Hardwick's activities and it had created a sombre mood.

'Did everythin' go as planned, Master?'

'Yes, thank you Matthew. As well as could be expected.' We were on our way to meet the lighterman who had rowed Ingram, Drummond, Turney and the late Don Alphonse away from the Chancel House on the night of his murder. I already suspected what he was going to tell me and I was tired and fed up with the whole affair, but something inside told me that I had to go through with it.

The rendezvous was a dingy inn on the Southwark bank directly overhanging the waterfront. The front of the building was pitched towards the river as though the constant sapping of the tide had gradually undermined its foundation, and it was only held up by a collection of motley posts driven into the clay bank. The three of us carefully climbed a fleet of slippery, broken stairs and entered the dim interior. The inn was noisy and smelly and, perhaps not surprisingly, appeared to be a haven for all grades of low life.

We edged our way through a crowd of undesirables trying not to attract too much attention. Eventually we found the waterman, whose name was Jerome Forkes, sitting by himself in a damp and mouldy corner. He was an aggressive individual with a dirty face and a foul mouth and I wouldn't have fancied suggesting to him a better route to take out on the river. After berating us for keeping him waiting, he demanded that I buy him three strong cups in quick succession before he would even consider answering any questions. Waiting nervously while he knocked back the beer, I concluded that by the time he did feel like talking he would be too drunk to remember anything. Fortunately, he could hold his drink and it also had the extra benefit of loosening his tongue. Once he started talking, I was barely able to get a word in.

'I remember the party well, all four of them. The night of the Southwark Fair. Three English gentlemen it were, and the foreigner with the big nose.' Don Alphonse's nose seemed to be his most memorable feature. 'Picked them up around half past the hour of ten and rowed them downstream. Left three of the gentlemen at the Paris Gardens in Southwark.' He leant back with a self-satisfied smile on his grimy face as if his night's work had been done, and offered his cup up for a refill.

'And there were definitely only four of them?'

'Are you rutting deaf. Like I said, three gentlemen and a big-nosed foreigner. Dusky brute. I didn't care for him in my boat much – looked like a Spaniard.' He wiped his dirty arm across his face and again indicated that his glass was empty. Ignoring this obvious gesture, I pressed on.

'The three men that left the boat, were they cordial with the foreigner when they left the boat?'

'Cordial? What the pox is that? Don't you speak rutting English?'

'Friendly. Were they friendly with the foreigner?'

'Two of the gentlemen shook his hand – the fat one and the one as was sittin' be'ind me. The one that looked like a bull ignored 'im – he seemed keen to get off to the night life, I suppose.' Forkes again indicated his empty glass by pushing it firmly in my direction, seemingly non-plussed by what English gentlemen got up to in Southwark. Paris Garden, where Drummond and Ingram had alighted, was a short walk away from the bear-baiting arena and only a few minutes from the inns and stews on Bankside where we now sat. I had been in the neighbourhood myself on the same night and for all I knew Drummond, Turney and Ingram may have been just across the street from me.

'Where did you take the foreigner?'

'Well that was the rum thing, weren't it? As soon as the others had left the boat, 'e said he wanted to go back where e'd just come from. Strange like. That's why I remembered it.'

'You turned round and headed back where you'd just come from?'

'Just said so dint I?' He turned to Matthew and Kyd. 'Is 'e bleeding deaf or someat?'

'What was his demeanour like?'

'His de-rutting what?'

'What sort of mood was he in?'

'Ah mood, why didn't you rutting well say so?'

Forkes rubbed his grubby nose on his equally grubby sleeve thoughtfully, and was about to speak, when a brawl broke out in the bar. All four of us took refuge in our corner as fists, bottles and tankards flew all around us. When it settled down, I started again.

'The foreigner – what sort of mood was he in?'

The fight had unsettled Forkes and he was losing patience with the questioning. 'I don't rutting know. Excited. An excited rutting mood. That's all I remember. Now if you want anything else you had better buy me another rutting drink.' I could see little option and signalled to the innkeeper, who had just found the courage to poke his nose out again. Forkes refused to say anything until the refill had been delivered.

'What happened when you arrived back at The Chancel House?'

'I never said we went back there, now did I?'

'You said you returned the way you had come,' I said, finding it hard to keep the frustration out of my voice.

'Yes, but I never said we went back to the house.'

'God's teeth! Where did you go then?'

'Now, don't you go getting uppity with me young gentleman. I said we headed back toward the grand house, but I never said we landed there.' Forkes turned and winked conspiratorially at Matthew. 'We were intercepted, weren't we?'

'Intercepted? By whom?'

'Another boat! What did you think I meant? A whale with bleedin' Jonah aboard?'

'Who was in the boat?'

'Can't say.'

'Well, how about – a man or woman?'

'Don't make me laugh,' Forkes spluttered into his beer. 'I'd like to see a woman rowing a boat on those tides.'

'So you saw a man. I mean you actually saw him?'

'Well, naturally. He wasn't invisible was he?'

'Then why couldn't you say if he was a man or a woman?' I said, between gritted teeth.

'Because, my clever young gentleman, he or she,' he laughed mirthlessly, 'was wearing a cloak over his head.' Forkes crossed his arms with a satisfied smugness.

'Can you tell us anything about him?'

'The Spaniard knew 'im. No doubt about that.'

'He wasn't a Spaniard. He was Portuguese.'

Forkes merely shrugged. 'Same difference.'

I described in as much detail as I could remember the man who I believed had been lying in wait for Don Alphonse that evening. As I did so, Kyd's mouth dropped open and Matthew nodded slowly as though I was confirming his own suspicions. When I finished Forkes rubbed his nose on his sleeve again and also nodded.

'Could be 'im. More than likely I'd say but, as I said, it were dark and 'e was wearing that cloak. There was definitely someat strange about him though.'

I thanked Forkes with exaggerated graciousness and we were about to leave, when Matthew surprised me by asking Forkes a question.

'You must know the river tides like the back of your hand. If a body washed up on the Rotherhithe bank at around seven o'clock in the morning, and had only gone into the river around midnight, where would it have entered the water?' Forkes seemed far happier with this question than with any I had asked him and set to thinking, with an expression which made it look as though he was trying to pass a particularly uncomfortable stool. Eventually the grimace left his face.

'You know what old man, that's a rutting question and an 'alf that is. Of course depends which rutting day it was but if it was in the last week or so I'd have to say not further west than the bridge. The tide just starts to turn around midnight at the moment but a body west of the bridge would take longer.' He thought again before concluding: 'anywhere east of the bridge I reckon, quite possibly the Bridge itself.' I patted Matthew warmly on the back. He was getting into this detecting business.

Soon after, we left the grizzled waterman to his corner of the inn, and it was then, that I explained to both Matthew and Kyd what I intended to do.

***

The logbook of the Santo Francisco and my father's diary! What mixture of feelings stir within me when I turn through these pages, twenty years after the horrific and life-changing events they record. Heartache, pity, anger all blend together, as I peruse my pathetic scratchings on the paper. True, there were adventures too, the forming of attachments, and some kindness, but it cannot be denied that it is always hatred that rises to the surface when I recall that history. A life-long desire for revenge nurtured in my bosom, which will soon be assuaged once and for all. And it is to that end, and the quenching of my life-long bitterness, that I now turn to these pages once again to record events. That particular business runs more smoothly than I ever could have hoped or expected. The Red Devil is so tied up in illegal activities that it is a wonder he has survived in his position for so long. I will enjoy exposing them for all the world to see and ruining his marriage into the bargain.

So what else shall I record here, besides the evidence of Hardwick's destruction? I see that I finished my last entry with my parting from Gbèré in Tangiers some twenty years ago. He died only last year, a rich, comfortable and fat old man at his home in Medis on the Barbary Coast. I still trade with his sons. It was Gbèré who gave me my first ship and started me on this journey. He was a wily and cunning man, and his vision of a trading network stretching from Timbuktu to the Baltic, with me acting as his instrument, was eventually realised. I suppose I have him to be grateful to for becoming the man that I am – nevertheless I am grateful.

I first came to these shores in the early part of the last decade. I suppose it was natural that I would settle here – there was nothing for me in my native Portugal, even less since it became annexed to Spain – and few other countries were welcoming, but nowhere else offered anything like the same opportunities as London. The greed of the merchants here is only topped by their naivety. All they can ever think of is outdoing the Spaniard to whom, though they would never so much as admit it, they feel such base inferiority. It was easy to turn their need to my advantage and thus have I lived upon their hospitality.

The English think I reside in their country in support of the Portuguese pretender, Dom Antonio. It is true I have made some advances in that direction, more as a matter of form than anything else, though I consider the man a fool. Can I honestly say, though, that I have any loyalty to his claim – the recovering of a country whose sons so cruelly abandoned me to the savages because of my faith? No, my reasons for living here are far more prosaic – money and, at last, the opportunity for revenge.

Cassangoe has stuck by me over the years, though I can't deny that our relationship has been strained at times. He hates this country; hates the weather, hates the people, who mistrust him and insult him in the streets, hates the businesses we are in. Most of all, I think he hates himself for putting up with it all and allowing me to become the man I am. When I first told him of my plot concerning Hardwick, he appeared to acquiesce with my plans, but now he has become truculent, hostile even. In particular, he is making a nuisance of himself about the girl. True, she is as charming as she is beautiful but what does her happiness matter compared to the murder of my father? Besides, I fancy that Leticia Hardwick is a survivor. Cassangoe is a fool to think of her so tenderly – it is as though she is the one beacon of light in the gloom that his life has become. He is becoming quite unstable, even beginning to dress like an Italian gentleman in the hope of attracting her eye. Frankly, he looks ridiculous. I often wonder if I should have brought him here with me – but, like me, where else should he go? Where else could he live without my protection? Of late, though, he is giving me much cause for concern. However, when the world learns – albeit falsely – that the great Sir Christopher Hardwick has been cuckolded by a Negro of all people – ha! I feel such joy to think of it!

Well, enough of that. Cassangoe's peace of mind can be dealt with once this other matter has been completed. Nothing must be allowed to stand in its way. The logbook of the Portuguese caravel Santo Francisco' – the one surviving link to my father, whose soul I feel within these pages – bear witness to the wrongs done to my family and my resolve to revenge them.

A de S. 1588

Chapter 36

'The devil is not so black as he is painted.'
(16th Century proverb)

The alleys of Queenhithe were cold and empty. Rotting wooden houses closed mournfully together, trying in vain to shut out the sharp gusts of frozen air that blew fitfully from the banks of the river.

Matthew, Kyd and I walked purposefully over rough cobbles, towards the covered passageway that Andromeda the cat had alerted me to on our first visit. As we reached the passage, I turned, and in hushed tones explained to them both what I wanted them to do. Kyd followed me down the passageway, while Matthew walked back down the street and round past the ancient, crumbling walls of the church dedicated to St Trinity. I had asked him to find a way to the back of the house and to wait there for a signal to enter.

The old house in the hidden courtyard was quiet and no light could be seen within. Motioning to Kyd to stand guard at the entrance to the passageway, I walked quickly across the exposed yard. The downstairs window had not been repaired and I had it open in a matter of seconds. I slipped quietly into the small parlour, trying to make as little noise as possible, and then crept to the foot of the stairs. Opposite the parlour, the door to the storeroom was wide open, but inside was only blackness. I put a foot on the bottom step of the stairs and it creaked ominously.

'Cassangoe,' I said in a stage whisper, loud enough for him to hear but not to scare him. The old house seemed to flutter for a second before sinking back down into stillness. There was no answer from above. I tried again.

'Cassangoe. It's Lovat. I've brought the diary.' Still nothing. 'Don Alphonse's diary. The one I found in the warehouse … before it burnt down. Before *you* burnt it down.'

Still nothing.

'Cassangoe.'

'Devil!' A shocking vision came swiftly out of the darkness of the storeroom – a face, dead and alive at the same time, locked in a silent scream of agony. My heart leapt into my throat and I tripped backwards onto the stairs.

The terrifying figure stood over me. Gone was the elaborate finery of an Italian gentleman. Instead, he stood above me naked, apart from a thin piece of material covering his loins and an array of beads and jewellery hanging around his neck – his body criss-crossed with scars, tattoos and a shiny, white paint. I couldn't see his face – from the neck upwards was only the dreadful wooden mask that had frightened the life out of me. Behind the mask Cassangoe let out his deep, monstrous laugh. In his hand he held a long, archaic-looking spear with a sharp, business-like metal tip poised inches from my neck.

'What were you doing in there?' It sounded ridiculous but it was all I could think of saying.

'Waiting. Waiting for the devil.'

Cassangoe jerked the spear towards me, tearing the skin inches below my throat and drawing blood. I began inching backwards up the stairs.

'Did you come alone, Devil? Or did you bring that old man to protect you? Who have you told about me devil?'

'I know about the lady.' He jerked to a sudden halt as though punched in the gut. 'Please. Take off that mask Cassangoe.'

'The lady? Don't speak of her. You are not worthy.'

'I have a letter from her to her lover. To Don Alphonse. She wasn't your lover was she, Cassangoe? Never was. It was all in your imagination.'

'Let me have the letter.' Cassangoe began moving ominously forward again, the spear twitching perilously close to my neck

'Did you want to be her lover? Were you jealous? Jealous of your friend? Is that what happened?'

'The letter, devil. Give it to me.'

'You wanted her but you couldn't have her.'

'Quiet devil.' Barely more audible than the low growl of the earth at night.

'Your friend had her instead. You had to leave the house when he brought her back here.'

'I didn't leave. I stayed … and listened. He wasn't worthy of her. He corrupted her. He used her for his own ends.'

'Is that what you hated? Is that what you had to stop?'

Cassangoe suddenly darted at me. I had gradually been inching backwards and I now fell over and sprawled onto the landing. Cassangoe laughed and motioned for me to keep moving. The door to the open hall on the first floor was shut tight. The only way was to continue up the stairs to the attic. Cassangoe started a low, guttural chant as he stalked me. I started talking more quickly.

'You met him that night, didn't you, on the river before he could reach the Chancel House? You had already tried to reason with him in the garden, but he had brushed you aside. You knew he would return and were waiting for him. You wanted to stop him disgracing the lady. To tell him not to shame her – to leave her out of it. He was going to introduce you to Hardwick as the man who had been cuckolding him with his wife. Disgrace him and his wife into the bargain. Is that what you had to stop?'

The chanting continued behind the mask – the sound of a bird trapped in the gates of hell. I reached the top of the stairs, my back pushing against a small wooden door. The spear had stopped wavering as if it had decided its point of entry. I could feel the cold sweat of fear running down my spine.

'But he wouldn't listen to you would he? He wanted his revenge. He didn't care about the lady. So you had to stop him. You didn't mean to. Before you knew what was happening your hands were at the chain around his neck – the chain he was flaunting as a gift from his latest victim. And like that time in the jungle all those years ago, those big hands of yours had a life of their own. They squeezed that chain tight till there was no more breath.' Cassangoe thrust the spear at me. I leapt backwards and galloped on with my speech, thinking it was the only way I could save myself.

'When he was dead you put him in a boat and then rowed towards the bridge. Then you launched the boat into the waterwheel.' It was partly guesswork on my part but it explained Don Alphonse's missing boat, the broken waterwheel and Don Alphonse's battered body.

'How do you know all this devil? Witchcraft?'

Cassangoe charged at me with the spear, letting out a shrill cry of anguish. I was saved by something on the floor that I tripped over backwards, the spear grazing my cheek as I fell. I grabbed it and hung on with all my strength. The masked man fell on top of me, as we fought over the spear between our bodies. I felt it snap, the sharp point in my hands, but it was too late to manoeuvre – I was pinned down by his weight advantage and those huge hands were at my neck. I let go of the spear and grabbed the hands instead. The mask had half come off and I could see his crazed, bloodshot eyes beneath. The air left my body in gulps. Numbness was creeping into my brain. I was drifting. Those manic, terrorised eyes were the last thing I would see.

Then the hands loosened their grip. The madness in the eyes seemed to die a little – some sense returning.

'Cassangoe?' I croaked, my mind starting to black out.

I'll never forget the anguish in his tone: 'I killed my friend.'

My mind was still foggy from the throttling. Everything happened in a blur. Mumbled shouts – hands grappling mine, grappling Cassangoe's – prising the fingers away from my throat. Other hands round the neck of my assailant, pulling him backwards. Choking on the floor as I watched Matthew and Kyd manhandling Cassangoe into a corner. Matthew holding him in a headlock while Kyd, totally out of his depth, tried to tie some rope round his wide arms and torso. Cassangoe's arms flailing – catching Kyd and sending him flying, shaking Matthew off roughly, his head cracking the floorboards sharply. Matthew grappling for a leg, Cassangoe taking up the broken spear head. Matthew holding on tenaciously. My desperate croaked plea as I saw Cassangoe swing the spear head in a great ark and drive it into Matthew's shoulder. Matthew's cry of pain. Cassangoe bursting from the attic. Matthew – good, honest, loyal Matthew – collapsing backwards in a crumpled heap.

* * *

It was many hours later when Kyd and I spoke of Don Alphonse's murder. I explained to him how during all his years in Europe, Cassangoe had descended into a state of lonely paranoia. How he had become both jealous of his friend's freedom but also contemptuous of his actions and motivations. How Leticia Hardwick had been the catalyst that finally pushed him over the edge – the beautiful object of his desires, which he could never have, but which his friend only wanted to corrupt. How on that night at the Chancel House, Don Alphonse had told Cassangoe to meet him in the garden after everyone except Hardwick had left.

'The plan was to confront Hardwick with Cassangoe and Leticia's jewellery and make him believe that Leticia had betrayed him with the moor – my brother and Anne were to bear witness. He would then have exposed Hardwick's plot to Robert and enjoyed the fall out.' I looked at the ring and brooch that were still in my possession. Leticia's wedding ring and wedding gift. I wondered if I should have returned them to her but it was a bit late now. 'Hardwick could just about bear the thought of Don Alphonse cuckolding him – but Cassangoe? Cassangoe wanted no part of it. He arrived earlier than expected, waited in the shadows of the garden and tried to reason with Don Alphonse one last time as he was leaving – the argument that Turney and Drummond overheard – but Don Alphonse angrily dismissed him and told him to wait till he returned. Instead, Cassangoe lay in wait on the river and strangled his friend in a fit of rage. He then pushed the boat with the lifeless body into the waterwheel under the bridge, smashing them as the body and boat were churned up in the powerful force of the wheel – not the work of drunken youths, as the engineer had thought, but the work of a crazy outcast, who had turned against the society that rejected him and the friend who had brought him in to it.'

I then explained how Cassangoe had tricked Hercules Smyth into believing he was being persecuted and into letting him hide in his workshop. How he had been there the night Matthew and I broke in and how he had later burnt the warehouse down in the hope of destroying the only evidence that showed his state of mind – Don Alphonse's diary.

'So it wasn't Ingram and his men who started the fire?'

'No. I was convinced that it must have been but it didn't make any sense after a while. They didn't need to destroy the warehouse. They had simply planned to move the goods to help incriminate my brother further – I suspect Nesbitt had suggested they do it.'

All the time we were speaking, Kyd listened with the intensity of an audience member watching the death of Heironimo in his famous play. Emmalina listened intently too, in between bouts of tending to Matthew, who lay on my bed, the wound in his shoulder wrapped in bandages. When Kyd and I had carried him back to my lodgings, the spear still sticking viciously from the wound, we had felt at times that his survival was touch and go. But he was a tough old fellow and Emmalina was a compassionate and competent nurse. She had successfully staunched the flow of blood, and was now trying to prevent him from getting fever as he lay wearily on my bed.

'What I don't understand is why Leticia Hardwick didn't tell you that her lover was Don Alphonse and not Cassangoe. Why did she let you believe it?'

I thought about my answer for a moment as I had done before. I hadn't wanted to believe Cassangoe's guilt from the beginning, even when my brother insisted, for his own ends admittedly, that he must be guilty. Why not, I thought? To spite my brother, certainly; to fight for the underdog, as always; but there was something else when I had learned that he had been the cuckold and not Don Alphonse. Something that I couldn't put my finger on, even now, but something that had stopped me from even closely broaching the subject with Leticia Hardwick. I had subsequently opened her letter to Don Alphonse and seen that he was clearly her lover after all, and not Cassangoe. 'I should have guessed,' was all I could say, weakly.

'How did you know he was guilty?'

'It's all in the diary, if you read between the lines, that is, and besides, too many things didn't make sense. And then of course there was the testimony of the lighterman.' I glanced over at the prostrate figure on the bed. 'Matthew did a brilliant job of finding him. Even in the darkness on the river, he caught enough of Cassangoe's description. Still, I wasn't sure until we went to the house – until he confronted me in his tribal mask. Finally, I understood his madness.'

I reflected for a moment on everything that happened over the last few weeks. 'From the beginning this has been a story about outsiders – Don Alphonse, Hercules Smyth, myself even, but Cassangoe – he was the biggest outsider of us all.'

Epilogue

'Fortune, seeing that she could not make fools wise, has made them lucky.'
'Michel de Montaigne'

On a bleak Monday in January 1589, Sir Christopher Hardwick was delivered to the river gate of the Tower, charged as a traitor to England and her Majesty. A few days later his accomplices, a Scotsman called Edward Dakers and a Frenchman called Étienne Vaillons, were hung without ceremony at Tyburn, convicted of the crime of giving aid to Catholic priests. They had all been arrested a month earlier, a few days after I had given the information to Walsingham. All had protested their innocence, but the evidence against them, not all of which I was expecting and which seemed to have been fashioned purely for the purpose in hand, was overwhelming.

Hardwick avoided execution, at least for the time being, by dint of his status in society. I wonder if he ever realised that the man who had set his destruction in motion was the same boy whose father he had murdered.

A number of other men had also been rounded up, including Ingram and a man called Frazier Inglecrook, who I later learned had a milky eye, set off by a livid scar running down his left cheek. There was no mention of anyone called Grayson. The Lady Merrydance had not returned to Rye and I could only assume that Buck had eventually achieved his wish of being set ashore in France. I wondered also about Karl Würtembatter –whether or not I would be able to honour my pledge to him and whether he would ever be reunited with his bird, Lucius, who Emmalina and I had made a gift of to my landlord's children.

Hardwick was joined in the Tower by Lord and Lady Asthor, late of Chillenham manor, who had been surprised by Walsingham's agents in the middle of saying Mass. Both the Hardwick and Asthor estates had been seized by the Crown and would no doubt be distributed as favours by Gloriana at some convenient time – I doubted if the man who had brought all of these crimes to light would benefit, however.

Of Lady Hardwick I heard only rumours. Exonerated of any involvement in her husband's crimes but nevertheless besmirched by them, she was finally turfed out of the home of her childhood, and had gone to live with relatives somewhere in the North. Not long afterwards, so the rumours had it, she had become the object of desire of half the county's bachelors and had taken her pick of the richest – and oldest.

I wasn't in England to witness any of this and only learnt of it later. A few days earlier I had set sail from Gravesend to France. Walsingham had been persuasive and there was little to keep me in London. Rather than show any gratitude for the good turn I had done him, my brother grew cold towards me, perhaps embarrassed that his base half-brother had saved the family name. He could not (or would not) find any work for me, and my visits to the Chancel House became evermore infrequent. I had some sympathy for him though. The scandal had done him some damage at court and he was side-lined from the action, which, for a man of Robert's ambition, was tantamount to a death sentence. He apparently haunted the Chancel House by day, bemoaning his fate and scaring the servants by coming upon them unexpectedly.

At least I wasn't the only outcast from the house. Nesbitt had removed himself and disappeared completely. Drummond had avoided prosecution but had been turned out by my brother. Tainted by his treachery and unable to get another patron, he was reputed to be drinking himself to death in the stews of Southwark.

This, and more, I learnt from a rapidly recovering Matthew, who was a regular visitor to my lodgings on the Bridge. For many nights after Cassangoe's flight, we would sit and discuss the strange case of Don Alphonse's murder, whilst taking it in turns to gaze at the stars hanging over the city through the simple eyeglass that had belonged to my father. One day he brought me a gift, wrapped in a velvet purse. I opened it to find a silver brooch and a short note thanking me for everything I had done and promising me a return to favour soon. It was written in Anne's neat handwriting

Of Cassangoe himself there was no news. The day after he fled from Matthew and Kyd's clutches, I visited the home of Hercules Smyth. I told him about everything that happened since we had last spoken and he listened to me patiently, with a thoughtful expression on his wrinkled old face. Afterwards he showed me to the door promising to inform me should Cassangoe seek help from him but there was plenty in his manner that made me doubt whether he would. As Cassangoe's only potential ally in London, I thought of staking out his house but there seemed little point. Events had overtaken Don Alphonse's murder and no one would thank me for bringing in his killer and besides I was weary of the whole affair. Wherever he was, I knew that he must be in torment and I also knew that some of that was down to me. Even if he wasn't hanged for the murder, at the very least he would be committed to Bedlam, where his colour and features would ensure that he would be right at the front of the entertainment for the passers-by on Bishopsgate Street. I thought it better to allow him to escape that fate and take his chances on the streets of London but I also told no one about the secret house in Queenhithe and also swore Matthew and Kyd to do likewise. Perhaps one day he would creep back there and find a modicum of peace.

I had passed Bedlam myself, arm in arm with Emmalina, only days before the departure to France, to visit Kyd in Norton Folgate. He introduced us to the man he shared the room with, a fellow poet called Kit Marley, who, during a marathon drinking bout in a nearby tavern, first delighted us with his wit and charm, and then scared us to death by drawing his sword and demanding to fight any stranger that happened to so much as glance in our direction. During one of the moments that Marley was in full-fight mode, Kyd turned to us in an aside to give us his understated assessment of Marley's character: 'brilliant but volatile.' It was the perfect night to remember London by.

And what of Emmalina? Naturally she got her way. There was little enough for her in London without her brother, only the prospect of returning to the unhappy home of her stepfather and the potential marriage to someone she despised. My landlord told me casually one day that men had been making enquiries along the bridge about a girl who had run away from home. We sensed that her stepfather was closing in. It didn't take much to persuade Walsingham that she might also be an asset to him in France. When he handed me the papers for my mission, including the permit to travel, there was also a permit for an Emmalina Bucklesbury. We will take our chances across the channel and search for her brother together. For my part, any reservations I had about her travelling with me quickly dissipated as I saw the happiness the prospect brought her, not to mention the thoroughness she put in to planning our progress, including numerous little details I hadn't thought of.

As it turns out I have been gifted the perfect travelling companion – resourceful, intelligent, and really quite beautiful. Goodness only knows what she is doing with an ass like me. As my adopted mentor Michel de Montaigne has written: 'Fortune, seeing that she could not make fools wise, has made them lucky.' Perhaps he had someone like myself in mind when he wrote those words.

Acknowledgements

My thanks go to Craig Cornock for his great design skills and for allowing me to learn how to use InDesign!